REYNARDINE

JUDITH LENNOX-SMITH

REYNARDINE

Hamish Hamilton · London

HAMISH HAMILTON LTD
Published by the Penguin Group
27 Wrights Lane, London W8 5TZ, England
Viking Penguin Inc, 40 West 23rd Street, New York, New York 10010, U.S.A.
Penguin Books Australia Ltd, Ringwood, Victoria, Australia
Penguin Books Canada Ltd, 2801 John Street, Markham, Ontario, Canada L3R 1B4
Penguin Books (N.Z.) Ltd, 182–190 Wairau Road, Auckland 10, New Zealand

Penguin Books Ltd, Registered Offices: Harmondsworth, Middlesex, England

First published in Great Britain 1989 by
Hamish Hamilton Ltd

Copyright © 1989 by
Judith Lennox-Smith
1 3 5 7 9 10 8 6 4 2

British Library Cataloguing in Publication Data

Smith, Judith
  Reynardine.
  I. Title
  823′.914[F]

  ISBN 0-241-12612-6

Typeset at The Spartan Press Ltd, Lymington, Hants.
Printed in Great Britain by
Richard Clay Ltd, Bungay, Suffolk

REYNARDINE

CHAPTER ONE

One evening, as I rode out
Amongst the leaves so green
I overheard a young woman
Converse with Reynardine.

(REYNARDINE)

*L*ONDON: brittle, seductive London, calling the enterprising
and ambitious to its learned, spendthrift court, its great
parks and playhouses, its gaming houses and bordellos. A cast of
a dice and a fortune's made or lost, a flick of a card and a
reputation tumbles.

If Giles Galliers had not been three parts drunk when he had
finally found his brother, he might have kept a better guard on
his tongue.

Embattled with a large quantity of anger, a peppering of
apprehension and an ever-present misery that made him want to
howl like a night hag, Giles had thus far found alcohol much the
best salve for his wounded heart. So he had drunk at Amyott,
before he had left home, his mother clucking and sniffing
somewhere in the background. And he had drunk at most of the
reasonable taverns on the long, hot ride from Essex to London,
remaining more or less upright in the saddle because of his
horsemanship, not his sobriety. At Epping he had found an inn
for the night, and dreamed, to his surprise, neither of Anna nor of
Richard, but of sea monsters that rose from the deep, and
gnawed away his limbs, neatly, one by one.

Breakfasted on ale, dined on ale, and fortified by more ale

I

during a tedious search of the more squalid parts of London, Giles had scratched irritably at the modest ruff he wore about his neck and had mentally added a scarlet blossoming of flea bites to his already considerable list of troubles. Had Richard the decency to keep a suitable London address . . . had Richard the decency not to reappear at this inconvenient time, newborn like some discreditable butterfly from a chrysalis of scandal and rumour . . . then he, Giles Galliers, might still be in Essex, perfectly content with his crumbling inheritance and carping mother, because he had Anna. But decency had never been Richard's failing, so Giles trudged from the Mitre to the Mermaid, from Cheapside to Holborn, a headache competing with the flea bites for his attention. In Holborn he found Esmé Molyneux and, after a pleasant meal and a jug of water to tip over his head, set off for the Dagger.

It was still light outside, an agreeably warm summer's evening. But the Dagger tavern was black, night black, as black as the rogues and scoundrels that infested it. It was also smoky and noisy; and famous equally for its dark, lethal Dagger ale, its pies ornamented with a representation of a dagger and a magpie, and the criminal nature of its clientele. You went to the Dagger if you wanted assistance with a venture that was rather less than legal; you went to the Dagger if you wanted to win, or lose, a large amount of money at dice and cards. The low-ceilinged room was crammed to the rafters with gamesters, their hungry eyes intent upon hazard, one-and-twenty, ruff, or primero. Giles's brown eyes travelled the width of the room, searching every crowded table, surveying a myriad of unknown faces in the hope of finding one familiar face. Assuming, of course, that Richard would still be familiar. Three years was a long time.

He saw him, in a far corner of the room, a dark head bent over a game of dice. Giles's hands, loose at his sides, fisted once, briefly, startling the pickpocket who had reached out fluid fingers to take the silk handkerchief that trailed so temptingly from his doublet. Then Giles elbowed his way through the whores, the cutpurses, the vagabonds and thieves to stand behind his brother's table.

2

Richard had not, he thought, seen him. But as Giles reached out to touch his brother's velvet shoulder (Richard calling and throwing a seven; the bearded man opposite him sliding, reluctantly, another coin to Richard's side of the table), his hand was stayed when Richard looked up and said, 'Giles. How pleasant.' As though it had been three days since they had met, not three years. So Giles, finding nothing to say other than his brother's name, quickly took a jug of ale from the passing pot boy's tray, sat at the table, and glowered until the penniless bearded man rose and left.

When he had consigned his dice and his winnings to his pocket, Richard looked across at Giles and said, 'You had my letter, then?'

Giles nodded.

Richard's letter had been his first communication with his family since he had ridden, so long ago, through Amyott's gates. *Madam, kindly accept my condolences on the recent death of your husband, Lord Amyott . . .* Lady Amyott had passed the letter to Giles without comment, and had continued her description of her latest malady. Only Giles, kind, uncomplicated Giles, had noticed the brightness of her eyes, the shiver in her voice.

'We received it about a month ago,' Giles said. He added hastily, 'Mother isn't very well at present.'

'Ah.' Richard leaned back in his chair, but his eyes, green-gold and lucent, did not leave Giles. 'Nothing serious, I trust?'

Giles shook his head and applied himself conscientiously to his ale. He thought Richard had altered – how, he was not exactly sure. He still looked the same – perhaps the sun-browned, high-cheekboned face was leaner, more fined down; perhaps the heavy-lidded green eyes were more experienced, more cynical – but it was not that. There was a reserve which, though it might mask the wildness of former years, hinted at something disquieting, dangerous, behind it. There were, of course, a hundred questions that Giles would have liked to ask, yet he found he could utter none of them. There were subjects that must not be touched on. A refusal in the clear, hard eyes made Giles, even though he was the elder by almost two years,

3

fall silent. Banalities such as *where have you been* and *what did you do* rose to the forefront of Giles's brain and were effectively drowned by another mouthful of sweet, dark Dagger ale.

'And Amyott?' said Richard, lazily breaking into what had seemed, to Giles at least, an increasingly awkward silence. 'Amyott still stands? Our neighbours – our friends – *something* must have happened since I left England. The Askews, the Deans, the Murrays –'

'I hope to marry Anna Murray.'

There, it was out, and Giles, putting down his tankard with a thump, experienced a wave of almost unbearable longing.

'To marry? You have finally forsworn the pleasures of the town, Giles?'

There was an edge of mockery in Richard's voice, but Giles ignored it, and staring down into the empty depths of the ale jug saw only Anna, with her thick chestnut hair and gentle grey eyes. 'I have been at Amyott since father died,' said Giles. 'The Murrays were at the funeral. And really, Anna is the loveliest creature . . .'

He fell silent again. The Galliers and the Murrays had known each other vaguely for some years, but differences of religion, coupled with Giles's absences and Anna's domestic duties (her mother had died when she was eleven, leaving her with a substantial assortment of younger siblings) had combined to keep Giles and Anna apart. Anna Murray was twenty-seven, only one year Giles' junior, with heavy family responsibilities and a father with increasingly Puritan leanings. But nothing of the spinster clung to her: she was tall, graceful, with a perfect clear skin, fine eyes, and yards of shining chestnut hair. Giles had been totally unprepared for the emotions that had swamped him when Anna Murray had called to offer her condolences after Lord Amyott's death in May. Giles had had many love affairs – he was good-looking, generous and easy going, with a streak of devilment in him that women found exciting. But he had coasted through these amours, writing perhaps a bad sonnet when the lady transferred her affections to another but shedding not a tear. But his feelings for Anna had been instant and irrevocable, and, best of all, they had been reciprocated.

From across the table, through a smattering of aggrieved argument from the benches at their side, Giles heard Richard prompt gently:

'And Brother George?'

'Oh, George Murray is in London.' Giles signalled to the pot boy to refill his tankard. 'George dices his allowance away quite nicely – keeping it well hidden from his father's ears, of course.'

'But not all gossip has been kept from John Murray?' Richard's clear gaze met Giles's troubled one. 'Come, Giles, if your suit with Miss Murray had met with any success, you wouldn't be drinking yourself to insensibility in the Dagger.'

Beside them, someone had lost once too often. Shielding himself from the sudden cascade of bodies, ale jugs and furniture, Giles said gloomily, 'Some bastard saw fit to remind him of your past career,' and he threaded his hands through his brown hair as he recalled John Murray, in a particularly self-righteous frame of mind, dismissing him from the doorstep of the Murrays' Saffron Walden house.

Richard's smile, Giles thought when he looked up, was that of a cat which has just cornered a particularly large and juicy mouse. 'Dear me, brother,' he murmured, flicking the undoubtedly expensive lace of his cuffs back from his long hands. 'Scandal takes a long time to die down.'

Giles ducked as a chair flew through the air, just missing his head. 'Well, you didn't time your reappearance too well, Richard,' he said, feeling justification in his resentment. 'You were supposed to be piloting a corsair's galley round the Mediterranean.'

The cat's smile became positively tigerish. 'Well, I always did have a penchant for large ships, my dear. But it was a pinnace, not a galley.'

In spite of himself, Giles grinned. 'Do you remember the Fens, when we took the eel trapper's boat? We were sailing for the Americas, I believe. You were pilot then, I was master, and –'

'– and Jeremy the ship's boy.'

5

The smile had gone, Richard's eyes were blank, devoid of warmth. Inwardly cursing himself, Giles reached for the ale jug. He heard Richard say: 'And our neighbour at Kingscote? The good Sir Nicholas Carleton – he is, I trust, quite well?'

The ale had gone to Giles's head, blurring the sound of the protesting gamblers, yanked forcefully from their seats and kicked into the street, blurring also the two whores, one fair, one brown-haired, who had taken their place. But not blurring the image of his brother opposite him, waiting, apparently carelessly, for an answer to an apparently casual question.

'Carleton is rarely at Kingscote,' said Giles, choosing his words with the artistry of one who has begun to see the yawning pits open before him. 'He is generally at Court.'

'So his fortunes continue to rise.'

And Richard, his dice nestled once more in his palm, no longer looked at Giles, nor at the fair-haired whore who edged steadily closer, nor at the tangle of thieves and gamesters who roared and heaved and sweated on the Dagger's scuffed wooden floor. Giles, watching him, answered some of the questions he had not been able to face asking. Richard had travelled South; his skin was not the colour of a man who has endured three northern winters. He was well dressed, his doublet a good black velvet, his shirt a lace-trimmed silk. But God, it should have been possible to talk to him, to meet those disconcerting, too familiar eyes, and say: The past is over, and should be forgotten. But it was not possible. There was a barricade between them, and Giles knew that even if he were to drink the Dagger dry he would not cross that barricade.

But the coldness had gone from Richard's eyes, his voice was flippant. 'So who else prospers in London, Giles? The Scottish faction were doing rather well when I left, I recall.'

Through an increasing haze, Giles considered the Byzantine intricacies of the Court of King James at Whitehall. 'If you mean Robert Kerr,' he said, grasping thankfully at the change of subject, 'then he has been made Earl of Somerset – and Lord Chamberlain. Oh, and he is married – to a Howard. *Frances* Howard – you remember her, surely, Richard?'

6

Outside, the sky had almost darkened. The heads of the revellers were framed black against the dark blue of the Dagger's small window panes. Their voices lost in the general uproar, they seemed to Giles like the writhing stylized figures of a dumb-show. Threading through the muttering, the shouting, the singing, was Richard's voice, soft and seductive.

'*There is a lady sweet and kind, was never face so pleased my mind . . .* Yes, I remember Frances Howard. But, Giles, she was married to the Earl of Essex.'

'Yes.' The brown-haired whore was smiling at Giles. He returned the smile, and three faces swam before him: the whore's, well painted to hide the pock marks; Anna's, dimmed and distressed through the window of her bedchamber; Frances Howard's, glittering and unobtainable on the arm of Robert Kerr, the King's Scottish favourite.

He collected his thoughts, and said, 'There was some scandal – the details are hideously complicated. Frances Howard married Robert Kerr in 1613. Last Christmas in fact. So the Howards are in even greater favour than ever. Are you –' his gaze returned slowly to his brother, discovering a new possibility in the silk, the velvet, the jewellery '– are you considering a career at Court?'

The dice tumbled from Richard's hand to the table. 'Now, *there's* a wager for you, Giles. For – let me see – the company of these two ladies for an entire night' the women giggled '– for that not inconsiderable pleasure, I will oust Robert Kerr from King James's heart – no? Perhaps not. Perhaps Kerr has qualities even I do not possess. Perhaps I should consider a different calling. What openings are there, Giles, for an impoverished second son with an expensive taste in women, alcohol and dice?'

'The Church', said Giles, helpfully. And then, entering into the spirit of things, 'No – you might turn Puritan, and God, life would be dull . . . An apothecary –'

'Too drab. Black robes and impenetrable mumblings about the constellations. Try again.'

'An alchemist –'

7

'*'Tis magic, magic that hath ravished me –*'

'A wherry man. Or are you obsessed with pinnaces? A rat catcher – a coney catcher – a highwayman!'

Richard's arm had curled about the fair-haired whore's plump shoulders. Giles felt a soft hand take his and begin to stroke his fingers very gently, one by one.

'Dashing in a black cloak and mask?' Richard's eyes, reflecting the tallow candle on the table, glinted. 'A touch theatrical, don't you think, Giles? But a good, steady income – although the penalty for failure's a mite distracting –'

The soft hand had been replaced by a mouth that kissed his palm, a tongue that flicked at the tips of his fingers.

Giles was inspired.

'A wager, Richard,' he said.

When Giles stood up, weaving unsteadily through the crowds to answer a call of nature, Richard Galliers raised his tankard in salute. 'Then let's follow darkness like a dream, brother,' he said, softly, and kissed the fair-haired whore on her painted lips.

'Damn the woman!'

Martin Grosse cursed as his horse slipped again in the pale Cambridgeshire mud. He righted himself in the saddle, pushed his sparse damp hair out of his eyes, and spurred on his bony and uncooperative mare.

'Damned flat place!' he cursed again, unwilling to admit even to himself that, in this alien and soaking county, he was lost. His eyes scanned the horizon for signs of habitation, his mind tempted by visions of hot ale, fresh bread and ham, and perhaps a kind and docile country girl on his knee. Then he remembered the Countess of Somerset, and looked instead at the track ahead for, even if he had had the luck to find a village with a warm and cosy inn, he could not have stopped. 'This is to be at Hinxton by nightfall,' she had said, pressing the letter into

8

his hand – and looking into her clear, hard blue eyes, he had not dared disobey.

It was getting perilously near nightfall now – greenish-grey clouds filled the darkening skies, and it was becoming increasingly difficult to make out the ill-defined path in front of him. The rain sheeted relentlessly down making the landscape even more featureless. He could just make out a blurred shape in the small copse a little way ahead of him – and it was moving, slowly. Grosse clutched his knife under his cloak, his keen eyes trying to pierce the rain and dark – and then relaxed as the shape formed into the figure of a bowed old woman.

'Alms for a poor beggar woman, sir, that has no home but the woods and ditches.'

Grosse glimpsed a pleading face, darkened by sun and wind, half hidden by the folds of a dirty old shawl. In no mood for charity, he was about to push the frail old body out of his path, when another vision of that warm and kindly inn prompted second thoughts.

'Am I on the road for Hinxton, old woman?'

As she hesitated, his hand searched through his pocket for a coin to help ease her memory.

In the unthinking moment of stooping to give the beggar her bribe, Grosse never saw how the knife reached his throat. He knew, however, that it was an Italian knife, long, thin, sharp, and utterly deadly, its tip scratching the skin over his windpipe, its handsome jewelled haft held unwaveringly by a young, strong, and unquestionably male hand.

Eyes that were not old and rheumy, but young, and a curious cat-like amber-green, stared coolly into his face.

'Your money and your jewels, sir,' said the voice softly. 'Now.'

If he had not been sent on what he considered to be a damn fool errand, if it had not been such foul weather for late August, if he had not been taken in by such an old and obvious trick, then Martin Grosse might not have lost his temper. After all, he knew himself to be carrying little of any value, except possibly the letter, which would be of no interest to a highwayman. But he had never been a placid man, and he had rarely been outmatched in a fight. He was heavy, too, his body far bulkier than the comparatively slight form swathed in dirty rags before him.

With a roar of anger he lurched backwards, kicking with his spurred boot to stab violently into the crone's side. Simultaneously, Grosse swung for the arm holding the dagger.

He had almost expected it to be easy. As it was, he had just long enough momentarily to respect the other man's skill in the split second between being thrown from his horse and his head making hard and painful contact with an old beech tree. Then, almost thankfully, he lapsed into unconsciousness.

In the shelter of the beech tree, the highwayman knelt by Grosse's prone body. Systematically, he began to search his pockets, removing what little coin and valuables he found. From an inside pocket of the soaking blue doublet he withdrew a folded and sealed piece of paper. The seal had broken in the struggle. He studied the seal for a moment, and then, pushing back the dirty cloth covering his head to reveal dark hair, slightly curled by the driving rain, he sat, his back propped comfortably against the tree trunk, and began to read the letter.

Cambridgeshire's reputation as one of England's drier counties looked to be forfeit that day. Four weeks of cloudless summer had suddenly given way to rain: unremitting, dreary, teeming rain. Everything dripped – hedges, leaves, the spiky brambles with their half ripened blackberries, the orchards heavy with small hard green apples. Rain streamed from overburdened gutters, flattened any strips of corn not yet harvested, tore the petals from the scarlet poppies that embroidered the waysides, bruising the silky fragments into a sodden pot pourri.

The roads, always bad, became intolerable. Large flat

yellow puddles hid the treacherous pot-holes from the unwary rider. At the verges, water and earth mixed to form a vile, glutinous mire perfidious to both man and beast.

Where the road followed up the slight incline lying to the west side of the Conways' large Belford estate a stream, opaque and fast running, gathered the water at the top of the incline and spat it downhill, where it created a new sea, fully six feet across, to plague the already over-tired traveller. To the small group of riders, half drowned somewhere between Ickleton and Belford, it seemed the final straw.

The first of the riders checked his horse, steaming and shivering at the edge of the offending puddle. He waited, water dripping from his hat, his nose, his hair, for the second horse to draw level.

'Your ladyship –' The man's words were addressed to the old woman who sat pillion on the second horse, but his eyes met those of the servant in front of her. 'There's a quagmire under this, your ladyship. With the burdens they carry, I fear the horses might sink too deep in the mud.' His voice faltered hopelessly, lost in the constant drumming rain.

Willis, the servant, caught his eye and nodded almost imperceptibly. 'Loader is right, your ladyship. And we should not still be on the road at this time of evening.' He gestured to the gently wooded darkness around them. 'Perhaps we could find a decent place for the night, and then set out early again next morning.' He pulled his cold, wet cloak further about himself.

'Nonsense!' The sharp autocratic voice rasped in his ears. Despite the appalling weather, despite being perched uncomfortably pillion, her bony arms clutching her servant's back as they jolted along waterlogged tracks and bridleways, despite the delays that had lengthened the duration of their journey, Lady Woodroffe was content. A small smile had hung incongruously on her old dry lips for much of the day, and her pleasurable thoughts had distracted her from some of the physical discomforts of the ride. 'Nonsense! Stop now? Certainly not!' The third horse, double burdened with another manservant and Lady Woodroffe's ancient personal maid, had reined in beside them. 'We must be within a few miles of Robert's house. I wouldn't dream of paying some crooked tapster a ridiculous price for a flea-ridden bed!'

Loader stared miserably, resentfully, at the ever deepening puddles. Resigning himself, he swung out of the saddle, his feet sinking into the soft mud.

'Then we had best walk the beasts across, your ladyship.'

It took a full twenty minutes, and several cold, slippery journeys to relieve the horses of panniers and people, and to carry luggage and women across the undividing Red Sea that blocked their way. It took a further ten minutes of numb fingers fumbling with awkward straps and buckles to reload the horses, kick some of the excess mud off boots and breeches, and lift Lady Woodroffe, still anachronistically resplendent in her early Elizabethan finery, back into the saddle.

The tiny cavalcade set off again in silence, the horses picking their way fastidiously through the puddles and pot-holes. Sheltered behind Willis's stocky body, Lady Woodroffe smiled to herself again. The thought had occurred to her that it would be even better to arrive late in the evening. Robert would have already made himself comfortable for the night, most of the servants would have already retired, and her late arrival would cause the maximum inconvenience. And the joy of it was that Robert would have to disguise every tiny bit of his irritation. She imagined her nephew's fat face straining to produce expressions of pleasure and welcome at her arrival. Ah, there were many compensations in wealthy old age, but this was the best of them. With six impoverished greedy nephews and nieces, Lady Woodroffe divided her time, comfortable in the knowledge that each one must attend instantly to her every whim, however unreasonable and inconvenient. The idea of making a visit unforwarned, and at an awkward hour, had been a superb refinement. Margaret had run about like an agitated hen when she had arrived, and then been equally agitated at her sudden unexpected departure earlier today, obviously terrified that her aunt had taken some unpredictable offence. Yes, it was a pleasant way to live out one's declining years.

The track diverted through oak trees. It was darker under the trees, but the low twisted boughs and heavy green leaves gave some protection against the rain. The horses stepped more easily over the moss and ferns, and their riders relaxed as the likelihood of being thrown into the churning mud receded. They should not have relaxed, however, for the branches of the trees did not bear only leaves and green young acorns. Like some unwanted manna from a malevolent heaven, the threat that fell from above was beautifully planned, exquisitely executed. Thud, thud, thud, the three bodies dropped almost noiselessly, two to drag the men to the ground, the third to land impossibly, and perch precariously, on the rump of Lady Woodroffe's unfortunate horse. Then the unreal silence broke – the lady's maid began to scream with hysterical shrillness, the horses, shocked and distracted, joined in the cacophony, and Willis, forcibly disarmed and dismounted, added a deep basso thump and grunt as his weighty frame mingled suddenly with the dead leaves on the ground.

Had they not already been tired and dispirited, they might not have been so easily overtaken. After all, they were not unevenly matched. The burly Willis must have had an advantage of two or three stones over the wiry dark figure who instantly wormed his way up the saddle to grip the reins of the agitated horse, and then held, business-like, a pistol an inch from her ladyship's withered chin. His two accomplices, similarly masked and cloaked, but of a wilder, ragged, more flamboyant style, their hats plumed and extrovert, their faces extravagantly whiskered, were neither of them giants. But their agility compensated for their lack of muscle, and Loader's one half-hearted attempt at reprisal left him with nothing more than a sore chin and a grass-stained rear.

Lady Woodroffe turned to look at her attacker. Her old face betrayed not a frisson of fear at the masked and hooded figure before her, and she ignored the intruding pistol. She noted that the man was young – she could tell that from the way he sat, gloved hand confidently holding the reins with the easy balance and assurance of youth she had long ago lost. From underneath the capacious hood of his cloak a little rough untidy hair peeked out. She thought it was red, a shade of hair she had always detested.

Softly, the highwayman spoke.

'Your pardon for the intrusion, my lady.' A young voice, slightly accented. 'Be so good as to let me have what money and jewels you carry, and you may continue on your way.'

Lady Woodroffe's grey eyes met his. Because of the mask and the darkness, it was hard to see the colour of the man's eyes – green, hazel, she could not be sure. But they were cold, and their cunning, knowing glitter betrayed an intimacy with life and death more appropriate to old age than youth. Despite her pride, Lady Woodroffe shivered. She had already had her threescore years and ten. With feelings of secure superiority she had watched friends and relatives die in childbirth, of war wounds, of the ague, the plague, the pox . . . death had many disguises, many deceptions, but her successful combination of selfishness and wealth had secured her safety over the years. But she knew now, looking into this man's inhuman eyes, that here was a possible death.

She was pleased that her voice was steady as she spoke.

'Willis. Do as the – gentleman – says.'

There wasn't that much, really. Some jewels, a purse, and for some reason he took the valuable copy of Seneca that she had filched from Margaret's library at Frog Bridge. An *educated* highwayman, thought Lady Woodroffe, some slight measure of confidence returning with the sneer. Then the pistol was removed from her vision, and she felt the warmth of his body disappear from behind and heard the slither of movement as he jumped from the horse's back.

One of the highwayman's two associates had dumped her servants' weapons in a ditch at the boundary of the copse, and had shortly returned, leading three horses. The maid still screeched. Lady Woodroffe eyed her with an emotion close to hatred.

14

The highwayman said: 'I suggest you give her a glass of brandy. There's a nice little inn at the next village.'

Then they were gone, the short drama played out as the three figures melted into blackness and the sound of their horses' hooves was lost in the distance.

Unwisely, Loader spoke. 'Shall I do as he said, your ladyship? Find an inn, I mean?'

Taking the heavy embroidered gloves that she clutched in her hand, Lady Woodroffe raised them and struck him about the head, over and over again.

Through lips that were almost paralysed with anger and shame she hissed: 'Fools! Collect your swords and ride on! And if you do not stop that noise this instant, woman, I will beat you also!'

The oak copse in which the unfortunate Lady Woodroffe had been parted from her possessions skirted the westernmost side of one of Cambridgeshire's largest estates. The estate was owned by the Conway family, and bore the same name as the nearest village, Belford. Belford House sprawled, rain-sodden, lumbering and untidy, just half a mile away, crouched like some enormous warty toad in the shallow, gently wooded valley.

Belford possessed none of the grace of a Hever nor the imposing might of a Bodiam Castle. Successive generations of Conways, all incorrigible individualists, had added to, adapted, and altered the original structure to suit their own tastes and purposes. No uniformity of design or decoration had succeeded in attaching itself to Belford: griffins leered uncompromisingly from the parapets, escutcheons teetered at slightly odd angles over the vast doorway, but all failed to give the building the majesty merited by its size.

But the estate was profitable. If Sir Thomas Conway himself had little interest in the day-to-day matters of field and stock, he had, at least, sufficient intelligence to engage an efficient, conscientious steward, and to pay him well. The soil was rich, the weather generally kind, and Sir Thomas's substantial fortune could hardly help but multiply.

Sir Thomas Conway was a handsome man in his late fifties. He was a true Conway, prone to short-lived, magnificent obsessions, great love affairs of the intellect only superseded by the next inevitably irresistible amour. Sir Thomas had looked set to be a confirmed bachelor until suddenly, when nearly forty, he had fallen hopelessly in love. Maire Conway had been Irish, small, black-haired, and entrancingly lovely. They had lived together, briefly, in perfect happiness, and Belford, if not beautiful, had at least been clean, tidy and full of laughter. But Maire had died in childbirth, eleven months after her wedding, leaving a tiny dark-haired daughter her single frail hostage to immortality. For a long time Sir Thomas had tried not to be aware of the child's existence, and had immersed almost all of himself in whatever study – natural philosophy, alchemy, astrology, anatomy – had had the possibility of offering some sort of oblivion. But gradually, the dark curling hair, the deep blue eyes, the quick mind, all so painfully like her mother's, had wormed their way into his beleaguered soul, and had become the new centre of his existence. From then on, until Mall was in her early teens, they had been almost inseparable. Sir Thomas sought to give his daughter what his wife, isolated in her Irish castle, had never had – an education. So he engaged the best tutors, and spared considerable portions of his own time so that Mall might learn music, languages, mathematics, philosophy. His efforts were well rewarded; she proved an apt and enthusiastic pupil. If her gowns were old-fashioned and ill-mended, Mall did not notice; if Belford's draughty and complicated passageways became littered with the ingredients of Sir Thomas's stranger experiments, she was not aware of it. And if the Conways' nearest neighbours – the Houldens, the Murrays, and the Askews – muttered that the Conway girl was growing wild for want of a mother, neither father nor daughter cared.

Then, when Mall was fourteen, Sir Thomas remarried. What transient return of spring prompted this step, no-one was ever completely sure. After his first wife's death, all the pretty, and not-so-pretty, young women of the county had called to offer their condolences. But they had received little encouragement, and had gradually accepted that Sir Thomas wished to remain a permanent widower. The years had passed, the old queen had died, and the Stuart king had succeeded to the throne. King James had gradually freed England of many of its Elizabethan shackles of economy and morality. A new licence permeated the playhouses, the great houses, the Court. But although London had changed into something more fascinating, more wicked, more dangerous, little had altered in Cambridgeshire. The disruption, when it came, was of an entirely different nature. One spring-like March day Sir Thomas was introduced to Alice Porter and within six weeks he had married her.

Alice was in her mid thirties, as different from his long dead Maire as was possible. She was blonde, her thick butter-fair hair fell heavily to her waist, her plump rounded figure was in total contrast to Maire's slight fragility. Alice was of yeoman stock, she exuded good health and placidity, and had none of the fey quality that Sir Thomas had sometimes found so disturbing in his first wife. She was kind to her difficult stepdaughter, she would obviously be a good mother, and her eyes followed Sir Thomas's every move in patient adoration, as if she were unable to believe in her good fortune.

A year after her marriage, Alice Conway's good fortune ran out. She gave birth, prematurely and with considerable difficulty, to twin sons. One of the babies died within a few hours of birth, the other survived – just. Ralph Conway, heir to the vast Conway estates in Cambridgeshire and Essex, plus the odd castle and bog in Ireland, inherited his fairness and his lack of intellect from his mother, with none of her physical robustness. At horribly frequent intervals he would acquire yet another childish ailment that would both threaten his life and further retard his unspectacular progress. He had just passed his second birthday, a miracle that seemed to Alice Conway a direct result of her own prayers and determination.

Her son's delicacy tied Alice Conway to Belford and separated her from her husband. For, as King James's reign progressed, he gathered the learned about him, seeking minds as agile and tastes as catholic as his own. Whitehall did not only draw the gilded young: it sought great intellects as well as pretty faces. The king might rise at dawn and chase the hare through the early morning mist with a score of Scots and English courtiers following behind him, but at dusk he would discuss theology, poetry, natural philosophy with the finest minds in the kingdom. Sir Thomas Conway, being possessed of a particularly fine mind, found himself drawn unexpectedly to a milieu he had previously despised. Able to discourse passionately on most subjects from alchemy to zoomancy, he had found himself welcome at a Court which considered the pursuit of learning as entrancing as the pursuit of pleasure. Sir Thomas, on his part, having no need for money and no wish for advancement, could not fail to enjoy the company of his intellectual equals, the stimulation of new books, the travellers' tales of foreign lands.

Knowing the dangers of the London in which Sir Thomas spent more and more of his time – the dirt, the noise, the overcrowding, and, worst of all, the plague – Alice Conway had refused either to take her son to the city or to leave him at home with his nurse and travel there herself. Ralph, tiny, fragile, teetering on a knife-edge between life and death, had taken her attention during the last two years, while increasingly numerous journeys to Court had occupied much of Sir Thomas's. Mall, doubly deserted by her father, with little in common with and a large natural resentment of her stepmother, had watched her unconventional, interesting world steadily disintegrate. True, there were not so many cobwebs festooning Belford's ceilings, and Mall herself had a wardrobe of reasonably well cut, respectable clothes, but something irreplaceable seemed to have gone, leaving her in a well dusted limbo.

The last few weeks had seen a return to some of the pre-Alice pleasures. Sir Thomas' latest invention – a wonderful, insane idea – was in the process of design. Mall had acted as her father's amanuensis, and it was in his study that they now worked. Sir Thomas intended to journey to London: he would leave Belford the following day, pausing to stay with his brother Leo on the way, and arrive in Whitehall by the end of the week. Hoping to enjoin the interest of his sovereign, he had prepared reams of notes, diagrams, discourses. Mall sat behind her father's desk, pen in hand, black hair falling untidily over her face, awaiting Sir Thomas' next dictation.

A vast pile of books and pamphlets, of varying antiquity and condition, stood before Sir Thomas; billowing clouds of dust surged into the air as he pulled more from the shelves. Triumphantly, he found the volume he had been looking for.

'Ah, here we are, my dear.' He opened the fragile text carefully, standing by the window to get the last fading light from the overcast sky. 'I will translate and you will write.' Sir Thomas cleared some of the dust out of his throat, and began to dictate. 'Mechanics are the paradise of mathematical science because –'

He broke off abruptly, and stared out of the window. 'We seem to have visitors, my dear.'

Mall rose, and stood beside her father, looking out into the torpid skies and sheeting rain. Three overburdened horses, two bearing the curious widened shape that indicated a pillion passenger, were slowly making their way down the winding path to Belford's front door.

'Do you know them, father?'

It was impossible to distinguish the riders' faces, or the colours of the servants' livery. Sir Thomas shrugged.

'I am not expecting visitors.' He turned back to the book he held. 'Alice can deal with them,' he said dismissively.

Inside Belford's Great Hall, Lady Conway attempted to entertain her unexpected guests. The Great Hall was one of the oldest rooms in the house; built in the late fourteenth century, the Hall still retained its original traceried windows, high oak-beamed ceiling and stone floor. A monstrous fire-surround and a curving stone staircase had been Sir Thomas's only concession to modernity. Neither made the room any more conducive to easy, cosy conversation. Punctuated by the howling draughts that issued from every door and window, ill-lit by flickering inadequate rushlights, conversation flowed stickily, alternate venom and honey from both ladies' lips.

For almost the first time in her life, Lady Woodroffe felt the full weight of her many years. Fatigue and disquiet had forced her, unwillingly, to take sanctuary. She was somewhat comforted in her defeat by the thought that she could send Willis to Robert's house, and require him to come to her assistance that very night. How he would detest having to ride out in such foul weather! Yet he could not refuse.

Sitting in the Hall's most comfortable chair, a glass of sweet wine in her hand, Lady Woodroffe could remember Sir Thomas Conway, but was surprised to learn he had remarried. Someone must have told her . . . it was odd how the events of twenty years ago could seem so much more vivid than those of the recent past. And, on meeting Alice Conway, flustered, disorganized, Lady Woodroffe had smiled to herself. What on earth had possessed the fool of a man to wed this twittering commoner? Her overblown physical attractions were evident, but her lack of education and breeding would soon irritate even an eccentric like Sir Thomas. Of course, thought Lady Woodroffe, watching as Alice Conway dispatched a manservant to convey her guest's situation to her husband, his first wife had also been a disaster. The men had found her pretty enough, and she had brought with her a large dowry, but anyone with any sense could have seen she would not outlive her first child.

The introductions and explanations over, Lady Woodroffe felt some of her accustomed equanimity return. She leaned back in her chair, and began to exercise one of the prerogatives of a wealthy old age: unpardonable rudeness.

'And how long have you been wed, Lady Conway?'

Myopic blue eyes met filmy grey ones. 'Oh – three years now, Lady Woodroffe.'

'And do you have any children?'

Lady Woodroffe noticed the white, surprisingly muscular hands clutch and twist at the handkerchief they held. 'I have a stepdaughter, Mall; she is almost grown. And a son.' A note of maternal pride tinged her voice. 'He has just celebrated his second birthday, praise the Lord.'

With unerring instinct, Lady Woodroffe caught the note of anxiety and burrowed for its source. 'He is a sickly child, then?'

Another twist to the handkerchief. 'He is a little frail, but we trust he will grow stronger.'

Lady Woodroffe sniffed, and the pitiless eyes fixed themselves on the younger woman. 'In my opinion, these weakling infants never make much of themselves. Even if they do survive, they are frequently physically or morally deficient. In my opinion, children like that should be –'

A new voice, clear and cold, interrupted her from the top of the stairs. 'Ralph will be neither physically nor morally deficient. He is a dear little boy, and will grow into a fine man.'

Lady Woodroffe looked up sharply at the figure descending the stairs. It was the stepdaughter – dishevelled, dust-powdered, barely concealed anger brightening her dark blue eyes. The girl clearly embodied the disastrous combination of her mother's appearance and her father's arrogance. Lady Woodroffe spoke with equal clarity.

'In my day, girls were taught not to interrupt their betters.'

Mall smiled sweetly. 'I never interrupt my betters, ma'am.'

Alice, recognizing the commencement of hostilities, broke in. 'Mall, this is Lady Woodroffe. Her ladyship was travelling to Mr Askew's house, when she was attacked by a highwayman. And just outside Belford's gates! Imagine!'

Lady Woodroffe's penetrating tones interrupted.

'And of course, Sir Thomas, as the principal landowner in this area, must assemble a party of men to search for the villains. Robert will be delighted to assist him,' she continued generously, 'when he arrives.'

The stepdaughter addressed her again, dark hair that badly needed brushing framing a pale oval face. 'But what did he *look* like, Lady Woodroffe – the highwayman, I mean?'

Unwillingly, Lady Woodroffe's mind was dragged back to the uncomfortable incident in the woods.

'He looked like a fox, girl, like a fox. Cunning, evil, cruel.' And she was surprised at the genuine, unavoidable shiver of fear that iced the surface of her withered skin. Anger returning with the memory of the humiliation, her voice became harsh again.

'That gown is a disgrace, child. I'm surprised your step-mother allows you to be seen in public like that.'

The clash was unavoidable, this time.

As Mall left the room on her stepmother's instructions, the dusty hem of her skirts sullenly brushing the stairs, Lady Woodroffe turned to Alice Conway. 'She will grow out of hand if you are not careful. I remember her mother, she was the same. How old is she – sixteen, seventeen? Is she betrothed yet?' Lady Woodroffe adjusted the shawl that covered her shoulders. 'Take my advice, my dear. Find her a husband, and soon.'

Sent humiliatingly upstairs, Mall discarded the dusty dress for a nightgown, but did not go to bed. Instead, she knelt, wrapped in a blanket, leaning against the window seat, watching the small group of men headed by her father and Robert Askew ride out through Belford's gates. She had every intention of waiting for their return. For they might well bring the highwayman, and keep him guarded in one of Belford's less pleasant rooms before transferring him to Cambridge in the morning. Mall wanted to see him, with his mask and cloak, and his cunning, wicked, handsome face like a fox. Kneeling on the floor, her head cushioned on the old brocade window seat, she looked out to where the yellow moon, newly visible through the thinning rainclouds, bathed the trees at Belford's boundary with an enchanted, glamoured light. Perhaps she would see him and speak to him. Perhaps he was not as wicked as the old lady had suggested, but had some dashing ulterior motive for his crime. Perhaps he would fall in love with her, and she would smuggle him from Belford and save him from the hangman, and together they would leave the country . . . and travel . . . sail the blue Mediterranean on a galley rowed by slaves with skins as black as night . . . ride to Muscovy's icy wastes on fleet-footed steppe ponies . . . Her head cradled comfortably on the cushion, Mall slept.

Lady Woodroffe having been parcelled, complaining, into one of Belford's less spartan bedchambers, Alice Conway retired also. But not to sleep. Lady Woodroffe's more memorable comments had hurt her deeply. A gentle woman, Alice would have killed to protect her fragile son. Although she knew the child to be a little backward for his age, she had every hope that he would catch up when his health improved. She had not allowed herself to be discouraged by Ralph's lack of speech or inability to toddle more than a few halting steps; many children were slow at first, and still managed to draw level with their brighter brothers and sisters. But there would be no brothers and sisters for Ralph. Alice had long resigned herself to that. Only a half-sister, Maire, whom the family called Mall.

Mall. Lying alone in the lumpy four-poster, Alice's tangled thoughts turned to her stepdaughter. 'She will grow out of hand – find her a husband.' The destructive words, with their horrible ring of truth, echoed in Alice's ears. For she did find Mall difficult, she had never understood her, and feared that she would never do so. When they had first met, three years ago, Alice had seen an undisciplined, untidy child. True, she had glimpsed flashes of a fiery nature, and rebelliousness, but she had put them down to the girl's isolation from the rest of polite society. Treated with firmness and kindness, Mall would behave better, and they would grow close – or so Alice had believed. Mall would become the daughter Alice would never have. But that had not happened. Instead, there was an undercurrent of hostility between them, rarely stated, but insurmountable, a thin palisade of mistrust and resentment. It was Thomas's fault, of course. He had ruined the child, giving her a ridiculously elaborate education – totally unsuitable for a girl – and allowing her to do more or less as she wished. Alice had been able to make some improvements. Mall dressed better, and was generally – with some regrettable exceptions – tidier. Indeed, when her hair was properly styled and her face painted, she could look quite lovely. But Lady Woodroffe had been right, and she, Alice, had evaded her duties too long. Mall must be found a husband, and preferably before she did something so outrageous that no respectable man would have her. Alice recognized that she had been too involved with Ralph, and had neglected her duties as the mother of a stepdaughter of marriageable age. And, if only Mall would refrain from displaying some of her less feminine talents (shooting, for instance, or swimming), then she surely would secure a creditable match. Yes, she would bring the subject up to Sir Thomas before he left for London.

At last Alice slept, most of her troubles forgotten. The only fear that haunted her dreams, as pale light glimmered over the horizon, was how on earth she was going to face that awful old woman in the morning.

Sir Thomas, packing books in his study the next day, was not in the best of tempers.

A sleepless night spent trailing round the country after some wretched highwayman, who was doubtless two counties away by now, was not guaranteed to improve his state of mind. The hunt, *ordered*, thought Sir Thomas crossly, by that appalling old woman, had, of course, found nothing. Together with Robert Askew, who had confided through gritted teeth to Sir Thomas that he wished the miserable rogue had done the job properly and finished off the old hag, he had scoured the borders of Cambridgeshire and Essex, becoming soaked and mud-spattered in the process. Had it not been for the fact that her servants had independently backed up her tale, Sir Thomas would have taken most of Lady Woodroffe's story for the self-obsessed wanderings of senility. To waste the best part of a night in some fruitless parody of a hunt for a fellow who was supposed to resemble a fox (the highwayman had already acquired the nickname of Reynardine), seemed to Sir Thomas to be the height of folly. The news, brought to the house by one of the maidservants, that Lady Woodroffe had not been the only traveller molested the previous night had shaken Sir Thomas slightly, but had not weakened his resolve to leave for London. Irritably, he went back to his books.

'Thomas?'

It was Alice, standing in the doorway of his study.

'Come in, my dear.' He waved at the chaos around him. 'I am just choosing a few books to take with me.'

'Oh – I wish you did not have to go!'

Her voice, usually gentle and undemanding, was untypically passionate. It annoyed him – the last thing he felt like now, after the frustrations of the previous night, was an emotional scene.

'You know I have to go, Alice.' He tried to sound jocular. 'After all, we cannot disappoint the king!'

'Of course, Thomas.' Alice was looking older this morning, lines beginning to etch themselves in the fair skin around her eyes and mouth. 'It's just that – Lady Woodroffe – and the highwayman – and . . .' her voice trailed hopelessly away.

Sir Thomas's vexation increased. After three years of marriage, Alice really should no longer have any qualms about dealing with an old battleaxe like Lady Woodroffe.

'Lady Woodroffe will be gone this morning. Robert Askew stayed the night, and will escort her to his home shortly. And the highwayman –' his voice was impatient '– the highwayman will be in another part of the country by now. I am taking enough men with me, all armed, of course, so that we will be a match for any fool that dares waylay us. Indeed,' the last book was placed on the pile with an unnecessary thump, 'I almost wish he would. It would give me an opportunity to exact retribution for last night's fiasco. But do make sure Mall does not ride abroad by herself. If she wishes to ride she must take several of the men with her.' He turned away, fastening a leather strap about the books.

Alice knew this was the moment to bring up the subject that lay like a pebble trapped in her shoe, allowing her no peace. She overcame her sudden reluctance to speak.

'It is about Mall I wish to speak, Thomas. I'm worried about her.'

She had his full attention at last.

'Worried? She's not ill, is she?'

'She is not ill.' Alice spoke firmly, angered into bravery by an awareness that Sir Thomas's ready concern for his daughter was rarely shown for his son. 'We need to talk of her marriage.'

'Marriage? What marriage?'

'It is high time a betrothal was arranged for Mall. Perhaps you could consider the subject while you are at Court. After all, she is a considerable heiress.'

'Mall's far too young for marriage. She's only a child – perhaps in a year or two.' He turned from her again, and began to sort out papers in a drawer.

Alice persevered.

'She is not too young, Thomas. Mall is seventeen, quite old enough to be wed. Many girls are married far younger than she. You will spoil her chances if you leave it too late. It would be an excellent thing for Mall to have an establishment of her own – and children of her own. You know how fond she is of Ralph. It would be the making of her – and she has not always been easy of late.' Instantly, Alice regretted voicing any criticism, however mild, of her stepdaughter. It invariably produced the wrong response.

Sir Thomas said coldly: 'It would be considerably easier to arrange a match for Mall if you were to accompany me to Court, as I have frequently requested.'

Tears sprang unbidden to Alice's soft blue eyes. 'You know that I cannot come with you, Thomas, however much I would like to. London would not suit Ralph.'

Sir Thomas faced her. 'But, as you said, Mall is of an age to be wed now, not in three or four years time. Ralph has a nurse. He will remain at Belford, and you and Mall will follow me to London.'

26

Unable to explain her conviction that the delicate thread of Ralph's existence depended on her own constant vigilance, Alice said faintly: 'No, Thomas.' She dabbed at her eyes with a tiny lace handkerchief.

Sir Thomas softened slightly. She cried so easily nowadays, yet she had seemed such a simple, happy person three years ago. It was the baby, of course. Alice should have had a nursery full of healthy babies to cosset instead of one constantly failing infant and a well-tended grave in Belford's churchyard. He took his wife's hand.

'Perhaps you yourself should consider Mall's future, my dear.'

It had suddenly occurred to him that if his daughter married a local squire he would, at least, still see her. After all, if he were to find Mall a husband at Court, she might eventually live as far away as Cornwall or Northumberland. Or, more likely, Scotland, for when James Stuart had left his native country in 1603, to succeed to the English throne, many of his countrymen had accompanied him on his leisurely progress south, and had then stayed, enjoying England's softer, more indulgent air. A local match might not be so prestigious, but, on the other hand, Sir Thomas would not lose Mall completely.

'Yes, there are several families not too far from Belford. The Askews, the Murrays –' He tried to recall the names of the neighbours he had ignored for years. 'Oh, yes, the Galliers. Giles Galliers would be a fine match now that he has inherited the title . . . though I did hear some rumour concerning him and the eldest Murray girl. And there is his younger brother, of course. He has recently returned to the country, I believe.'

Alice frowned doubtfully. 'I seem to recall there was some unpleasantness –'

'Oh, women's tittle-tattle!' Sir Thomas tied a ribbon round the collection of papers. 'The lad was just a little wild, I expect. He'll settle down, I don't doubt. At least he had a few brains in his head – which is more than can be said for most of the empty-headed jackanapes at Whitehall!' The papers were thrown into a bag. 'Yes, you put your mind to it, my dear, and

27

when I return, perhaps we will see if something definite can be arranged.' He shut the drawers of the cabinet.

'But that will mean entertaining.' Alice put her hand on her husband's velvet sleeve. 'Not by myself – I couldn't, Thomas.'

With sudden inspiration, Sir Thomas smiled down at her. 'Then I will ask Leo to visit Belford for a while. He will keep you company, and host whatever occasion you wish. You know he will be delighted to stay – he may use my library, and he enjoys the company.'

For the first time that morning, Alice's brow cleared, and she smiled back at her husband. Leo Conway, Sir Thomas's younger brother, was a bachelor and a scholar. He was pleasant and undemanding, and played with Ralph for hours, reserving for the child an undivided, patient attention. And he would be good company for Mall. Alice had not realized how greatly she was dreading the husbandless weeks ahead, until Sir Thomas presented her with this solution. Leo would play chess with Mall – a game Alice had never been able to fathom – and they could share their mutual obsession with books. Lightly, Alice kissed Thomas on the cheek.

'Yes. That's the very answer. Tell Leo we will be delighted to see him.'

The heavy rain was short-lived. The oppressive late August heat returned all too soon, drying the puddles almost as quickly as they had appeared, turning the mud back to dust within a few days. The heat multiplied the insects; wasps, as bad-tempered as the humans they scourged, buzzed inside the festering fruit of the orchard, and gleaming aquamarine flies swarmed in kitchen and midden.

Along with Alice, and most of the other female inhabitants of Belford, Mall had spent much of these last, unbearable dog-days of the too-long summer in the kitchens, fighting the flies and heat to make jams and jellies, and bottle plums, pears, apricots and damsons. It was while they were wrapped in capacious jam-spattered aprons, their hair tied unbecomingly back from their perspiring foreheads, that Alice had broached the subject of marriage to her stepdaughter. She had, thought Alice, introduced the topic with the utmost tact and consideration, but the conversation, instead of becoming an adult, woman-to-woman discussion, had, of course, gone utterly wrong. To Mall, prickly with heat and dread, the idea had seemed appalling. Alice's phraseology, never her most notable asset, had been unfortunate, and Mall had seized upon the notion that she was to be shunted out of the way and into the arms of some fat, bucolic squire while her father resided, in blissful ignorance, in London. The scene had ended with tearful protestations on Alice's part, and sarcasm on Mall's, and the jam-making had been relinquished to the capable hands of Dorcas, while one woman retired to her chamber with a sick headache and a strong infusion of feverfew, and the other fled to the comparative coolness of the orchard.

In the orchard, divested of her sticky apron and seated comfortably on a wide apple tree branch, Mall began to realize that she had, perhaps, been a little hasty. After all, Alice had not tried to *force* her into anything, she had merely suggested that Mall was, perhaps, of an age to marry. And it was not exactly the prospect of marriage itself that had horrified her. Indeed, the thought of an establishment of her own, and perhaps the trips to Court that Alice's reluctance to visit London denied her, was quite appealing. And she was fully seventeen, and knew very well that the number of years of freedom a girl could expect declined in inverse proportion to the size of her dowry. No – it was simply that the choice of prospective bridegrooms was so depressing.

Mall wormed her way up the branch, and pulled off a particularly attractive apple. From her superior position she could see the front of Belford House, the courtyard from which her father had ridden out at the beginning of the week, and the stables and outbuildings. Behind her lay the dark coolness of the oak copse. The oak copse . . . The highwayman had not been found. As Martin Bartlett, one of the stable boys had said, Reynardine would hardly be hanging about waiting for them.

He would probably be in London, selling her ladyship's baubles in one of the city's less salubrious areas, enjoying his ill-gotten gains in the stews and taverns. Crossly, Mall bit into the apple. She did not expect love in marriage, but just the tiniest bit of romance would have been welcome. Cunning, evil, cruel . . . like a fox. That was how Lady Woodroffe had described Reynardine – but he had also been young, agile, a little cleverer than the average footpad. And with what sort of man would Mall Conway share her bed and the rest of her life? Well, there was Robert Askew . . . fat, boring Robert Askew. He would probably be a keen contender – until that dreadful old aunt of his died, he must be chronically short of money. Then there was Matthew Houlden, from Ickleton. A picture of Mr Houlden, taciturn and lugubrious, rose unfavourably in Mall's mind. But no, Matthew Houlden had recently and improbably married a pretty Essex girl. Ann Farrow – half her husband's age, her brightness and charm lost and wasted in that cold, damp, house. Was that the fate that awaited her, Mall Conway? The trouble was that she knew so few people. Sir Thomas, intolerant of all but his few intellectual equals; Lady Conway, nervous of accidentally revealing her own humble beginnings to those she still unconsciously considered to be her superiors – both had unwittingly conspired to keep Mall isolated from the rest of the world. The Murrays, from Saffron Walden? George Murray was at least young, but Mall could remember no more about him. Not a Roland nor a Sir Philip Sidney. The chances of a verray parfit gentil knight residing within fifty miles of Belford seemed remote indeed.

Mall threw the apple core neatly over the wall. Down the slope, in the stable yard, she could see Martin Bartlett, sitting on the doorstep of the tack room, unenthusiastically polishing bits and stirrups. In more liberal times, before Alice's arrival had jerked the household into something nearer conformity, Mall and Martin had passed many profitable hours together. Martin had taught the girl to fish, to shoot, to jump her horse, to row, to pick locks, and to play some rather dubious card games. When Sir Thomas had remarried, Martin had been in the process of teaching Mall to use a rapier, something at which, unrealistically, he fancied himself to be an expert. As swordplay necessitated the wearing of breeches, not skirts, this enjoyable if unfeminine pastime had been halted most emphatically by Mall's newly acquired stepmother. Martha, the buxom and obliging kitchenmaid, now wandered, water bucket in hand, across the courtyard in front of Martin's besotted gaze. Martin's attitude to Mall was generally one of amused, elder-brotherly tolerance; he was almost six months older than she, and an entire foot taller. But as for Martha – Martin rearranged his pose, rubbed harder at the leather, and called out greetings in what he hoped was a casual voice.

Mall, up in her tree, saw Martha smile slowly back, and continue her lazy amble to the kitchen. Sliding down off the branch, Mall walked, head flung back, Martha-like out of the orchard. But it was no use – Martha had thick chestnut hair and sly little hazel eyes . . . Mall's black hair curled also, but in impossible ringlets that would spring disobediently out of whatever net or ribbon was intended to contain them. And her eyes were blue – she had practised before her mirror looking knowing, like Martha, but it had not been convincing. But worst of all – Mall looked despairingly down at the flat void of her bodice. Where Martha spilled out in profusion, she had next to nothing. No wonder Belford was not besieged with the flower of the kingdom, all clamouring for her hand.

With sudden inspiration, Mall picked up her grass-stained skirts, and ran towards the stables. Martha had gone, Martin had put the saddle aside, and was staring, with an utterly ridiculous expression on his face, into the distance.

'It's no use, you know.' Martin jumped. 'She'll be in the kitchen, drinking ale with the rest of them.'

Martin swore, and threw the saddle back into the stable. 'I've had enough of this. It's too damned hot.'

'Then let's go for a ride.' Mall summoned her sweetest smile. 'Just think, Martin – cool woods, a breeze in the air –'

Martin looked suspicious. 'Her ladyship said you wasn't to go out on your own.'

'Lady Conway won't know!' Mall cried impatiently. Then, softening her tone, she added cajolingly: 'She'll be in her bedchamber for the whole afternoon. She'll think I'm in the library. And I won't be by myself – you'll be with me.'

Martin shook his head. 'I don't know, Mall –'

'I'll give you some of my ribbons for Martha – you know Sam gives her trinkets.'

Martin scowled, thinking of his rival. 'Scarlet ribbons? She likes red.'

'Every colour of the rainbow, my dear boy, if you will only take me out of this inferno!'

Finality in her voice, Mall went into the stables. Martin stood for a moment watching her retreating back, and then swore again, picked up two saddles, and followed.

They rode south, Mall on her small bay, Polly, Martin on a bad-tempered piebald hack capable of taking his ungainly height. Martin had appropriated a pistol from the armoury before they left – in case of highwaymen, he had said, optimistically.

Away from Belford, cantering through Essex's green and rolling plains, some of Mall's irritation of the last few days began to disperse. A few blue butterflies hung lazily in the late summer haze, echoing the colour of the scabious that mingled with the dust covered daisies at the side of the bridle paths and fields. A slight breeze rustled through the remaining strips of wheat and barley. Bareheaded, racing Martin into the open country, thoughts of marriage, of Alice, of her father, left Mall.

At length, on the brow of a hill crowned with a tiny circle of horse chestnuts, Mall reined Polly in, and waited triumphantly for Martin.

'Bitch of a horse,' he said crossly, swinging his long legs over the saddle, and looping the reins around a tree.

'Martin – that highwayman,' Mall wiped the sweat from her brow with a dusty hand. 'How did he do it? Rob Lady Woodroffe, I mean?'

Martin grinned, rolled back the sleeves of his shirt, and placed the pistol carefully on the grass.

'Watch.' He began to climb, finding feet- and hand-holds in the smooth lichen-covered trunk of the nearest horse chestnut. When he was about ten foot up the tree, he lowered himself on to the long, dipping branch, and began to edge along on his stomach.

'See, Mall!' Showing off, delighting in a captive female audience, he swung monkey-like under the branch, hanging in mid air, suspended by his crossed hands and ankles. Mall watched, half amused, half impatient, as the weird animal sounds Martin felt appropriate to his performance echoed across the silent valley. Then, righting himself, he called down:

'Move Polly in a bit – that's right – and keep her still.'

Polly had more sense than Martin. As the boy dropped inelegantly from the branch, whooping, 'Your money or your life!' the bay mare shied, reared, moved three places to the right, and watched unconcerned as Martin hit the grass with a thump.

Being seventeen, and having limbs made of rubber, only his pride was hurt. 'Poxy animal!' He lurched to his feet, knocking the earth off his breeches. 'Well, that's what they did – more or less – they jumped on to the horses' backs from the trees – oh, stop laughing, Mall!'

'Let's go to the pool.' She was hot, she had laughed too much for comfort, and the lure of the green opalescent glimmer in the valley below could not be resisted. Without waiting for Martin to reply, Mall mounted her horse and rode down the hillside to the ring of hawthorn and willow that enclosed the pool. It was a perfect circle, a deep, translucent bottle green edged with reeds and purple loosestrife, its surface as still as glass, flecked with gold and sapphire dragonflies dancing on the dark water. This was Kingscote land, Carleton land, but Mall Conway had been hot, dusty and sticky all day, and she intended to be hot, dusty and sticky no longer.

Kicking off her shoes, Mall dipped her toes in the ice cold water while the mare drank placidly beside her. The valley looked deserted, they had never encountered a soul here; only a few rabbits, stupefied in the hot sun, trembled on the hill above them, and a kestrel wheeled high and lonely in the azure sky.

At her side, Martin was fingering the pistol in his belt. His mind on other temptations, he said quickly:

'I'll join you in a minute, Mall. I'm going to that copse to try the pistol – Joshua's Joe hasn't let me near a gun lately.'

Very sensible of Joshua's Joe, thought Mall, absently, and began to unlace the front of her bodice. The gown, a dusty jam-stained silk, was soon discarded along with a linen petticoat at the circumference of the pool. Mall, clad only in her shift, waded into the pond, the water deliciously cold on her hot, bare legs. When the water had reached her waist, she struck out for the centre of the pool, and then turned, floating on her back. She was a competent swimmer; Martin had taught her years ago in the weed-filled mud of Belford's lake.

If she half closed her eyes, the dark trees wheeled in a circle about the lapis lazuli sky, the white hot sun the burning epicentre. Mall shut her eyes completely, her arms slowly scythed the water, her feet moved gently to keep herself afloat. Turning on her stomach, she peered down into the black depths of the water. The pond was deep; who could know what treasures, mysteries and monsters lurked in its foetid bed. Well, there was only one way to find out.

Taking a large gulp of air, Mall duck-dived, plunging down into the darkness. A few bubbles rose to the green surface, circular ripples swelled through the smooth stillness of the water. And it was those small evidences that caught the eye of one of the men, the older dark man who rode along the nadir of the valley and around the one semi-circular side of the pond. Then his gaze moved slowly to the blue gown lying bundled and neglected on the feathery reeds. His companion was younger, his hair an even more glorious gold than the corn stubble of the fields behind him, and he watched from behind as the older man nudged his horse to the bank.

'I hadn't realized country rides were to your taste, Nick.' He wiped his brow with a fine lace handkerchief.

34

It was the older man's reply that Mall first heard as her head pierced the mirror-glazed water above her.

'You are not quite conversant with all my tastes, my dear Lucas. Still, if you are bored, you have no need to stay.'

Wiping the water from her face with her hands, shaking her head to clear her ears, Mall opened her eyes. The bright colours, the jewels, the silks and satins and nodding plumes contrasted blindingly with the dark water and trees. Mall blinked rapidly, the moisture in her eyes blurring the figures before her. They were out of place: gorgeous alien creatures in the commonplace waving corn, peacocks amid the crowlike Essex countryside. And the nearest man, the one with the dark, pointed beard, was looking, inescapably, at her, with disturbing eyes that gazed into her soul. Transfixed momentarily, Mall was suddenly aware that she was half naked, her dripping wet hair plastered to her head, an anonymous stranger in unfamiliar territory, perhaps this man's territory.

The bearded gentleman said nothing. Slowly, he raised one hand and lifted his hat, inclining his head towards Mall in perfect courtesy. Then he pulled at the reins and guided his horse up the bank and away from the pool. His golden-haired companion followed him.

The dark-haired man waited until he was out of earshot of the pool before speaking again.

'Now who, I wonder, was *that*?'

Lucas, his profile classically perfect again the deepening blue sky, drew level with him.

'Some slut from one of your yeoman farms, Carleton. Probably the nearest thing she's had to a wash in years.'

Sir Nicholas Carleton did not reply. He, unlike Lucas Holland, had noticed that the gown thrown so carelessly on the reeds was of good quality material, and that around the neck of the unknown bather had hung a thin gold chain.

Carleton smiled. 'I don't think so, Luke. And as I said –' he took in the boy's petulant frown '– you are not yet conversant with quite all my tastes. If you begin to find Kingscote tedious, perhaps you had best return to London.'

He still smiled, but there was no humour in his dark, narrow eyes.

The boy hastily protested: 'Not at all – I simply meant that I am more at home in the withdrawing room than behind a plough.'

Sir Nicholas said blandly, 'I had not thought otherwise, my dear.'

They had reached the crest of the shallow escarpment. The two riders paused, looking down into the valley to where a house, large and breathtakingly graceful, rose, moated, from the Essex grasslands.

'I hear that Richard Galliers is back.' Luke's voice was casual, but his beautiful blue eyes were cunning.

Almost imperceptibly, Carleton's face changed, something dangerous incised on the handsome Spanish features.

'Dear Luke. I have *that* information already. But I believe Mr Galliers can wait. I have discovered further business to keep me at Kingscote. I think we shall delay our departure to London for just a little longer.'

Then Carleton spurred his horse and rode for the house, and the words he sang under his breath were inaudible to Luke's jewelled ears:

> '*Beauty sat bathing by a spring*
> *Where fairest shades did hide her.*
> *The winds blew calm, the birds did sing*
> *The cool streams ran beside her.*
> *My wanton thoughts enticed mine eye*
> *To see what was forbidden . . .*'

CHAPTER TWO

A few weeks after his memorable evening in the Dagger tavern, Giles Galliers had, unwillingly, to return to London. Unwillingly, because, after stubborn but gentle persuasion on Anna Murray's part and many avowals of virtue and industry on Giles's, John Murray had grudgingly agreed to allow his daughter to become betrothed to Giles Galliers. Unwillingly also, because there were aspects of that evening he had spent with Richard that Giles had since begun to contemplate with a distinct unease.

But one of the conditions of his betrothal had been that Giles make good Amyott's tottering finances. To do that, it had been necessary to go to London to put his Town house up for sale. His business complete, Giles would have left for Amyott that very afternoon, had he not received a somewhat cryptically worded note from his brother – their first contact since an intoxicated leave-taking in the Dagger. It was with an unpleasant premonition of impending catastrophe that Giles entered the Red Bull playhouse in Clerkenwell to keep his appointment with Richard that afternoon.

Inside the playhouse, Giles soon realized, first, that the play was unlikely to reach its natural conclusion, and, secondly, that

Richard was nowhere in sight. Through the orange peel and apple cores, the jeers and catcalls, Giles searched for the familiar dark head. He swore under his breath. The stage – but there was only one man seated on the stage, a glorious sunburst of orange silk, the cruel orchestrator of the crowd's ridicule . . . but not Richard. Giles had sufficient humanity to feel fleeting pity for the actors, especially the boy who played the heroine's part, mocked and mimicked by the seated gentleman.

Giles turned to leave, and then remembered my lord's room. There was, of course, the faint possibility that Richard had done the conventional thing and taken one of the best seats in the house. Hot and exasperated, Giles made his way up the stairs. But my lord's room was almost empty: an oasis of quiet in the mounting hysteria of the playhouse. Only one of the cushioned seats was occupied. A man, gorgeous in turquoise satin, a ruff of impossible dimensions circumnavigating his neck, lounged, eyes half closed, barely glancing at the stage below. Again, not Richard. But in spite of himself, Giles smiled.

'Esmé.' Seating himself on an adjacent stool, he tweaked the ruffled and embroidered sleeve. 'Esmé. It's good to see you.'

Oyster-coloured eyes opened a fraction and a distant, weary trace of a smile enlivened the thin, intelligent face.

'Giles, my dear. How wonderful to see you. London has been moribund without the Galliers brothers.'

'Have you seen Richard?' Giles mopped his perspiring forehead with an inadequate silk handkerchief. 'Is he here? He sent me a note.'

Esmé Molyneux shrugged. 'I have seen nothing of Richard for at least a fortnight, I am grieved to say. He is not here. The last time I saw him was at a *wonderful* banquet. His behaviour was atrocious.' The long, ascetic face looked wistful. 'It was the best evening I have had in years. Anyway, Giles, enjoy the play. It's a tragedy, and quite amusing . . . although whether they will be allowed to finish it, I really can't say. It's a shame, there's nothing I enjoy so much as a bad tragedy.' He rearranged the perfect lace of his cuffs. 'When they take up the lathes and tiles and throw them,' Esmé's bored gaze surveyed the riotous, baying crowd 'that will be the end of it. The lad is new to this game, and will not endure much more.'

Looking at the stage, Giles saw that Esmé was right. There was a suspicious tremble in the heroine's voice, a more realistic quiver than the boy's dramatic talents seemed to imply.

'That fellow –' Esmé lowered his voice a little, and flicked his fan in the direction of the man on stage '– that fellow began it. He yawns, he mimics, he mocks – the audience adore him.'

Giles frowned. 'Who is it?'

The thin mouth made an expression of distaste. 'His name's Ellenby. Some distant cousin of the Howards, I believe. Doubtless he hopes to rise to wealth and glory on the backs of their present good favour with the king.'

'Then he cannot be as brainless as he appears,' said Giles, letting his gaze wander over the orange-clad figure on the stage. 'Perhaps he possesses a little of the Howard cunning. There can be few neater ways of securing your family's supremacy than by marrying the king's favourite.'

'Some say Frances Howard married for love, Giles.'

The corners of Giles's mouth twitched in a smile. 'I doubt whether she would have wed her precious Robin if he had been a pot boy or tapster.'

'I doubt,' said Esmé Molyneux coolly, 'whether her great-uncle Northampton would have let her. What more gorgeous bait could there be than the lovely Frances? What more bitter pill for his enemy Pembroke to swallow than to see a Howard wed to Robert Kerr?'

Giles nodded. 'Useful, to be friendly with the Howards.'

Molyneux spoke softly from behind the spread segments of his fan. 'Although perhaps not quite as useful as it once was, Giles. The Howards may at present be indisputably the most powerful family in England, but they will not necessarily remain so. You have been incarcerated at Amyott too long, Giles, and have missed the latest excitement. His Majesty's attentions have been wandering – in the direction of Mr George Villiers, placed conveniently centre stage by our revered Archbishop of Canterbury.'

39

Giles's brown eyes still inspected the auditorium in a fruitless search for his brother. 'Villiers? Do I know him? Should I know him?'

The habitually bored features betrayed some animation. 'If you had seen him, you could not forget him. He is the handsomest creature you ever saw – and there is a little more in his head than Kerr's.'

Giles grinned, and rested one booted foot on the wooden balustrade. 'I doubt whether Lady Somerset or the king himself fell in love with Kerr for his intellect.'

'Precisely.' Molyneux waved away a persistent fly. 'Apparently the Earl of Somerset and his lovely and virtuous wife are unhappy about Villiers. His lordship sulks, and the lady's temper is even less certain than usual. It should brighten up the winter – a nice, sordid little dogfight between the Howards and the Pembrokes – plus the Archbishop, of course. And as the willing pawns, those two beauties, Kerr and Villiers. Perhaps it will relieve boredom – I shall be in need of a distraction if you and Richard are not to be about?'

Giles shrugged. 'I can hardly answer for Richard. As for myself, you know that my affections –'

The rest of his sentence was lost, drowned in the crowd's frenzied howl. The lovers had left the stage, the boy almost in tears. Comic relief had arrived in the variegated patchwork form of the Fool. An anarchic parti-coloured motley of reds and yellows, his costume layered, ragged, slashed and frilled, his white, wicked face half seen under his hood, it had taken the Fool just one topical and utterly obscene remark to recapture what the previous players had lost: the audience's attention. Then followed a short extemporized song, that mocked the rowdier elements of the yard and finished with indecently pointed ridicule unmistakably directed at Ellenby, the man seated on stage. Giles leaned forward, eyes narrowed in an attempt to peer under the enveloping hood and identify the pale, mercurial face. There was something familiar about that damned figure.

Esmé, too, was curious. 'Tis not de Salis – nor Jack Cates – he sometimes plays the Fool. I doubt if our friend will like to be usurped.'

Giles's gaze travelled to where Ellenby, galled by the fickle allegiance of the crowd, had drawn his rapier and begun to wave in imitation of the Fool with his bauble. The crowd roared their approval: orange peel, nuts, ladies' and gentlemens' fans, less permanent fixtures of the playhouse itself, lunged into the air, scattering the stage like colourful hailstones.

It took the Fool only a few whirling, somersaulting seconds to reach Ellenby's side, and only a few more to take, to the audience's horrified delight, a thin dagger from the swaggering folds of his costume. With one deft flick the dagger sent Ellenby's rapier soaring into the air, a glittering succession of silver arcs, ending neatly, flourishingly, with the filigree hilt in the Fool's outstretched hand. Bowing excessively to the ecstatic audience, he turned and tossed the rapier back to Ellenby.

There was angry humiliation on Ellenby's face as he rose from his stool, rapier in one hand, grabbing the Fool's dirty yellow sleeve with the other. The laughter and excited expectation of the crowd swamped Ellenby's words, but the attitude of his rapier, the attitude of challenge, was unmistakeable.

The silence, as the Fool turned to Ellenby and smiled, was instantaneous. A duel on a public stage – the Red Bull was better than ever this year.

The Fool's bauble, and Ellenby's hat, gloves, cloak and boots were tossed to the side of the stage.

'A sword to a dagger,' said Esmé softly. 'An unequal challenge. He is therefore either truly a fool –'

'Or very good,' finished Giles absently. He tried to remember the note he had received that morning. What had it said? 'See me at the Red Bull this afternoon.' *See* me . . . and Giles's eyes went back to the stage, as the duellists made their brief formal salute.

'En bloody garde,' muttered Giles to himself. 'Hell, Esmé, that's Richard.'

The oyster-coloured eyes focused on him, and then on the stage as the Fool's hood fell back uncovering dishevelled dark hair beneath. Molyneux smiled. 'The devil – this play is becoming most enjoyable. I have no knowledge of Ellenby's capabilities, but, Richard, I seem to remember, is a genius. Oh, this is *most* interesting.'

'*Interesting*!' Giles's voice, reverberating in the roofless circle of the playhouse, was louder than he had intended. 'He may be killed – or he may kill the fellow – on a public stage! In front of –'

'Only about five hundred, my dear. Audiences are always low at this time of year.'

'Christ.' Giles, his mouth set in a thin, hard line, planted his elbows on the balustrade in front of him, and prepared to watch the fight.

The dagger that Richard Galliers held lightly in his left hand was fully fourteen inches long, the blade of stiletto fineness. The hand that gripped it was sun-browned, strong and skilful, and Galliers possessed a tumbler's speed and agility. But a sword to a dagger was, as Esmé Molyneux had said, poor odds. Ellenby's rapier was more than twice the length of the other man's weapon, its point needle sharp. Green eyes wide in the dead white face, luxuriant sleeves pushed back, Galliers edged sideways, parrying the flickering rapier. His enjoyment was plain: he revelled in the fight, all but taunting Ellenby with his expertise in slipping away from the darting blade. But Ellenby's temper, scoured with humiliation, had worn thin. As Galliers turned to crack a joke with the audience, Ellenby closed in, anger lending him courage. The rapier whirled, catching the afternoon sun. Galliers' free hand snaked out, grabbing a metal salver used in the previous scene, blocking the downward, headward, impetus of the rapier. The makeshift shield diverted the sword, Galliers moved forward, dagger in hand, his foot jabbed, and Ellenby fell to one knee, his fine silk shirt ripped from shoulder to wrist.

The rapturous, terrified gasp of the audience ebbed as Ellenby staggered to his feet, and the two parted and circled again.

'I think the years abroad have taught him new tricks,' whispered Esmé, and Giles, sweat beginning to gather on his brow, was forced to acknowledge that Richard had spent time in another school than that of the drunken old fencing master of their childhood days.

It was Ellenby, however, who drew first blood. Spurred by shame, and with the advantage of a longer reach, he hit the dagger aside, and thrust his rapier forward into his opponent's face, just below the eyes. One yellow-clad arm lunged out, the plate spun between Ellenby's legs, and the gallant sprawled on the stage as a thin line of red disfigured Richard's mocking white face.

'Come *on*, Richard.' Giles forgot his anxieties in the tension of the moment. 'Get the bastard.'

Crouching, the knife held steady in his left hand, Richard's voice echoed derisively around the playhouse.

> *'Ile lay me down – and bleed a while*
> *And then Ile rise – and fight again.'*

Giles, watching, knuckles gripped white on the wooden balustrade, muttered, 'He can't do it – Ellenby'll never let him in close enough.'

'They'll need to finish it soon.' Even Molyneux's urbane voice betrayed some tension. 'Some killjoy will have gone for the watch. Richard will know that.'

Richard Galliers, of course, knew perfectly well that it would be unwise to prolong the fight. His hair curled to his forehead with sweat, a thin red trickle of blood running down his cheekbone to mingle with the red patches on his clothing, his gaze jumped once, rapidly, to the entrance. Ellenby's discarded cloak still lay downstage. Galliers stooped, grabbed it, and flicked it round his right arm. Bright in the pool of sunlight through the open roof, the cloak spun in a flaring ellipse around the outthrust rapier, muffling the blade. Galliers closed in, and as the entire audience of the Red Bull watched in collective disbelief, the dagger stabbed into Ellenby's stomach. Giles stared, mesmerized, sick horror in his throat as Ellenby made one peculiar gargling noise, slid to the floor, and lay still. Richard calmly replaced the dagger under the motley folds of his bloodstained costume. And it was his voice that broke the silence. He hooked his hands under Ellenby's shoulders, and dragged the body through the curtains to the rear of the stage. '*I'll lug the guts into the neighbour room*', he announced clearly, and a woman laughed somewhere, hysteria in her voice.

'Will you,' said Esmé Molyneux succinctly, 'assist him in leaving the country, Giles? Or do you wish to disassociate yourself completely?'

Giles could not speak. Somewhere in his dazed brain, John Murray's outraged Puritan voice could be heard echoing through the pandemonium of the theatre: Your brother has killed a man in a *playhouse* . . .

'*Giles.*' It was Molyneux again, urgency keeping the accustomed drawl from his voice. 'Giles, we may consider Ellenby slain in a fair fight, but I doubt if the Howards will. They will be baying for Richard's blood before the day is out. And his reputation will not exactly assist him through the scandal. If we are quick, we can get him to Gravesend and ship him out of the country before it is too late. *If* you wish to help.'

Anna. Richard. The new love and the old alliance.

Giles and Esmé battled their way to the tiring house at the side of the stage. By means of grim desperation and elbows, they succeeded in forcing their way through the mob. Heads turned, phrases pierced the jumble of sound. Giles seized the opportunity to whisper a few words in one of the player's ears and to slip a few coins into his palm.

Inside the tiring house it was scarcely any quieter. Smoke and curses issued from one corner of the room where a card school contended a disputed win. The obscure classical army of the first act were removing swords and bucklers from their sides. The red-eyed heroine unlaced the bodice of his gown, flat-chested beneath the stiff buckram. Through plumes, silks, satins, gilt and glitter there appeared to be no sign of the cause of the havoc. Then, just as Giles was beginning to believe that Richard had done the sensible thing and quickly left the playhouse, he saw him. Seated on a stool in the centre of the

44

room, talking, apparently calmly, to two of the players, he was the single still centre of a wheel of activity. He had removed the multi-coloured finery of the stage, and was dressed in black breeches and hose and a plain white shirt, and was engaged in wiping off the white stage paint with a piece of rag.

'God's teeth, to sit like that when you have just killed a man!' exploded Giles, battering his way through the throng to his brother's side.

'Richard!'

Galliers looked up. His skin was pale against the thin red line of the rapier cut. He smiled slowly.

'How pleasant to see you, Giles. Let me introduce you to my fellow players. Benedict –' Richard waved a hand '– and Nathaniel,' a tall, thin spider of a man. 'This is my elder brother, Lord Amyott. Did you enjoy the performance, Giles? It was a little more histrionic than I had intended it to be, but –'

It was Esmé Molyneux's poorly concealed snort of amusement behind him as much as Richard's words that drove Giles to violence. Seizing his brother's shoulders, he shook him hard, as, almost incoherent with anger, the words hurtled from his lips.

'Jesus Christ, Richard, you sit there – calmly disrobing yourself – if you have no thought for the idiot that you have just killed – or for our mother – I had believed you would still have some vestige of self-preservation.'

'Calm yourself, Giles –'

Giles hissed: 'The man is dead! The fellow was a protégé of the Howards. You must get yourself to France *now*, while there is still time!'

Richard's long hands grasped the arms that shook him unmercifully, and stilled them. Wide-eyed, he said innocently:

'What? Exile myself for winding an Ellenby? It seems a severe sentence.'

If his arms had not already been held, and if Esmé Molyneux had not just then placed a restraining hand on his back, Giles would have happily have hit his younger brother. As it

45

was, he stood up, hands clenched by his sides as he heard Esmé say carefully:

'Richard. I saw your knife go into his stomach.'

Richard shook his head. 'No. You thought you did. Look.'

The dagger was still in Richard's belt. He withdrew it, and, to the small crowd that had gathered in hopes of witnessing another fight, held out the pearl-inlaid shaft in his right hand. He balanced the stiletto tip in the outstretched palm of his left hand. Then he pushed. Giles took one sharp inward breath and watched, hypnotized, as the dagger sank partway to its hilt. There was no blood, and no sign of pain on Richard's face. Then the left hand was removed, and the blade of the knife sprang out. With no expression in his eyes, Richard said gently: 'A pretty toy. Ellenby is vomiting in the privy.'

Giles's knees had suddenly become inadequate for the task of bearing him. He collapsed to sit on top of a wicker basket and almost inaudibly, in the renewed chatter and laughter that had broken out, whispered:

'My God, Richard, I could kill you for that.'

Richard was pulling on black riding boots. 'That would hardly assist your suit with Mistress Murray.' He laid an unnecessarily solicitous hand on Giles's shoulder. 'Don't fret so, dear brother. Unparalleled disgrace – well, no more than we already suffer – is not about to fall on our noble family. For your sake I will even debase myself and make my peace with Ellenby. He must have finished disgorging the contents of his stomach by now.' And he was gone, leaving the tiring room by a side door.

Giles looked at Molyneux and shook his head. Esmé brushed invisible dust from the immaculate silk of his doublet.

'He will do as he says, Giles. Richard is possessed of considerable personal charm when he chooses to exercise it. He will persuade the ass that it was all a game, an entertainment of their joint divising, and the fellow will fall in love with him.' He removed his hat, and began to tweak the disrupted feathers into place. 'He will, Giles,' he added, almost to himself. 'After all, we all do.'

46

Giles laughed, a sound devoid of any amusement. 'Damn it, Esmé, I'm going to get drunk.'

There was a bottle of wine, half full, next to the discarded Fool's costume. It occurred to Giles, as he pulled out the stopper and began to drink, that Richard might also have been slightly drunk. There had been something about his eyes, and a luxuriance in his voice, but it was hard to tell. The wine was sour, but Giles proceeded to drink it conscientiously. He thought briefly, painfully, of Anna, experiencing a sudden intolerable longing for her uncomplicated company.

'And this is my elder brother, Lord Amyott. Giles, unwrap yourself from that appalling bottle and greet Mr Ellenby.'

Giles stumbled to his feet, knocking over the bottle, and the thick dark dregs of wine dribbled over the rush-strewn floor. He made a sketchy bow to Ellenby – *Lionel* Ellenby, Richard politely informed him. The man did not look too much the worse for his experience. He walked a little stiffly, perhaps, and was somewhat pale about the jaw, but no more so than Richard, whose bright, dark-shadowed eyes belied the quietly courteous façade, and did nothing to reassure Giles's troubled mind. He noted, as he made conventional, meaningless remarks to Ellenby, that Molyneux had been, sickeningly, right. Ellenby's heavily ringed hand touched the white silk of Richard's shirt, and his soft, slightly protruding eyes did not leave Richard's face.

Richard added a quilted black velvet doublet and a wide-brimmed hat to his earlier outfit, and walked with Ellenby out of the tiring room, oblivious of curious stares. A kindly word, a friendly clasp of the shoulders, a benign smile, and Ellenby was dispatched on his way. Giles scowled after the retreating figure.

'What, still not content, Giles?' Richard's voice, gentle and mocking at his ear. 'I understood you wished me to make friends with him.'

Giles felt outmanoeuvred and irritable, and in need of another drink. He pulled Richard aside. 'I didn't say you should make him your *dog*. Merely – not *kill* him – oh, what's the use?'

Richard's expression was distressingly angelic. 'But it's a nice dog, Giles. A helpful, *useful* dog.'

'You can befriend whom you like, you can bed whom you like, you can kill whom you like – but for God's sake do it in private in future!' Giles took a deep breath. 'And now we have business to discuss, Richard.'

Heavy-lidded eyes scanned the still crowded playhouse. A small riot had broken out in one corner of the yard, and two colourfully dressed whores sought for trade in another. Some eyes, particularly the women's, turned to Richard Galliers, examining questioningly the rapier cut that he wore like a banner on his face. Giles grabbed his brother's arm.

'Not here, then. Somewhere quiet.'

The somewhere quiet proved to be Esmé Molyneux's lodgings, in Holborn Street, a reasonably short walk from the Red Bull. They squeezed through the crowds and stage wagons and sedan chairs that blocked the narrow streets. The route, darkened by overhanging buildings, was constricted and crooked, winding past the cook shops, the street sellers, the carriers' carts that threatened to obstruct the road entirely.

Even though he had already managed to achieve a state of mild inebriation, Giles felt surprise, as he always did, on entering Esmé's rooms. He knew Esmé to be a man of comparatively little fortune, with no surviving close relatives. He knew him also to be intelligent, witty, a sympathetic listener. But the rooms – restrained, sober, almost austere – were totally out of character with his opulent appearance. The only visible indications of luxury were the books that lined the walls, and the large silver mirror that stood to one side of the fireplace. Molyneux had one manservant, an emaciated old man who had the look of a distinguished scholar fallen on hard times.

Wine bottles were opened, glasses found, and Esmé, who had discovered a small stain on the glorious turquoise satin of his doublet, excused himself, and left the room.

48

'Dear Esmé. Always so tactful.' Richard perched himself on the edge of the table in front of Giles. 'Before you become totally crapulent, Giles, I believe we had a wager.'

Giles's head jerked up suddenly, and his gaze fixed, with uneasy fascination, on Richard's hand as his brother withdrew a small package from an inside pocket of his doublet.

'You lost, I'm afraid.' Richard took Giles's hand, upturned the palm, and something slithered from the package, glittering, sparkling in the late afternoon sun. Giles's fist clenched suddenly shut, and his eyes, alert now, stared wide at Richard.

'It belonged to our mother. She was always a poor card player. Perhaps you can return it to her, somehow.'

'*Christ* – who did you –? how the devil –?'

Richard put a warning finger to his lips. 'Hush now, Esmé returns. Unless you want him to know of our little wager?'

Giles groaned and shook his head. 'Oh, God, no – *nobody* –' He hastily thrust the object into his purse. His alcoholic inclinations rapidly transformed into a quest for amnesia and, with a bottle of Esmé's excellent wine to hand, he set about pursuing his goal singlemindedly.

The evening passed pleasantly enough. Slightly animated with drink, Esmé described the epic poem he planned to write that would compare man's four humours with the four seasons of the year. Giles, fired with intoxicated enthusiasm, discoursed upon crop rotation, a subject which had recently become dear to his heart. Richard Galliers, lounging on Esmé's daybed, tuned the old and temperamental lute that had lain untouched in a corner of the room for many months. And when his long fingers, with their one small green-stoned ring, began to play, they caressed the old strings and coaxed melody from the unprepossessing catgut and pearwood with perfect co-ordination. Pieces of tunes at first, fragments of ballads, of airs, and of dances. Then a gentle song of Dowland's that Giles recognized as a favourite from years past. There were words to that song, but he had drunk too much to remember them. He frowned into his glass, but found no inspiration there. The music changed again, to a tune of Richard's own composing. The words were

Sir Thomas Wyatt's, and softly, Richard began to sing them. Somewhere in the confused fuddle of Giles's brain, there was a bass to Richard's tenor. Light broke, and Giles, pleased with himself, also sang.

Esmé Molyneux closed his eyes to hear better. He himself had no voice and no ear – but just for a moment, listening, he could lose himself . . . Bass and tenor threaded above, below, and round the intricate accompaniment, and a short stillness followed the song. The spell broke with three loud chords, and Giles laughed and launched drunkenly into a long and increasingly indecent French ballad.

Somehow Giles, losing the order of the verses, managed to bring the song to a reasonably satisfactory conclusion. He leaned back in his chair and, laughter still in his eyes, loosened the laces at the front of his doublet. 'Our mother taught us that one. Do you remember, Richard? Only the first verses, of course – the rest came from somewhere else –'

Like curtains closing, the amusement vanished from Richard's face. He stood up and carefully replaced the lute in its corner.

It occurred to Esmé, watching, detached, that a change of subject was called for.

'I have my epic, Giles has his fields – how have you occupied yourself since your return, Richard?'

Richard turned to face him, one hand on Giles's shoulder.

'Oh, I have found amusement enough, have I not, Giles? Come, don't choke, dear brother.'

Giles made an inadequate attempt at mopping up the spilt wine with his handkerchief. Richard seated himself on the daybed again after refilling the glass.

'I have a little – unfinished business – from three years ago to see to. Apart from that – I shall probably return abroad again quite soon. As our dear mother does not see fit to receive me –'

'She does,' interrupted Giles opaquely, looking up from the glass. 'I mean, she will. In October, that is, when she returns from the Murrays.'

His eyes met Richard's.

'Worthy Giles. Labouring away on my account. Or did you wish to see a united family for your glorious nuptials next year? Was that it? It will take longer than a year to achieve that, I fear.'

Giles felt his face redden. Memories of the long and bitter discussion with his mother, in which he had eventually managed to secure an agreement from her to see Richard, lingered in his mind. He frowned and rubbed his eyes. The square mullioned panes of Esmé's window were shifting awkwardly.

The thin-stemmed glass slipped from his hand and shattered on the floorboards. Giles's head slid slowly, inevitably, downward, and stilled, cradled in his inert arms on the wine-pooled table.

Richard moved forward and gently adjusted the heavy head. 'That was always Giles's failing. Reasonably coherent one minute, totally unconscious the next. How pleasant to be able to achieve oblivion so effortlessly.' Rearranging the lifeless arms into a more tenable position, Richard replaced his brother's head.

Esmé stooped to pick the shards of glass from the floor.

There was a bitterness in Richard's voice that he had not heard before. He poured more wine, and said gently:

'You were not kind to Giles. He means well.'

'*Child of glorious great intent*. I know. But he will receive his just reward – estate, wife, children – the present Lady Amyott to nurse through her disappointed old age.'

Esmé looked up at the dark, arrogant face. The only sign of emotion was a faint tension in the muscles around Richard's mouth. And you are not drunk at all, he thought, but said nothing.

Richard, bottle and glass in hand, dropped full length on the floor at Molyneux's side, his hands propping his head. 'Now, my dear, I wish you and I to have a little talk.'

With an amused ironic awareness that Richard had manoeuvred this scene to suit his needs precisely, Esmé asked, 'About anything in particular?'

'Oh, definitely. And with my brother – dead to the world, shall we say – we can talk more freely.'

Esmé's eyes widened, and his painted eyebrows lifted a fraction. 'I noticed the frequency with which you filled Giles's glass. And what, Richard, are we to talk about?'

Richard closed his eyes. 'Of our betters. Their tastes, their friends, their peccadillos – their scandals.' A small smile. 'In particular, I should like to talk about the Howards. A remarkably successful family, the Howards. There was – let me see – Henry Howard, the Earl of Northampton. Dead a couple of months past, I hear, but he was both Robert Kerr's friend, and Lord Privy Seal. And then there's Thomas Howard, the Earl of Suffolk, doing rather well for himself as Lord Treasurer just now. Oh, and Frances Howard, his daughter, of course. Formerly Frances Devereux, Countess of Essex, but now, I am told, Frances Kerr, Countess of Somerset. A rather impressive career, don't you think, Esmé, for a girl not twenty-three years old? Although –' and the long, mobile mouth curled a touch at the corners '– it is also a little confusing. How can Frances Howard have wed Robert Kerr while her first husband still lives? You must enlighten me, Esmé – it all sounds the most *delightful* scandal.'

'Delightful,' said Esmé, dryly. 'Especially for the unfortunate Earl of Essex. Frances Howard claimed that her husband was impotent – that the marriage had never been consummated. That she was a virgin.'

'And was she?'

Esmé chuckled. 'Richard, Frances Howard was no more virgin than you are. She just wanted Robert Kerr very badly – for his influence or his looks, I am not sure. The remainder of the Howard brood – Northampton in particular – wanted the Kerr alliance in order to guarantee their ascendancy with King James.'

'So the marriage was annulled?'

Esmé inclined his head. 'Frances Howard obtained her divorce from Essex a year ago. Robert Kerr was created Earl of Somerset in the November of 1613, and he and Frances

Howard were married – with the king's blessing, of course – at the end of December. Somerset is weak – the lady is not. Doubtless Robert Kerr does what his wife tells him to. And she is ambitious – a lovely face, but a fearful cold heart.'

Richard said dreamily, 'I saw her once, before I left the country. Honey-coloured hair, and eyes of blue ice. A beautiful girl.'

Esmé's tone was dismissive. 'She has the face of an angel, that is not disputed. Richard – to obtain her annulment, she had to prove her virginity. She achieved this miracle (heavily veiled, of course) despite rumours abounding of her frequent love affairs. Our late Prince Henry referred to her as a "used glove" – and he was right, I have no doubt of that.'

'And this marriage – was it easy? Were there objections – objectors?'

Esmé glanced down at Galliers, but the lidded eyes told him nothing. 'Plenty of objectors, dear boy. There was Pembroke, of course, who simply loathes the Howards – and George Abbot. Now, George Abbot was a most notable objector. As Archbishop of Canterbury, he was one of the commission examining the case for the annulment of the Essex marriage. King James had to enlarge the commission in order to counter Abbot's influence. Whether Abbot was affected by moral scruples or by factional interests, I really cannot say. Whatever his motives, his objections were overridden, and the happy couple were wed. A magnificent wedding – the bride wore her hair down, to prove her maidenhood.' Esmé glanced down again, and took a short, calculated risk. 'Oh, and there was poor Sir Thomas Overbury, of course.'

'Why "poor"?'

The gamble paid off: Richard's eyes opened a fraction, minutely betraying interest.

Molyneux's voice dropped. The manservant had come into the room to light the candles. 'Overbury had been an associate of Kerr's for many years. Some say their relationship was much as that between Kerr and King James. As you know, Kerr has a brain somewhat less agile than that of a snail, so it was

Overbury who penned Kerr's love letters to the then Lady Essex.'

'He was a friend of the Howards?'

Esmé shook his head. 'No. He loathed them. I expect he found it appealing to act as procuror for their daughter. Overbury never thought it would come to marriage. He was happy for Frances Howard to become Kerr's mistress, but he tried to dissuade Kerr from marriage. He must have been somewhat tactless, for he presently found himself in the Tower. And in the following September –' Esmé paused, and Richard looked up.

'Yes?'

'In the following September, he died.'

'Ah.' There was a small silence, and then Richard said softly, 'I see. How convenient – and coincidental.'

'Quite. At the end of that month the annulment of the Essex marriage came through. And on the twenty-sixth of December, the King gave his blessing, and the happy couple were wed.'

There was a muffled groan from the table. In one fluid movement Richard was on his feet. 'And Overbury – he died of a broken heart, the measles, the King's Evil –'

Giles groaned again, and raised a creased face from the table.

Esmé stood, one jewelled hand touching Richard's shoulder. 'And *your* interest in this delightful affair, Richard?'

'Oh – nothing direct.' Richard faced him. 'Merely a sprat to net a mackerel, a springe to catch a woodcock . . .'

'A noose to loop around someone's neck?' Esmé's voice was very quiet. '*Whose* neck, Richard?'

There was no friendship, no warmth, in the hard emerald eyes. 'My affair, Esmé. Mine, and mine alone. Understand?'

Esmé inclined his head. 'As you wish. But one word of advice, whether you want it or not. You are treading on very dangerous ground. Be very careful. There are rumours –' He broke off abruptly. Giles's eyes were open. He rubbed at them with one hand, and moaned again.

'Oh my God. I feel –'

'As if a hundred badly trained horses have been kicking at

54

your head?' Richard looked at him unsympathetically. 'That, my dear Giles, is the effect of intemperance.'

His normally neat hair disordered, Giles tried unsuccessfully to relace the loosened front of his doublet. The slight, discomforting weight of the package given to him earlier by Richard did not improve his spirits. He watched with unaffectionate eyes as Richard picked up his hat and gloves.

'Dear me, if only the fair Anna could see you now, brother. I must regretfully take my leave of your fascinating company – I have a call to make. I'm sure Esmé will be delighted to throw you on a horse tomorrow morning, and point it in the direction of Amyott. Oh, and don't forget –' he lowered his voice slightly 'my reward for winning the wager.'

'Bastard.' Giles stumbled uncertainly to his feet, propping himself one-handedly on the table. 'Who the hell are you intending to see at this time of night?'

Richard was at the door. He turned, smiling delightedly. 'Why, my new admirer, of course. That "dreme of joye", Lionel Ellenby. Goodnight.'

Giles, suddenly horribly sober, wondered if he was going to be sick. It would be a fitting end to the day, he thought grimly, striding to the window and flinging it open to breathe some fresher air. From the window, he watched Richard's progress up the street and out of sight.

Disgust in his face, Giles turned back into the room. The buzzing, circular motion of his head, the hopeless confusion of his thoughts – there was only one answer.

'Esmé,' he said, weakly, 'can you put me up for the night?'

CHAPTER THREE

He's kissed her once, he's kissed her twice
Till she came to him again
And boldly has she asked him
Pray tell to me your name.

(REYNARDINE)

*D*ESPITE the heat, Belford was busy. Apples and pears were
picked, blackberries, elderberries and sloes gathered for
wine; trees cut and stacked in vast piles of logs as an insurance
against winter cold.

To Mall, captive in the airless parlour with needle and
thread in hand, life had become unbearably dull. It was barely
a month since Sir Thomas had left, but it seemed like six. There
had been no word from London, nor was any expected, delivery
of a letter relying on some neighbour or acquaintance returning
from the city. Martin Bartlett was, like the rest of the servants,
extremely busy, and Leo Conway had not yet arrived.

The seat covers which Mall had, in a rare moment of
altruism, volunteered to help sew, were intended for the
dining-room chairs. The chairs had long needed recovering,
and in view of Alice's fermenting plans for entertaining, the
task could be put off no longer. There were forty of them, all
bearing an identically unattractive design of griffins, unicorns
and other more obscure mythical beasts. Mall stabbed her
needle into the vacant eye of the unicorn. It was bad enough
being incarcerated in Belford with an increasingly flustered
and disorganized Alice (if the mere *idea* of entertaining

produced such panic in her, how on earth would she cope with the occasion itself?) It was even worse, thought Mall resentfully, to have to consider the dismal prospect of her eventual marriage to some ale-bellied, uneducated squire, whose only topics of conversation would be the health of his pigs and the state of his fields. But what made life so utterly infuriating and intolerable at present was that distraction was at hand now – and she, Mall Conway, was to be denied it.

For the past fortnight, the fair had been at Stourbridge. It would remain there, temptingly, within easy riding distance of Belford, and then be gone for another year. And in a year's time – Mall pulled her French knot unnecessarily tight – who knew where she would be? She would be married, possibly miles away, perhaps with a child of her own, or one on the way, perhaps with a husband who felt fairs to be undignified, or sinful. And Stourbridge Fair was glorious, the most famous in the land. It did not only sell the bales of woollen cloth and more exotic lengths of material for which it was renowned. It sold everything from jewellery to gingerbread, from bridles to bonnets, from cutlery to cockerels. And the sideshows! Puppets, dancers, tumblers, jugglers, players, lutenists, pipers, fortune tellers, balladeers – it was as good as London, some said. Once Mall had watched an Indian at Stourbridge, his smooth brown body naked except for turban and loincloth, a curious bulbous pipe held to his lips. And when he had played, a snake had risen, entranced, from its basket.

But this year Mall would see no snakes, no tumblers, no lengths of silk and brocade. That morning Martin Bartlett had waylaid her on her way to the pantry to tell her that he was to visit the fair tomorrow to buy a horse. Joshua's Joe had seen the animal, and he, Martin, was to be sent with a purse of money to pay for it and bring it home. Mall had groaned with the unfairness of it all, and resolved to ask Alice if she could accompany Martin. So later, in her most dulcet voice, with her most dutiful expression, she had put her request to Alice. Alice had looked at her vaguely, hardly seeming to see her, and had said distractedly, no, she didn't think they could spare the men.

And when Mall, desperately trying to keep her temper, had pointed out that she would have Martin to escort her, Alice had replied scathingly that, in her opinion, Martin Bartlett's sense of responsibility was scarcely more developed than a child's, and she was surprised that Joshua's Joe thought fit to entrust him with buying a horse. Then she had replaced her spectacles, and returned to her hopeless, myopic sewing.

Mall had stood there for a moment, paralysed with fury and despair, yearning to say all the unforgivable words that she knew would come all too easily to her tongue. Then she had blinked back the angry tears, and, unable to bear the sight of Alice's painstaking, inaccurate row of stitches, had almost snatched the half finished seat cover from her stepmother's hands and left the room.

Alone in the parlour, it had given Mall some small revenge to unpick the sprawling, uneven stitches, and replace them with her own neat handiwork. Arguing with Alice, she thought angrily, would be like arguing with the donkey in the stables – a totally pointless exercise. If only her father would come home! If only Leo would arrive! If only something, anything, would happen to rescue her from the hot, dull, unending tedium!

It may have been the forest – cool, green and dark – that protected Kingscote from the cloying heat the rest of the country endured; it may have been the moat from which the house emerged, weathered and mellowed from the clear, cold water. But whatever the reason, Kingscote, with its square paved symmetry, its soft golden stone, its crenellated gatehouse and gently bowed bridge, its flowering courtyard and sparkling fountains, remained tranquil, unfevered, harmonious.

Built in the fourteenth century by Gilbert Carleton, Kingscote was unmistakably a manor house, with few concessions to a defensive purpose to mar the symmetry of its line. It was a symmetry echoed in the golden-haired, slit-eyed person of Lucas Holland, perched gracefully on a window seat overlooking the courtyard. Dressed in beautifully tailored light blue doublet and hose that emphasized both the elegance of his figure and the colour of his eyes, Holland was satisfied that his lack of birth and fortune were amply compensated for by the desirability of his person. Picking himself an orange from a silver bowl, Lucas began to peel it.

'But Nick, the whole thing sounds utterly appalling. The man's a half-wit – and the woman! The daughter of a yeoman farmer, y'know, and to prove it she looks remarkably like a heifer.' He split the orange into segments. 'No wit, no breeding, and their wine will probably be quite disgusting. I can't think why you wish to go.'

Sir Nicholas Carleton turned to face him. Thirty years old, tall and good-looking, Carleton had, in twelve years, restored Kingscote to the perfection its architecture merited. Paintings, sculptures, tapestries, carpets, furniture – Sir Nicholas had only added the best to the house's already impressive collection.

'I am calling at the deplorable Conways' house for one very good reason, my dear Luke,' said Nicholas Carleton, drawing a crimson stocking on to a well-shaped calf. 'Sir Thomas and Lady Conway may well be a pair of tiresome boors, but they have one wonderfully redeeming feature – they are extremely rich. Besides, thankfully, Sir Thomas is presently at Court, so I will only have to tolerate the fair Lady Alice.'

He picked up the lavishly embroidered and bejewelled doublet that lay on the chair to his side, and put it on over the silk shirt. On the window seat, Lucas Holland's famous blue eyes narrowed still further. He placed the peeled and pipped segments of orange in the bowl, and said carefully:

'Sweet Nick, of what possible interest can the state of the Conways' fortunes be to you?' Feline, he walked softly over to Nicholas Carleton, and placed his ringed hand on the older man's shoulder. 'After all, you're not planning to pilfer the house, are you? Far too active for you, my dear.'

Carleton did not look at him, and his dark eyes were impassive. 'The item I am interested in is, how shall I say? – on offer. Yes, on offer. To the highest bidder, I strongly suspect.'

Warily, Holland smoothed out a non-existent crease on Carleton's immaculate velvet back.

'Another miniature? Some Florentine glass, perhaps? Although I would hardly have considered Conway to be a connoisseur of objets d'art.' His lovely face, responsible for countless broken hearts, looked troubled.

Carleton laughed, and took a diamond earring from a lacquered box. 'A connoisseur? Hardly. No, the extremely valuable item I am interested in happens to be their daughter. Now, Luke,' he chided reprovingly, as the younger man's hand slipped from his shoulder, 'don't look so horrified.' The diamond earring was carefully positioned. 'You must realize a man of my standing needs a wife – especially a wealthy one.'

Crossly, Holland turned away from him. 'If she favours her mother she will be fat, cow-eyed, and without a brain to her head. To wake up with that beside you in bed in the morning!' Unwisely, he sniggered.

Carleton said softly:

'Were she sixty years old, and afflicted with gout, and the daughter of a tinker, I would still be dressing myself in my best to call on her appalling mother today. Mall Conway has an enormous dowry, my beautiful but stupid boy, and even better, between her and an extremely lucrative inheritance lies only a half-senile old man and a sickly infant. Sir Thomas cannot live for many more years, and the child will die of some ailment before he is out of long clothes. Now run along and amuse yourself, dear boy – you bore me.'

As Holland left the room, discontent marring his classical features, Carleton put the finishing touches to his toilette – a plumed hat, a jewelled cane and a pair of embroidered gloves. What he had said to the boy was true. A wealthy heiress might be the perfect solution to the financial problems that had become just a little too awkwardly pressing of late. It could also free him of a dependence he had lately come to find a little inconvenient.

But he had not spoken the whole truth. There was another reason for this call. Beauty sat bathing by the stream; white shoulders, great dark blue eyes, water polishing the smooth planes of a slender boyish body. An image that disturbed his dreams, causing him to wake, hot and impatient, filled with a destructive, terrible emptiness that threatened to overwhelm him.

It had taken only a few discreet enquiries to discover the identity of the unknown bather. And if Sir Thomas Conway's daughter had annihilated his peace of mind, then he would possess her. He would.

Under one of the tallest oaks in the copse that edged Belford's boundary stood a horse, a neat bay mare. The rider of the horse was a girl, black-haired, blue-eyed, fair-skinned, pretty in any setting, in this green wood, a beauty. The horse was frisky, anticipating movement and adventure as readily as Mall herself: she calmed it with a pat. This was *the* oak copse – Reynardine's oak copse – cool, unlike the heavy, heat-soaked fields beyond, dark and silent. Here, Reynardine became the black half-man, half-beast of fairy stories.

> *'There was a shepherd's son,*
> *He kept sheep on yonder hill;*
> *He laid his pipe and crook aside,*
> *And there he slept his fill –'*

Mall smiled to herself. Martin. As she had expected, she had not had long to wait. The sound of horse's hooves and Martin's pleasant voice echoed through the copse.

> *'He looked east and he looked west,*
> *He took another look,*
> *And there he spied a lady gay*
> *Was –'*

The singing stopped. Martin rounded the corner, his knife unsheathed.

'It's only me,' said Mall, impatiently. 'Put that thing away, Martin, you might hurt someone.'

'God's wounds, Mall. What on earth are you doing here?' Relief mingled with disappointment on his face as Martin sheathed the knife. 'I'm carrying a lot of money – I thought you were a footpad.'

Mall had a brief tempting vision of herself as a female highwayman – highwaywoman? – and discarded it with some reluctance.

'Don't be silly, Martin. I'm coming to Stourbridge Fair with you.'

Martin eyed her warily. 'And does her ladyship know?'

'Of course not.' No, a sudden wonderful flash of inspiration in the early hours of the morning and she had forgotten the heat, the boredom, the future. 'Although,' she added pensively, 'I think she may have worked it out by now.'

Martin still looked doubtful, 'There'll be hell to pay.'

'I don't doubt it.' Another argument, further tears and protestations from Alice, nothing more. 'Come *on*, Martin, just in case she tries to send someone after me.'

Martin had a small, easily quashed, moment of indecision. Of course, he should escort Mall back to Belford. But that would make him late to buy the horse, and Martha was to be at the Fair that morning, and it wouldn't do to miss her.

He kicked his horse's sides, and together they rode out into the bright sunshine. Mall's voice joined with Martin's as they galloped over the patchwork fields.

> '*She said, Sir, don't touch my mantle,*
> *Come let my clothes alone,*
> *I will give you as much money*
> *As you can carry home . . .*'

Stourbridge Fair was one of the largest trading fairs in Europe. Every September, after the harvest had been gathered in, the tents and booths gathered on the fields that lay to the north-east of Cambridge. Rows and rows of miniature streets sprang up selling everything man or woman could desire. Braziers, fishmongers, grocers, mercers, goldsmiths, pewterers – they were all there, their goods laid out before them to be touched, examined and bartered over. Such was the fame of the fair that some of the rich and great even rode up from London to inspect its wares. Some came in coaches, braving the ruts and potholes and puddles; others arrived on horseback, brightening the countryside with their gaily plumed hats and gaudily coloured clothes. With the traders came the other ingredients of a good fair. Bakers, piemen, ale sellers, gingerbread sellers, showmen, gipsies, whores and pickpockets. The Vice Chancellor's Court was always busy in September.

Mall and Martin looked first for the horse dealer. They found him, small, dark and wrinkled, comfortably ensconced in a colourful caravan. Dressed in a shirt that might once have been green, worn leather breeches and an embroidered waistcoat that gave him an incongruous air of frivolity, he showed them the Barbary roan stallion. It was, as Joshua's Joe had said, an exceptionally beautiful horse. It stood fully sixteen hands, a magnificent rich sorrel mixed with white. Its eyes were lit by pride and temperament, a spirit excited but undaunted by the noise and bustle around him. Mall talked gently to it, stroking the arching neck while Martin discussed payment with the horse dealer. If he could knock the man down a crown or two, Martin could pocket something for himself to spend. The ale looked tempting, the smells of baking that hovered in the warm air made his stomach cramp with anticipation – and there were countless trinkets that might appeal to Martha. If he were to buy her one of those scarves with gold in them, or maybe some beads, perhaps she would treat his courtship more seriously.

Business was done. One of the remaining crowns was offered to the horse dealer to look after their three beasts for them until they chose to leave, and the other two crowns went into Martin's pocket.

Mall had brought money, and she intended to spend every last farthing of it. Resolutely, she pushed troublesome thoughts out of her mind, and slipped her arm through Martin's so as not to lose him in the crowd. The sun was shining, the fair beckoning. Food first; there was a gingerbread stall nearby. Martin could take the edge off his appetite, and Mall could buy a gingerbread horse for Ralph. Alice might not allow him to eat it, but the gilt harness and tossing mane would delight him. Then hot mutton pies, slightly burnt, impossible to hold, but delicious with a mug of ale, warm from the sun-heated barrel.

A group of tumblers whirled through the air, their hair black as night, their skin the colour of earthenware, their writhing tattooed arms exotic against the flat Cambridgeshire earth. Then a fire eater, hook-nosed and tangle-haired, the light from the flaring torches flashing diamond-like in the sweat that gathered on his brow and chest. Lastly, some gipsy dancers, haughty and alien, dangling silver bells, skirling ribbons bright against the heavy skies.

Weaving through the crowds and noise they found the Cloth Exchange: endless bales of materials banked one on top of the other: brocades, velvets, silks, satins, damasks, in every shade of yellow, orange, plum, crimson, blue, purple, scarlet, lime, gold and silver, and the woollens, more soberly coloured, heaped row upon row under the awnings. You were spoilt for choice. Eventually, after a dozen bales had been pulled out for her to see and touch, Mall chose a rich red velvet for herself, and a watchet blue silk for Alice. A peace offering.

Mall's purchases were wrapped and given to Martin to carry. They paused to listen to a ballad singer giving a spirited rendition of a tangled Scots saga of love and betrayal. A coin to the balladeer, and back to the stalls, Mall's money still weighting her purse. She bought honey, face powder, an ivory box containing oil of musk, and an engraved egg which claimed to have the entire story of the Bible etched upon its smooth freckled surface. And there was the haberdasher's stall, a paradise of needles, pins, thread, ribbons, laces, braid and thimbles. The look of glazed boredom settling on Martin's face was best ignored. Leaving him in the narrow pathway, Mall pushed her way to the crowded edge of the stall. Combs, lace, needles, a silver thimble – and gloves. Wriggling along to where a glovemaker sat cross-legged behind a basket on the ground,

64

Mall bought two pairs of gloves of perfumed Spanish leather. And next to the glovemaker was a cutler selling pairs of the new pivoted scissors, so much better for needlework than the shears Mall and Alice used. Only one pair of those – they seemed ridiculously expensive – and Mall looked round for Martin to hand some of her bulkier purchases to. She could not see him. Some of the smaller items went into her purse and pocket. Mall wormed back through the crowd. Martin must still be near the haberdasher's, leaning against a tent post, waiting impatiently for her. But he was not there – neither by the tent post, nor sprawled on the grass, nor attempting to charm the buxom pock-marked girl who sold pins. A small tight feeling of panic began to form in Mall's stomach. She looked quickly round; surely that was him? No, it was a different boy, the wrong face. Someone knocked into her, and Mall clutched her purse, automatically afraid of the pickpocket. She searched the seething crowd before her. He must be there, he could not have gone far.

A voice at her side said, 'Lost something, sweetheart?', and Mall saw small colourless eyes, and felt a dirty hand touch her sleeve.

'No –' She pulled away, her packages slippery in her slightly perspiring fingers. 'I'm just looking for my brother.'

'Sim'll help you find him, dearie.' A coney-trimmed jacket topping layers of torn, ill-fitting garments, too short black hair, a face faintly tinged with insanity.

Summoning as strong a voice as she could muster, Mall said coldly:

'There's no need, thank you. I can see him now.' And she walked off as fast as she could, heading away from the haberdashery.

Strange how a place she loved could suddenly have become so menacing. There must be someone she knew in all this crowd, some neighbour or friend who would keep her company until Martin reappeared, who could make the world seem safe again. But she saw no-one, and as she threaded her way through the crowds, constantly looking for Martin, the women's faces had become painted and grotesque, the children's wizened and prematurely old, the men's brutal and lascivious. Even the weather had altered; the clear skies of the morning had thickened, threatening greenish-grey clouds gathered over the flat swampland of the Fens. The temperature had dropped, and the sharp, dry breeze made Mall's plain thin gown inadequate.

'Found your brother yet, darling?'

The same sickening voice, and she could smell his foul breath on her cheek. All semblance of dignity dispelled in panic. Mall hissed fiercely 'Go *away*!', and picked up her skirts and ran. A woman laughed mockingly, 'Won't he wait for you then, pet?', and another voice cackled in reply.

She no longer knew where she was running to, she only knew, or thought she knew, for it was difficult to tell against the frantic beating of her heart, that the man was still behind her, chasing her. Cannoning in her headlong flight into a boy with arms full of rabbit skins, Mall dropped her gloves and scissors, and the boy cursed her as he stooped to pick the skins out of the mud. Once she paused to look into an ale booth, thinking she saw Martin's back, but it was not him, and the men jeered and whistled at her. Here she was not Mall Conway, heiress, daughter of one of Cambridgeshire's wealthiest landowners; here in her dirty unremarkable dress, with her hair in disarray, with no servant to accompany her, she could have been any young girl without the necessary protection of a man. And he was still there, that nightmare figure with the coney-trimmed jacket and the hungry eyes. She could not run any further, her legs were of jelly, and her breath came in great gasps. She leaned against a tree trunk, her lungs tight and painful, watching as the colourless eyes fixed themselves upon her and came steadily closer. If he touches me or speaks to me again, Mall thought, I shall just scream.

But there was no need to scream. Just as Mall began to take a shuddering inward breath, she saw, only a few yards away, the horse dealer. Feeling suddenly foolish, she smoothed her hair with her hands, and stumbled towards the caravan, feet sliding in the mud. The horse dealer looked up at her from a complicated game of patience.

'Afternoon, miss.'

'Has the boy I came with this morning been back?'

The man shook his head, not bothering to take the straw from his mouth. 'Not seen the lad since this morning, miss.'

Mall looked at the fair, and then up at the darkening sky. She made a rapid decision. Searching in her purse for a coin, she said:

'Would you saddle the horse for me, please? And when Martin – the lad – does appear, please tell him that I have already left.'

'This one, miss?' The horse dealer patted Mall's bay mare.

Mall glanced at Polly, and then her eyes moved to where the Barbary roan stallion stood, shifting nervously in the straw. She smiled.

'No – that one.' She pointed to the stallion, proud and excitable after too many hours' confinement.

The horse dealer looked at her, seemed about to speak, then thought better of it, and contented himself with spitting in the straw. He saddled the stallion, cupped his hands for Mall to mount, and watched her leave the fair. Grudgingly, he had to admit not only that she was nearly as bonny as the Drogheda lass he had loved nearly twenty years ago, but also she knew how to ride a horse. But what had the boy done to deserve her stealing his master's stallion? The horse dealer chuckled, then spat into the straw again.

Mall gave the horse its head along the plain between Stourbridge and the Gog Magog Hills. The stallion, frustrated with the day's inactivity, revelled in the freedom, the opportunity to use its strength and speed.

Her fear had dispersed, lost in the escape from the fair and the glory of riding the roan, but not the anger. The taut ball of her own fury, coiled in the pit of her stomach, matched the stallion's tense strength, enjoying its speed. Not only had Martin Bartlett succeeded in giving her one of the most unpleasant hours of her life, thought Mall as she jumped the

67

horse over a deep ditch, but he had supremely justified every bit of Alice's lack of faith in him.

Mall felt the beginning of rain as, caution at last beginning to return, she slowed the horse to wade through a stream. It would not be a light shower – heavy drops hit the shallow water, and the unsettling wind rustled the elms and reeds at the bank. Mall looked back at the sky behind her. The clouds were no longer greenish-grey; they were black, ominous, surging from the Fens in the north to oppress the gentler south of the county. A thunderstorm . . . and a distant drum-roll sounded a warning overture.

The horse shied, edging sideways in the water, the whites of its eyes showing as it stirred. The rain fell more heavily, soaking the shoulders of Mall's thin gown, darkening the stallion's sorrel coat. It would be quicker to ride through the wooded side of the hills than to take her usual route through the fields. That should cut a mile from her journey: pulling at the reins, Mall directed the horse through the tall trees ahead. Suddenly she wanted nothing more than to be back at Belford, away from the increasingly slippery paths, out of the reach of the almighty thunderstorm that would break any minute, safe from the nervous, temperamental stallion.

Nearing the Gogs, it was evident that whatever the roan's finer qualities, a placid temperament was not amongst them. The first flaring crack of lightning had sent the creature near to hysteria, and it was as much as Mall could do to control it. The day, so promising at its beginning, seemed to be rapidly dissolving into an object-lesson in folly. Trusting Martin Bartlett, taking the Barbary roan – if only she had ridden her own Polly back to Belford! Another loud crack of thunder, and the animal attempted to rear. Perhaps she should stop and shelter under a tree until the worst of the storm was over. If she hobbled it to a branch with the reins, at least her bones would remain unbroken. But not here – anywhere but the Gogs.

For there was a vague, undefinable unease about this place. It had been used by the ancients, named for their twin god- giants; and some memory of that distant, forgotten, magic lingered.

68

Darkened by the gale, the tall trees blocked the sky from view. Mall slowed the horse to a walk, clinging grimly to the reins as it skittered and shied. Rain dripped from the end of her nose on to her sodden gown, but it was better to concentrate on the physical miseries of the journey, and not think about the nameless terrors that lurked unseen behind the black trees covering the hillside. When I get back to Belford I shall be *good*. I shall do whatever Alice tells me; I won't argue any more, nor make fun of her, nor deceive her . . .

But Mall's virtuous thoughts went unrewarded. In her hurry to reach home, she had forgotten one important rule: that you do not ride through tall trees in a thunderstorm. Whichever God (the Christian one of Belford's draughty chapel or the older pagan one) held sway on those rain-soaked hills chose that moment to bring the storm to its height. The lightning that struck the tall oak tree ahead split the proud thick trunk as easily as an axe splits kindling for firewood. The cannonade of thunder that followed almost immediately after the lightning was deafening, masking the noise of the rain, the wind, and the terrified neigh of the horse. Mall had no chance of keeping in the saddle. The horse reared violently as the world erupted into fire and sound, and, tossing its rider, bolted from the horrors before it.

Mall did not move after her head struck the tree stump that stood at the side of the path. The Gods, having achieved catharsis in the sacrifice of the oak tree, let her lie beside the track, the softer rain touching her smooth white cheek, her wet black hair mingling with the mud and old broken leaves.

It had been a trying day for Alice Conway. First, the discovery that Mall was missing; it had been halfway through the morning before Alice had realized that she was not there, was not in the library, nor playing the spinet in the Great Hall, nor hiding in some obscure corner of the garden. It had not been hard to guess where she had gone, of course. Alice's first reaction of anger had been rapidly followed by one of fear. If any harm came to her stepdaughter, it would be she, Alice, that Sir Thomas would blame. Oh, why did the child have to be so difficult? Lady Woodroffe had been right, Mall was becoming impossible, and something must be done about it.

The second trial of the day had been the unexpected visit of Sir Nicholas Carleton. Sir Nicholas had never called before, and, had her husband and stepdaughter been present, Alice would have been delighted to receive him. As it was, she did her best, hoping she did not appear flustered or gauche, remembering to offer the correct refreshments, explaining to her guest that Sir Thomas was in London, and Mall indisposed – nothing serious, she had added hastily, blushing a little at the lie.

Sir Nicholas explained, between sips of the Conways' best wine, that he had been riding in the area, and that as he had never congratulated Sir Thomas on his second marriage – most remiss of him after three years – he had taken the opportunity to do so today. And although he was devastated that Sir Thomas was not present to receive his felicitations in person, he was much consoled by the loveliness and charm of Sir Thomas's new wife. He enquired after Mall's health, and admired, for some considerable time, the portrait of her mother. Perhaps he could have the honour of making Miss Conway's acquaintance some other time. If she had half the beauty of her stepmother, the task would hardly be onerous. Alice had dimpled at that, and become very bold. Mall was certainly said to be very pretty, and, of course, she would be well provided for when she married. And if Sir Nicholas would like to meet her, why, nothing could be simpler. Alice had intended to arrange a dinner for her neighbours in the near future – they entertained too rarely at Belford – and nothing would give her greater pleasure than Sir Nicholas's attendance.

Sir Nicholas had implied that an invitation would be well received, and had made his farewells shortly afterwards. Alice watched him ride up the path to the main gates, the triumph in her heart only slightly diminished by an uneasy feeling that she had not at all understood what the conversation had really been about.

The next arrival was Leo Conway, hot and dusty after his long journey from Enfield. He arrived alone, in the late afternoon, to an increasingly anxious sister-in-law. Alice, looking at the weather, was really beginning to worry. Mall must be home soon – surely she, if not that foolish boy, would notice that there was soon to be an almighty thunderstorm?

Leo, three years Sir Thomas' junior, and of a sanguine, unexcitable temperament, attempted to allay Alice's fears.

'She will be back soon, my dear.' He embraced his sister-in-law. 'Mall can look after herself very well – she has done so for most of her life. She'll be home in half an hour, having had a fine old time, and in better spirits than you've seen her for months. Besides, she has Martin with her. He'll look after her, he's fond of the girl.'

Alice tried her best to be comforted, and settled the scholar, tired after his long ride, in a chair by the fire. Wine and food was brought, and Ralph fetched down from the nursery to sit on his Uncle Leo's knee and play with his straggling grey beard and bushy eyebrows. Alice made valiant attempts to talk as though nothing was on her mind, politely enquiring about Leo's health and prospects. But her eyes wandered increasingly to the window, watching for riders to appear at the gates. It began to rain heavily, thunder and lightning disturbed the heavy black sky and frightened Ralph, who buried his head in his uncle's lap. Puddles formed on the path and amongst the paving stones of the courtyard – the more fragile plants in Alice's garden would be crushed by the violence of the storm. In a single afternoon, the season had changed from summer to autumn. Mall would be soaked. Alice hoped she had had the sense to take a cloak with her, and reminded herself that the girl was tougher than she looked.

Her heart leapt when she saw the horses come through the gate. Two horses – and then elation and relief turned instantly to horror as she realized that the lone rider was Martin Bartlett, and that the horse he led by the reins was Mall's own bay mare, Polly.

'*Leo!*'

The tone of her voice made him disengage the child, pass him carefully to his nurse, and hurry to Alice's side. He strained to see through the relentless rain. 'That's Martin –'

'Leading Mall's horse!' Tears were flowing unchecked down Alice's plump, white, cheeks. 'Oh, Leo, what can have happened to her? What are we to do?'

Leo Conway was disturbed to find that he, too, felt troubled. He sat Alice down, called for her maid, and instructed a footman to show Martin Bartlett to him immediately.

Martin's face, as he entered the Hall, reflected the fear on their own.

'She's not here, then, sir?'

Leo shook his head, feeling some pity for the boy who stood before them, drenched, panic in his eyes.

'I lost her at the fair, sir – one minute she was there, the next she'd gone. And she took the new horse –'

'Martin.' Leo interrupted as calmly as if he were giving a discourse on logic to one of his pupils. 'Sit by the fire, and tell us *slowly* exactly what happened. Then we can best decide what to do.'

Martin sat down, unable to meet Alice's anguished eyes.

'I wasn't away for more than a minute, sir, honest! So I looked all round the fair for her, but I couldn't see no sign of her. Then I went back to the horse dealer – we'd left the horses with him that morning – and he told me she'd already gone home, but she'd taken the stallion, not her own Polly. It's a big, powerful horse, sir – not at all the horse for a girl!'

'And did the horse dealer tell you how long she'd been gone?'

'About half an hour, he thought,' said Martin, miserably. 'So I rode home the usual way, thinking perhaps I might catch up with her. But there was no sign of her, so I was sure she'd be here . . . .' his voiced trailed off.

'And she isn't,' said Leo crisply, turning to Alice. 'How long will it take to get a search party ready?'

*

72

It was black, very black, and there was a steady insistent drumming in her ears. With difficulty she located her eyes and opened them slightly, but still could not see. Such darkness – dim, misty objects formed and reformed before her, and the drumming noise ebbed to her own heartbeat. Mall began to remember what had happened – the fair, the horse, the thunderstorm. Her head rested on broken leaves and twigs, and she could smell the acrid scent of the charred remains of the tree; it jarred her stomach, making her feel sick. Mall moved her head, slowly, cautiously, anxious not to disturb the raw pain in her left temple. Heavily, tangled by soaking skirts and limbs that felt as though they were made of clay, she sat up, leaning her back against the tree stump that had struck her. Fighting nausea, she brushed off some of the leaves and mud. There was something on one side of her face, something warm and wet and sticky. She touched her forehead, and there was blood on her fingertips, black in the lightless, starless night. 'Oh hell' said Mall wearily, and began to look for her handkerchief.

It was not there, of course. Her handkerchief was gone, and so was the horse. All she could distinguish were the twigs and branches scattered on the ground around her like spillikins. The tall black trees crowded in, threatening shapes waiting for her in the darkness. If she called for help no-one would come, no-one . . . It must be miles to the nearest village, miles of staggering, injured and desperately cold, through this horrible, menacing place. Mall tried to stand and failed; the nausea returned, swamping her in waves of unnatural heat that did nothing to quell her shivering. Her stomach heaved again, despised tears came to her eyes, and she rubbed at them uselessly with the wet sleeve of her gown. They would not be staunched, however, and flowed unchecked down her cheeks, mingling with the dirt and the gentle rain that still fell, masking the sound of the black mare that stepped delicately through the fallen debris of the oak tree.

> ' 'Westron wynd, when wilt thou blow
> The small rain down can rain –'

73

The song stopped suddenly.

'God's teeth, the former occupant of the horse. And a girl – well, this is a pleasant surprise.'

Mall's tears had halted as soon as she heard the voice. It was young and male, and she knew the words of the song he had been singing. It was indecent. She stiffened, wiped her nose and eyes on the back of her sleeve, pulled her dishevelled skirts into some semblance of decency, and tried to focus on the figure before her. It was too dark to see clearly: a vague shape of horse and rider, darkly cloaked and hooded, swam confusingly before her.

'Now I had expected to find a man – 'tis a treat to discover a pretty girl.'

The voice was light, pleasant, slightly accented. Irish, thought Mall, remembering a long distant visit from her Irish grandmother. With an uncontrollable tremble of relief in her voice, she asked:

'Do you mean you have found my horse, sir?'

Cloaked and hooded as he was, she could not see his face. He dismounted from the mare.

'I most certainly have, my sweet – if that ill-tempered monster I have tethered half a mile away is really your horse. Not a suitable mount for a lady at all, I would have thought – not at all.'

Relief gave way to irritation at the implied criticism, unnecessarily galling at the end of such a disastrous day. She said crossly:

'I only borrowed him. If it had not been for that damned thunderstorm, I should be home by now.' At too much of a disadvantage seated on the ground, Mall staggered to her feet, squinting in an attempt to see her rescuer's face.

'Close your eyes. That's a nasty cut – but I think you were lucky not to have broken your neck.' Mall felt his hand, surprisingly gentle, touch her forehead, and a handkerchief dabbed at the cut.

'You'll live. And it is not deep enough to impair your beauty.' And then his finger was tracing the line of her jaw, finishing

74

almost at her lips. Mall's eyes opened quickly, and she drew back, but he had already turned away from her.

'If your ladyship would be so good as to mount my horse –'

He was laughing at her, mocking her because she was alone and unprotected. Like that dreadful man at the fair, thought Mall angrily. But no, not like him at all . . . because the fear was not there, only a faint betraying frisson of excitement.

Ridiculous thoughts. Impatiently, ignoring his outstretched hand, Mall managed to scramble inelegantly on to the back of the black mare that stood more placidly than the roan stallion ever would. Silently, the man handed her his handkerchief, and she held it against the cut, stemming the thin trickle of blood, whilst he led the horse through the woods by the reins.

'And what might you be called, sweetheart?'

It would be childish not to answer. Mall replied stiffly:

'My name is Conway, Mall – Maire – Conway. I am from Belford – that is about five miles from here, I think.'

'Ah, yes, to be sure, I know it. A grand house. But I had thought the Conways were fair . . . oh, but I remember now, there was a black Conway –'

> '"I can love both fair and brown
> "Her whom the country formed and whom the town –"'

'And you, sir,' Mall interrupted the flow as curiosity overcame her irritation, 'What is your name?'

'My name?' Mall caught a tantalizing glimpse of a smile, white teeth, and a long, well shaped mouth. 'My name is Fox. Robert Fox.'

Fox. The name meant nothing to her. It was difficult to place him. He was not terribly well dressed; the hooded black cloak he wore was of a rough woollen stuff. But the voice – and the poetry. Perhaps he was some traveller connected with the fair.

'And do you come from round here, Mr Fox – or have you business in this county?'

He sighed heavily. 'Alas, it is business that brings me here. I have business to do in Saffron Walden – with the Murrays. Do you know them? What a shame that duty calls. Otherwise, my

75

beauty, we could while away many pleasant hours together. I have always had a fondness for black hair and blue eyes, and a temper like the devil.'

There was really nothing to say to that. Anger would only prove him correct, so Mall sat proudly on the black mare, and attempted to treat his remark with the dignified scorn it merited. If only she could see his face. The hand that held the reins was ungloved, strong and brown, and, although she did not care to admit it, there was something undeniably attractive about his voice. But he should not be speaking to her like this – sympathy, concern, chivalry, were what was appropriate – not flirtatiousness. And surely this gentleman, if gentleman he were, was being flirtatious to the point of rudeness.

'And I like a woman with spirit,' continued the infuriating voice. 'Not many girls will steal a horse, ride through a thunderstorm, and –'

'I did not steal the horse!' Angered into speech, Mall glared furiously down at the hooded head at her side.

'Your pardon. I forgot. You borrowed it. Well, *borrow* a horse, and ride it through a thunderstorm alone and unprotected. But it was not wise, my dear. I would not recommend you to do it too often.'

'It is no business of yours what I do! I am indebted to you for guiding me to my horse, Mr Fox, but if I chose to steal an elephant and ride it single handed to Cathay, that would be my affair, and mine alone.'

Her answer was a low chuckle. 'There. I said you had a temper. What a pity that we both have to rush off, you to your doubtless distraught family, me to my business. With your spirit and my experience, just think what we could do together.'

'Sir,' said Mall tightly, 'would you see me to my horse and direct me on the right path home? That is all I wish.'

He sighed again. 'What a shame. It is not all I *need*. Ah well, here is your horse, and down there is the path to Belford. I'm afraid I cannot escort you to your home, as my business is rather urgent.'

He gave her his hand to dismount the horse. How it

happened, Mall was never afterwards completely sure. Suddenly, she was in his arms, and he was kissing her, crushing her slight frame against his warm body. Firm lips met hers, knocking the breath out of her. Then he had released her, turning away to unloop the reins of the Barbary roan from the branch of a tree. His voice floated over to her, through the dark.

'*And softly said, Dear heart, how like you this?* . . . and could that possibly be your rescuers, my dear?'

Mall stood, shaking with anger, cold and exhaustion, and some other nameless emotion, her stupefied brain registering the sound of horses' hooves in the night and voices calling her name. She spun round as she heard heavy steps coming towards her. But it was not the unknown, teasing face of Robert Fox that she saw, pushing through the thicket, but the familiar, kind ugly features of Joshua's Joe. Wildly, she turned again, searching the darkness.

But he was not there. He had gone.

Alice no longer saw the chameleon she was embroidering; instead, a horrible vision of a riderless horse and a broken body in a ditch metamorphosed before her eyes. Sometimes the vision was replaced by a different nightmare – of Mall, bound and gagged, held prisoner by brigands who demanded a fortune for her safe return. Alice prayed for Mall's life as she had prayed so many times before for Ralph's, her prayers repeating themselves ritually in her head.

They had given up standing by the window, although Leo, under the guise of stretching his legs, frequently went to peer out into the dark and the rain. It was during one of these excursions that he saw the riders return, their lanterns glowing in the rainswept night. Leo was out of the door and down the path as fast as a man half his age. Alice did not rise, but her sewing slid from her nerveless fingers, and the prayer repeated itself more urgently. *Please God, please God* . . .

'She's all right, Alice! She's safe!'

*

Mall woke in the morning, having slept surprisingly well, with no worse after effects of her misadventure than a splitting headache. Lucy brought her breakfast in bed, chattering continuously as she pulled back the curtains to let in the feeble sunlight. Mall found herself unusually ill-disposed to conversation. There were certain incidents of the previous night she had not made general knowledge. The Fair, the appropriation of the horse, and her fall she had admitted to fully. But she had left a tactful blank over subsequent occurrences, picking up her story at the arrival of Joshua's Joe. It had not been a conscious decision to lie, just a strong suspicion that the episode concerning Robert Fox would not go down too well with the elder members of the Conway family. Besides, how could she explain what she herself did not fully understand? She had given much thought to her own behaviour, and found it incomprehensible. Why had she let that man kiss her? It would not have been easy to stop him, but she had not exactly tried very hard. '*Dear heart, how like you this . . .*' – and why had his every word etched itself upon her brain as indelibly as the Biblical pictures had been engraved upon the egg she had lost in her fall? But whatever the reason, she need think about him no more. Robert Fox would presumably have completed his business in Saffron Walden, and be on his way back to wherever he came from, and she need never meet the unsettling gentleman again. Crossly, Mall pushed the slight lingering disappointment out of her mind, and tried to concentrate on Lucy's chatter.

'The highwayman – you remember, Reynardine – *he* did it –'

She had not been paying attention. Mall buttered some bread and said absently:

'Did what, Lucy?'

'Broke into Mr Murray's house – I told you, mistress, Martha heard it. She'd been to see that young man of hers. She said they knew it was Reynardine, because some old witch saw him riding away. He had a black cloak and a black horse, and she was feared she'd seen the Devil! Anyway, that Lady Woodroffe said he had a black cloak and rode a black mare, so they reckon it was the same man. Wicked, isn't it, mistress. He'll be here next, that's what my mother –'

A black cloak and a black mare. Carefully, Mall cradled her cup in her hands. '*Whose* house did you say, Lucy?'

Lucy sat on the edge of the bed, her pinched little face flushed with excitement. 'Mr Murray's house, mistress, in Saffron Walden. *You* remember Mr Murray – he visited here once.'

I have business to do tonight in Saffron Walden. With the Murrays. Robert *Fox*. How stupid of her not to guess! Her rescuer, her black-cloaked, impudent stranger had been none other than Lady Woodroffe's cunning, wicked highwayman. So it was Reynardine she had encountered on the hills.

And Reynardine who she had kissed.

The cup from which Mall had been drinking slipped from her hand, its contents spilling in drips and rivulets all over the coverlet and on to the floorboards.

'Mistress!' Lucy began to mop the floor with her cloth. 'Mistress! Are you ill? Shall I get her ladyship?'

Mall managed to shake her head. 'There's no need – it was just a mistake.' She forced herself to smile. 'You go now, Lucy, and I'll have a rest.'

Lucy left, but Mall did not rest. She climbed out of the bed and began to search through the pockets of the gown that lay bundled on a chest by the fire. Yes, it was still here, where she had thrust it on Joshua's Joe's appearance last night in the Gogs. The handkerchief was not a pretty sight, bloodied, rolled into a ball in the corner of her pocket. She flattened it out. It was not a tradesman's handkerchief, unless the gentleman traded in Valenciennes lace. Neither did it seem entirely appropriate for a highwayman. It was undoubtedly a gentleman's hand-kerchief – a square of formerly white silk, edged with a thick border of the finest lace. And in the corner – in the corner, embroidered by who knows what patient female hand, was an initial. Mall stared at it.

Footsteps pattered outside, coming towards her room. Only one thing was certain, thought Mall, as she stuffed the handkerchief back into the pocket and jumped into bed.

The ornate R that decorated the corner of the handkerchief did not stand for Robert.

A week later, Alice set about the formidable task of composing a guest list. A major social event was something Alice Conway approached with dread, but she had forced herself to put her duty before her inclinations. Unable to resist the sneaking hope that Sir Thomas might, after all, be able to attend, she had set the date for the end of November. Leo had agreed to act as host, new china and glassware had been ordered: Alice was merely required to formulate a list of sufficiently sparkling guests to ensure the occasion's success. As many eligible young – and not so young – men must be invited as possible, plus an equal number of women to make the numbers even.

And there lay the problem. It was hard to recall which neighbours Sir Thomas was on speaking terms with, and which had taken irretrievable offence during his long years of hiding from the world. Mall's assistance was necessary. She had been sent for, and Alice watched from the window as her step-daughter crossed the garden below. She appeared to have recovered quickly from her adventure on the Gogs. The wound on her head had almost healed, and would leave no scar. She had accepted her punishment of a day confined to her room with surprisingly little argument. But something had changed, and it had crossed even Alice's unimaginative mind to wonder if she had been told the entire truth about that night. Mall had been quieter, more subdued, spending long hours playing the virginals in the gallery, or reading in the library. And once, when Mall had not noticed Alice's presence, she had not even been playing, she had simply been sitting there, staring out of the window, a lost expression on her face. Alice had worried that the blow to her head had perhaps had some hidden ill-effect, but on tactful enquiries to Leo had been informed that Mall could still beat him at chess, and that her grasp of Latin and Greek had become almost as good as his own. But Mall seemed less approachable, thought Alice unhappily, even less the close companion she had originally hoped for in a stepdaughter. She did her duties conscientiously – when she could be found – but, frequently, Alice had to repeat her requests more than once. Let the girl be found a good husband, for the responsibilities of a home and family would give her something on which to concentrate her mind.

Alice raised her eyes from the blank piece of paper as Mall came into the room. 'Perhaps you would write this for me, my dear.' Mall's neat script was so much of an improvement on her own untidy scrawl.

Alice stared dim-sightedly out of the window, looking for inspiration in the garden she loved. It would be so much nicer to be out there, weeding and pruning, potting the less hardy plants.

'We will ask Lord Cheseborough. I know he is a little old for you, Mall, my dear, but it would be considerably to your credit if he were to propose. He has been a widower for some time now, and he may think of remarriage –' She stopped. Perhaps the remarriage of widowers was not an entirely tactful subject. But Mall made no comment, in fact, Alice suspected that she had not been listening at all. '*Mall*. I said perhaps we should ask Lord Cheseborough –'

Mall made an effort. 'And his daughter, Eleanor. Eleanor was a friend of my mother's.'

Alice thought again, fragile lines forming on her brow. 'And the Murrays. Your father had no quarrel with them, I believe? We will invite the eldest daughter, Anna, and the eldest son – now, what was his name?'

'George,' said Mall, writing it down. 'What of their father? He's a widower too. Perhaps all these ancient widowers will propose to me, and then –'

'*Mall*,' said Lady Conway, more sternly this time. 'Yes, we will invite Mr Murray, but I do not believe he will come. I hear he has grown very religious of late.'

Mall added the name of John Murray to her list. George and Anna Murray – they had visited shortly after her father's and Alice's wedding, to offer their felicitations. Both had been tall, dark and grey eyed, and Anna Murray had been memorably pleasant to the miserable, scrawny fourteen-year-old that Mall had then been.

'If we are to invite Miss Murray, then we must ask Lord Amyott,' continued Alice. 'Lord Amyott is betrothed to Anna Murray. So perhaps we should also invite his younger brother –' she paused, frowning. 'Or perhaps not.'

'Why not?' cried Mall impatiently. 'After all, if the elder brother is already betrothed to Miss Murray, he is hardly likely to offer for my hand as well. Unless Lord Amyott intends to set up a harem, I think we might as well have the other one also. My marital prospects,' she surveyed the list in front of her, 'do not look too exciting as yet. Or is he fifteen, pock-marked and feeble minded?'

Alice shook her head. 'No . . . I have heard Mr Galliers is very handsome – and clever. It is just that . . . he is not quite . . .'

'Not quite *what*?'

Alice's eyes refused to meet those of her stepdaughter. 'His reputation is rather bad, my dear. I am not sure of the exact details –'

Mall put the pen down. 'Oh, he's probably lost too often at dice or cards, or had the odd love affair. All the more reason to invite him – he might make things a little less dull.'

Alice said tactfully: 'I have heard that some of Mr Galliers' love affairs were a little odder than most. Still, Sir Thomas suggested I ask him . . .'

'So we will have him.' Mall, bored with the discussion, picked up the pen. 'What's his first name?'

'Richard, I believe.'

Richard. Another R. Mall's mind returned, as it so often had over the past week, to the scrap of silk and lace (now washed and white again), that lay in the corner of the chest in her bedchamber. Richard – or Ralph, or Roland, or –

'Mall!' cried Alice for the third time.

The ink had gathered at the end of the quill, and flooded to make a large and ugly blot on the paper. Crossly, Mall sprinkled it with sand, and wrote carefully under the last name: Richard Galliers.

CHAPTER FOUR

Follow her whose light thy light depriveth.
Though here thou livest disgraced,
While she in heaven is placed,
Yet follow her whose light the world reviveth.

(CAMPION)

*I*T was October, and Giles Galliers stood in the front courtyard of Amyott House, watching the rain, the windswept, golden-leaved trees, and the lone rider retreating ever smaller into the grey distance.

Richard had come and gone; a mere, disastrous, twenty-four hours that would leave a sour taste in Giles's mouth, and anger in his heart. He had arrived yesterday at midday, evil-tempered, with a cold and cutting tongue and a dangerous, presageful glint in his eyes. Perhaps if Richard had been forewarned about the neglect to which the late Lord Amyott's last, most self-destructive years had brought the house and estate, his sense of outrage at a tarnished and unhappy homecoming might have been allayed. But it had not occurred to Giles, who had seen his birthplace at reasonably regular intervals over the years of its decline, that, to one who had been absent, the missing roof tiles, the crumbling stonework and overgrown gardens might come as a profound shock. Whereas Giles could see the improvements his few short months of work had begun, Richard witnessed only his father's neglect. And Richard, all too practised at concealing what he really felt, had no inclination to share his shock with Giles.

Even Giles, however, was sufficiently aware of Richard's state of mind to wish to avoid being present at the interview between Lady Amyott and her younger son. And when his mother had welcomed Richard with the words, 'So one of my sons has come back to me' – not the most tactful phrase under the circumstances, thought Giles, his stomach dropping to the region of his boots – Giles had left them to exchange barbed and frozen pleasantries.

Dinner had been appalling, indigestible and overloaded with innuendo. Richard had looked superb, dark hair brushing his immaculate silk shoulders, fine lace at his wrists and neck, and a considerable sparkling of well placed diamonds. But not, most definitely not, the penitent prodigal son whom Lady Amyott had no doubt expected. The defences were up and, although he remained polite, there was a brittleness about him that made him totally unapproachable. If only, thought Giles angrily, if only Richard had seen fit to exercise just a little of the charm and wit he was currently wasting so lavishly on Ellenby and others like him. If only he had made the slightest effort to respond to what lay beneath Lady Amyott's unforgiving façade. But he had not; Richard had been proud, arrogant, almost insolent, everything Giles had always detested in him.

But Giles, with a brother's lack of perception, had not noticed Richard's hands, white-knuckled as they gripped the twisting stem of his wine glass. Neither had he understood the following morning the dark-shadowed face, consequence of an endless, sleepless night. All he had seen was Richard's over-ornate, flourishing bow to his mother, his cold, formal salute of her hand, and his failure to offer to visit her again.

Giles had walked with him to the stables, where his black mare stood saddled and expectant, waiting in the courtyard. Richard had turned to him, rain beading the wide brim of his black hat, Ellenby's rapier scar still marring his pale passionless face, and had said:

'Well, Giles – and was that the joyous reunion you had hoped for? Errant son clasped to mother's large and forgiving bosom?'

He put one elegantly booted foot into the stirrup, and swung

84

on to the horse's back, looking down at Giles, a small smile curling his lips.

Giles was silent. His inclination was to turn on his heel and go back to the house; but the certainty that, if he did that, he would never see Richard again stopped him.

Richard bent his dark head to speak to Giles, controlling the eager mare with a gentle pull at the reins.

'It's no good, you see, Giles. No more the happy loving family. "*Thy brother by decree is banished*" – remember?'

Giles said flatly: 'So will you go to the Conways in November?'

'I don't think so.' The infuriating smile reappeared. 'Another quotation for you, Giles: "*A friend loveth at all times, and a brother is born for adversity*." I must leave you to your adversity, brother. I have an assignation with my ever-loving friend tonight – Lionel Ellenby, of course.'

He spurred his horse and cantered through the gates. Eventually Giles turned, walked through the courtyard, back into the house and up the stairs towards Lady Amyott's bedchamber. He paused at the top of the stairs.

'Well, God damn you to Hell, then,' he said, tightly, and went to comfort his mother.

The Countess of Somerset's house at Blackfriars, glittering, festive, graceful, shone like a beacon of light in the damp autumn air. Crowded with candles, alive with music, it extended its tentacles like a gorgeous sea anenome, sucking in the rich and beautiful from the dark London streets. The banquet had been fit to surfeit the Five Thousand; the masque, a tangled rendition of the fable of Persephone, had reached its triumphant conclusion, the mouth of Hades was dismantled and the mourning countryside heaved noisily away. With the finale of the masque, the dancing had begun: galliards, corantos, and voltas in the rich splendour of the Countess's Great Chamber.

The dancing figures turned, jumped, bowed and curtseyed; patterns of silks, satins, gold and silver, pearl and ruby, woven to the music of viol and lute. Lines crossed, transient acquaintances were made or renewed, and then fragmented again. Circles formed, circles within circles, clockwise and anti-clockwise, hands linked and then parted. And at the centre of the dance, splendid in pale blue satin, her honey-coloured hair threaded with emeralds the size of peas, was the Countess of Somerset herself.

Frances Kerr, formerly Devereux, née Howard, was twenty-two years old and married to one of the most influential men in the kingdom – Robert Kerr, King James's Scottish favourite. Queen in her own house, the steps of the dance brought her in turn to Lionel Ellenby, pursuing his Howard connections in hopes of favour and fortune; to George Murray, brother of Giles Galliers' adored Anna, hoping for nothing more than good wine and a decent game of dice; to Richard Galliers, whose face the Countess had not recalled, but who had arrived, uninvited, on the arm of her distant cousin Lionel Ellenby. She had assessed her unexpected guest with a practised eye, and, though perfectly aware that Richard Galliers was at least half way to being gloriously drunk, had decided to accept his presence with equanimity.

It occurred to George Murray also, as the measure finished and the dancers left the floor and collapsed, temporarily exhausted, in chairs arranged round the circumference of the room, that Galliers was not completely sober. He was by no means alone in that; at Blackfriars, wine flowed as freely as the waters of the nearby Thames, and many of the company were already a little the worse for wear. No, Galliers' insobriety was no cause for censure; it was his encouragement of Lionel Ellenby that surprised George. Ellenby possessed neither wit, nor intellect, nor looks. What, then, was the attraction?

The Murrays and the Galliers were, when in the country, relatively close neighbours. The two families had known each other vaguely for many years, and following the betrothal of George's elder sister Anna to Lord Amyott, the relationship would become regularized by marriage. George, unlike his father, was wholeheartedly in favour of the match – Giles Galliers had been a convivial drinking partner in the past and

86

Richard was a damned good dice player. And if there had been some scandal years ago – well, Anna was in her mid twenties now, and had looked to waste herself in spinsterhood. George was fond of his elder sister; she could be relied on to keep rumours of George's indiscretions from their father's censorious ears. To George, twenty-three, good looking and blessed with a generous yearly stipend, London was a pleasure ground, a treasure chest of delight to be plundered at will.

Hazard . . . the game of hazard was George Murray's joy, his obsession. The dancing was temporarily succeeded by a lutenist, perched on a stool in the centre of the Great Chamber; backgammon and chess boards had been placed discreetly around. Through the liquid notes of a fantasia, the laughter that had accompanied the end of the dance dimmed temporarily to a low hum of conversation, spiced with the clink of wine glasses – and, sweeter than Dowland to George Murray's ears, the click of dice cast on a polished wooden table. He watched as Lionel Ellenby, increasingly unsteady on his feet, slid slowly backwards in his uncomfortable farthingale chair, and stayed there, his mouth wide open to the air like a transfixed carp. George grinned to himself and crossed the room.

'My dear Galliers,' he made a perfunctory bow. 'I thought you might be in need of company.'

'As my present company is rendered speechless?' Indifferently, Galliers surveyed the prone figure of Ellenby, now gently snoring. 'Do you know, Murray, I don't believe it makes a great deal of difference. His capacity for holding his drink seems roughly equal to his skill with the sword.'

George's smile widened. He signalled to the manservant to refill their glasses. 'I heard rumours about that. Unfortunately, I am not much of a theatre-goer myself.'

'I think the playhouse has begun to pall for Ellenby also. And I have a sufficiently conspicuous souvenir of the occasion to absent myself from the Red Bull for a while. Or they might request an encore.'

The scar was indeed still noticeable, a thin straight line drawn across the sculptured cheekbone. To one who did not know him, Galliers did not look particularly drunk, but George was observant enough to recognize the very slightly less than perfect arrangement of his clothes, and the unnatural brightness of the sleepy-lidded green eyes. Richard Galliers inebriated – that was promising.

'You and your – friend –' George nodded towards the unconscious Ellenby, 'have been celebrating?'

At Galliers' side, a woman's fan had fallen to the floor unnoticed, a multi-coloured fragment of silk and ivory. Galliers stooped and picked it up, spreading its delicate segments once before returning it, with a bow, to its owner. He smiled unpleasantly at Murray.

'Dear George. I have just undergone the unalloyed joy of spending a day at Amyott – twenty-four hours cradled in the bosom of my loving family. *Not* an experience to be repeated.' He drained his glass of wine. 'Most definitely not. So I felt it propitious to hasten back to my more natural milieu – the dens and stews of London.'

Murray's brows lifted a fraction, and his eyes travelled the length of the room. Only the presence of the king himself could have made a more prestigious company. Silks and velvets of ochre, rose and amethyst, frosted with gold and silver lace, bodices and doublets slashed, inset, quilted, embroidered, encrusted with jewels, all multiplying and magnifying the lights from the bright fire and from the ranks of candles that crowded every spare inch of the room. The changing light flickered across the faces of the guests, softening the effects of age and over-indulgence, transforming plain faces into pretty, pretty into beautiful. George Murray said gently:

'I hardly think the Countess's Great Chamber could be described as a den or a stew, Galliers.'

'Perhaps not. And she is a ravishing woman, don't you think, George?'

In the centre of the room, at her musician's side, stood the Countess of Somerset, a shiver of ice blue flicked with the

88

reflected light of the fire. 'Exquisite, Richard,' said George Murray with approval. 'One cannot but help envy Somerset, with that to warm his bed each night.'

'And she is plainly skilled in the art of the well connected marriage.' Galliers' insoucient gaze caressed the jewelled amber hair, the voluptuous body. 'Her husband is now Lord Chamberlain, her father Lord Treasurer. What more could a beautiful and ambitious woman want?'

A shadow had fallen across the Countess's face, darkening the light eyes, the bright hair. Murray said softly, 'As long as the king does not entirely switch his allegiance to George Villiers. He has not lost interest in him.'

The lutenist had begun to play again, but the delicate notes were lost in the rising hubbub. Richard Galliers brought out a pair of dice from his pocket. '*What fools these mortals be* – but no concern of yours or mine.' He tossed the dice invitingly in the air, and George's eyes brightened. 'It is a long time since we played, George. You shall cast. With Lady Amyott's tender words still ringing in my ears, I am feeling magnanimous.'

Bets were made, Murray called a nine, and won the throw. The music, the banquet, the company was forgotten. All the clever and vicious chatter, all the alcohol-loosened licence of a London evening, retreated to the choice of a number, a twist of the fingers, and chance, glorious chance. The vast Great Chamber contracted to a pair of dice on an inlaid table; the throng of guests narrowed to one opponent, generally danger-ous, but now, surely, impaired by drink. In the light from the nearby fire the gamblers' faces were red lit, intense. George's eyes were dark with concentration: he called again. He felt excitement rising in him like a whirlwind, blocking out a woman's high pitched laughter from the next table, blocking out Richard Galliers' lazy, bored face opposite him.

The certainty he always experienced at the beginning of a game, that this night was to be his night, that those tumbling ivory cubes would fall the way he wanted, evaporated as the throws began to go against him. He could not lose – he had had a good run of luck recently. Richard was drunk, and George, for

89

once, was stone cold sober. He could not pinpoint the moment when he realized that his instinct had been wrong: all he could see was a hand, ringed and lace cuffed, rolling the dice with a casual skill.

It was when the pile of coins on George's side of the table had diminished to almost nonexistent size, and when Lionel Ellenby's head had slipped from the back of the chair to loll, still open mouthed, on his yellow satin shoulder, that Sir Nicholas Carleton and Sir Thomas Conway were ushered through the wide doors of the Great Chamber. George Murray, a fine sweat beading his forehead, a tense knot of panic forming in his stomach, did not notice the late arrivals. But Richard Galliers did: his gaze travelled once to the doorway, and then followed the two men as they made their apologies to the Countess. But his concentration did not slip; he returned to the game, wine glass in one hand, dice in the other, calling the throws, thought George Murray sourly, with the accuracy of a clairvoyant.

The noise simmered, bubbled to fever pitch; a crash of broken glass, a burst of mocking applause, and George twisted round in his seat and saw Sir Nicholas Carleton, faultless in quilted black velvet, moving through the bustle of gaudy colours to stand, gloves in hand, just behind Murray's seat.

'My dear Galliers! After all these years how – *surprising* – to see you.' Edged with the scarlet of the nearby fire, Carleton laid a careless hand on George's shoulder. 'Yes, I had thought we were to be permanently deprived of your illustrious company. I was devastated –'

'To hear I had returned?' The last of Murray's coins slid to the other side of the table, and Galliers looked up, a pinpoint of red light in each blank eye. 'Comfort yourself, Carleton. It may not be for long – the company abroad was frequently more to my taste.'

Carleton smiled, his dark gaze taking in the dice, the empty glasses, Ellenby. 'Seals, sea serpents, and other crawling things. I don't doubt it, Galliers.'

'*But the serpent was more subtil than any beast of the field . . .*'

Galliers scooped the coins off the table, and leaned back in his chair, the thin line of the scar vivid in the candlelight. 'But then you are not a beast of the field, are you, Carleton? Stalking in chambers is more in your line – great chambers, withdrawing chambers, bed chambers –'

Against the increasing howl of the revellers, Richard Galliers' soft voice was almost inaudible. But Carleton heard it: he leaned forward, his hand gripping George Murray's shoulder like a hawk's talons, his face distorted into grotesque by the firelight. 'I would have hoped, if nothing else, the experience of a few years struggling exile would have taught you your manners, Mr Galliers, but it seems my expectations were misplaced; you are obviously little improved. I hear you have hardly been sober since putting into Dover. Still –' and Carleton's voice was clear and precise, '– what can one expect from the son of a drunkard and a whore?'

That remark jolted even George Murray out of the sickening misery of defeat. But – and he glanced quickly round him – no heads were turned, no eyes drawn, shocked, to the bitter verbal duel that George Murray had found himself forced to witness. A man and a woman danced, slightly unsteadily, just behind them; in the nearest corner of the room, half hidden by shadows, a couple embraced, the man's gloved hand clawing the woman's back. And, looking back at Richard Galliers, George saw that he was unruffled – no, more than that, he was positively welcoming Carleton's invective. The boredom had gone from his face: Richard Galliers was enjoying himself. *This* was what he was here for.

'Dear me, Sir Nicholas, did you intend that I should spend my years abroad in honest toil, earning a crust by the sweat of my brow? I hate to disappoint you – but as you know full well yourself, it is perfectly possible to profit quite nicely using much less strenuous methods.' He stood up, his russet silk slightly crumpled, lace cuffs and collar somewhat askew. 'But I'm afraid I must deprive you of my company. You know George Murray – George forgot that I play hazard better when drunk. He is in need of some liquid consolation. Oh, and here is Mr

Ellenby.' Ellenby gave a loud snore and slipped further down the chair. 'Mr Ellenby is another admirer of mine – think what fun you could have discussing my charms. He might even challenge you to a duel. Now you must excuse me – that lute is sadly out of tune.'

He rose, and for one long moment Murray thought that Carleton would try to bar his way. But the grip on his shoulder relaxed, and George watched Galliers thread his way through the tables. The fan was dropped to the floor again, deliberately this time, and George saw Galliers pick it up, and its owner totter unsteadily against him. A whispered conversation, and the woman's hands stroked at the russet silk, her eyes fixed on Galliers' face, and she laughed again, the sound high and uneven.

George put his dice back in his pocket. There was a foul taste in his mouth, even though he had drunk little wine, and his lungs felt clogged with the chamber's thick, overheated air. Not very far away, he could hear someone being sick through one of Lady Somerset's mullioned windows. He saw that Richard Galliers had pulled away from his admirer, and saw also the frustration on the woman's face as her empty hands clutched air.

Murray watched, and Sir Nicholas Carleton watched, as Galliers stood before the Countess of Somerset, and bowed. A brief conversation, a smile from the Countess, and the lute was passed to Richard, who sat on the musician's stool, and began to re-tune the instrument. George Murray pulled at the constricting ruff round his neck.

'At least his skills with the lute are not quite so ruinous to the pocket. A drink, Sir Nicholas?'

> 'Let now the chimneys blaze
> And cups o'erflow with wine;
> Let well-tuned words amaze
> With harmony divine.
> Now yellow waxen lights

Shall wait on honey Love,
With youthful revels, masks, and courtly sights
Sleep's leaden spells remove.'

The door of the small withdrawing chamber was gently closed, shutting out both the singer and the song. Frances, Countess of Somerset, turned to Sir Nicholas Carleton.

'Your Mr Galliers has the face of Lucifer – and the tongue of an angel.'

Carleton said smoothly, 'And the soul of the devil. And he is not *my* Mr Galliers.'

The firelight caught the emeralds in the Countess's hair. 'But I saw you deep in conversation with him, Nicholas.'

'The man would sell his own brother – as you know. He is worthless – he is nothing.'

Underneath the beauty, behind the poise and serenity, there was steel, and a hard, cold, intelligence. Frances Kerr said softly, 'Worthless, Nicholas – or dangerous? And if he is dangerous, then dangerous to whom?'

Their eyes met, and the ghost of a smile lit Carleton's face. 'To both of us, perhaps, your ladyship.'

There was a brief silence, and then the Countess said:

'Then I had better bring my cousin to heel – and you, Sir Nicholas, should consider the possibility of eliminating the danger – soon.'

Carleton touched the Countess' pearl-encrusted sleeve. 'Listen, Frances – it was not of Galliers I wished to speak. You know that – and you know why I'm here.'

'Of course. And I also wished to speak to you. For instance, I am interested to know why you arrived with – who is it? Conway? – and not your lovely golden-haired friend.'

Carleton's grip relaxed slightly. 'Sir Thomas Conway is not important. My bringing him here has nothing to do with our – association. His land lies near mine – we have business to discuss, that is all. The fellow made the cardinal error of marrying the daughter of one of his yeoman farmers. Besides, he is something of a freak – he is building a boat that will sail under the water. As for Lucas – Lucas is confused by some of the finer points of friendship. He has a very jealous nature.'

Frances Kerr took hold of the importuning hand, and clasped it in her own small white one. Gently, she said, 'But I also have a jealous nature, my dear Nick. And perhaps, if you wish your property to be returned to you, you should discover a way to demonstrate your loyalty. Yes?'

It was not in his nature to beg, to grovel. Raising her hand to his lips, Sir Nicholas Carleton bowed. 'As you wish, Frances.' He held open the door for her to leave the room.

She inclined her graceful head to him once more, contentment in her light blue eyes. 'And now escort me to Sir Thomas Conway. I have a fondness for madmen.'

Only one man in the Great Chamber had guessed the conversation between Sir Nicholas Carleton and Lady Somerset to be anything more than a friendly dialogue concerning the weather, the troubles with Parliament, or the rebuilding of the new Globe theatre. The russet silk of his doublet was spotted with wine, the superb lace of his shirt lay open and slovenly, and he knew, finally, that he had drunk too much to play the lute with the perfection his soul required. But Richard Galliers had seen the fire and ice in that encounter, and he had also seen the lady cross the crowded room to the side of Sir Thomas Conway. His gaze moved between the three of them – the Countess, Sir Thomas, Carleton – and his long hands gripped the fretted neck of the lute they were no longer capable of playing.

It was not until the early hours of the morning that the last of the revellers, gorged with food and wine and dancing, left the house in Blackfriars. Richard Galliers was one of the last to leave – alone. The Countess of Somerset had roused her stupefied cousin and spoken to him privately a little after midnight, and Galiers had not seen him since. Neither had Sir Nicholas Carleton stayed long: after two short hours he had returned with Sir Thomas Conway to the dark autumn night.

But the festivities had continued, accompanied by lutes, viols, and citterns, another impressive array of dainties (quince jelly, gingerbread, hippocras, biscuits, spice cakes and suckets) had been served to tempt the appetites of the glutted.

Richard Galliers had neither played nor danced. He had sat on a bench in the corner of the room, his legs stretched lazily out before him, his jewelled hands comfortably cushioning his dark head, a glass of wine at his side. Occasionally, when the music had demanded a chorus, he had sung, the words only slightly slurred. And sometimes one of the prettier ladies had sat beside him, and spoken to him for a while.

He had taken his unsteady leave of the Countess a little before three in the morning, enthusiastically saluting her small white hand. The night air was damp, but not actually raining; the watch was nowhere in sight as Galliers wove his lurching way up the twisting, silent street.

> '*All do not – all things – well:*
> *Some mea – meash –* damned word *– measures comely tread.*'

He adjusted his cloak, which had slipped from one shoulder to trail on the filthy ground, and rounded a corner.

> '*Some knotted riddles tell,*
> *Some poems – shmoo – shmooth –* oh, God's teeth!'

Beset by sibyllants, he stumbled over a pothole in the road, steadying himself against the overhanging wall of a house.

And yet the street was no longer – quite – silent.

To the two men who, like wraiths from the underworld, clung to and dissolved in the shadows around him, Galliers gave no indication that he had heard anything. The tottering, intoxicated gait was unchanged; the blurred, disjointed singing still echoed haltingly in the cramped unlit alley. But the face altered: the cat's eyes were suddenly alert and wary, and the lips parted slightly in anticipation.

> '*The Summer – hath – his joys . . .*'

95

There were – how many? – two of them behind him. They had attached themselves to him when he had turned the corner, not too close, not too far away. The hilt of his main gauche dagger was already touching Galliers' perfectly steady hand as he crossed the alleyway, slipping drunkenly in some of the filth that lay underfoot.

'*And Winter hish – delights –*'

But, if possible, he must avoid using the dagger. As a threat, perhaps, but a man with a knife in his belly did not tend to be over informative. They were waiting – for what? For him to turn the next corner into the small, windowless courtyard ahead – an ideal spot for a short, silent murder. Galliers could not have chosen better himself. His eyes caught a minute flicker of movement ahead of him. Especially if assistance was waiting . . . perhaps odds of two to one were not good enough. Four, five, six to one, and his own chances of survival did not seem too promising.

The knife was in his left hand now, the thin reassuring hilt balanced in his palm. He slowed his pace still further, and heard his shadows likewise slow theirs.

'*Though Love – and all his pleashures – are but toys –*'

Not footpads then; common thieves would have attacked by now, and either he or they would be sprawling bloodied in the gutter. *Whose*, then?

Aye, there's the rub . . . and if their knives found their target before his, he would never, ever know. All these years, all that misery and hatred to end squealing and ignorant at the side of the street.

Before the courtyard, then. Galliers stumbled again, pinpointing the position of his assassins as he glanced quickly backwards, grasping the side of a stone horse trough for support. They were near enough now.

'*They shorten – tedious nights –*'

They were not ready. They had expected it to be easy, to slaughter a drunken man. The first, kneed in the groin with annihilating force and then struck sharply under the chin, never knew what had hit him. The second had time to grab the slippery russet silk, to shout, to use his fists, and then finally to make a short, muffled gasp as his head ricochetted off the plastered wall behind him, and he slithered unconscious to the mud below.

The main gauche knife flew through the air, whirling, incandescent in the moonlight, finding its deadly mark in the chest of the third man as he emerged from the courtyard. To the fourth, taking in the confusion and carnage before him, the game was lost before it had begun. He turned and ran back into the courtyard, then through the maze of alleyways and paths beyond, dissolving into the shielding darkness.

There was no point in attempting to follow him: to find the correct route through that rabbit warren would require a miracle. Richard Galliers walked to the prone figure at the entrance of the courtyard. He knelt down beside it, his breathing harsh in the renewed silence of the street, his dark hair clinging to his forehead with sweat.

He swore softly. The man was dead, the knife still protruding obscenely from his chest. Galliers pulled it out, wiped the blood from the shaft, and returned it to his belt. There would be, of course, no clue to the identity of his assassins, no emblem, no livery, no indication as to who had sent them. They were dressed with anonymity – old jerkins, breeches, nameless, unknown faces.

It would not do to be found here in this street. Neither would it do to return to his lodgings – after the fourth man's retreat there could always be another, larger reception party waiting for him. And with a split lip, a torn doublet, and, he suspected, an incipient black eye, it might be best to find shelter for what was left of the night with someone who did not ask too many questions.

Without a backward glance at the still figures in the street behind him, Richard Galliers set off for Holborn.

97

Esmé Molyneux, an habitual night owl, had long since returned from his evening at the Mermaid, sent his manservant to bed, snuffed out all the candles but the pair in his study, and thrown a fur edged wrap around the superbly cut shoulders of his doublet. He had been working on the epic poem for over a fortnight; progress was good, if slow, and conceits and devices were beginning to come more easily to his pen.

The sound of the rapping at his door was not loud, but it was definite. With only the faintest frown at the interruption, Esmé first found a loaded, primed pistol, and then went to open the door.

He took in the situation at a glance, beckoned in his unexpected night-visitor, and softly closed the door behind him. The pistol was replaced, carefully, in the chest from which it had been taken, the visitor shown into the study where a feeble fire still glowed, and a bowl of water and pieces of linen fetched.

'Let me see, Richard.' Esmé moved aside the writing materials and books, and placed the bowl of water on the desk. 'You won once too often at hazard, your latest dramatic performance went sadly awry, or a lady was not receptive to your advances?'

An expression of pure delight lit the spoilt, ravaged face. 'None of those, Esmé.' Richard Galliers plunged his head into the water, and emerged gasping, fully sober for the first time that night. 'No – but I have had a very interesting evening.' He rubbed his face and hair with the towel that Esmé held out to him.

'You are going to have the most *ornamental* black eye – and that suit is quite ruined. What a waste – it was a good silk.'

Under the blood, the bruises, Richard's face was elated. 'Never mind about my clothes. Don't you wish to hear about my interesting evening?'

Esmé threw a log on to the faltering fire. 'If you wish to tell me, Richard. One never knows.'

Galliers sat down in the chair behind him, dabbing at his bloodied lip with a corner of the towel. 'Four cut-throats, sent most deliberately, placed most artistically, were awaiting my solitary drunken departure from the Countess of Somerset's house tonight.'

'You thought to be their stalking horse? You expected them, of course.' The question in Esmé's eyes needed no answer. 'A dangerous game, my dear – your hunters might have been better skilled. Four, you say? And what became of these unfortunate assassins?'

Galliers grinned. 'Three are probably still lying in the mud. The fourth turned tail and ran.'

'Understandable in the circumstances.' Esmé rose and poured a cup of wine. 'Did you know them? Have you any idea who sent them?'

Richard shook his head absently as Esmé offered him the cup. 'There was no means of identification. And unfortunately I was drunker than I thought – my knife went through the third man's heart instead of his shoulder, as I had intended. A pity – a conversation could have been useful. I arrived at Blackfriars earlier in the evening, with Ellenby. I left without him, and I have a strong suspicion that his company will no longer be available to me.'

Esmé frowned as he jabbed at the fire with the poker.

'Yes – I think he has been warned off – by the Countess herself, of course. But *why*?'

'Who else was present tonight?'

The good humour vanished from Galliers' face, the excitement turning coldly to calculation. 'Carleton was there. And Sir Thomas Conway. It's many years since I've seen him. What do you know of him, Esmé?'

'A little. He is something of a scholar, we have spoken occasionally of mutual interests. He has a large estate in East Anglia – you must know Belford, it cannot be that far from Amyott. I believe he has an infant son, and a daughter who is almost grown.'

'A pretty, dark-haired, little thing?'

Esmé shook his head. 'I've never met the girl, Richard. Conway keeps her hidden in the depths of Cambridgeshire, although he's frequently at Court himself. He's a brilliant man —but too eccentric for this world.'

Richard was silent for a moment, gazing somewhere into the heart of the now roaring fire. 'I have an invitation to the Conways' house for the end of November. Perhaps I shall accept it after all.'

CHAPTER FIVE

And if by chance you should look for me
Perhaps you'll not me find
For I'll be in my dream castle
Enquire for Reynardine.

(REYNARDINE)

*I*NEXORABLY, relentlessly, Belford's day of reckoning had come. Everything that should have been done was done or never would be: plate, silverware and glassware had been shone to hitherto unimagined brightness, and the dust of centuries swept from under furniture and behind hangings.

Preparations for Belford's largest culinary occasion since Sir Thomas's second marriage had been under way for several days. Pies, cakes, tarts, almonds, olives, marzipan, preserved fruits, custards, dates, currants, all kinds of roasted and boiled fowl from tiny pigeons to gigantic geese, loaded the monstrous kitchen table. And at the spit, already thoroughly overheated, sat Martin Bartlett, mechanically rotating the heavy iron handle, his mind far away from the chaos of the kitchen. The disaster of the Stourbridge Fair had blown over with no worse consequence for Martin than a severe thrashing, the bruises of which were long gone and forgotten. Requisitioned from the stables early that morning, he had been assigned the dullest task of all – turning the overburdened spit with its load of roasting beef, venison, whole roast pig, and, Sarah's speciality, a kid with a pudding in its belly. Yet, despite the heat, the cook's bad temper, the noise, and his strong aversion to indoor work, Martin was happy. His gaze wandered to Martha, her arms flour-dusted as she rolled out sweet pastry for pies. Smiling to himself, he thought again of the straw and horse-smelling stables where last night he had spent a most agreeable hour. Martha had abandoned her previous sweetheart, and had finally turned her attentions to Martin, rewarding him most handsomely for his persistence. And tonight, when all this nonsense about banquets was over, she would be waiting for him in the stables . . .

'The kid's burning.' The cool voice in his ear made him jump, swear, and hastily resume turning the spit. Mall stood behind him.

'Just think, Martin, if I hadn't to be found a husband, you could be outside now.'

Martin grinned, his task lightened by a vision of Mall, walking slowly down the aisle of the church on the arm of the ancient and rheumatic Lord Cheseborough.

'Which one of 'em are you going to choose, then?'

She grimaced. 'I don't think *my* choice will have much to do with it.' Her temporary good spirits evaporated with the recollection of the day's festivities. 'You, Martin Bartlett, may be sitting there wishing to God you were back in the stables grooming the horses, but remember: you can marry whom you choose – even though –' she finished maliciously '– it'll probably be a fat dimwit like Martha. Still,' Martin's face had taken on an even deeper hue, 'there's no accounting for taste. The pig's scorching now.'

Helping herself to some biscuits from the table, Mall escaped from the heat of the kitchen. She had some distant memory of having promised to help Alice with something – but she had forgotten precisely what it had been – and besides, the thought of more time spent preparing for this horrendous feast was not remotely appealing. She had woken that morning feeling particularly flat and low in spirits, and with a longing to be anywhere but Belford. It was not that she, like Alice, was dreading the banquet itself. No, it was the thought of the day's inevitable consequences that Mall found lowering. Last night she had dreamed of Reynardine again, a dream that had lingered after she had woken. The silk handkerchief still lay neatly folded in the corner of her chest. She knew, of course, that she should have thrown it on to the fire long ago, just as she should have told someone – Leo or Alice perhaps – what had really happened that night. But the handkerchief remained unburnt, just as the haunting, teasing, words of the song remained unforgotten. *Therewith all sweetly did me kiss, And softly said, Dear heart, how like you this . . .?*

They had met, briefly; he had kissed her thoughtlessly, once; and left her with no other token than a beautifully initialled silk handkerchief. But he had also left her with a dream of what might have been. She had encountered her dark, dangerous man, her sly bold Reynardine, and he had given her no taste for what reality had to offer.

But these were foolish thoughts, only underlining the need for today's occasion. Surely – Mall looked out of the window to the cold frosty garden – surely with her future settled and a wedding in the offing, she would be rid of these plaguing fantasies of a stranger's kiss. After all, she had not even seen his face . . .

Richard Galliers, riding that morning along the frost-hardened tracks of Essex, had also found the last few weeks frustrating. The more visible souvenirs of his encounter following the Countess of Somerset's banquet had faded, but so too had any trace of a hint as to the identity of his attackers. Worse than that: it had seemed to him that certain doors had become closed to him, that just as Ellenby was no longer soliciting his company, so had his presence become imperceptibly less welcome in other circles. And in worldly, restive London it seemed unlikely that sudden offence would have been taken at his less than spotless past – more probable that someone, that same someone who had warned off Ellenby, had whispered influentially in other ears. That was interesting in itself, but had produced a defensive silence Galliers was unable to breech. The last two days had been particularly unsatisfactory – one entire twenty-four hours wasted with an old drinking crony of Overbury's, who had, like George Murray, a passion for hazard, but a passion unmatched by talent. It had been damned difficult, Galliers reflected ruefully as he forded a small ice-fringed stream, to lose and keep losing, to ply the fellow with drink and to keep the game going long enough to loosen that miserly tongue with alcohol or victory. The dice had been infuriatingly uncooperative: Galliers had been driven to substituting weighted dice for the pair they played with, and using them against himself. And in the end the man had told him nothing – nothing that could not equally well have been picked up in any alehouse or taproom. It had been as much as he could do to remain civil, and keep sufficiently sober to find solace in a warm bed and a soft, comforting bosom.

But although lovemaking offered a pleasurable diversion, it did not allow him to forget that the opportunities, that had begun so promisingly that wet afternoon in August, were narrowing inexorably to one last chance. It was ludicrous, he thought to himself as he eased the mare over an icy patch on the path, that the thought of this day should have cost him sleepless nights. He recalled his words to Carleton at Lady Somerset's banquet and, incongruous in the grey Essex countryside, one memory, echoed and re-echoed since in nightmares, re-asserted itself. The gentle rolling downs dissolved into the glaring blue of the Mediterranean, and he was back once more on the deck of the corsair's vessel. A short, sharp, disastrous sea battle, and he had been left to fight for his life with whatever came to hand. And it had been his skills, the sweat of his brow that had saved him then. The corsair's pilot had been lost in that same slaughter, and Galliers had bought his reprieve by his ability to pilot that ship through the treacherous straits and into the safety of the Atlantic. He had navigated that damned pinnace for nearly a year; he had seen things that, even now, woke him in the early hours of the morning, his body running with a cold sweat. He had lived by his wits, he was indeed – he smiled bitterly – everything Carleton could accuse him of. He had prostituted himself, sold his skills, his looks, his cunning, anything to remain alive.

It was cold enough to snow, the bare branches of the trees signalled the beginning of a hard winter. He tried to remember his last, long distant visit to Belford. The place was huge, he recalled, a cumbersome maze of chambers and antechambers, winding staircases, belvedere towers, kitchens and galleries. Suddenly his quest seemed impossible: like searching for a single flea on a dog's back. And if he found what he was looking for, what then? Nothing – except finally facing up to the fact that he should never have returned home. And that, of course, accounted for the sleepless nights. Whatever happened today would dictate his course of action over the next few weeks, months, years – perhaps the rest of his life.

And if there was nothing – if the contents of Conway's desk and cabinets proved as innocent as Murray's had been, that would make, by a process of elimination, what he had hoped and dreaded these last few months so much more likely. Then –

Then the game would really begin.

As the gloom of the weather matched her mood and thus made walking or riding undesirable, Mall had headed for the familiar solace of her father's library. There was always something comforting about the untidy dark room, with its small mullioned windows hung with rather dirty green curtains. There was little furniture; a desk, a couple of chairs, a cabinet, several chests. Two of Belford's less distinguished tapestries attempted with a squint-inducing lack of perspective to adorn the walls, and the fire surround was an over-ornamented chalk monstrosity. But the most important furnishings of the room were books: the high shelves were crammed with them, some vertical, some horizontal, some squeezed into double rows, a few slipping loose backed to the floor. And on the rush matted floor, more books, piled under the desk, behind the chairs, almost obliterating the linenfold wainscotting. Some of the books were covered with a liberal layer of dust, evidence of Sir Thomas's reluctance to let outsiders in to clean the room, but others were dustless, open, and obviously well read. Sir Thomas's table was piled high with still more books, papers, pamphlets, writing and drawing materials. The chests, too, were full almost to bursting point. The one under the window contained maps, collected partially by Sir Thomas, who had been an enthusiastic traveller in his youth, but also by Grandfather Conway, whose austere representation gazed at Mall from the portrait by the door. Mall had spent many long and happy hours poring over the collection. Maps studded with names whose very resonance suggested the exotic, the adventurous. Goa, Siam, Cape Verde, Astrakhan, Cathay – magic words with the power to assuage childhood sorrows.

But it was not to the maps that Mall went today. Gathering a pile of cushions and a thick rug – for the room was always cold –she settled herself in one of the better lit corners, and drew from the top of the pile where she had last placed it, a well worn copy of the *Iliad*. Several times during the morning she emerged briefly from the sounds of clashing swords on shields to hear, echoing dimly in the distant recesses of the house, a name, possibly hers, being called. And once, the door had been pushed open slightly and a servant's head peeped in and failed to see her in the retreat behind her father's desk.

Then, just as Hector was about to perish, the door was pushed abruptly open, and Lady Conway, hands on hips, blonde hair pushed anyhow under a badly pinned cap, peered short-sightedly into the room.

'Mall?' Breathing heavily with the effort of the long tortuous staircased route to the library, Alice stumbled over one of the larger piles of books and jarred herself painfully on a chair. Pain, fatigue, and anxiety made her speak less gently than usual.

'Mall! Are you in here?'

Mall stood up, annoyance at the interruption clearly written on her face. Carefully picking her way round books and furniture, she bent to rescue the pile of books Alice had knocked to the floor.

'I was reading, stepmother.' Her dark head bent over a broken book. 'The spine's cracked –'

'*Reading*!' Alice's voice rose in a shriek. In spite of a letter hinting that he hoped to return to Belford by the end of November, Sir Thomas had not appeared. And although Leo was only too happy to help, it would have made all the difference to Alice to have had the support of her husband at the banquet.

'*Reading*? When half the county is coming to dinner today? When you know that I especially requested you to help with the set piece because Sarah's hand is bad again – you must have known Martha would make a disaster of it – and she has!'

Mall shifted guiltily, vague memories of quickly made and as quickly forgotten promises returning to her. Lady Conway, having replenished her breath, continued:

'And Ralph! The poor little mite has been crying for you all morning. How could you neglect him so? Sitting here, reading books, when you know that the poor angel is only just over his last chill. It's not right, Mall, it's not natural –' She broke off, aware that concern for her son, and panic about the banquet were causing her to breach her already fragile relationship with her stepdaughter.

But it was too late. Mall's head had begun to throb again, even the *Iliad* had not yet succeeded in distracting her from thoughts of marriage, of the future, of Reynardine. Guilty of semi-deliberate neglect of the culinary arrangements she might be, but Alice's charge of neglecting her tiny half brother Mall knew to be deeply unjust.

'My apologies, Lady Conway.' Mall put down the broken book. 'I had forgotten you could not manage.'

The older woman gaped, and then gasped incoherently as the force of the insult struck her. 'Could not manage? I don't know why I do it! I invite half of the most eligible men in the county – to try and find you a respectable husband – Good God!' The lace cap finally lost its precarious hold and slipped to the floor. 'Look at you! Who'd be fool enough to have you, even with all your money? Your hair's in a mess, your gown is torn, and your nose is always in a book. A man doesn't want a wife who won't put herself out to please anyone. He wants –'

'Yes, *your ladyship*, what does he want?' Through the annoying tears that threatened to blur her vision, Mall knew that she must control her tongue, yet could not. 'You know what a man wants, don't you? You must do – you persuaded my father to marry you. How did you do that? A man who'd hardly looked at a woman since my mother died. Go on, why don't you tell me – should I bed them before I wed – is that the way to do it? You should know!'

With her own unforgivable, irretrievable words echoing in her ears, and the sight of her stepmother's pretty face reduced to plainness before her eyes, Mall fled. She ran out of the room, and down the stairs, but the rustle of her skirts, the noise of her footsteps, the sound of furniture being shifted in the Great Chamber below, all failed to muffle the terrible, despairing sobbing from the library.

An hour later, in the peace and sanity of her own room, Mall stood in front of her old curtained mirror. She had gone to Ralph, but he had been asleep in his cradle, one thumb in his mouth, the other chubby hand clutching his favourite worn piece of blanket. Teething, his nurse had said, a few hours sleep would put him to rights. Then Mall had left for the kitchen, and expertly, mechanically, resurrected the set piece. An over ambitious edible arrangement in the form of a galleon, it had, as Alice had said, been a disaster. And if it would never be seaworthy, it was at least now possible to tell what it was intended to represent.

Declining Lucy's offer of assistance, Mall had then returned to her chamber to dress. She had, she thought miserably, never felt less like festivities. But if nothing else, this morning's appalling scene had highlighted the need for her removal from Belford. Clearly, there was no longer any point in pretending that she and Alice would ever do any more than barely tolerate each other.

Mall looked at her reflection in the mirror. She had dressed herself in her beautiful new gown, made from the red velvet she had bought at the Stourbridge Fair. A few proposals of marriage might give the lie to some of Alice's criticisms, which had stung more than Mall would admit even to herself. And although she knew she was too small, too thin, too pale, with the new gown and her hair dressed in a reasonably fashionable style, she no longer saw the reflection she was used to.

A different image, older and unfamiliar, looked back at her from the mirror. And somewhere in the blurred, burnished depths another shadow hovered, almost seen.

Reynardine.

It was going well, thought Alice. Dressed in a pale blue silk that floated over a large and elaborate farthingale, she felt the equal of any woman present. She glanced across at Leo, distinguished in a long shag robe, and felt a momentary pang of misery at the absence of her husband. But how delighted Sir Thomas would be if she were to arrange a good marriage for his only daughter. Mall – where was the child? Yet again, Alice looked around the Hall, her myopic eyes narrowing in an effort to see her stepdaughter. She couldn't have disappeared again, thought Alice, panic and the heat generated by the heavy farthingale causing her palms to become damp with sweat. No, she surely wouldn't do that – oh God, if only there had not been that dreadful scene in the library. Paint and powder had successfully camouflaged the redness of her eyelids, but deep down, Alice felt something akin to despair. It had happened, the unspeakable had been said and could not be retracted. And it had been her own fault, Alice acknowledged, smiling acceptance as the servant filled her glass of canary. She had been unfair in accusing Mall of neglecting Ralph, and unforgivable in openly criticizing her appearance and behaviour. Fear had led her to act foolishly: fear that this banquet should be a disaster, fear that Sir Thomas would consequently be ridiculed for his second marriage, fear that Ralph's tears were heralding yet another illness. And it could only be her own failings that made her unacceptable to Mall. After all, the girl had never known a mother, it was not as though Alice had attempted to replace some still fond memory. It was too late, though, the scene in the library had made that abundantly clear. The best Alice could do for her stepdaughter now would be to find her a good husband.

Perhaps she should send one of the servants to look for her. More people had come than she had dared hope. The Murrays, the Houldens, the Deans, Robert Askew, both Giles and Richard Galliers – and Sir Nicholas Carleton. His presence was particularly gratifying. If he should make an offer for Mall, what a coup that would be! And Thomas had mentioned in his letter that in London Sir Nicholas had made certain discreet enquiries concerning Mall's marriage settlement. But, of course, he had been one of the most eligible bachelors in the district for some time now, and had succumbed to none of the lovely daughters that scheming mothers had put in his path. So she must not become too optimistic. But he had definitely shown interest . . .

And there, at last, was Mall. Alice breathed a heartfelt sigh of relief. Slowly, Mall was descending the staircase, and she looked magnificent. Her red dress was ornamented with silver lace and irregularly shaped pearls. Her hair was brushed into a smooth and glossy black knot, and threaded with another rope of pearls. Alice stole a glance around the room. Every man's eye was on her stepdaughter, from the sixty-year-old Lord Cheseborough (who really should have been past that sort of thing) to the unsuitable and phlegmatic Robert Askew. And Sir Nicholas Carleton – those dark Spanish eyes were staring at Mall with an intensity that even Alice found surprising. Unobtrusively, she moved to his side.

By the fireplace, George Murray, unwillingly involved in a

somewhat abstruse debate between Leo Conway and his old adversary, Doctor Lucey, was looking for a diversion. Financial strictures – he had had a bad run of luck since that ruinous game with Richard Galliers – had obliged him to return, temporarily, to Essex. There had been little prospect of amusement at a country dinner but, to please both Anna and his father, he had been happy enough to escort his sister to Belford. At the party Anna had long since deserted him for Lord Amyott and, feeling superfluous in that company, George had somehow become embroiled in this appallingly dull conversation. A glaze of boredom had settled on his handsome, regular features, and he stifled a yawn.

Then Miss Conway appeared from some dark distant corner of the house, and instantly his ennui had evaporated. Somehow, he had still expected to see the scrawny child of several years ago. Hellfire, what an unexpected delight. When had he last seen her? Not that long ago, surely – but then she had been a skinny little thing in an ill-fitting gown, too absorbed in the game of chess she had been playing to pay much attention to him. That would have been just after Sir Thomas had remarried. Yes, that must be it, Alice Conway had transformed her stepdaughter into the enchanting creature he saw before him. Politely, George made his excuses to the two older gentlemen, and manoeuvred himself to a convenient position at the bottom of the staircase.

'Miss Conway, you cannot have forgotten me.'

Mall looked at him, and smiled. 'Mr Murray?'

The afternoon began, suddenly, to show promise. 'Miss Conway, you look ravishing.' His grey eyes devouring every inch of her, George bowed, and kissed Mall's hand. 'We must make up for lost time, Miss Conway. We have been neighbours all our lives, yet have seen so little of each other.' Taking Mall's arm, Murray escorted her away from the stairs. 'A glass of wine, my dear? I see that you have assembled a good company here.'

The hall was indeed crowded. Customarily sombre in appearance, it was beginning to appear positively festive as the brightly coloured silks and velvets of the guests, their feathered hats, the jewellery, the gold and silver lace and many coloured ribbons caught the thin sunlight let in by the high windows. And the faces – old, young, pretty, and plain – some Mall had known all her life, others she could not recall ever having seen.

'Was your sister able to come today, Mr Murray? I remember her well; she was very kind to me.'

'Anna is the soul of kindness. A person would have to be villainous indeed for Anna to talk harshly of them. Look, there she is, by the fireplace.

Mall peered through the crowds, and saw a tall, chestnut-haired woman. A man stood beside her – tall, like Miss Murray, dark and dashing. It was plain that whatever the noise and distraction around them, those two saw none but each other. Mall had learned a little of their story from her chambermaids. It had been love at first sight, Lucy had said; one glance and the hitherto untamed Lord Amyott had eyes for no other woman. Mall suppressed a sigh. George Murray was pleasant and good-looking, but she had yet to fall desperately in love with him.

'Come and meet Anna and Giles. Do you know Lord Amyott? They are to be married next September –'

He had not expected to experience that ache of longing again. But it had hit him, like a blow to the stomach, just as when he had first seen her, bare-shouldered in the pool. She was different in this setting – different, but no less covetable. In this ugly, badly proportioned room she was no longer the naiad that bedevilled his dreams, but a beautiful, infinitely desirable creature. She had nothing of her father in her, thank God: in this assembly of country hayseeds she stood out like a fleck of gold dust in common earth. And she was so young – innocent, unspoiled, unsophisticated. He would mould her into whatever he wanted. A boy's half-formed body, fragile, spare, with the small collectable perfection of a Hilliard miniature. Black hair, translucent skin, and those extraordinary dark blue eyes. And, he hoped, not totally brainless, unlike the overfed, overdressed creature hovering at his side.

'May I have the honour of introducing my stepdaughter to you, Sir Nicholas?'

If he wished to pursue the daughter he must continue to find favour with the stepmother. Smiling, Carleton turned to Alice and murmured an assent.

Where, then, was the disreputable younger brother? Richard Galliers had been invited, he had subsequently accepted but, looking round the Great Hall, Mall could not find the face to fit the description. Very handsome, Alice had said – well, so was Lord Amyott handsome, and she could find none that bore a brotherly resemblance to him. Who was Alice speaking to? A tall, dark-haired man, his face hidden from view. And how on earth was she ever going to face her stepmother again? The headache still throbbed in Mall's temples, and she forced a smile to an enquiry of Miss Murray's.

The dark-haired man turned so that his profile could be seen. A strong face, dark eyes, a beard – Mall choked on her wine. A kindly word from George Murray, who was only too pleased to pat her sympathetically on the back, and then fetch another glass of wine. Restored to superficial composure, Mall glanced across the room again.

There was no doubt about it. That was indisputably the man who had watched her in the pool – that glimpse of another world – with the golden haired boy behind him. Here, at Belford. As if this whole occasion were not sufficiently intimidating, that man, witness of her past folly, was here also. Mall touched George Murray's sleeve.

'Mr Murray – the gentleman with the beard – over there, speaking to my stepmother. Do you know him?'

It was not George Murray that answered, but Lord Amyott.

'Carleton. I am a little surprised to see him here.'

'Yes, he is seldom away from London.' Murray smiled. 'You are honoured, my dear. Sir Nicholas Carleton only attends the greatest occasions and seeks the company of the greatest ladies.'

Yet Sir Nicholas Carleton had called at Belford at the end of September, on the same day as Mall's ill-fated visit to the Stourbridge Fair. Alice had spoken of it incessantly, Mall had taken little notice, being far too troubled with memories of another encounter. So he had called *after* he had seen her in the pool . . . No, she would not follow that train of thought. Draining her glass of wine, Mall tried to listen to the conversation.

George Murray was speaking. 'Yes, I saw Carleton quite recently. Talking to Richard, incidentally, Giles.'

Giles smiled, slightly sourly. 'Indeed? So which of them ended with the knife at his throat?'

'Neither.' George shook his head. 'A few muted insults were passed – sotto voce, you understand – but Richard was unusually restrained.' He looked around the room. 'By the way, Giles, where is that devil of a brother of yours? I understood he was to be here.'

'Oh, he is. But in a particularly foul temper. I think he is attempting to console himself with the lovely Mrs Houlden.'

Mall followed the direction of Lord Amyott's gaze. In a distant corner of the hall stood a man and a woman. The woman Mall recognized as Ann Houlden, young and pretty bride of the cheerless Matthew. The man she did not know. Dark-haired, slender, beautiful in black velvet, he lounged against the wooden panelling, Mrs Houlden's hand in his. Since the composition of the guest list, Mall had taken the trouble to discover exactly what it was that Mr Galliers was supposed to have done. Her chambermaid, Lucy, had as ever been an inestimable source of rumour and scandal. Mr Galliers had lost three fortunes at dice and cards, had founded a colony of atheists in the New World, had run a brothel, had been the catamite of some Eastern princeling . . . all that in three years. Well, thought Mall, focusing on the neat, dark figure and pale, slightly exotic face, perhaps he did look tired.

George chuckled crudely. 'Mr Houlden had better look to his wife. Perhaps you should do the noble thing, Giles, and intervene. Besides, I would like to speak to Richard – he damned near robbed me blind the last time we met, and I need a chance to even things up.'

Giles Galliers did not answer at first. Then his eyes met Anna's, and he shrugged, and said, 'Of course. Let me introduce my brother to you, Miss Conway'. He passed his empty glass to a manservant and made his excuses.

It occurred to Giles, as it had to Mall, that Richard looked a little weary. His dress was immaculate, the black velvet richly yet soberly ornamented with black pearls and fine lace. A few carefully placed diamonds caught the pale winter sunlight. But his skin was a bad colour, dark shadows smudging his eyes. He looked, thought Giles with a faint vengeful satisfaction, as though he had spent several weeks in a Southwark brothel. And that, in itself, argued a possibility of retaliation.

Giles said innocently, after initial greetings had been exchanged: 'And am I permitted to enquire as to how you have spent the past few weeks?'

Richard smiled nastily. 'You are permitted to enquire, Giles, but you will not be told. But it will doubtless cheer you to know that two days ago I lost most damnably at dice, and am at Belford in hopes of more rewarding pleasures.' His eyes travelled over Mrs Houlden, and she giggled.

Giles's gratification increased considerably. 'Two days losing at dice, Richard? You must be losing your touch.'

Richard turned back to Giles, and gave him the full benefit of his malicious green gaze. 'Perhaps I should have been more precise. I spent one day losing at dice, and the next receiving comfort from a close friend of mine, Kate Gilbert. *You* remember Kate Gilbert, don't you, Giles – after all, I think you knew her also.'

Giles glanced quickly back at Anna, still talking to Miss Conway, and decided to change the subject.

'George Murray wishes to speak to you, Richard – and perhaps you should meet Miss Conway.'

Richard glanced lazily across the room. 'The black-haired girl?'

'That's right.' Suddenly, Giles felt vaguely uneasy. Mrs Houlden looked more than sufficiently experienced to deal with any advances Richard might care to offer, but Mall Conway was so young . . . And, as Esmé Molyneux had once memorably pointed out, Richard could be perfectly charming when he chose. But perhaps not today – he was already more than a little drunk, decided Giles, and in a blatantly uncooperative frame of mind.

Disconcertingly, Richard appeared to have read his thoughts.

'Don't fret, Giles, schoolgirls never were to my taste. Besides –' his hand played with a lock of Mrs Houlden's fair hair – 'I prefer blondes.'

'Mr *Galliers*. My husband –'

'My dear, your husband is far too busy discussing the sins of the parish with Lady Whitfield and Mr Dean. He will not notice the sins taking place under his nose.' Offering her his arm, Richard led Ann Houlden across the room.

Her mind still preoccupied with the problem of Sir Nicholas Carleton, Mall inspected Lord Amyott's younger brother. It was his eyes that were unusual, she thought, as Giles Galliers made the introductions. They were slightly slanted and green – not the warm friendly green of the fields or a calm sea, but a cold olivine green. Hawk's eyes, cat's eyes, predatory –

'Mr Galliers. I don't believe we have met before.'

The dispassionate gaze widened a fraction. 'Oh, but we have, Miss Conway.' He raised her hand to his lips. 'I had occasion to visit your father, many years ago. You appeared halfway through the hour, covered in duckweed. I believe you had been learning to row.'

Richard, you bastard, thought Giles angrily. Losing a game of hazard offered no excuse for embarrassing this girl. Dammit, she had been looking uneasy enough as it was.

'I'm sorry, Mr Galliers.' Mall's voice was perfectly polite. 'I remember the rowing lesson very well, but you do not seem to have made such a lasting impression.'

Ouch, thought Giles, and failed to hide his smile.

Years of practice, thought Mall, thankfully taking another glass of wine. I have had years of practice, Mr Galliers, at the insult, subtle or otherwise. Lady Conway was always too easy a target – but you, Mr Galliers, with your long, mocking mouth, and your unpleasant eyes, look fit to be my equal. Mall lifted the glass to her lips. Two glasses of wine already, both to blur the headache that had gathered like a tight constricting band about her forehead, and to quell the panic that had gripped her since she had seen Carleton. If only he had not come. What if he should make some reference to that hot summer's day. How the obnoxious Mr Galliers would enjoy that – providing he could drag himself away from his claret and that stupid giggling Ann Houlden, how much more scope for ridicule that occasion would give him than a mere rowing lesson!

Alice was bearing relentlessly towards them, Sir Nicholas Carleton at her side. Unless she suddenly dropped dead or disappeared in a puff of smoke, there was nothing Mall could do to avoid the meeting. Finishing her drink rather rapidly, Mall clutched George Murray's arm for succour.

'Sir Nicholas, may I present my stepdaughter, Mall?'

A bow, a curtsey, and if Mall had not, as she rose from her curtsey, looked up to his face, her worst fears might have been allayed. The elegant bow and murmured pleasantry gave nothing away: it was the faint flicker of recognition in his dark eyes that betrayed him. He knew *exactly* who she was: and just for an instant those disturbing eyes looked at her precisely as they had done in the pool, seeing her as she was beneath the velvet, the jewels, the unaccustomed finery.

Had the manservant not arrived to usher the guests into the Great Chamber for the banquet, it would have been difficult to save herself from complete confusion. As it was, Mall took the arm held out to her, and allowed herself to be escorted by Sir Nicholas Carleton, out of the Great Hall.

The Great Chamber, swept and polished to a hitherto unprecedented degree, was one of Belford's more impressive rooms. Its proportions were vast, and succeeding generations of Conways had left on it the mark of their own wildly individual tastes. From the lozenge-patterned ceiling numerous multi-coloured beasts stared down from the confines of each diamond shape at the unfortunate diners below. The fireplace was immense, carved in wood, and frenziedly allegorical. The cold November light filtered sluggishly through the narrow windows on to the long oak table and sturdy chairs, all uniformly resplendent in their identical matching seat covers.

Alice sat at one end of the table, Leo at the other. Alice had managed to place Sir Nicholas Carleton to one side of her, Mall on his other side. This is my stepdaughter, Sir Nicholas. She not only bathes almost naked in pools on your land, she also has a rather large dowry. She neglects her household duties, and some people think she has a temper like the devil, but don't let that put you off.

What appetite Mall had, had long evaporated in tension and misery. Even the consort of musicians (two scratchy viols and a crumhorn, specially hired for the occasion) seemed out of tune. And she had drunk too much – three glasses of wine – and the noise of the chatter around her had become distorted, unnatural, forcing her to concentrate in order to make sensible conversation. George Murray was on her other side, thank God. Every so often his hand felt for hers under the table, but that seemed more of a reassurance than an imposition. Matthew Houlden was seated opposite Mall, then his wife, more sober in his presence, then the awful Mr Galliers. Conversation stumbled in jerks and pauses, punctuated by the necessary business of eating and drinking. Plates were soon full to overflowing; beef, ham, capon, overcooked mallard, a surfeit of rich and succulent food.

At Mall's side, Carleton spoke: 'My dear Galliers – it is some weeks since we have met. I thought perhaps you had been forced to leave the country again – or met some untimely accident.'

A pause, while Richard Galliers calmly refilled his empty wine glass. 'Fallen among thieves perhaps, Carleton? No, not dead or even departed, merely –' he glanced at Mrs Houlden '– discovering country pleasures.'

Ann Houlden, her eyes on her husband, stifled another giggle.

Alice, who, like Mall, had found it necessary to fortify herself with an unaccustomed quantity of wine, cried enthusiastically: "Perhaps your affections are also engaged, Mr Galliers? A double wedding would be so romantic!'

Savagely, Mall stabbed her knife into a stringy piece of pheasant. If Alice had nothing sensible to say, she had better keep quiet instead of providing that dislikeable man with ammunition for his tongue. But Richard Galliers merely made a polite negative, and Carleton took up the conversation again.

'Then what can it be, Galliers? Have you acquired some new interest in estate management – or farming – or –'

'– or hunting?' For the first time in the short exchange he looked up at Carleton. Galliers leaned back in his chair, elbow on the chair arm, knife in hand. 'Now, hunting is a fascinating sport, don't you think? The thrill of the chase, the hunted animal at bay, the finding of the quarry . . . do you like to hunt, Sir Nicholas?'

Another silence, and then Carleton speared a whole roast pigeon from a salver in the centre of the table. 'Sometimes, Galliers. I particularly like to hunt the fox.' He dismembered the pigeon with his shapely ringed hands, pulling wing from breast, splitting the fragile ribcage in two. 'The fox is, after all, but vermin, to be hunted to earth without quarter. The sight of a fox torn apart by a skilful pack of hounds can be a most edifying experience.'

Ann Houlden tittered nervously. Alice, conscious of her duties as hostess, said tentatively: 'Mr Murray – I heard that the highwayman – Reynardine – broke into your house.'

The goose leg Mall was eating became tasteless, sickening. She put it down, and her hands clenched under the carved apron of the table.

'That's right, Lady Conway. The rogue took off with a few of Anna's trifles – nothing of great value.' George grinned cheerfully. 'They were all found, though – in a copse on the edge of our land. In a fox-hole, would you believe!'

A small ripple of laughter disguised some of the musicians' bad notes. Alice put down her glass and addressed Sir Nicholas Carleton at her side.

'We have all been afraid the villain will strike here next, Sir Nicholas. Belford is well-guarded, of course, and the Court cupboards are safely locked, but we would all sleep easier if we knew Reynardine had been taken and hanged. You simply don't know what to do for the best. Mall has some lovely jewellery, don't you, my dear? Her mother left it, and it would be a great temptation for any thief.'

Mall gave up all pretence of eating. Why not, she thought angrily, do away with all this talk of jewellery and money, and simply auction her off to the highest bidder? That might be quicker and far less aggravating.

'Perhaps you should consider a few well placed fellows with muskets, Lady Conway,' Carleton said smoothly. 'The sight of a firearm can be remarkably discouraging to a would-be thief.'

Alice's brow creased, 'I have always been a little nervous of firearms, Sir Nicholas. One of my brothers was badly wounded by a pistol that misfired.'

Oh, you stupid, stupid woman –

'Every grown man at Belford knows how to use a pistol correctly. Not all country dwellers are incompetent dunces.'

And in one of the many small sour private quarrels between herself and Alice, Mall's outburst would have been unkind, but comparatively harmless. Here, witnessed by the flower of East Anglia's gentlefolk, all prinked and preened and with manners to match, it was completely indefensible. Too many pairs of unsympathetic sharp eyes looked first to Mall, and then, expectantly to her stepmother. Lady Conway's complexion deepened to a painful shade of red, and the pinkness returned to her eyes. As she took a quivering breath a man's voice said gently:

'A firearm can be a danger even in the most experienced hands. Lady Conway is quite right. I have seen a man who has used a flintlock for twenty years lose a hand due to a flint unexpectedly fracturing. And after all –' Richard Galliers' words were addressed to Alice, but his cold eyes had fixed themselves mercilessly on Mall. '– the attraction of the country-side is surely its peace, its tranquillity. Musket shots echoing throughout Cambridgeshire would hardly preserve that. Place a few men with rapiers around your boundaries, Lady Conway, and I'm sure you will not be troubled.'

Some of the colour died away from Alice's cheeks. If Mall had not seen the slight trembling of her stepmother's hand as she lifted her knife, she might have believed that Alice had forgotten the insult. And if there had been any way Mall could have decently left the table and fled to the cool, silent peace of the library, she would have done so without hesitation.

It was not until the guests were invited to rise and take the next gargantuan course of the banquet in the small withdrawing room to the side of the Great Chamber, that Mall was able to make her escape. Then she made her excuses to George Murray and ran to the tranquillity of the Gallery. Leaning her aching head on the cold glass of the windows, Mall looked out into the distance. It would snow tonight: heavy yellowish clouds were massing on the horizon, and the morning's frost still silvered the ground. *Therewith all sweetly did me kiss, and softly said, Dear heart, how like you this . . .?* We would all sleep easier if we knew Reynardine had been taken and hanged . . . Oh, if only this dreadful day were over!

But the nights had been no better recently. Long white nights, and this night would be worse: that awful remark she had made to an audience of forty would echo over and over again in her guilty ears . . .

'Miss Conway.'

She had not heard the footsteps behind her. Mall jumped and straightened. Richard Galliers – oh, this was the last straw.

But he had not come to tease her. He said simply:

'I believe your father possesses a telescope, Miss Conway. I should very much like to see it. Lady Conway said you might be willing to show it to me.'

It was more of a demand than a request, thought Mall, irritably. But she would not be childish. Not again.

The more manageable and reasonably sized of Sir Thomas's treasures were kept in a small damp room next to the library. Before Alice's arrival, they had been scattered haphazardly over the entire house. But Alice had, not unreasonably, taken exception to sharing her bedroom with the dried head of a gibbon and had, with consummate tact, removed all the less pleasant objects to one of the more obscure corners of the house. The small chamber, Mall pointed out shortly in reply to Mr Galliers's question, was next to Sir Thomas's library.

The box containing the precious telescope nestled between a rather dirty alembic and two phials containing something that looked like dried blood, evidence of Sir Thomas's brief but passionate flirtation with alchemy. Gently, Mall lifted the box from the dust covered shelf and unwound the piece of velvet covering the device. Sir Thomas had made a special journey to France to purchase the instrument, and together he and Mall had looked at the stars one magical frosty December night. Mall felt unexpected tears prick behind her eyes at the memory. If only her father would come home . . .

Mr Galliers' fascination with the telescope was undisguised. The heavy-lidded eyes were alert now, squinting through the instrument out into the frosty kitchen garden. The long hands, quick and precise away from Ann Houlden and the claret, adjusted the telescope skilfully. Mall waited impatiently for him to replace it in its box. This room was too tiny, she felt too close to him. The slashed and silk inset sleeve of his doublet brushed Mall's shoulder as he lifted the box back on to the shelf.

Without facing her, he said smoothly: 'Marvellous though the telescope is, I must confess to some deception. The real purpose of this interview is that you and I should have a little talk.'

Mall reached for the doorknob. She said, coldly, 'I don't think you and I have much to talk about, Mr Galliers.'

Without warning, his hand grabbed her wrist, halting her flight. 'Ah, but we do, my dear. I have some advice to give you.'

Mall looked down, disbelieving, at the hand that imprisoned her wrist. Three rings, she noted absently. The stone in the small delicate ring was a chrysoberyl. Her father had shown her a chrysoberyl once, long ago when she was a child. You could recognize the gem by the twist of light that lay frozen in the green-gold stone. Cat's eyes, she thought. How appropriate. She took a deep breath.

'I don't think I want your advice.'

'But I'm afraid you're going to get it anyway, Miss Conway.' Galliers released her wrist and, leaning against the door in such a way that any attempt to leave on Mall's part would be made embarrassingly awkward, he continued:

'You would do much better, Miss Conway, to accept the fact of your father's second marriage, and cease kicking against the traces. Sir Thomas and Lady Conway are man and wife; you cannot change that, you can only make them unhappy. Your stepmother is not stupid, and you are making a serious error in treating her as such. She is a little ignorant perhaps – but, after all, she did not have your manifold advantages. She is a kind hearted, well meaning woman – you could have done much worse.'

The headache was becoming intolerable – and she would not cry in front of this dreadful man. 'And what, sir,' said Mall tightly, 'gives you the right to comment on my behaviour? How can someone with a reputation as black as yours have the arrogance –'

'Dear me, so tales of my misdeeds have penetrated even this outpost of the kingdom.' There was no offence in his voice, only mild amusement. 'It is precisely my foul and muddied past that gives me the right to offer advice. Keep to society's laws, Miss Conway, avoid eccentricity or nonconformity, and your life will be considerably easier. Remember, I speak from experience.'

'And having delivered your lecture,' Mall was surprised to

find that she was trembling, 'perhaps you would allow me to leave? That is, if you have finished meddling in affairs which are no concern of yours.'

Galliers looked down at her, the amusement gone from his face. 'No concern of mine at all, Miss Conway. Only a purely intellectual regret that someone like you might find herself married to the first to offer – be he old or infirm, or simply in need of your fortune – just because your stepmother cannot bear to live with you for another day.'

Mall's furious inability to think of a suitably crushing reply was interrupted by a sharp knock at the door. Unhurried, Richard Galliers opened it. Sir Nicholas Carleton stood outside, and it occurred to Mall that the two men were not dissimilar. Carleton was heavier, taller and older, and had a stillness Galliers lacked. But both, she suspected, were possessed of considerable resources of intelligence and culture. And underneath the thin, perfectly polished veneer, that acted as a palliative to convention, lay something ruthless, almost frightening. Mall suppressed a shiver not entirely due to the coldness of the room.

Blandly, the bearded man spoke.

'If you have finished inspecting Conway's – treasures – my dear Galliers, the madrigals are sorely in need of another tenor.'

Offering Mall his arm, he escorted her back to the Gallery.

CHAPTER SIX

She said, kind sir, be civil,
My company forsake
For in mine own opinion
I fear you are some rake.

(REYNARDINE)

*T*HE last of the Conways' exhausted, dyspeptic, inebriated guests had ridden through Belford's gates, leaving the servants to clear up the debris, and the family to heave a collective and weary sigh of relief. Leo Conway raided his brother's library for the appropriate text to research his contretemps with Doctor Lucey before retiring thankfully to his chamber. Alice escaped to her favourite corner of the damp, faded garden, standing in the dark and luxuriously breathing in the cold air still perfumed with a lingering scent of chamomile and rosemary. In the end, she thought, it had not gone too badly. She had not let Thomas down, despite her lack of birth and education. Tranquil for the first time that day, Alice stood for a few minutes, enjoying the solitude, and then went to kiss her fragile son goodnight.

It was going to be a cold night. The snow had begun to fall: small, delicate flakes that blurred the sparse woods and fields around Belford house, dissolving as they touched the ground. The clouds hid the moon, and only a faint dim candlelight glowed dully behind a few of Belford's many windows.

In the stables a solitary candle shone, stuck in a jar at a safe distance from the heaps of dry straw. The horses in their stalls stood quietly, undisturbed by the efforts of Martin Bartlett, his fingers fumbling inexpertly with the ties of Martha's bodice, the tedium of the morning forgotten. Martha was happy enough to assist when necessary, not pausing in her lengthy ramblings about the afternoon's entertainment.

'. . . and that Mr Murray. He'll want to wed Miss Mall, I'm sure . . . and he's a handsome gentleman, though a bit of a lad, I've heard . . .' clogs were kicked off, and Martha's best blue gown tumbled to the stable floor. 'I saw them holding hands. He couldn't keep his eyes off her . . . hold me a bit closer, dear, it's ever so cold in here –' the first of many layers of petticoats went the way of the gown. 'That Mr Galliers – you know, the younger one, not his lordship . . . don't do that, Martin, you naughty boy . . . Sarah says she saw him kissing Mistress Houlden. She's a hussy, though,' continued Martha virtuously, breaking off to kiss Martin's demanding lips, 'she's a bad one, and no better than she should be. I know, my sister's her maid, and Jane says – oh, do that again, Martin, that was nice – Jane says she's had three lovers already and they've only been married six months! Mind you – I'll give you a hand with that, Martin, don't fret – mind you, I can't blame her fancying our Mr Galliers. If I were her, I –' she broke off suddenly, resisting Martin's efforts to pull her down into the straw.

'Someone's out there, Martin – in the kitchen garden –' She shook away the boy's hand.

'So?' Martin kissed the soft flesh at the back of her neck. 'Nobody's going to bother us.'

'*No*, Martin. I mean it wasn't nobody from Belford.'

'Nonsense, sweeting. It was probably Ned Carter back drunk from the alehouse. Come on, we've better things to do than stand round talking like a clutch of old wives.'

Martha broke away from him and went to the stable door. 'It was a thief, Martin, I'm sure it was. It could be that Reynardine! You know her ladyship was worried he might come here next. We could all be murdered in our beds if you don't do nothing about it.'

With chagrin, Martin noticed her use of the pronoun 'you'. Unwillingly, he moved beside her and gazed out into the darkness. There was no movement, no sound. But, as he watched, a candle guttered fitfully in the library window. Martha saw it at the same time.

'See, Martin – I told you.'

Squeezing her plump waist, Martin made a last ditch attempt to save himself. 'I expect it's one of the family – Mr Leo, probably. Anyway, it's no business of ours.'

Pushing him away, adjusting what remained of her dishevelled clothing, Martha said with some asperity:

'You know they've all gone to sleep, Martin Bartlett! The house was quiet when I left it. Just you go and find out what's going on. Sam Hollis would go – are you afraid?'

His masculine pride appealed to, Martin had no alternative. In an anguish of hardly bearable frustration, he bad-temperedly relaced his shirt and jerkin, tucked his knife into his belt, and ran towards the house.

But Martha was wrong in one thing. Not all the family were asleep. Mall was wide awake, her jewels removed, a silk shawl round the low neck of the red velvet gown, the window open to let the cold, snow-laden air bathe her hot and aching forehead.

The entire day had been a disaster, from the morning in the kitchen when she had forgotten her promise to help Alice with the set piece, to the moment the last guest had left and she had been able to drop the false smile from her face and flee to the refuge of her bedchamber. It really could hardly have been worse; she had been thoroughly unpleasant to Alice, twice, and there were two men amongst that company she never, ever, wanted to see again. Whether her future husband had attended the banquet she could not be sure; George Murray had seemed to like her, and most of the other gentlemen had been courteous and complimentary. With one notable exception, but Mall had no wish to see desire for herself in those cold green eyes.

The headache was getting worse. Perhaps she was sickening

for something – she, who was never ill. If only she had been on better terms with Alice she might have had some valerian, or feverfew, and then she could have slept. Mall leaned out of the window, finding some relief in the icy touch of the snow upon her skin.

And then, Mall saw, as Martha had, the single, betraying candlelight.

So there was someone in the library. From her chamber, its position in the jutting wing of the house almost the mirror image of the library opposite, Mall watched. The candle was still, as if someone was sitting at the desk. Leo, perhaps, searching for another book? But Leo had been halfway asleep when Mall had gone to bid him goodnight, worn out by the rigours of the banquet. And not Alice – Alice hardly ever went into the library. Neither did the servants, except by Sir Thomas's particular request. Her father, unexpectedly returned from London with some new enthusiasm that would not wait until morning?

Sliding her feet into slippers, Mall closed the window and drew the curtains. She took the candlestick from the table and left the room. It was a considerable distance to the library, and Mall, clutching her shawl about her, was glad of the candle's reassuring light. She could, of course, wake Joshua's Joe, but the prospect of adventure, however small, was attractive, a distraction from the day's megrims. Belford was very quiet: the only noises the sounds of the minute creaking of the furniture, and the susurrant rustle of Mall's velvet skirts as she walked.

Her courage did not falter until she reached the library door. Here, she realized, she was too far from the rest of the household to be heard if she did cry for help. It *must* be her father – he was, after all, due to return any day. And what sensible thief, she asked herself sternly, would rifle the library when the court cupboards in the Hall were crammed with silver, and, as Alice had mentioned, the casket in Mall's own chamber was full of jewels?

Mall took hold of the doorknob with a slightly nerveless hand, and gently pushed open the door. Despite the candle in her hand and the other one in the room, it was still dark, too dark clearly to distinguish the figure by the cabinet. One of the cabinet's secret drawers was open, and the candlelight reflected palely on the papers within it. But as her eyes adjusted to the light, Mall realized, too late, that it was not her father's well loved face that looked at her, but a stranger – no, almost a stranger. He was masked this time, but he was unmistakable in the black cloak and hood of the Gog Magog Hills. One of his bare hands rested lightly on the hilt of his sword, the other held the pistol that pointed, unwaveringly, at Mall.

'Oh my God,' said Mall faintly, as the doorknob slid from her shaking hand. '*You.*'

Under the mask, inside the hood, Reynardine gave a small, rueful grimace. 'Yes, me. We seem destined to encounter each other under circumstances of extreme mutual embarrassment, Miss Conway. It appears I was not as quiet as I had intended.'

That same lilting accent – but somehow, through the almost irresistible desire to run and shout for help, something naggingly familiar about his voice.

'I saw your candle.' Mall tried to keep calm. 'My chamber is opposite the library.'

'I see – careless of me.' She could sense the anger in his voice as he moved towards her. The gaping mouth of the pistol still pointed at her, but Mall stood her ground, her mouth dry with fear. Shorn of Robert Fox's thin disguise, with no hint of flirtatiousness to lessen the tension, he had become dangerous, threatening.

At her side, he said softly: 'Are you deciding whether or not to scream, sweetheart? I would advise against it. I do not believe anyone would hear you, so the effort would be quite wasted.' Under the mask, his eyes glinted in the candlelight. 'If you would be so good as to sit in this chair, my dear –' he held out his hand to her '– I will then temporarily imprison you and speedily take my leave.'

Mall did not reply. She was staring, like a hare cornered by hunting dogs, at the hand Reynardine held out to her. Both well shaped and strong, it lightly held her fingertips to guide her to her father's chair. And on the fifth finger it bore one small, insignificant piece of jewellery.

A chrysoberyl ring.

And at the same moment as Richard Galliers noted and correctly interpreted Mall's horrified gasp of comprehension, Martin Bartlett, fortified by the sinewy shape of Joshua's Joe, flung open the door.

'God's teeth, the cavalry' muttered Galliers, and in one neat movement dragged Mall in front of him, clamping his left hand hard over her protesting mouth, while his right hand held the pistol to her cheek.

'I regret, sweetheart' he whispered in Mall's ear, 'that you and I will have to take a little walk.'

Then, louder, in Reynardine's voice:

'Put your weapons down, gentlemen –' A pause, and then Martin's knife and Joe's sword clattered to the floor '– and I will not harm a hair of her pretty head. I merely –' he pushed Mall towards the door '– wish to guarantee my safe exit from this charming house.'

But it was all too much for Martin. It had been a long, frustrating day. The combination of the hours of tedium in the kitchen and the evening's debacle with Martha, had reduced his normally even temper to tinder dryness. Mall Conway may not have possessed half of Martha's allure, but they had known each other since they were infants, and in spite of their dissimilarities in birth, Mall had been a friend to him. With a howl of rage and anguish, he hurled himself at Reynardine with some ill-planned intention to wrest the pistol from his grip. But he was not fast enough. In the space of a few seconds, which seemed to Mall to take on the horrible frozen immobility of a nightmare, Galliers swore, kicked Martin aside, and the pistol fired, resulting in nothing but fallen plaster and masonry, but waking the entire household. And as Richard Galliers, never releasing his grip over Mall's mouth, rapidly replaced the spent pistol with the main gauche dagger, and Martin Bartlett groaned on the floor, the family and servants rushed to witness the closing scenes of the drama.

The next few minutes were hopelessly confused for Mall. She was aware of faces – Leo's dazed, Alice's shocked, others angry, a few secretly enjoying the excitement. Then they were out of the door. Galliers had taken his hand from her mouth, and was pulling her across the darkened grass in a way that made her arm feel as though it was coming out of its socket. Then she was shoved unceremoniously through a small side gate, and beyond the gate stood Galliers' black mare, cropping grass, blithely unaware of the imminent chaos that threatened to overtake her owner.

'Mount. Quickly,' said Galliers, curtly, holding the horse's reins.

Mall stared at him, her eyes round with disbelief. 'You can't mean –'

'I can – and I do.' He cupped his hands for her to step in. 'And if you don't hurry, I'll throw you over the saddle like a sack of corn.'

Somehow, she scrambled on to the brim of the saddle. Mall felt her captor climb up behind her and spur the horse. The cold, snow-dusted air was filled with the sounds of their pursuers battering against the stout garden gate that Galliers had thoughtfully locked, as the black mare, burdened by her double load, picked her way carefully through the trees and out into open country. Jammed ludicrously and uncomfortably on the saddlebow between Galliers and the horse's mane, her arms pinioned to her sides, it seemed to Mall that perhaps she would have done better to have stayed timidly in her room that night. She shifted awkwardly to try and make her position more comfortable, and Galliers' voice hissed in her ear. 'Don't move a bloody inch, sweetheart. Don't assume I would hesitate to use this knife.'

Stronger than discomfort, stronger even than fear, was the white hot, barely containable anger. So it had been Richard Galliers all along. Richard Galliers who had rescued her, muddied, hurt and horseless from the wood on the Gogs, Richard Galliers who had wiped the blood from her forehead with his beautiful lace handkerchief, and finally, intolerably,

Richard Galliers who had kissed her. Oh God, it was unbearable, quite, quite, unbearable.

And now Richard Galliers, his chin jammed over her head, his hurried heartbeats echoing through the material of her gown, with whom she was, unbelievably, fleeing all her home comforts and annoyances, to be taken God knows where.

They were being pursued. Horses' hooves thundered behind them, and Mall heard a voice call, 'There they are now, Joe! Get him now, while you can see the bastard's back!'

There was the crack of a pistol shot. Mall heard Galliers swear unrepeatably, and felt him dig his heels hard into the horse's flanks. Another shot – and abruptly he lurched forward in the saddle, forcing Mall sharply against the horse's neck. The mare slewed, then Galliers straightened and pulled at the reins to guide them through a copse.

She was fast, this mare of his, and it was plain he knew the countryside as well as Mall did. He would, of course, thought Mall angrily, shutting her eyes and holding her breath as they jumped over what looked like an impossibly high hedge. After all, he had lived not far from here for most of his life . . . The snow was thickening. She dared not twist round to look behind her, but she could no longer hear anything but the sound of Galliers' mare's hooves, pounding the frost-hardened earth.

No villages, only the occasional glimpse of a solitary cottage or farmhouse. Strange bridleways and footpaths; hedgerows, ditches, spinneys, looming up suddenly out of the darkness and then disappearing again, shadowed and confusing. They had lost Belford's servants long ago in that mad dash through field and copse. The falling snow would soon obliterate any prints for trackers: and Mall herself no longer recognized the surrounding countryside. Her sense of direction had gone, lost in the whirling snow. Even her anger had left her. There was only the unceasing motion of the horse, and a mind no longer able to think with any clarity.

Galliers rode expertly, efficiently, the hands that gripped

the reins never faltering. But he spoke no more, and Mall, crushed against him, became aware that he was holding his body stiffly. Without warning, he reined the horse in, and Mall struggled to reorientate herself in the dancing snow, the unfamiliar blackness.

Twisting in the saddle, Mall saw that Galliers was reloading the spent pistol. He had removed his highwayman's mask, but his face was still darkly shadowed by the deep hood. He poured some powder from the horn into the barrel.

'I'm afraid you are going to have to get off and walk now, Miss Conway. My mare is exhausted, and this country is too difficult for her.'

Too difficult? Stupidly, Mall looked around her. Instead of grass to the side of the track, there were reeds; instead of the familiar pattern of field and wood, there was water, black and gently rippling, ice-fringed at its edges . . .

'Yes, you are in the Fens, my dear. Now, I would play the gentleman and help you down from the saddle, but with your faithful servant's bullet in my shoulder, I'm afraid my capacity for chivalry is limited.'

She stared at him, uncomprehending. 'You were shot?'

'Perhaps you thought they were setting off a celebratory feu-de-joie? Yes, your steward is a fine marksman.' Completing his task with the pistol, Galliers looked up at Mall. 'But do hurry up and dismount, sweetheart. I'm all for polite conversation in its place, but if we don't reach my sanctuary soon, I will probably faint for loss of blood. And then you, my dear, will perish of cold.'

He had dismounted, nimbly for a man with a bullet in his back, before he had finished speaking. Clumsy with cold, Mall scrambled off and stood beside him.

Galliers was looking around him, eyes narrowed, searching the gloom as if to find his bearings. He glanced at Mall, small and shivering beside him, and he laughed.

'Dear me, you are not dressed for adventure! What's this – scarlet velvet and silver lace – with a highly unsuitable neckline, my dear – no cloak, no boots, no gloves?'

Mall said stiffly, 'A gentleman might lend a lady his cloak.'

A low chuckle in the darkness. 'But I, as you have surely realized, am no gentleman.' He unclasped the cloak awkwardly and, unwillingly, she pulled it over her shoulders. 'And I'm not altogether sure, sweetheart, that you are a lady.'

Glad of the sheltering night, Mall felt the blood rise to her cheeks. He was, no doubt, referring to that unfortunate September evening on the Gogs.

'Not much further now.' Galliers led the mare by the reins as they stumbled along the narrow path. He began to sing, low and flippant under his breath.

> *'Come live with me and be my love*
> *– and we will all the pleasures prove –'*

How much longer? All sensation had gone from Mall's hands and feet, all thoughts from her mind except a dreadful desire for warmth. Surely Richard Galliers must be almost as exhausted as she: and if Joshua Joe's bullet had caught his shoulder, more so. As they penetrated deeper into the dark silent Fen, lights flickered in the distance, dancing spectrally on the murky waters. Corpse candles – and Mall shivered uncontrollably. The cold was intolerable, paralysing; Mall's only source of warmth the man's close but despised body beside her.

'Ah, home,' he said suddenly, and stopped, letting the reins of the horse dangle from his hands.

Mall looked around her for signs of habitation, but could see nothing, only an empty expanse of black water, a few scrubby trees, and the inevitable endless gently moving reeds.

Galliers clapped the mare hard on its flanks, so that it skittered away into the snow. His voice floated over to her.

'How useful that you can row.'

Vague memories of an earlier irritation, a lifetime ago, stirred in Mall's cold-dulled brain. She stared at him blankly.

He was at the edge of the water now. 'Miss Conway – I need you to row.'

Perhaps delirium had set in – perhaps he was insane. Yes, insanity would explain a great deal.

He walked to her side, put one hand on her shoulder, and shook her gently. 'Mall. Are you listening?'

Jerked out of her numbness and confusion, she looked up at him.

'The hut is on an island. Unfortunately we cannot walk on water, therefore, unless we are to roam eternally about this God-forsaken country like a pair of latterday wandering Jews, then you must row. I,' he added with simplicity, 'am wounded.'

Under a clump of willows, bobbing slightly in the icy water, was a small skiff. Slowly, painfully, shuddering with fear, cold and exhaustion, Mall made her way to the boat. Galliers held it still for her while she stepped in and felt for the oars in the inch of icy water that covered the bottom of the craft. Somehow she managed to push the skiff from the bank out into the blackness of the lake.

'Over there, see? There's an island.'

She looked to where he pointed, and at first saw nothing: only the snow, the water, the darkness. Then, gradually, a shape emerged out of the gloom: a small wooded island, no more than twenty yards across.

Pulling at the oars, clenching her teeth, Mall reminded herself that Marco Polo and Vasco da Gama had endured worse than this, and that back at Belford, she had foolishly wanted adventure. How she ever managed to complete that nightmarish journey she was never afterwards sure. Although the childish escapades to which Galliers had untactfully referred had turned Mall into a competent oarswoman, she had reached that trough of physical and mental distress where she would have been thankful to slide beneath the icy waters of the Fen and never be seen again. Had Richard Galliers not been sitting opposite her, always watching her, she would have lain in the boat and slept, and never woken. But something in that challenging, cynical face made her grip her frozen hands to the oars, and force the boat to the island.

Galliers was out first, wading to the bank to loop the skiff's rope around the overhanging branch of a willow. Reluctantly, Mall took the hand he held out to her, and almost fell out of the boat. She felt no other emotion than mild surprise when her knees buckled under her, and she sank to her thighs in the cold, black water.

'No, my dear, no use hiding from me there.' He hauled her out to the bank. 'You've a fire to light and a meal to cook before you can sit down.'

Easy tears of humiliation and exhaustion gathered in Mall's eyes. He was laughing at her again: he actually seemed to derive some perverse enjoyment from this ordeal. She shook herself free of his hand, and made her unwilling legs bear her up the slight incline towards the hut.

It was only an old turf-cutter's hut – tiny, one-roomed, and primitive. The walls were of turf blocks, two feet thick, plastered with mud outside. Inside were two small horn-paned windows, a pile of peat turfs, a chest and a small trestle bed. And miraculously, gloriously, in the centre of the hut there glowed a fire.

Mall went immediately to the fire, crouching over the smouldering peat, warming her white, numbed hands over its glowing heart. Gradually, feeling began to return to her limbs, and she was able to pay some attention to her surroundings. One bed, with several rather grey sheepskins on it. Well, she would have that bed – to herself. With Richard Galliers' cloak still around her shoulders, Mall moved over to the bed and sat on it, pulling sheepskins over herself for warmth. *He* could make what shift he chose on the floor – she had not asked to be taken to this dreadful place.

Mall's eyelids were becoming heavy: exhausted by cold and fright, sleep was not far away. She watched dreamily as Galliers knelt, feeding the fire's glowing warmth with small pieces of turf, nursing the flames to catch and grow. Irrelevant, disjointed thoughts flickered briefly through her overtired mind – the banquet – Sir Nicholas Carleton – 'should I bed them before I wed, stepmother, is that the way to do it?'

And then, as he turned his back to her, she was jolted abruptly from the brink of unconsciousness. Through the quilting of the faded black doublet spread a large stain,

136

somewhat resembling the map of the Americas Mall had seen in her father's library, its source the torn, ragged area of Galliers' shoulder, its end in the region of his waist. 'Oh my God,' said Mall, involuntarily, and when he turned she saw how white his face was, the eyes glittering and darkly shadowed.

Joshua's Joe's bullet had not *winged* his shoulder; that was no surface wound to be patched with a handkerchief or the frill of a shirt. That wound was deep, painful and life-threatening – and yet he had ridden with it, sung through it, teased her in spite of it.

'It's only a little blood, my dear. At least you have not fainted.'

Mall said with some dignity, 'I do *not* faint. I was going to offer to bandage it for you.'

He smiled wolfishly. 'Very civil of you, sweetheart, but I can manage perfectly well myself.'

'Oh, don't be ridiculous!' It was becoming very warm in the hut; Mall unclasped the cloak. 'Your shoulder is badly hurt, Mr Galliers. I could make a much better job of bandaging that than you.'

'Dear me, such concern.' He began to unlace the front of his doublet.

'Not at all, Mr Galliers. I simply have no wish to wake with a corpse for company tomorrow morning. And you are the only one of us to know his way out of this wretched place.'

'I assure you, Miss Conway, I have every intention of surviving until morning.' He grimaced as he began to pull off the sleeves of the doublet. 'I have managed without a wetnurse for a good few years now, my dear.' The cold, sardonic eyes looked up at her again. 'I am not averse to ladies watching me remove my clothes, but I doubt if your stepmother would approve.'

Blushing furiously, Mall turned away from him and lay on the trestle bed with her face to the wall. Sleep, postponed so many times that endless night, began to overtake her again. The last coherent, faintly wry thought that crossed her mind before she sank thankfully into oblivion was that at least, if nothing else, her headache had gone.

At first she could not remember where she was. Then, as she saw the daylight sluggishly showing through the tiny windows, the peat fire, and the man lying sleeping beside the fire, she remembered only too well. The preposterous events of the previous evening came back to Mall in their complete, appalling, colourful detail, and she was suddenly very wide awake.

Slowly, she sat up. Every bone, every muscle in her body ached as she moved. She looked down at herself. Much of the skirt of her beautiful scarlet gown was caked with black mud; the silver lace hung in dirty shreds; her feet and ankles were bare and filthy. She must go home. She had sickened of adventure: it was far too uncomfortable and frightening.

Last night it had been too dark to tell where she was. Today, in daylight, she might be able to see some village or hamlet she could walk to. She glanced across at the inert body by the fire. Richard Galliers had reclaimed his cloak; he lay curled under it, his face to the fire. Quietly, Mall stood up and walked over to the door.

Pushing it open, she peeped outside. There was nothing. Nothing but water, reeds, the occasional isthmus and spare, featureless island. No house or village between herself and the low, bleak, horizon. And to make matters worse not only was there no sign of habitation, but the snow had thickened overnight and settled. 'Pox on it,' said Mall, inelegantly, and shut the door.

And Richard Galliers? Standing by the closed door, Mall watched him as he slept like the dead, only the gentle rise and fall of his chest indicating that he was indeed, still living. He had dressed his wound; the remains of his shirt lay beside him, presumably used for a bandage. It shamed her now, in the cold white morning light, to remember that she had offered to help dress that damaged shoulder. How foolish – for, as the two

138

separate identities, Reynardine and Richard Galliers, merged indistinguishably into one, her ignorance of either man was forcibly brought home to her. If he were to die from loss of blood or from a fever caused by the injury, that might well be to her benefit. For she was a danger to him: that was why he had taken her away from Belford. Richard Galliers dead, even though it left her isolated in this cold and inhospitable country, was surely less of a threat to her than Richard Galliers alive. Because he had, of course, a simple way of ensuring that his secret remained safe. A body drowned in this distant and unpeopled Fen would lie undiscovered until it was unrecognizable. And the dark-haired man sleeping so soundly before her could simply return to life as Richard Galliers, debauched and irresponsible younger son of a declining noble family, of no possible connection with the bold highwayman Reynardine.

Mall shivered, despite the sticky warmth of the hut. But there was a way of guaranteeing her safety – one way. Richard Galliers had a pistol, and Mall knew how to use a pistol. Martin Bartlett had taught her. If she could get hold of it . . .

She looked round the hut, trying to discover where he had put it. It was not in the chest; that only contained a bottle and a little food. Softly, Mall crept over to the unmoving figure by the fire. Galliers still appeared totally unconscious, the mocking eyes lidded, the vivid face relaxed in sleep. Having lost blood, he ought to be difficult to rouse. Mall could now see the flintlock: it lay at his side, half covered by the cloak, the hand with the betraying chrysoberyl ring lying loosely over its inlaid butt. With infinite delicacy, Mall stooped, lifted a corner of the mud-stained cloak and moved it aside. Her fingers touched the barrel, her hand gently brushed his. Now she could slide it away –'

Too quick for any escape, the hand snaked out and grabbed her wrist.

'Darling Mall, were you lonely?'

She was jerked forward with surprising force, until her face almost touched his. His lips parted in a feral smile and then, as suddenly, the smile disappeared, and Mall tried to shrink back.

He said softly: 'If you ever try that again, my dear, I shall tie you up. Imagine, all day, tied to the bedpost, dependent on my caprice for everything. How would you like that?'

Mall's stomach contracted sickeningly, and her heart thudded in her chest. 'Not at all. I will not go near you again.' Her voice sounded annoyingly feeble. She tried to regain some of her composure. 'Now let me go.'

Slowly, he released her hand. With legs that would not quite obey her, she moved back to the trestle bed, watching in silence as Galliers rose and began to rebuild the flagging fire.

She did not offer to help.

Around midday, Galliers knew that Mall was awake. She had not moved, had remained a sulky and offended bundle of dirty scarlet velvet, her back to him, her face to the wall; but he knew that she was awake by the changed pattern of her breathing, and the small deliberate movements that replaced the abandoned attitude of sleep. He had been harsh with her in the morning. She had not spoken to him since then, but had first sat on the trestle bed, glaring at the ceiling in black-browed disapproval, and then, eventually, had given in to weariness and boredom and fallen asleep. He did not care whether she slept or woke providing she did not harass him; he had almost ceased to care about the farce of the previous night's events. Indeed, it was becoming difficult to think of anything other than the increasing pain in his shoulder. He had not dared look at what lay beneath the bandage he had applied last night, but it did not feel right; the throbbing, sickening waves of pain were ominous.

The only medicine available was the bottle of aqua vitae taken from Hosea's chest. Galliers had unstoppered the bottle half way through the morning, and at first the fiery liquid had offered some relief. But now – he rubbed at the rough stubble on his jaw, and his hand came away damp with perspiration. A bloody awful mess, he thought, and that small, sullen passenger on the trestle bed could only make things ten times worse.

'If you can bear to look at me again,' he said indifferently, 'I think perhaps you should eat. There's food here.'

Onehandedly, he pushed up the lid of the bog-oak chest. He did not particularly care whether she spoke to him or not: conversation with a resentful, prattling schoolgirl was something he did not need. But she should eat – he had not quite sunk to starving little girls. Thank God there was food in the chest – sensible, organized Hosea.

The chest contained a dusty loaf of black bread, half a cheese, and some dried fish. 'Eel, I think,' he said casually, noticing that Mall had shuffled off the bed and sat resolutely opposite him, across at the other side of the fire.

The eel did not look particularly edible. 'Perhaps,' said Mall, coldly, 'we should boil it or something.'

There. At least she had spoken. So a hunger strike was unlikely to be imminent. The thought of food, he found, turned his stomach: it was only drink he needed, Hosea's half-bottle of aqua vitae and its attendant offer of insensibility, if not oblivion. He shrugged. 'Boil it, roast it, marinade it in a ginger sauce if you so wish – my thirst is greater than my hunger.' He swallowed a mouthful, put the bottle aside, and took his dice from his pocket.

Mall took his knife and hacked herself a piece of black bread. Yesterday she could have had her pick of any delicacy she chose, and yet she had not enjoyed a single mouthful. Today, improbably, she was ravenous.

The bread was not as bad as it looked, the cheese was unexpectedly pleasant. She sat for a while and ate in silence, her eyes fixed firmly on the fire. But soon curiosity overcame her, and she glanced furtively across at her captor. He looked dreadful; it was hard to believe him the same person as the glittering, hard-edged stranger of Alice's banquet. The jewelled doublet and single earring had gone, replaced by clothes that had been old and faded to begin with and now, after the snow and the bullet, were more fit for the common criminal he had pretended to be. His hair curled damp and tangled to his forehead, and the dark shadows under his eyes had deepened,

141

marking like thumb-prints a skin that was flushed and sheened with perspiration. He lounged against the wall of the hut, the bottle at his left side, the dice nestled in his restless right hand. He neither spoke to, nor looked at Mall: his eyes glanced repeatedly at the door, edgy, agitated, as if waiting for something that failed to happen. He ate nothing.

The silence was unsettling. Mall, used to Alice's chatter or her father's somewhat more focused conversation, found sitting mutely with another human being – even this frightening wreck of a man – thoroughly unnatural. And he was drinking far too much. She eyed the rapidly falling level of the bottle with some misgivings. The prospect of spending the remainder of this hitherto extremely unpleasant day incarcerated in a tiny hut with a drunkard was not appealing. Haughty with disapproval, Mall asked:

'Do you intend to spend the entire afternoon drinking, Mr Galliers?'

Putting down the bottle, he directed his uninterested gaze approximately in her direction.

'Well, and how else should I spend the afternoon, Miss Conway? What distraction could we enjoy together to pass the time? A few airs on the lute, perhaps, or a round of one-and-twenty? Or hazard – do you play hazard, Miss Conway? No? A pity. I would teach you, but –' the dice slid from his fingers to the rush-strewn floor '– perhaps another time.' His eyes, brilliant in the dim light of the hut, wandered back to the door.

He thought of Kate Gilbert, whose warm bed he had left the previous morning, whose neat fair locks he had loosened from their net so that they drifted one by one over her naked shoulders. And then, unaccountably, his mind drifted to the Countess of Somerset, that shining, self-possessed, pale-eyed beauty, her hand touching and discarding his as they wove through the lines of galliard and volta, in and out, circling round and round, until he felt dizzy. He sang softly under his breath, '*Let my whispering voice obtain, Sweet reward for sharpest pain . . .*' and the room blurred briefly and darkened a little.

The girl's sharp words brought him back: he blinked, and re-focused on her small, angry face.

'You seem to be singularly ill-equipped for bad weather in this hideaway of yours, Mr Galliers. However, there are a few minor matters we should discuss. Such as –' and he saw her attempt to catch his unsober stare '– how long do you intend to keep me here? When can I go home?' And she was unable to keep the treacherous tremor from her voice on the word 'home'.

His gaze travelled from Mall to the door, and back to Mall again, but he did not notice the sudden brightness of her eyes, the distress in her voice. He merely said, apparently amused, waving the bottle of aqua vitae in the air in a misjudged attempt at a salute, 'Go home? My dear, you have only just arrived! There are infinitely more interesting topics of conversation, if it is conversation you desire.'

It was too hot in the hut. The ruins of his shirt lay on the floor beside him; one-handedly he loosened the laces of his doublet. 'You could, for instance, tell me about your father's little hobbies. What does he do in that amazing room of his? And why does he spend so much of the year in London? Your stepmother's charms should be enough to keep any man happily at home. Or –' and he fleetingly recalled that there was something important he had to say to Mall Conway '– we could consider your marital prospects. Does Lady Conway really intend to marry you to one of that collection of numbskulls and senile old men?'

Mall bristled angrily. 'I assume you do not include yourself in that description, Mr Galliers.'

A mistake, that one. Richard Galliers smiled, briefly and nastily. 'No, my dear, I did not come to Belford in search of a *wife*. I leave connubial bliss to Giles and others like him.' He paused for another drink. 'I was there for entirely other reasons. To study the layout of your house – for my nefarious night-visiting, you understand.'

'But *why*?' Mall's voice rose impatiently. 'It was you all along, wasn't it? You robbed that messenger in August – and Lady Woodroffe –'

'And the Murrays. After we met. Remember?'

'So why the play-acting? Why call yourself Robert Fox? Why not merely introduce yourself as Richard Galliers and direct me to my home? Or,' she looked hard at him, dark and slovenly by the fire, 'I suppose it must have been amusing – especially at the banquet. You must have thought me a complete fool, not recognizing you.'

'No.' Her face was clear at last; fleetingly, he remembered kissing her in the rain-soaked silence of the hills. 'I did not intend you to recognize me. And I was careless – damned careless.' For he knew that when he had ridden through Belford's gates yesterday morning, his nerve had already been half gone. There had been Giles to face for the first time since October's disaster. And Carleton, of course: to pretend civility to Nicholas Carleton it had been necessary to be drunk, necessary also to have the distraction of Matthew Houlden's pretty wife. And with an aching head and a fatal lack of concentration, the fiasco of the evening's little venture had been an inevitability.

She was watching him, he knew that, waiting for – what? Explanations? He shifted uncomfortably – if only he could find one position where this damned shoulder did not torment him like a mouthful of badly drawn teeth . . . With an effort, he collected his thoughts. The escapade on the Gog Magog Hills was one thing he *could* explain to the wretched girl.

'When we met, I was not dressed as a gentleman. I was alone, with no servants, and no plausible excuse for being about on such a night. How long would it have taken you to suspect a connection? You did later realize that you had encountered Reynardine – didn't you?'

He saw Mall's fingers pleat the red folds of her dress, and her head bow so that he could not see her face. 'So . . . I suppose the way you behaved was – part of the disguise, so as to speak?'

'Something like that.' His voice was becoming unsteady, and he looked hazily at the bottle in his hand. 'Damn thing's finished – not enough. Never is enough.' Infuriatingly, the alcohol that had blurred his thoughts had failed to mask the pain at all. He shook his head once to clear it, and wiped his forehead with the back of his sleeve, struggling to unravel his tangled thoughts. 'To return to your suitors. George Murray is a wastrel. I would warn you against him, but there is no need. George will not marry you because he is enjoying life far too much to let a wife get in his way. And he has a large allowance and cannot yet have squandered it all on women or dice.' He looked across at Mall, and saw the anger in her eyes, a perfectly natural resentment of his criticism of charming, carefree George Murray. 'I speak from experience, Miss Conway: some of George Murray's fortune lines my pocket.'

The heat was oppressive: every bone in his body had begun to ache in perfect polyphonic harmony with the raw pain in his shoulder. Wiping his face with a less than clean handkerchief, Galliers frowned and stumbled to his feet. He heard Mall say indignantly, 'Sir Nicholas Carleton, then – he's hardly senile or an imbecile,' and the words he should say jumbled in his head, twisting and turning like those glittering bright figures that had danced in the Countess of Somerset's Great Chamber. He moved towards Mall, swaying gently.

'Perhaps I could modify your opinion of Sir Nicholas Carleton just a little bit. He is not – quite – the model of English manhood he appears to be.'

But then – Nicholas Carleton – how to tell this pretty innocent of Nicholas Carleton . . . And if only the girl would remain still. Two, no, three images of those fiery blue eyes swam confusingly before him.

But her voice was still lucid. 'That really is incredible, Mr Galliers, coming from you!' He saw her move back, away from his oscillating, sweat-soaked figure. 'Does Sir Nicholas Carleton rob old women? Does he attack honest servants and leave them for dead?'

'Does he kidnap young women and carry them off to his lair?'

His voice would not behave: it shook, and Mall watched, scowling, as he staggered over to the door and opened it, leaning against the jamb for support while the land that he knew so well heaved like a stormy white seascape before his eyes. 'Probably not.' He felt an almost hysterical desire to laugh. 'Well, Carleton's preference lies in kidnapping young men –'

She was at his side now, her eyes blazing, her words like scourges on a body that had been misused for too long.

'You – how can you say such things? Your reputation is worse than anybody's. You baselessly accuse Carleton of things everyone knows *you* to be guilty of. You are just attempting to reduce everyone to your own level of foulness and depravity.'

A hit, a palpable hit. For just a fraction of a second, Mall saw pain in those passionless eyes. 'And look at you,' she cried with disgust, 'you're so drunk you can hardly stand up!'

She was right, he was barely able to remain upright. The pain had taken over his entire body: he turned from Mall, her final words echoing in the chaos of his mind, while he stared, brightly unfocused, out into the snow. Then, thickly and incomprehensibly, he muttered, 'Hosea Dockerill, why don't you *come*?' and with consummate grace slid slowly down the door jamb and collapsed, a crumpled and unconscious heap, on the floor.

Had it not been for the fact that Richard Galliers was propping open the door, letting in the cold and vicious wind that blew across the Fens from the North Sea, Mall would have probably left him lying where he had dropped. As it was, it was necessary to haul her inebriated kidnapper into the hut so that the door might be closed while she collected her few belongings. Hooking her arms under his shoulders, Mall pulled. And then she stopped and looked at her hands. They were red: his doublet was wet, soaked with blood. She felt his forehead. It was burning.

So it had been fever that had made him shake, and pain that had made him drink. But that made no difference to her. He must have known what risks he took when he had started on his life of crime; he had, after all, been armed, and it was he, and he alone who had forced her to this dreadful place, away from her home and family. All she had to do was to find the pistol, take his cloak and the tinder and what little food was left. The boat would still be there, the Fen was not frozen yet, she could row well enough to take her a mile or so.

But although Richard Galliers had been armed, he had not used the pistol. He had not shot Martin Bartlett for his clumsy attempt to save her. And, somehow, Mall suspected that Richard Galliers was as good a shot as Joshua's Joe.

And when she herself had been lost and injured, he had helped her. He had taken the trouble to search for a stranger's body, tossed by a bolting horse, at a time when it must have been supremely inconvenient to do so.

Mall sat down, looking at the prone figure beside her. In sickness he looked untypically defenceless. The unconscious face, beaded with perspiration, the dark hair clinging in tiny wet tendrils to the sculptured cheekbones and forehead, did not look so wicked, so dangerous. And if she left she would be leaving him to die, of course. With no-one to feed the fire, it would soon go out; with no tinder to re-light it, he would freeze to death. If he did not perish from loss of blood or fever first. He would die, alone, comfortless, uncared for. If he were not to survive there should at least be a fellow human being with him to close his eyes and cover his face. She looked down at him, angrily. He had no right to do this to her: he should not have brought her here, forcing her to make these awful decisions. She should go.

And yet she could not. In spite of what he had done, to leave would be inhuman. For if she were to stay, he would have a chance. Not much of a chance, she thought grimly, but a chance, nevertheless.

With a sigh of exasperation, Mall hauled Galliers fully into the hut, and closed the door. Then, with some difficulty, she began to pull off his doublet, rolling him on his left side as she did so. Then, thanking God he was unconscious, she removed the bandage he had made the previous night.

147

The linen was soaked with blood, the edges of the wound were open, raw, beginning to swell. There was no sign of the bullet. He must have removed it himself, fighting against pain and fear, forcing himself to stay sentient long enough to complete the task and stem the bleeding, twisting round at an impossible angle. And yet she had offered to help, and pride or mistrust had persuaded him to reject her offer. It looked as though tonight he might pay for his pride.

But Mall had never given up anything without a fight. One of her best linen petticoats would have to go. She removed it, tore it into strips, and began to rebandage the wound. He began to stir as she finished re-tying the bandage. His eyes opened but did not see her, and she knew that the fever was rising rapidly. She cushioned the hot and heavy head with sheepskins, and began to bathe his face.

It was going to be a long night.

Outside the hut, the snow fell thickly, blanketing the silent Fen in a white shroud. Ice formed out of black water, trapping the myriad minute darting creatures beneath. Mall had never felt so alone, nor so powerless. It was fear that motivated her to fight for Richard Galliers' life: fear of being abandoned in this desolation with a dead man made her forget her own exhaustion and will him to remain alive. Fear of isolation from the rest of humanity – that, and another new emotion that crept up on her unawares as she bathed his hollow shadowed features and smoothed back dark, wet locks of hair from fever-brilliant eyes. Periodically, she checked the bandage covering the injury. It had stopped bleeding, that was one success. But the fever might still kill him, just as a fever had killed her own unremembered mother so many years ago.

He became increasingly restless, unable to find any comfortable position for his aching limbs, struggling against invisible bonds for freedom, oblivion; mumbling confused phrases, fragments of songs and poems. Occasionally he seemed to see her; for a fraction of a second his wild eyes would focus on her before reality slipped and dissolved again. But more often he did not recognize her, and his increasingly tortured conversation was addressed to listeners other than Mall.

A few of the names Mall knew – Giles (that was his brother of course), Frances – a mistress, perhaps? – and once, while he attempted hopelessly to sit up, her bearded onlooker's name: Nicholas Carleton. But the names and even the language became incomprehensible, tangled strands from an unhappy past, blurred and confused with the ballads, the poetry.

'– *make for me a winding sheet* . . . *wrap me up in a cloth of gold* . . .' Pushing Mall away, he struggled into a sitting position, his back to the wall, his eyes covered with his taut hands. '– *and see if I can sleep* – no, that's not right – I've forgotten –' His hand slipped and his eyes, wide open and luminiferous, stared in horror. '*Mother, mother, make my bed* – no, not that one – don't want that one –' The hand went back to his face, and he shivered violently, huddled against the wall.

Mall crouched by his side, ignoring his attempts to push her away. He shook his head, muttering the same words over and over again, inaudibly at first, and then louder, despairing. 'My God, why did I bring him home? Why did I bring him home?', and his long fingers clutched Mall's arm until it hurt. And then the song again, tormenting him. '*Mother, mother, make my bed – make for me a winding sheet –*' his voice painfully cracked and harsh, so changed from the clever singer of Belford's madrigals. And Mall began to sing her own songs, as much to comfort herself as to quieten him, for that tormented voice was worse than the desolation and the loneliness and the snow, and it frightened her. Gradually, miraculously, he quietened, and she saw the heavy eyelids droop, and his head lean back against the wall, exhausted.

Mall sat with Richard Galliers until she was sure he slept, feeling his damp hair against her face, and the still warmth of his sleeping body close to her side. Eventually, gently, she lowered him to the ground and covered him with his cloak.

Her own eyes ached with tears: they coursed slow and silent down her cheeks.

She awoke with a start a few hours later. She was not sure what had woken her – the cry of a bird, perhaps, or simply the silence of the snow-covered Fen. Mall rose, and went to check her patient. His breathing was deep and regular, his forehead cool to the touch. Sleep was what he needed, so she would be quiet and let him sleep as long as possible. Feeding the fire with small pieces of turf, Mall thought about the events of the previous night. Everything had changed now, irrevocably altered by what she had done. Who would understand why she had voluntarily stayed in this squalor to nurse her kidnapper, a highwayman? She could have been back at Belford now, in a clean gown instead of the filthy mud-stained rag that her red velvet dress had become, with decent food to eat instead of dried eel and mouldy bread.

However, whenever, she saw her home again, she could no longer tell the whole truth. Some lie must be concocted to protect both herself and the dark-haired man still sleeping by the fire. There was no point in saving a man from a quick death from fever, to consign him to a lingering demise courtesy of the local Assizes and the hangman's noose.

But it was better not to think of these things yet, better to find herself some breakfast, and get more water ready. There was very little food left; perhaps she would have to shoot wildfowl with Galliers' pistol. An enticing thought. Mall picked up the metal pan, wrapped a sheepskin about herself, and pushed her feet into Galliers' over-large riding boots.

Outside, the snow had stopped falling. The sky was white, and a pale sun glowed feebly through a thin layer of cloud. The horizon was invisible, lost in whiteness, land and sky melting into one. Mall quickly scooped some snow into the pan, and retreated back into the warmth of the hut.

It was while she was sitting by the fire tearing the remaining half of her petticoat into strips that Mall looked across and saw that Richard Galliers was awake, his eyes open, watching her. She poured some water into a cup, and went to his side. With difficulty he struggled into a sitting position and grimaced apologetically when his hands shook and spilt some of the water. '*I* will hold it for you,' said Mall firmly, knowing he had no strength to argue. His face was drained of colour, exhaustion showing the structure of the bones beneath the skin, his hair lank and untidy. You looked better in your black velvet, thought Mall, but kept silent.

Finally, with considerable effort, Galliers spoke.

'I was ill last night –'

'You nearly died,' said Mall flatly, putting the cup back by the fire.

He frowned, confused, and then said:

'You could have gone – taken the food and the pistol.' His eyes had not left her face. 'It would have been better for you.'

And you, Mr Galliers? No, better to leave that question unasked. But it seemed important to be honest. 'I nearly did leave.' Her voice was sharp. 'I changed my mind.'

A pause. He looked away from her, slowly taking in the bandaged shoulder, the torn remains of her petticoat, the old and battered doublet she had washed out and put to dry over the chest.

'But why – why stay? You owe me nothing.'

Therewith all sweetly did me kiss, and softly said . . . Mall stood up, busying herself with the water and the linen, her back to him.

'*Owing* doesn't come into it, Mr Galliers. Perhaps I thought I would miss the sound of your voice.'

It was a feeble attempt at humour, and she knew it. But he said nothing more, and, thankfully, she returned to practical matters.

'I'm afraid I shall have to change your bandage, Mr Galliers.'

'There's no need. I can –'

'Manage perfectly well yourself? You may not want a wet-nurse, my dear man, but this time you are going to get one. I doubt if you have the strength to change so much as a lute string at the moment.'

The pride came back, a hint of anger as well. And then he smiled weakly, and inclined his head, and Mall felt the tension go from her hands as she began her task.

The next day he was better still. He had moved, prompted by relentless nagging on Mall's part, to the relative comfort of the trestle bed; Mall spent the night cushioned on sheepskins by the fire. He had slept well and eaten a little. It could only be a little; their meagre supply of food was exhausted. He still tired easily, however, dozing off disconcertingly in mid conversation. It was during one of those naps when Mall, too, was almost asleep in the thick heat of the hut, that she heard the footsteps.

At first she thought it was her imagination. But then, as her heart began to pound in unison with the steps, she knew that someone was outside, the heavy tread crunching the snow, coming towards the hut. Friend, enemy – or rescuer? Whoever it was, Mall knew that she would feel safer with the gun in her hand. She drew the pistol out of the bog-oak chest, and cocked the trigger.

With horrible slowness the door of the hut was pushed open. Through the doorway, Mall could see, bobbing in the narrow unfrozen centre of the Fen beyond, a flat-bottomed boat. And before her terrified gaze stood a man, a giant who seemed twice the size of Richard Galliers, his enormous frame completely filling the doorway. A knitted cap of indeterminate colour covered his head, moleskin breeches and coat and long wading boots enveloped his body. An undisciplined adornment of matted grey whiskers sprouted from his lined, walnut-coloured face, and two sharp weaselly eyes peered from under straggling grey eyebrows. Mall's terrified gaze strayed from the knife in his right hand to the spear in his left, and she tightened her own trembling grip on the pistol. Shooting rabbits with Martin was one thing, aiming to kill at hairy marauding giants was most definitely another.

'Don't come in. Go away. I'll shoot you if you come any nearer.'

She pointed the heavy flintlock as where she thought the intruder's heart might be, praying that the apparition might leave, that Richard Galliers might wake up, that she would be magically transported back to Belford on one of her father's less likely inventions.

And then, incredibly, the giant began to laugh.

'Ooh, mightn't you ha' known it!' His entire frame quivered with whistling asthmatic amusement. 'Mightn't you ha' known it, he's got himself a maid to keep house for him! Well, I knew Mr Galliers couldn't be without a lass for long –'

Fear metamorphosed to fury with astonishing speed. 'Oh, for heaven's sake!' Mall's grip on the pistol relaxed slightly. 'Who the hell are you anyway, bursting in here like this? And what do you mean by –'

There was a gentle cough from the bed behind her.

'Miss Conway, may I introduce you to Hosea Dockerill? This hut, and all its facilities, belong to Mr Dockerill.' Carefully, Galliers swung his legs round to sit on the edge of the bed. 'Hosea, may I present Miss Mall Conway, of Belford. She is – how can I put it? A *guest* of mine.'

Dockerill had glanced sharply at Mall on hearing her name. He looked disapprovingly at Galliers. 'Half the county's looking for that maid. There'll be trouble if she's found here.'

'Then she mustn't be,' said Galliers briefly, and looked up innocently at Mall. 'Were you really going to fire my pistol? I know you must have been longing to empty it into *my* guts – but would you really have used poor old Hosea as a substitute? I must confess I was a little perturbed when you went over to the chest to retrieve it, but –'

'My God, you let me go on thinking you were asleep!' If he had not been wounded already, she would probably have hit him. 'I could have been murdered, or – or –'

'Raped?' asked Galliers smoothly. 'I don't think Hosea is the raping type, are you, Hosea? Not on eel-spearing days, anyway. However, you should be glad that Hosea has paid us a visit. He might have brought us some more palatable food. Not water rats, I hope, but then I don't believe it's the water rat season. So

153

put the pistol away, *please*, Mall, and come and sit down and make pleasant conversation.' He patted the bed beside him invitingly, and with some reluctance, Mall put the pistol back in the chest.

Hosea Dockerill put his glaive aside, crouched on the floor, and opened the reed bag he wore slung over one shoulder. A loaf, a bottle of ale, and part of a roasted goose were placed on the floor in front of them. Mall felt her mouth water and her stomach begin to rumble. When had she last eaten properly? That dreadful banquet at Belford, she calculated, two days ago.

Richard Galliers was obviously similarly delighted. 'Oh, Hosea, wonderful, *wonderful* Hosea! You are indeed a man of truly admirable qualities!'

Hosea pulled out his knife, and began to hack the goose into pieces. 'One of my lads found your mare roaming in the Fens. I've been away for the last few days – hunting.' His eyes travelled to the bandage under Galliers' unlaced doublet. 'I see you've gone and got yourself hurt. Fighting, was it? Or maybe the maid's family wasn't so keen on handing their jewels over to you?'

So Hosea knew of Galliers' little diversion, thought Mall, washing down the goose with a mouthful of ale. She looked covertly at Richard Galliers, and was pleased to see that he looked a little ashamed.

'I have to admit, Hosea, my latest scheme did not go to plan.'

Hosea snorted disapprovingly. 'Well, it was always a damn fool game. You should leave well alone, and stop meddling in what doesn't concern you, or you'll end your days swinging from the gibbet.' He spoke crossly, but the concern in his small sharp eyes belied his tone. 'What was it, a pistol or a sword?'

Galliers grimaced ruefully. 'It was a pistol. I'll take care never to cross Miss Conway's steward again – he's too good a shot. But it's nothing much. A day or two, and I'll be out of here.'

Hosea said dryly, 'If you can't stand up, man, I doubt if you can ride a horse. Still, I'll keep folks away from here – no-one'll know you're here, I'll make sure of that.' He stood up, pulling the bag over his shoulder, and picked up the glaive. 'I'll bring you some of Lizzie Balham's caudle – that cures anything.'

He turned to go. Galliers stood up, holding the wall for support. 'Hosea? Listen, will you – find out if they're looking for her this far north – and have the horses ready in case we need to go quickly. And – thank you.'

His only reply was a grunt as Dockerill left the hut.

Galliers swayed and sat back on the bed, exhausted by the effort of standing. But he had enough strength to say to Mall, 'Come. Aren't you glad you didn't shoot him?'

But this time Mall saw the laughter in his eyes, so she banished a sharp rejoinder, and contented herself with throwing a sheepskin at him, and retreated to her position by the fire.

Outside, the dying embers of the sun were reflected in the flat stillness of the Fen. The wind, readying itself for the night, rustled amongst the bare reeds and willows. And as Mall drifted off to sleep, she remembered what Dockerill had said. 'You should stop meddling in what doesn't concern you.' So what was Richard Galliers meddling in? And why had his meddling brought him to Belford?

Overnight a searing blizzard from Russia's far distant wastes blanketed the east of England in snow, and froze the water in the Fens. Mall was wakened in the middle of the night by the noise of the storm. The room was dark, her feet and hands numb with cold. For a moment she lay still, listening to the roaring monster of the snowstorm outside, unable to fathom what was wrong. And then, with a shock, she understood the reason for the cold and the dark. The fire was almost dead: only a feeble red glimmered at its heart, surrounded by grey ashes. She had fallen asleep without rebuilding the fire. The temperature had dropped during the night, and the peat walls of the hut had lost their warmth.

Fighting panic, Mall wrapped a sheepskin around herself, and crawled over to the hearth. She knelt down and blew at the embers to try and revive them. Briefly the fire flared and then died, leaving her in total darkness. With hands that felt dead with cold, Mall groped for the tinder and failed to find it, her scrabbling fingers touched nothing but the cold rough floor and the pile of peat turfs she had forgotten to use the previous evening. The courage that had helped her survive the last two days deserted her; she choked down the sob that rose in her throat.

Then a voice at her shoulder, calm in the dark, said:

'Mall? Here's the tinder. If you can strike it, we can light some kindling.'

She took the tinder from Richard Galliers' outstretched hand, and sat shivering as he found some dry rushes. But her hands had no strength, the sparks would not come, and the tinder seemed a feeble, useless weapon against the almost tangible darkness.

'Dear me, perhaps we should combine our efforts.' Galliers sat next to her, his shoulder brushing Mall's, halting the panic. 'You will strike, and I will hold. And perhaps a prayer to the elements.' Mall struck again as his voice murmured close to her ear, '*Ignei, aerii, aquatani, terrani, spiritus, salvete*,' and magically the tinder sparked, the dry rushes caught, and a yellow light flickered in the gloom.

'See? The heathen gods have answered us.' Carefully, Galliers lit the small heap of dry sticks and straw he had gathered in the grate. Mall felt him take the tinder from her, his warm hand touching her ice cold one. His fingers lingered: he put down the tinder and took her hands in his, chafing them, trying to drive away the cold.

'Christ, you're frozen.' He helped her to her feet, and hugged her, saying, 'Poor Mall. Your curiosity becomes too great for you, and you find yourself almost frozen to death in the Fens. Get into the bed, my dear. It's damned cold and it will take a while for the fire to heat the room.'

Mall could not move. She had never felt so tired nor so cold, and the impulse to burst feebly into tears was irritatingly strong. He had let go of her: she felt deserted, forsaken, and she shuddered again, blinking rapidly in the sheltering darkness. She felt two tears roll slowly down her cheeks, blurring the shadowed image of Richard Galliers, crouched again on the floor, building the turf around the fire.

He glanced back at her, and she heard him say impatiently:

'Get into the bed, Mall. I can attend to the fire.'

'I can't.' Sniffing noisily, Mall shook her head. 'You can't sleep on the floor. That would be –'

'I have no intention of sleeping on the floor. We will share the bed.'

We will share the bed . . . The tears stopped as suddenly as they had begun, and Mall's eyes fixed on Richard Galliers' face, unreadable in the poor light. We will share the bed . . . a simple statement of intent, neither a request nor a proposition. She watched him rise and come towards her, and felt him place his hands lightly on her shaking shoulders.

'Come, it's not worth crying about, my dear. I realize the thought must be somewhat repulsive to you, but you have my word that sleep is more attractive to me at present than lovemaking.' He grinned, his scarred, vivid face demonic in the firelight. 'Look upon it as a practical solution, Mall. Unpleasant to you, no doubt, but possibly less so than contracting an ague.'

Taking her hand, he led her to the bed. It was only a narrow trestle bed, barely wide enough for one person, but with Mall's head cradled on Richard Galliers' good shoulder, there was just room enough for two. Lying there, his cloak pulled over them both, she could see the soft roseate light of the fire, feel his heart beating against her cheek and his arm around her, holding her to him. She still shook, but no longer with cold. She heard him whisper, 'My poor girl. You've had enough of the hoary winter's night, haven't you?', and he held her more tightly, so that she was warmed by the heat of his body. At last the shivering lessened, but she did not sleep: no, staring with wide open eyes into the darkness, she was glad that he could not see

157

her face, read her thoughts. As his arms relaxed, she adjusted her position, so that she could see Galliers' face. He was asleep already, his eyes closed, a lock of hair falling across his face. *You have my word that sleep is more attractive to me at present than lovemaking* . . . In the dim light of the fire, she could see the line of his profile, the slightly aquiline nose, the faintly clefted chin. Gently, Mall brushed back the dark hair from his forehead, and let her finger trace the path of the rapier scar. And then she caught his abandoned hand in hers, and bringing it up to her lips, kissed the long fingers, one by one.

> *Therewithal sweetly did me kiss,*
> *And softly said, Dear heart, how like you this . . . ?*

CHAPTER SEVEN

Oh no, my dear, no rake am I
Brought up in Venus' trade
But I'm seeking for concealment
All on the lonesome plain.

(REYNARDINE)

*A*LWAYS that split second of confusion when he could not remember where he was: France, Italy, Amyott, the Dutch corsair's pinnace . . . and then, almost immediately following, memory flooding back, bitterness and relief combined. But this morning it was a little different: which bed, which girl? Whose small soft warm body had he held sleeping in his arms, whose wild black hair had he kissed as he woke, looking for a familiar solace? *Christ, that my love were in my arms and I in my bed again . . .*

And a few seconds' peace before he recalled who she was, and why he had brought her here. And then his arms left her body, his mouth no longer caressed her tangled hair, and he drew away from her as though she were fine glass and he a clumsy servant. Carefully he climbed out of the bed, and knelt by the pan of water, drinking great cold mouthfuls of it, letting it wash over his unshaven chin and trickle down to the collar of his crumpled, dirty doublet. But the water could not wash the foul taste from his mouth, nor the knowledge that, despite the bullet wound, despite the fact that Mall Conway was little more than a child, he had felt desire for her, closeted so close to her in that tiny trestle bed.

His shoulder was stiff and sore: pitilessly, he forced himself to flex his fingers and move his arm, knowing that there was only one solution to the bed and the problem it contained. *You reduce everyone to your own level of foulness and depravity* . . . He looked back at the trestle bed, wiping his damp face with the back of his sleeve, brushing back the ragged hair from his eyes. Mall was still asleep; he could see the slow rise and fall of her breast, the frill of torn grey lace about her loose hands. And he knew that lies must be thought of, something to cover his tracks, something to make good the careless mistakes he had made. And he must run, soon and quickly, before his mistakes multiplied.

He went to the door, assessing the weather, trying to think clearly. He saw that the snow had been followed by a frost, and that silvered fringes of ice had formed round the bare willows and reeds: a forest of white, light crystals, and damnably, damnably inconvenient. Pulling on his boots, Galliers walked to the edge of the island, feeling the strength of the frozen Fen beneath his feet, seeing the dusting of snow that gathered in drifts and eddies about its borders. There was no horizon, only a bare white plain where a horse, or a dark cloak, or a girl's scarlet gown would stand out like spilt ink on blank paper. If they found him here, there would be nowhere to hide.

He heard the creak of the door behind him, and looked back to see Mall, a sheepskin round her shoulders, framed in the doorway. He could see, damn it, happiness on her face, and hear happiness in her voice as she let her sleepy gaze travel over the sky, the Fen, the island, coming to rest, unmistakeably, on him.

'Isn't it beautiful, Mr Galliers?'

He walked back towards her, cradling his arm, conscious that the icy air had exaggerated the ache in his shoulder.

'Beautiful, Miss Conway,' he said. 'A poet would write a sonnet. But damned ill-timed for me.'

'You are not a poet, then, Mr Galliers?'

He heard himself say, 'No, Miss Conway. A poor player that struts and frets his hour upon the stage, perhaps, but not a poet,' and he pushed past her into the hut, remembering the Red Bull, Ellenby. Ellenby's eyes following him as this girl's eyes followed him now: and he saw, all too clearly, a new danger in the events of the previous night. He had taken Mall Conway's hands in his, he had slept with her the length of the night in one bed, he had called, with her, upon the heathen gods to light their fire. Crook your finger, Richard Galliers, he thought bitterly, say the right words, and she will follow you as Ellenby followed you, as Jeremy followed you . . . He may have felt desire often enough to know its transient deceit – but had Mall? Mall was ten years his junior, had lived all her life in Cambridgeshire's sheltered plains; how might she interpret what he knew to be of no significance?

And the last thing he needed now, in the net of intrigue into which he had cast himself, was a schoolgirl running after him, devotion in her pretty blue eyes. He knew that his indifference had piqued her, he could feel her eyes upon him as he took the main gauche knife from his belt and tried to exercise his arm into some sort of efficiency. He cursed as the knife slipped through his irritatingly fumbling fingers, and he heard Mall say, her tone an incongruous compound of hurt and common sense:

'Your shoulder is getting better, Mr Galliers. You must let it alone and it will heal properly.' He saw her throw the sheepskin on to the bed, and begin, crossly, to try and twist her hair into some sort of a knot. 'You cannot hasten the healing of a wound like that. You will just have to be patient.'

'I cannot be patient. We have been here too long.' He watched her hopelessly scrabbling at the thick mane of her hair, saw her set mouth and narrowed eyes, and knew that they had indeed been alone too long. She had got too close to him, had somehow wormed her way under the defences he had so carefully laid. 'They will be starting to look further afield for you, Miss Conway,' he said, attempting to be rational, practical. 'And besides, there's a limit to how long *I* can conveniently disappear without some people beginning to ask awkward questions.'

He saw her abandon the unequal struggle with her hair: it tumbled untidily down her back. She said sharply:

'I don't see how either of us can leave here unless you can ride, Mr Galliers. But perhaps you could tell everyone that you were at some protracted orgy or something – I'm sure they would believe that.'

He had bent to pull one of the laces from his discarded shirt, and could not see her face. 'For your hair, Miss Conway,' he said, holding up the lace. 'Let me.' And he took the heavy fall of her hair in his hands and looped the lace around it, trying to force the nerveless fingers of his right hand into some sort of sentience. He said, as patiently as he could, 'When Hosea comes today I had better tell him to bring the horses. It will be better for us both to get away from this place as soon as possible. *You* may have greater tolerance, my dear, but I shall go noisily and embarrassingly insane if I have to stay in this bloody cell much longer.' He pulled the lace into a knot. 'One more day and this damn shoulder should be sufficiently healed, and you will be able to return to the bosom of your family. And I will take ship and never see this God-forsaken island again.'

Mall swung round, stray tendrils of hair already escaping and drifting over her face. She said, clearly:

'Perhaps if you had not lived so hard in the past, Mr Galliers, you might be recovering quicker now.'

He looked up at her: she had pulled away from him and stood against the wall of the hut, her arms tightly folded and her eyes bright with anger. He felt an anger to match hers, and intense resentment that this girl – this child – should see fit to upbraid him on the unhealed wound of his past years. He said, as coldly and casually as he could:

'And what, miss, do you know of my sordid past?'

He had crossed the room to stand in front of her. Mall drew herself up to her fullest height, but even so, her eyes were not even level with his chin.

'Oh – gambling – and a brothel –' she said, looking at anything but him. 'And –'

'And Satan's right-hand man in Hell?' He moved away from her, knowing that his own temper was barely controlled, knowing that the air in the hut had become over emotional, oppressive. He picked up his cloak from the bed, and said, half-heartedly attempting to appease her, 'I suppose I have only myself to blame – ransacking your house and dragging you here to this benighted spot. A lecture on my morals is the least I deserve.'

She was not to be appeased. He heard her answer, her voice taut with sarcasm:

'Yes, Mr Galliers. I have been meaning to ask you – why were you ransacking our house? I quite understand that you are a penniless younger son, but I do find it hard to believe that you had to take to highway robbery to make ends meet. Perhaps a few profitable games of dice or cards would have been simpler?'

'Perhaps.' He flung the cloak over his shoulders and walked towards the door. 'Please be satisfied with the assurance that I will pay no more uninvited visits to your home, Miss Conway. And now, if you will excuse me, I am going to walk the bounds of our prison.'

As he reached the door he felt her grab at his cloak, stopping him from leaving.

'God's wounds, you really are the most infuriating creature I have ever had the misfortune to meet! Do you think I am a child, to be satisfied with your damned "assurances"? *You* brought me here – you involved me – you surely cannot expect not to tell me *why*!'

He swung round to face her, conscious of the stifling heat of the hut, and the unrelenting pain in his shoulder. 'I realise how much I am in your debt,' he said, softly. 'I also realize how foolishly I have entangled your life with mine, and I regret it to the bottom of my heart. But none of that gives you any right – any right whatsoever – to insist that I involve you more.'

Galliers looked down at her, cold indifference in his eyes, and felt her hand slip from his cloak. 'How old are you? Fifteen – sixteen – a child, no more. In spite of your interest in gossip, Miss Conway, I assure you that you know *nothing* of my affairs. As soon as I can arrange it, Dockerill will escort you back to Belford, and you can tell what tale you wish to your family. I shall be as far from here as I possibly can.'

He left the hut, stepping out into the snow, circling the margin of the island until he stood behind the hut, looking out to where a flight of wildfowl broke the silent whiteness of land and sky. The wind was bitter, whipping up the dry snow from the ground, forming it into small hills and furrows. It would snow again before nightfall: the heavy glaucous clouds were already massed on the skyline where the fragmented swampland of the Fens dissolved into the cold North Sea. The snow would make riding difficult, and lessened the chances of finding a vessel at one of the eastern seaports to take him – where? Northern France, perhaps, the Netherlands . . . it did not really matter. But it would be dangerous to stay in England now. Mall knew Reynardine's true identity.

He became aware that his hands were still fisted, his jaw still clenched. He had lost his temper with that girl; she had succeeded in getting under his skin.

The wind howled from the east, intensifying the ache in his shoulder. He pulled the hood of the cloak over his head and moved down to where the silver-white reeds rose from the ice. And yet, he had been unkind. He turned away from the Fen, and began to walk back to the hut. He must get Mall away from here today, with Hosea as an escort if necessary.

Galliers pushed open the door of the hut, kicking the snow from his boots.

She was not there.

The hut was empty: her shawl and slippers were gone. Galliers swore, and spun round, eyes raking the arctic scene outside. It was not difficult to find her, of course: his gaze fixed on a streak of flapping scarlet in the distance, running awkwardly, slipping on the ice of the silver Fen.

She was already too far away to hear him call her name. Galliers ran after her, anger and fear returning in double quantity. The ice might be solid here, but that was no guarantee of its thickness elsewhere. And if Mall went through thin ice, he might never return her to her family . . .

It hurt to run, but he ignored the pain, his eyes fixed on her peculiar flat-footed, sliding gait, necessitated by thin slippers on a treacherous surface. He called her name, his voice lost in the raw wind, drowned by the sad distant noise of the curlew. Christ, she must be cold.

And then he was level with her; he grasped her shoulder, pulling her round, clutching her arm when she tried to drag away from him again.

'Mall – what the hell do you think you're doing? In God's name, where do you think you're going?'

She did not answer at first; then he heard her mumble something about getting away, her face shadowed by the shawl she had wound round her head.

'But for Christ's sake, you idiot girl –' He took one of her hands in his, trying to drag her back with him towards the hut. 'How long do you think you'd last out there? You are frozen already.' It was true, her hand felt like ice, and she shivered like the reeds that fringed the Fen. She did not appear to understand the dangers of this country, in this weather. 'Mall, if you didn't put your foot through thin ice, or get lost in the snow, you would simply perish of cold long before you reached Belford. Dammit, my dear, you are not even going in the right direction! Now, come back with me, there's a good girl, and as soon as I can arrange it, Hosea will take you home.'

Mall jerked away from Galliers' restraining hand, her feet stumbling on the ice. She said incoherently, 'Let me go – you just think I'm an inconvenience.'

Exasperated, Galliers said impatiently, 'Inconvenient or not, you're coming back with me even if I have to pick you up and carry you –' and then he broke off suddenly. The shawl had blown back in the wind; he could see the tears that stained her face, her eyelashes frosted, eyelids already red and swollen with weeping. He groaned softly. 'Oh, my God, you're crying.'

She stood shivering on the ice, her hands fisted like a small child's, pressed against her wet face. Galliers pulled the cloak off his shoulders and wrapped it round her, drawing the hood over her head, fastening the clasp under her chin. He drew her close to him, cradling her head against his chest, trying to make sense of the unintelligible phrases gasped out between fresh bouts of sobbing. 'You'll go back to your family today, Mall, I promise you.'

Instead of calming her, the howls increased. 'It's not that – I don't want to – oh, you *stupid* man!'

He stood back from her, still holding her, his dark hair lashing his face in the icy wind. 'Sweetheart, what are you talking about? Of course you want to go home – that's why you're crying – isn't it?'

'*No!*' The words broke from her lips, a wail of misery cutting the cold air. Mall rubbed her face with the cuff of her sleeve. 'I'm crying because you – you –'

'Because I think you are an inconvenience?' He frowned and shook his head, and then began to lead her back towards the hut. 'Well, so you are an inconvenience, my dear. In other circumstances a totally delightful one, but here a damnable inconvenience. But I should not have been so boorish as to tell you so, I agree. The art of gallantry appears to be something I have forgotten.' Galliers glanced down at her blotched, wind-lashed face, and, putting his arm about her shoulders, said, 'I have lived among rogues and vagabonds for many years now, and seem to have picked up their manners. And I lost my temper back there in the hut. My only feeble excuse is the inactivity. I have never been any good at waiting.'

It was, Mall knew, the nearest thing to an apology she was likely to get. Galliers helped her up the frozen bank and on to the snow-covered grass. He kicked open the door of the hut, and followed her inside; and seeing that she was blue-tinged and shaking with cold, began quickly to build up the fire. He poured some ale into a cup and put it into her trembling hands. She drank a little, and then said unsteadily:

'It's just that – I don't understand. All these stories about you – even *Alice* had heard them . . . and you yourself do not deny them. But you are not a *bad* man, Mr Galliers. So why rob the old lady? And why break into my home?'

'Especially when your stepmother was kind enough to disregard my infamous reputation?' He smiled crookedly as he sat down beside Mall, back against the wall. Abruptly, he thought almost painfully of the fragile body he had held in his arms the previous night, of the feel of her silky soft skin. She was right, of course, he could not escape it. He must tell her something, repay at least a little of his debt – and, after all, he would not see her again.

'Of my past, some of the stories you heard were true, some were not. I had better keep to the incident that concerns you.'

Mall put the cup down. Her colour was more normal, a faint wash of pink lit her cheeks. 'The highwayman.'

'Yes – sly, bold Reynardine. That was the result of a wager, originally, I'm afraid. I was somewhat at a loose end – I had returned from the Continent and spent a month or so in London. The pleasures on offer there were beginning to pall, when Giles reappeared. He and I passed a pleasant evening together in one of Holborn's less salubrious haunts – the Dagger tavern. When I awoke the next morning – feeling fit for the gallows, I recall – one event of the previous night was clear in my mind. Somewhere in the course of a rather crapulent conversation about my future career, I had accepted a wager from Giles to commit highway robbery. So,' he went on, calmly, 'I did. One dull August evening I attired myself in the most ludicrous disguise I could think of and haunted the road between Amyott and Cambridge. I then waylaid the first unfortunate traveller to cross my path – a messenger, riding from London.'

Warmed by the fire and the ale, Mall's curiosity was returning. 'A wager? You risked your life for a *wager*? And what was the prize?'

'The prize?' Galliers grinned. 'The prize I will keep to myself. Definitely not suitable for your maiden ears.'

Mall rapidly changed the subject. 'Very well. So you robbed the messenger for a wager. But why Lady Woodroffe? Surely you didn't have to accost *two* people to win your disgusting wager?'

His eyes narrowed, two slits of gleaming green-gold between luxuriously lashed lids. 'Ah, but I did. Did you know whose messenger that was?'

Mall shook her head, trying to remember those late wet August days. 'No – I think he was someone's servant . . . He didn't take long to recover – as soon as he could ride, he was gone. He must have been in rather a hurry.'

A small, calculating smile. 'I don't doubt he was, my dear. Our simple messenger was carrying an urgent and incriminating letter from the Countess of Somerset.'

Mall let out a long breath. 'So you found a compromising letter from Lady Somerset in your first victim's possession?'

'He put up more of a fight than I had expected,' Galliers said ruefully, 'and I ended up having to knock him unconscious. Afterwards, I went through his pockets for valuables – some evidence of my success for Giles, you see. He had damn all. I was going to leave him with what little he had, but once I'd read that letter I realized I'd better take something to make it look realistic. Opening that bloody letter –' he grimaced '– it was like disturbing a hornet's nest. All sorts of nasty things flew out.'

'But I still don't see why that meant you had to rob Lady Woodroffe. And what was in the letter? And what on earth has all this to do with finding you in the library at Belford?'

He stood up to put more peat on the fire, and patted her black curls. 'Patience, child. I will explain. First, I thought it best to waylay another passer-by so that it would be plain to any suspicious parties that the despoiling of Lady Somerset's messenger was merely the work of a simple highwayman, a naughty rogue who relieves innocent travellers of their excess wealth. Lady Woodroffe happened to come by at the right time – well, the wrong time for her – and fall neatly into my lap like a ripe plum from the branch. Besides –' he grinned wickedly at Mall 'I had a score to settle with the old dragon. She used to play cards with my mother, and invariably won. It seemed – how can I put it? Appropriate.'

'So Lady Woodroffe was attacked to make the whole thing more credible. Reynardine, baulked of fabulous gains from the impecunious servant, lurks nastily in the undergrowth, waiting for a richer prey.'

Galliers inclined his head. 'Exactly right, my sweet. Lady Woodroffe was merely an alibi – rather an enjoyable one, I must admit.' His eyes sparkled. 'I had assistance for that venture – she had three men with her, whereas Lady Somerset's man was alone. Also, I chose a different patch of undergrowth to lurk in – your oak copse at Belford, I'm afraid. Anyway, after committing that particular crime, I came first here, to the Fens, to lie low for a night, and then returned to London to find Giles.'

'And claim your reward?' said Mall, dryly.

'Precisely.'

'And the letter?'

'Oh, yes, the letter.' His voice was no longer light hearted. 'The letter implicated the Countess of Somerset in murder – murder most foul, strange and unnatural – murder successfully carried out in the not too distant past. The letter said: "*Remind my dear friend that I bear evidence of his past assistance in ridding me of my enemy. His coldness has not escaped my attention. Let him not forget, dear Anne, that if the tree falls, so also will the branches.*" It was a threat, you see, Mall. I would guess that the lady was very angry when she wrote it, and it was intended to bring our friend to heel.'

'"Anne" – who is she?'

'The letter had no address.' Galliers poked at the fire with a stick. 'However, by copiously plying a creature of the Howards with drink for a few nights when I arrived back in London, I concluded that the letter was intended for Mrs Anne Turner. She usually lives in London – she makes love potions for the infatuated, spells to repel the unwanted, that sort of thing. She has long been a confidante of Lady Somerset. And the interesting thing is –' his hand absently traced some design in the ash on the floor of the hut '– the interesting thing is that in August she was a near neighbour of yours. She was staying with her family in Hinxton.'

'Hinxton? But that's only –'

'– a few miles from Belford. Anyway, I decided to attempt to discover the identity of the erring friend.'

'But why? Why not just re-seal the letter, put it back in the messenger's pocket, and forget all about it?' Hosea's comment of the day before sprang to Mall's mind. 'As Mr Dockerill said, it was none of your business. Or, if you felt you had to do something, why not tell the king and leave him to decide what to do about it – surely *that* would have satisfied your conscience?'

Galliers frowned. 'I have no great wish for advancement at Court just now, but to accuse, by inference or association, Robert Kerr of murder, could be construed as suicidal. No, Mall, I will need more than one somewhat confusing letter to convince King James of the Countess's guilt. And remember, Frances Howard belongs to one of the most powerful families in England. If I cannot manage to keep my suspicions to myself, I shall very probably end up in a ditch with a dagger in my back. I have already had one interesting encounter with someone's hired assassins. And besides –' he shrugged, 'I was bored. Investigating my neighbours' seamier secrets appeared an altogether more fascinating pastime than getting blind drunk every night, or competing with numerous other young men for the rather dubious favours of our king.'

Mall looked at him sharply. 'Then – you mean to say that I have just endured the most exhausting and uncomfortable three days of my entire life simply because you were *bored*?'

Galliers poured himself some ale from the bottle, and said casually, 'I remember that when we first met, in September, you had stolen a horse, and left your distraught family with no clue as to your whereabouts. What was your motive – altruism?'

There was no suitable reply to that.

Galliers continued: 'To return to the letter. I concluded that the enemy Lady Somerset disposed of was Sir Thomas Overbury. He opposed the lady's second marriage to Robert Kerr, and ended up in the Tower for his trouble. He died, in considerable agony, over a year ago and there are rumours that he was poisoned. I would guess that Lady Somerset is becoming worried, and the letter was an attempt to plug one hole in an increasingly leaky boat. I became interested in the role of the deserting ally. Someone who lives not too far from Hinxton, frequents the Court, has possibly dabbled in alchemy if poison was involved –'

Mall squeaked incredulously, 'My father! You thought my father was involved in murder! That's preposterous!'

'Is it?' Galliers rested his head back against the wall, and watched Mall. 'On the contrary, your father seems a very suitable candidate. He attends Court regularly. He is known to have frequent audiences with the king, and will therefore know the Somersets. He also has a well publicized interest in alchemy.'

'Well publicized, but decidedly out of date!' Anger blazed in Mall's dark blue eyes. 'His interest in alchemy waned long ago. He has an entirely different enthusiasm now – he is building a boat that will sail under the water!'

Richard Galliers did not even smile. Instead, he continued smoothly, 'There were other possibilities. I visted the Murrays in September, after our little interlude on the hills. I found nothing to implicate George Murray, and to be honest, I doubt if he has sufficient intellect for intrigue. When I attended your stepmother's banquet, it was with the intention of looking round your house. Also –' he appeared to be absorbed in scraping some of the layer of mud from his boot with the blade of his dagger, 'to ensure that the little lost waif I had found against a tree stump in the Gog Magog hills had fully recovered from the experience.'

Galliers was silent for a moment, staring into the smoke that rose thickly to the hole in the roof. He looked weary again, exhausted by the effort of talking. 'You will ride home with Hosea this afternoon. I shall leave England, and Reynardine will never be seen again.' Almost to himself, he added, 'I should never have come back, and I should have forgotten the contents of that letter as soon as I had read them.' He rose, and walked slowly over to the door. 'It is not as though Overbury was any loss, by all accounts. And even if the Howards and Kerr were to leave the stage, as they surely will without my assistance, George Villiers is already waiting in the wings.'

He opened the door, and Mall watched him step out into the snow. What comfort she could offer she knew he would not accept; his need now was to be alone.

Galliers was back in the hut almost immediately. By the altered expression on his face she knew there was something wrong, badly wrong.

'Hosea,' he said shortly. 'And in a considerable hurry.'

Mall hurried to her feet, her stomach squirming in certain premonition of danger. Following Galliers out of the hut, she stood beside him at the edge of the reed-fringed ice. She could see Dockerill on horseback, with a second horse on a leading rein at his side, riding along the snow-covered track to the side of the ice like some enormous twin-bodied centaur, slowing the animals as he neared the island. One of the horses Mall recognized – it was, she realized, the black mare on which she and Reynardine had made their escape from Belford.

Dockerill dismounted, leaving the horses shivering, looped by their reins to a willow, on the far side of the ice. Galliers crossed over to him. 'They're looking for her,' Mall heard Dockerill say. 'My lad's sent 'em round by the Wildmere Fen to slow them down a bit and give you some time – but it won't hold them for long. Some bastard saw hoof prints here a couple of nights ago and put two and two together in hopes of a reward.' He paused to recover his breath.

'Then we must leave now.' Galliers was already on his way back into the hut. 'Hosea, you must take Mall back to Belford. If you head south now, you should have time enough.' Inside the hut, he buckled on his sword, and pushed the pistol into his belt. 'Take Mall to the outskirts of her estate – it will be dark by the time you get there, no-one should see you. Make sure she gets within the gates and then go, and return here. That way there'll be nothing to connect you with me.'

Dockerill said doubtfully, 'And can you ride, lad?'

'I shall ride as if the devil's behind me – which he will be if we do not hurry.' Tossing the cloak over his shoulders, he threw their few belongings in Hosea's bag and extinguished the fire. 'There. Not much evidence of habitation now. With any luck our pursuers will be stranded sufficiently long in the marshes for the embers to cool before they arrive.' Picking up one of the sheepskins, he left the hut. Mall, standing by the clump of willows that hid the ice-bound skiff, watched Galliers turn and give further instructions to Hosea. For a long dreadful moment she thought that he might leave with no further word to her, and that would be truly, utterly unbearable. But suddenly he was at her side, wrapping the sheepskin around her shoulders.

'It's not very elegant, I'm afraid, but it might keep you warm.'

Mall looked up at him, trying to memorize his face, as an insurance against the bleak days to come. He held her gently by the shoulders.

'Mall – Mall, you will have to concoct your own story. I had hoped for a little more time.'

She tried to smile reassuringly, but her features would not obey her. 'Don't worry – I am a practised liar.' Her voice trembled annoyingly. 'And you – what will you do?'

'Oh, I know many circuitous routes out of here.'

Fleetingly, his lips touched her forehead, and then he said firmly: 'Now, go and mount the horse with Dockerill. It's time to leave.'

Mall did as she was told, climbing on to the broad gelding behind Hosea, trying to put aside the emotions that crowded in on her. It was over – a few short days that had changed her life out of all recognition. She should be feeling joy at the prospect of returning to her family – but she was not. She felt empty, forsaken, as desolate as the forbidding landscape of the Fens that surrounded her.

Richard Galliers, cloaked, booted, and spurred, was at her side, mounted on his black mare, the reins held loosely in one hand. She could not look at him, could not persuade her lips to frame trivial and meaningless goodbyes and expressions of good luck. Then she felt one of his hands touch hers; something was pressed into her palm, and her fingers folded about it. She glanced across at him.

His green eyes dancing, his dark hair blown about in the cold breeze, he smiled at her. 'A memento,' he said. 'It betrayed me most resoundingly once. Perhaps you should keep it, lest *you* betray me now.' And then, as speedily as the bridegroom to his bed, he was gone.

Mall watched him until he was a black speck on the horizon. It was only then, as Dockerill skilfully guided the horse along the winding path, that she opened her hand.

In her palm lay the chrysoberyl ring.

CHAPTER EIGHT

Follow still, since so thy fates ordained.
The sun must have his shade,
Till both at once do fade,
The sun still proved, the shadow still disdained.

(CAMPION)

*T*HE ship on which Richard Galliers made his escape from England was an ancient single-masted pinnace. Her name, the *Eglantine*, was scrawled across her bows, but no scent of wild rose clung to the vessel, only the stench of pitch, newly applied to her rotting hull, and the smell of salt water on soaking sailcloth. Looking at the patched sails and caulked timbers, Galliers was forced to admit to himself that his need to leave the country was greater than his mistrust of an obviously unseaworthy ship. There was little choice, of course – the wind had picked up, and in such vile weather few masters would wish to risk their ships, their cargoes, or their lives. But, when with a nagging pain in his shoulder and a burden of bleak thoughts, he had stood on the quayside and looked up at the pinnace's heaving decks, Richard Galliers had known that choice for him had narrowed to the unglorious *Eglantine*.

So he had hailed the man that slept standing on the fore deck, his rat-tailed head resting on the gunwale, his hands, one still clutching a half empty bottle, flung out beside him. With the aid of a small pebble the man had woken, and after staring wildly at Galliers as though he were some demon from the deep, had swayed off to fetch the *Eglantine*'s master.

The master of the *Eglantine*, a black-bearded, one-eyed man, had made little demur about taking a passenger on board, and had pocketed the crowns Galliers had offered and rowed him on board the vessel. The remainder of the crew – too small a number, surely, for such a night – had taken little notice of the new arrival, but had worked silently in the gathering snow and wind. Only the pilot, the bottle now cradled to his chest, had clasped Galliers' arm with a shaking hand, and, asking him his name, had forgotten it instantly.

His only condition of passage had been that he stay on deck. The *Eglantine*'s cargo must be illegal, he realized, but that was of no concern to him. Men involved in smuggling or gun running were unlikely to talk too loudly about an unexpected passenger. He watched the sails tighten in the breeze as the ship pulled away from the quayside, and saw the master shake the pilot and shout at him, his words lost in the crying of the wind. The hard ride from the Fens had tired Galliers more than he had expected, and all he wanted was some reasonably sheltered corner of the pinnace's shabby after deck, and sleep. But there was little shelter to be found: the snow cut across the little ship like a sword thrust, teasing the cold ache in his shoulder into new life. Crouching by the pin rail, his cloak wrapped around him, his knees drawn up to his chin, Galliers felt no regret on watching the flickering lights of the harbour fade into the horizon, only a sense of relief in leaving behind the accumulated complications of his life.

He saw the master leave the pilot to stand at the starboard bow and look out to sea with a practised, wary eye. When the pilot tottered over to crouch at Galliers' side, Richard accepted a mouthful from the almost empty bottle, thankful for the temporary relief from pain that the spirits provided. He felt too tired to plan coherently. When the ship docked he would buy a horse to replace the black mare he had sold to a gipsy – *that* had caused him some regret, she had been a good horse – and he would ride south. Where to, he was not sure: it did not matter, anywhere away from the biting wind and bitterly cold nights . . . to sleep, away from the Howards, and his family, and Nicholas Carleton – *especially* Nicholas Carleton. And away from that little girl who had tangled herself into his life in such a troublesome fashion. He had been unwise, again, there . . . to sleep. The cries of the sailors (hard out – hard out, before the wind – before the wind) became the substance of dreams, and his dark head, hidden inside the folds of his cloak, fell against the pin rail.

'Man overboard!' The cry that woke him, uncertain whether he was indeed awake or still dreaming, still produced the automatic reaction it always had. He was on his feet, and by the gunwale before his mind had fully accepted that this was reality, this creaking vessel, this howling wind, this black night.

'It was the pilot!' The master had to shout to make himself heard above the noise of the wind. 'Too much to drink again, God rot him! The rail is broken – there – and he fell against it. Well, that's be his last bottle – we'll never find him in this.'

Richard Galliers, staring out into the seething waves and dark, starless night, was forced to agree. The man would probably be dead already, stunned by the shock of the cold water, battered into unconsciousness by the power of the sea. There was as little hope of finding a drowning man as there was of plucking a mermaid from the sandbanks they had just passed. He turned to the master.

'Then there's nothing we can do?'

The man laughed, bitter humour in his Cyclops eye. 'Oh, there is, my friend – we can pray. We have lost our pilot, and we are heading into a gale.' He glanced pointedly at Galliers' wounded shoulder. 'Yes, perhaps you should make your peace with the Almighty.'

Richard Galliers grasped the man's soaking jerkin as he turned away. For just a fraction of a second, the prospect of sleep followed by a gentle and inevitable death had seemed less unpleasant than the thought of spending the night coaxing this damned hulk into some sort of a harbour. But the memory of someone who had not given up so easily invaded his mind, and would not let go. At least he would have no time to think.

'Keep your prayers, man,' he said, roughly. 'You have a pilot.'

They put into harbour in the early hours of the morning, at a fishing village between Dunkerque and Calais. Walking down the quayside, Galliers reflected that, had he access to a cannon, he would have quite cheerfully stove in the *Eglantine*'s side, sending her to the watery grave she so fully deserved. The master, fortunately, had known his seamanship, and the crew had known they were fighting for their lives, but that ship was a leaking, top heavy pig, and he hoped to God he never had the misfortune to sail one again.

He managed to find a horse by the simple expedient of hammering hard on the door of the first tavern he saw, and cursing in fluent and idiomatic French when the patron proved unwilling to leave the comfort and warmth of his bed. The horse was the equine equivalent of the *Eglantine*, spavined, ill-tempered, and slow. It was a mount, though, and riding was preferable to walking, even though every rise and fall of the animal's movement sent arrows of pain through his shoulder. He had long since, on the pinnace's heaving deck, lost all sensation in his hands and feet, and the discomfort of soaking wet, ragged clothes had become almost customary. He had only a vague idea of where he was heading – ride south, that seemed the right thing to do. The horse slipped on the icy track again, and Galliers' mouth compressed into a thin hard line as pain jolted through his body.

The snow started as he reached Calais, settling on the ancient walls. He knew the town well, but in the early half light his tired brain could make no sense of the twisting alleys and passageways. He had forgotten why he was here, he had forgotten why he existed. Calais took on the unreal familiarity of a nightmare, made more dreadful by the weird red sun that hung ominously over the churning sea.

The horse failed completely as he came within sight of the harbour. It had limped more severely for an hour past, and at last it shed the shoe that was the partial cause of its discomfort. He only just managed to keep his seat as the creature stumbled, and the mocking cries of the boys that had followed in his wake since he had passed through the walls of the town echoed confusingly in his ears. He had known their language since he was a child, but it was ceasing to make any sense. He left the horse where it stood, unable to face the ordeal of finding a blacksmith or a buyer for the beast. He walked along the road, his frozen feet slipping on the cobbles. The boys' mockery became more comprehensible: they imitated the unsteady gait of the drunkard, brandishing imaginary wine bottles in his face.

At last he realized he could go no further. *You are just attempting to reduce everyone to your own level of foulness and depravity* . . . and she had been right, and he would die in a foreign gutter, alone and nameless. He leant against a doorway, his breath coming in great clouded gasps, steadying himself by holding the iron lion head that served as a door knocker. His tormentors were nearer now; they would take the silk handkerchief from his pocket, and the few coins, and then, emboldened by his lack of resistance, his rapier, dagger, and pistol. And he did not care. Then, he could sleep.

But there was something familiar about the door. He had found his way, unthinking. A little more battered and weatherworn than when he had seen it last, but the lion's head was the same. With what remaining strength he had, he beat his ice-cold fist on the wood, praying that Madame Berthe would still be in business, that she would not yet have left Calais for the little farm she had so often spoken of.

It took several minutes for the door to open, and for Galliers to make out the hazy, swirling, figures of the concierge and Madame Berthe. He had just time before he clattered to the floor in front of them to reflect, with wry amusement, that three years ago he had arrived here in a very similar fashion.

Only, that time he *had* been drunk.

'Méchant fils!' Madame put down the tray she had been carrying. 'You should be in bed.'

Richard Galliers pulled his shirt over his head. 'I will gladly return there, chère Berthe, if you will come with me.'

Berthe, blond, plump and forty, sat beside him on the edge of the bed, taking his long brown hand in her small white one. 'Malheureusement, I have the baker and the butcher coming this morning, and Toinette will not dust the parlour properly unless I watch her all the time. Perhaps in the afternoon, mon petit, and then we will know you are fully recovered.'

Berthe watched him as he fastened the black doublet, now neatly washed and mended, over his shirt. She had had no hesitation about taking Richard Galliers in and giving him one of her best rooms, after finding him soaking and exhausted on her doorstep. She owed the *beau anglais* a favour; there had been the episode of the sailor who had not felt he had been given his money's worth, all those years ago, and Richard Galliers, newly arrived, silent, and unapproachable, had prevented him from venting his spleen on one of Madame Berthe's prettier girls. Besides, even if it had not been for that, she still retained a weakness for a handsome face. There were new scars on his body; she had seen that when, unaided, she had stripped him of his wet clothes and put him in her comfortable bed. And there was the shoulder wound – neatly bandaged, but the result of a pistol shot, there was no doubt about that. He had slept for two days, and she had let him, for by a glance at the pale, darkly shadowed face, she had suspected that it was sleep, rather than physic, that he needed. She had kept the girls from the room, much to the frustrated curiosity of Marie-Ange, Georgine and Hortense, because she had a strong suspicion that when a gentleman from England arrives alone, horseless, and injured, in a foreign country, he is unlikely to wish to broadcast his coming too publicly.

'Are the ships putting out to sea yet?' Galliers, fully dressed, looked out of the window. The gale, of which the *Eglantine* had only caught the beginnings, had reached its terrible height over the last two days, and now, having battered moored ships against the quayside, seemed to have spent itself.

'I think so, petit. The men from the *Henrietta* left this morning.'

'I wish to write a letter.' Galliers turned away from the window. 'Do you know of anyone I could trust to take a letter to England?'

She thought for a moment. 'I will find out for you, chéri. A letter, perhaps, to be delivered in person?'

His eyes glinted. 'And a reply to be waited for. I will pay well, of course – there is gold sewn into the hem of my cloak.'

Berthe smiled, and nodded her fair head. 'I know, Richard. I have unpicked it and put it away safely for you. You do not know what sort of a person you may find in a place like this.' She opened the door. 'There is writing equipment in the bureau. I will find someone to take your letter for you.'

It was a very short letter, terse and uninteresting, and it was addressed to Lord Amyott, of Amyott Hall, Essex, England. It assured him that his brother was well, and hoped that his lordship was in a similarly happy condition. It then went on to enquire as to the health of their neighbours, and finished by asking whether it would be acceptable for the writer of the letter to pay a visit to his home. It was signed, simply, R.G.

The brevity of the letter gave no indication of the amount of thought that had gone into writing it. On waking in Madame Berthe's bed in Calais, and finding himself recovered, and with an arm that felt almost capable of holding the reins of a horse, or the hilt of a dagger, Richard Galliers' immediate impulse had been, still, to go south. His sense of having only just avoided disaster was strong; it seemed preferable in every way simply to abandon friends, enemies, his country of birth, rather than attempt to continue to untangle the Gordian knot of his past. It was not that the thought of travel filled him with pleasure, or excitement. But he could find friends if he wanted company, he knew women if he wanted lovers, and there were still new places to see if he wanted interest. There were some other places, ports particularly, he must be careful to avoid, but that should not prove difficult. He would return to England no more, there had been nothing for him there, and he had been foolish to think there might have been. As soon as the weather improved he would go to the harbour and find a suitable, seaworthy boat.

But he had not done so. Instead, as his strength increased, so had the small nagging memories that he had pushed to the back of his mind. A black-haired girl, with the dark blue eyes that only those of the Celtic races possessed; himself saying to her, 'You will have to concoct your own story . . .' and a smile that fought against tears as she told him not to worry. A child, no more, but there had sometimes been a strange peace in her company. And an awareness that, although he had not lied to her, neither had he told her the whole truth. Particularly, an uneasy suspicion that he should have warned her more specifically against Carleton. He had a vague memory of trying to do so before he had collapsed with the fever, but he could not recall exactly what he had said. He could remember what he had *intended* to say, but was uncertain how much he had actually spoken. And later, when he had realized he must explain the whole messy business of Reynardine to her, he had cravenly baulked at reliving the affairs of three years past. There were things he had not even told Giles. But somehow, over the course of the last week, his conviction that it was none other than Carleton who was the disaffected accomplice of the Countess of Somerset had become unshakeable. The distance from Hinxton to Kingscote, and his own unacknowledged ambivalence in facing the implications of the possibility, had combined to distract him from the truth. But someone – Carleton, Conway or Murray – had wished to rid themselves of him at the Countess's banquet, and someone had warned Lionel Ellenby to have no more to do with him. And if it was Carleton, it fitted with what he already knew of the man's character and finances. Carleton would be the first rat to leave any ship that showed signs of sinking. Mall Conway must be told of his suspicions, and, reluctant though he was, he must no longer shirk the task of telling her of Sir Nicholas's past involvement with Amyott.

One more trip to England was therefore required, providing

his masquerade had not been uncovered, and he was still free to come and go without fear of the hangman. The letter to Giles would ascertain that, and if a visit proved feasible, he would go and see the Conways under some pretext.

Taking the letter, Galliers left the room and went down the narrow crooked staircase. The house was quiet – it was midday, and most of the establishment's business took place at night. Two of the girls were seated at the foot of the staircase, sharing a plateful of biscuits between them. Hortense, red-haired, hazel-eyed, and incurably greedy, looked up at him as he stopped behind them.

'Monsieur has recovered?'

He smiled and inclined his head.

'Fully recovered, thank you, Mademoiselle,' he said in French. 'I am looking for Madame. Can you tell me where I can find her?'

Hortense patted the stair next to her. 'Madame is in her parlour. But perhaps you would like to sit with us for a while?'

Galliers shook his head, his slanting eyes meeting Hortense's hazel ones. 'It would be a pleasure, Mademoiselle, but no. Madame and I have business to discuss.'

She moved aside and he stepped between them, and went to knock on the parlour door. Before he closed the door behind him, he heard Hortense's indolent voice:

'Quel dommage! Comme il est beau – et ardent!'

And Marie-Ange added in her gentle voice, 'Which is why Madame will keep him to herself, chérie.'

Inside the parlour, Madame, wearing a loose cream robe trimmed with lace and pale blue ribbons, was seated at a small table.

'You have written your letter? Good. I have found someone to take it for you. You will pay him ten louis d'or when he leaves, and ten more when he returns with your reply. The weather is uncertain at present, you will be here some weeks, I think.'

She took the letter Galliers handed to her, and put it into her bureau drawer. 'But we will pass the time quite agreeably, n'est ce que pas? First, you will share a little dejeuner with me, and then –' Berthe's plump hand stroked the side of his neck, and continued down inside the linen shirt that he wore, gently caressing the shoulder that had halted the flight of Joshua Joe's bullet. 'Then I will see whether you have really recovered your strength . . .'

It took almost a month for Giles's reply to be delivered into Richard's hands. Quite an agreeable month in some respects, if you had no objection to colourful days and even more colourful nights. Madame Berthe's business ebbed and flowed with the tides: a fair wind, and the lion's head door knocker would beat a drumroll of military proportions; a storm, and custom would trickle away like sea water from the bilges as the mariners ran out of money.

During Richard Galliers' stay, the weather had been particularly poor. He had melted as easily into the life of the Rue St Louis brothel as he had three years ago, helping Philippe kick the more cantankerous customers into the street in the early hours of the morning, amusing the girls on dull wet afternoons. In the course of the month the wound in his shoulder had healed completely, and he had continued, much to the chagrin of Hortense, to occupy Madame Berthe's best room. And Madame Berthe herself, with only a fleeting regret for youth, beauty and lost illusions, had been content enough to administer what advice and good French food he would take by day, and what physical comfort they both required by night.

The letter, when it arrived, was as brief and dull as Richard's own. It assured him of the health of his family and all their neighbours, and intimated that a visit to Amyott would not be inconvenient. It was signed, succinctly, *Amyott*, and sealed with the family's emblem. Richard looked at the letter for a moment, then crumpled it into a ball and threw it in the fire.

He had had some new clothes made for him whilst in Calais. Now he threw his few possessions in a bag, and went downstairs to take his leave of Madame Berthe.

'Madame – the *Falcon* sails for England on the next tide. I will go with her.'

She studied him shrewdly. 'You are impatient to go back to her – your "Mall". I understand.'

Annoyance flickered in the green eyes, and Galliers frowned. Berthe put her hand on his arm, and said comfortingly:

'Do not glower so, petit. You spoke her name in your sleep. I was uncertain at first of whether it was a man or woman of which you dreamt – these English names are so strange – but I think it must be a woman.'

He pulled her towards him. 'Mall is just a girl,' he said, dismissively. 'But *you* are a woman, Berthe, and I will miss you desperately.' He hugged her, and saluted each plump white cheek. Then he was gone, and she watched from the doorway as he strode, bag in hand, towards the quayside.

Most men were regarded by Madame Berthe with a sort of amused tolerance, but for Richard Galliers she found she felt a little more.

'A girl? Pouf!' she said, and shut the door.

The *Falcon*, a decidedly superior vessel to the unlamented *Eglantine*, reached Dover in the late afternoon. Richard Galliers found a passable tavern in which to spend the night, and bought a horse – a lively, good-tempered bay – to take him to London the following day. He would go to Holborn and see Esmé, he decided. Esmé would put him up for the night, and fill in the events of his month of absence. Then, if all went to plan, he would set off for Cambridgeshire early the next morning and call on the Conways. Somehow he should be able to find a few moments alone with Mall, warn her against Carleton, and then, his conscience appeased, he could return to Dover, calling briefly, perhaps, at Amyott, en route.

The ride to London was pleasant enough; although the weather was still very cold, there was little wind, and only a light sprinkling of snow on the ground. The streets of London were busy – it was New Year, Galliers realized – and he was relieved to see the candlelight showing dimly through the old shutters of Esmé's rooms.

His welcome was warm. He was given food and ale, and offered a seat next to the fire. Molyneux wisely refrained from asking too many questions, talking instead of the news of the past month. Giles was also in London, Richard was told, and might call at the Holborn Street rooms that evening. He himself had not been short of visitors – Sir Thomas Conway (Richard was acquainted with him?) had called on him that very morning, staying some considerable time. Esmé shared an interest in the revolutionary ship Sir Thomas was constructing, and Conway had visited to show him the plans as soon as he returned from the country. Yes, Sir Thomas had been absent from town for some weeks – a family celebration, Esmé thought.

At that, Richard Galliers had put down the tankard from which he had been drinking, and had requested, pleasantly, further information as to the nature of the celebrations. Molyneux was not sure. A wedding, perhaps?

It took Galliers only as long as it takes to clasp on a cloak and cover his head with a hat, to discover Sir Thomas Conway's London address. Then, courteously thanking Esmé for the half eaten food and the scarcely drunk ale, he departed, leaving Esmé staring after him with a troubled expression on his face.

It did not take him long to reach Sir Thomas Conway's house on the North Bank. He had pushed and shoved his way through the crowds, the unpleasant cold fear in his stomach giving him little patience with any delay. And the anger in the hard emerald eyes, and the hand that hovered, itching, near the hilt of his rapier, encouraged those who saw him to move quickly from his path.

He was admitted to a large timber and plaster house, and shown to Sir Thomas's study. Conway was seated at the desk, correcting some papers. He looked up when Richard was announced.

'Mr Galliers? Come in – fetch some wine for us, if you please, Hobden.'

The servant left, and Galliers walked over to the desk. His voice was perfectly calm, but a more observant man than Sir Thomas might have noticed the lack of a smile or conventional greetings.

'I attended Lady Conway's banquet at Belford at the end of November, sir. I had the pleasure of meeting your daughter there. I hear that she is married now?'

Sir Thomas put down his pen. 'That is correct. Mall was married three days ago. I have only just been able to return to Court.'

'And who, sir,' interrupted Galliers, his mouth dry, 'is the happy bridegroom?'

Sir Thomas' eyes returned to the papers. 'The bridegroom? Oh, she did well, there, very well. After that business of the highwayman – Reynardine, you've heard of the scoundrel? I had expected her to remain a spinster for the rest of her days.' He frowned. 'The foolish girl would not say where she'd been, who he was, or – or what he'd done. Well –' the door opened, and the manservant entered the room carrying a tray. 'Who would wed her after that? Anything could have happened. I had not expected such behaviour of Mall, I must admit. But in the end, to our surprise, she did well.'

Sir Thomas paused, shuffling through the papers in front of him. Galliers resisted the temptation to shake the information from him.

Sir Thomas looked up. 'Yes, she did well, Mr Galliers. Just three days past Mall was wed to Sir Nicholas Carleton.'

When the heavy oak door closed behind him, and Richard Galliers stepped out into the street, Esmé was waiting.

It was snowing again; white crystals gathered on the gold braid of Molyneux's hat, and settled in the many-layered folds of the cuffs of his plush suit.

'Richard?'

For just a fraction of a second, looking into the dark, arrogant face, he thought that Galliers was going to hit him.

'I merely wished to assure myself that you were – all right.'

Galliers smiled humourlessly, violence brightening his eyes. 'Perfectly all right, my dear Esmé. In fact,' he covered his ruffled hair with his hat, 'I'm going to celebrate.'

It would not be wise to place a comforting hand on that taut shoulder. 'Perhaps,' said Esmé carefully, 'perhaps Giles and I might share your celebrations.'

'I don't think so.' Richard spoke softly, almost unheard above the cries of the street-sellers, and the laughter issuing from a nearby tavern. 'I, my dear Esmé, am going to get utterly and stinkingly drunk. Alone.'

And he was gone, disappearing into the black of the London night before Esmé could follow him.

Simeon Merrowby, from his shadowed corner in the main room of the Dagger, eyed the dark gentleman again. He undoubtedly was a gentleman – the cut of his clothes and the elaborate filigree work on the hilt of his rapier told Simeon that, and his purse was indisputably full. He had played one short game of hazard an hour or so after his arrival in the tavern, disastrous for his opponent, and he could not yet have drunk quite all of his winnings away. He had drunk a considerable quantity, though. Simeon watched him covertly, noting the dark green front of his velvet doublet, and the good quality lace trimmed silk shirt beneath. The hat was good, too. Simeon's thief's eyes brightened as he saw the pearl clasp that held the plume to the felt. And the gloves – embroidered, tasselled, and jewelled – must alone be worth a good few crowns. He lounged like a drunken man, one arm around one of the prettier whores, and ordinarily, Simeon Merrowby, cutpurse, would have felt the time was ripe.

But there was something about the dark-haired gentleman that made Simeon hold back. He was reminded of a big cat he had seen in the menagerie at the Tower; prowling, watching, waiting for an excuse to kill. A short while ago an inebriated wintering soldier had slipped, accidentally, against the gentleman's arm, knocking the tankard that he held. The man's other indolent, beringed hand had gone instantly to the thin dagger sheathed at his side, and there had been no hint of any slowness in his reaction. And Merrowby had noticed, with his thief's keen observation, the murderous look in the gentleman's eyes, the glint of pleasure at the prospect of an outlet for violence. As it was, the soldier had been merry, had made his apologies, and had bought the gentleman another tankard of thick, dark Dagger ale. And the gentleman's eyes had flickered once, and emptied themselves of hatred or any other emotion, and he had allowed the fair-haired whore to caress him again. No, he would wait, thought Simeon Merrowby. He had seen others like that, and sooner or later the man would drink his anger into unconsciousness. Then the whores and the cutpurses would divide the spoils between them. But he, Simeon Merrowby, would have the clasp from his hat, he would make sure of that.

It took Giles Galliers, coming alone into the smoky dark fog of the Dagger, several minutes to see his brother. He stood in the doorway, his hand on the hilt of his sword, his brown eyes searching the room as they had already searched similar rooms in the Mitre, the Mermaid, and the Three Cranes in the Vintry. There he had found nothing, and he had been beginning to conclude that Richard's inclination to drink alone must mean several bottles in some whores' slum or the quickly rented room of a tavern. But the Dagger, of course – when Giles had remembered the Dagger's existence, he had been almost sure of finding him there.

He saw Richard, on a bench at the back of the room, his green velvet slovenly, a dark-haired girl filling up his tankard to one side, and a fair-haired one nestled into his shoulder on the other. The rest of the tavern was as crowded as on Giles's last visit, and the clientele looked no more salubrious than on that occasion. Setting his mouth, no humour for once on his pleasant face, Giles crossed the room.

Richard looked up as Giles approached. 'God's teeth, another nursemaid.' His speech was still clear, only the faint note of exhilaration confirmed Giles's suspicion that Richard was, as he had promised, stinkingly drunk. 'Ladies, let me present my elder brother, Lord Amyott. There's a dark one for you, Giles, and a fair one for me. If you remember, I prefer blondes.'

Giles ignored him. 'Esmé was concerned for you. Perhaps you should come back to his lodgings.'

Richard stretched out his legs to rest them on the low table in front of him. 'As you see, Giles, I am quite content to remain where I am. Beautiful ladies –' he indicated the women at his side, '– unlimited liquor, and a good prospect of a fight before the evening is out. What more could I want?'

Giles lowered himself to sit on the edge of the table. He said, quietly, so that none other in the crowded room should hear it:

'And I suppose tomorrow you'll leave the country again, and we'll not see you for another three years.'

'Ten, this time.'

'Well, that'll be no great loss to any of us. It was always your answer, to run away, wasn't it, little brother?'

Richard's eyes hooded instantly, but Giles saw the tightening of his hands. Carefully, Richard placed his tankard on the table, and then leaned back and looked up at Giles.

'I merely happen to know when I am not needed, a quality in which other members of our illustrious family are sorely lacking.'

But Giles would not let go. He knew he had angered Richard then: had needled him as effectively as when in long wet childhood days they had fought over a broken toy, a half imagined slight. But now the causes were not trivial, not imagined.

Lovingly, Giles twisted the knife. 'Did England fail to offer sufficient excitement for you, brother? A little tame after the Continent, perhaps? The Red Bull's stage wasn't big enough – you needed a wider audience, didn't you, Richard?'

Giles stood up. 'So you are content to sit here and drink Miss

Conway's – sorry, Lady Carleton's – health. Well, I'll leave you to it. It must be gratifying for you to have arranged that match so successfully.'

He made the mistake of turning away before he had finished speaking. Richard's hands were around his throat before Giles fully understood the significance of the table that crashed to the ground, soaking the floor with ale, and the curse from the fair-haired whore as she slipped to the floor, landing hard on her bony rump. Giles managed to jab an elbow into Richard's stomach, and to twist round during the momentary slackening of his grip. Breathing heavily, light in his narrowed brown eyes, he hissed:

'You wanted a fight, Richard. But perhaps not in here – unlike you, I am not used to washing my dirty linen in quite such sordid surroundings.'

The grip on his neck slackened, and Richard's hands fell to his sides. He glanced once round the room – at the thieves who waited to seize any rich pickings from a quarrel, at the gamblers who had barely paused in their games at the sound of a struggle, at the tapster who stood, cudgel in hand, ready to prevent any damage to his property. Richard nodded slowly, picked up his hat from where it had fallen to the floor, and, pushing past Giles, headed for the doorway.

Simeon Merrowby watched the two gentlemen leave the tavern. He felt sorry to have lost the pearl hat clasp, but did not regret failing to filch it earlier. There would be blood spilled before the night was out, and he was glad that it would not be his.

Out in the street, there was no sign of the watch. It was still snowing, a light dust that floated through the cold air, barely settling. Giles and Richard rounded the corner until they were out of sight of the Dagger, and then faced each other, their breath turning to white vapour in the cold night air.

'Perhaps we should discard our rapiers.' Giles's hands fumbled with the resisting metal buckle. 'After all –'

'Another bloodied son deposited on Mother's doorstep might not be such a good idea?' Only Richard's small crooked smile could be seen: the rest of his face was hidden under the dark shadow of his hat.

'I did not mean –'

He never finished. Richard's rapier and his Italian dagger thudded against the stone side of the horse trough. His cloak and hat fell in the filth at the side of the street, and the blow that landed in Giles' stomach knocked most of the breath from his body.

'I do not intend to *kill* you, Giles – just to ensure that you keep to your estate, making love to your obliging lady friend, leaving me to whatever sty I choose to wallow in.'

Giles, prone in the mud, his guts threatening to spew themselves from his body, felt all his anger and resentment return in double quantity. Spitting the dirt from his mouth, he pulled himself into a sitting position.

'What, only insults this time, brother? No apt quotation? I thought you had a poem for every occasion, a song for every misfortune – isn't that right, Richard?' Giles's face was ugly as he staggered to his feet. 'What song for this occasion, Richard? There must be *something* about seducing little girls, and leaving them to suffer the consequences.'

The satisfying sensation of his fist contacting with Richard's jaw gave Giles immense pleasure, and the blood that Richard wiped with the back of his hand from his split lip delighted him. The contemptuous smile had already gone from that too-familiar countenance by the time Giles hurled his greater weight and height on top of his brother, and they both fell to the ground, heedless of the snow and mud.

It was a gutter dwellers' fight; nothing of the courtier remained as they grabbed whatever came to hand, slipping in the thin dirt, shadowed by the overhanging walls of the houses that lined the road. The back of Giles's head reverberated painfully on the cobbles, his boot kicked Richard's knee, his hand clutched dark hair to batter the side of that infuriating face into the plastered wall.

In the end, it was Giles' sobriety and his recent work of supervising the construction of a fallen stable roof that won the fight for him. Weeks of helping to haul heavy timbers to the top of a ten-foot wall gave him a superiority over an evening of heavy drinking and a month in a French whorehouse. They had gained their feet again, their boots failing to grip the churned-up surface of the street, when Giles, his breath coming in great heaving gulps, managed to hit Richard exactly where he wanted to – under the chin. He caught him as he slipped, half stunned, grabbed the slight green-velvet shoulders, forced him to his knees, and thrust the dark, muddied, bloodied head through the thin layer of ice that covered the water in the horse trough.

Giles, gasping for breath, held him there until the struggles quietened, and he himself became conscious of the pain that drummed, cold and previously unnoticed, at the back of his own head. Then, when the threshing limbs had just relaxed, he took a handful of cold, soaking cloth, and hauled Richard out.

'And if you ever say anything – *anything* – like that about Anna again, I will bring you back here, and make damn sure to keep you under water for a good five minutes more!' Giles sat down, his back to the horse trough, one hand gingerly feeling his ribs to see if they were still intact. Richard collapsed beside him, his hair plastered wetly to his head, the blood that flowed from his lip and forehead mingling with the icy water that dripped from his face. Eyes wide open, his shirt torn, the green velvet muddy and crushed, he stared at Giles, struggling, half-drowned, for breath.

'God, Giles.' He pushed some of the wet hair out of his eyes. 'You always did like to make your point.'

Giles' eyes, still angry, met Richard's. He took in the sodden clothes, the battered face, and felt something close to triumph. He groped for his handkerchief, and dabbed it cautiously at the back of his head. 'I've wanted to do that several times over the past months. You can be so damned insulting.'

Richard shook his head, spraying droplets of water into the cold air. 'I apologise for the remark about Anna.' He staggered to his feet, holding the edge of the horse trough for support, brushing some of the mud and filth from his clothes. 'It was unnecessary – and untrue. But for the record, Giles –' unsteadily, he picked up his weapons from the ground, and began to buckle on his rapier '– I did not seduce Mall. I swear I didn't lay a finger on the girl.'

But that was beside the point. Giles said harshly:

'But you abducted her, didn't you? *Why*? I know the wager was as much my fault as yours, but why not stop it there? You seem to have lost all sense of decency, Richard. Have your sport with Ellenby and others like him if that is what you have come to, but for God's sake, you have ruined that girl's reputation. She was alone with you – God knows where – for three days and three nights!'

The anger had gone from Richard's face, leaving only hopelessness.

'In other words, it doesn't matter a damn whether I deflowered her or not, the result is the same. Reynardine would have raped her, Richard Galliers would have debauched her.' The split lip was beginning to swell, blurring his speech as the alcohol had failed to do. 'Giles. Mall found me searching her father's study. She recognized me, so I took her to a place I know in the Fens – to buy some time. I had intended to send her back immediately, by which time I should have been on my way to France. But her steward was too damned good a shot, and the whole thing went wrong.' He began to walk up the street. 'It was an unutterable bloody disaster . . .' He turned to Giles, and, hat in hand, made a flourishing mockery of a bow. 'What should I have done, Giles? Gone down on one knee and offered her my hand in marriage? Protected Miss Conway's sullied name by offering her my own?'

They both heard the footsteps behind them, and saw the yellow glow of lanterns. Picking their cloaks out of the mud, Giles drew level with Richard, and said patiently, 'I doubt if you will repair matters by drinking the Dagger dry. And I still don't see why you were at Belford in the first place.'

They turned the corner, away from the watch. Richard caught the cloak that Giles threw at him. 'It is too late to repair matters. Mall was wed to that bastard Carleton three days ago, and I – I, in my conceit, miscalculation, and stupidity – as you so rightly pointed out, forced her to it.' He smiled thinly. 'You see, it is not only the Ellenbys of this world who will throw themselves at my feet if required. Mall seems to have acquired some sort of attachment for me – it appears she wished to protect me. Thinking to save her sly, bold highwayman from a colourful if uncomfortable end at the gibbet, she told her father nothing of what happened in the Fens. And her father, fearing further scandal, was only too thankful to give her to that most opportune suitor, Sir Nicholas Carleton.'

The back of Giles's head hurt, and he had the uncomfortable suspicion that one of his ribs was cracked. He said, irritably:

'So why lose your temper when you find out she had been married to Carleton? You don't want the girl, so of what consequence is her marriage to you? It's considered to be a good match. Carleton may have improved somewhat over the years.'

'My God, your memory is short!' Richard spoke bitterly, lowering his voice as a group of revellers passed them, singing as they went.

Giles looked at him sharply. 'I did not mean that I had forgotten Jeremy – or his involvement with Carleton. But we are all different people from what we were three years ago. You were away a long time, Richard.'

'And yet Carleton still flaunts Jeremy's latest substitute.'

'Lucas Holland?'

Richard nodded.

Giles frowned and said: 'But if he has taken a wife no doubt he means to finish his involvement with the boy.'

Richard's eyes met Giles's. 'Does he? In my experience, Carleton does not willingly give up any of his collection.'

The conversation had taken an uncomfortable turn. Giles had to force himself to reply.

'He gave up Jeremy.'

Richard's words, as he strode ahead of Giles, turning the corner into the next alleyway, were almost inaudible.

'And made damn sure no other would want him.'

And made damn sure no other would want him . . . Giles stood unmoving, frozen not by the bitter cold, but by a suspicion that had remained unvoiced, trapped at the back of his mind for more than three long years. Richard was almost out of sight: Giles ran forward and grasped his shoulders, forcing his back against the wall, searching for the unwelcome truth in those changeable green eyes.

'What in hell are you saying?' The dialogue had become unreal, obscene against the background of laughter and song that issued from a nearby tavern.

There was something almost akin to laughter on Richard's face. Almost.

'God damn it, Giles, did you believe Jeremy's death was an accident? An anonymous street fight, with Jeremy as the chance victim?'

Giles could hardly speak. 'Go on.'

His taut hands still gripped wet green velvet, but Richard did not struggle.

'Not an accident, Giles – oh, no. They did not hurt *me*, Giles, did they? They held me and made me watch while they beat him almost to death. Jeremy was a good looking boy – you remember *that*, don't you, Giles? – but he'd lost his looks forever by the time they'd finished with him. And not a scratch on *my* face – clever, that, wasn't it, Giles?'

The calm broke: Richard flung off Giles's hands, and hissed:

'It was Carleton, I tell you, *his* men, sent with very specific instructions, carried out to the letter!'

The colour drained from Giles's bruised face. His hands dropped limply to his sides. 'Carleton – was responsible for Jeremy's death –' His voice was odd, not like Giles's.

'Carleton did not only corrupt Jeremy. When he found he could no longer have him, he murdered him.'

The tension suddenly went from him, and Richard said flatly, 'I knew one of the faces. I couldn't place it at first, but then I saw the man talking to Carleton's steward. By that time, Carleton could afford to be careless – even to taunt me, if he wished. He knew that he had won.'

196

Giles still did not move. He said, 'So you knew this – before you went away?'

A pause, and then Richard nodded: a single, damning assent.

'And you did not see fit to tell me?' Giles's fist beat once, heavily and uselessly, against the wall. 'For God's sake, Richard – he was *my* brother too!'

He closed his eyes, resting his forehead against the chilly plaster of the house. It was sickening – foul.

Richard said softly at his shoulder:

'I don't recall there being much rational conversation at that time. Our mother was hysterical, our father blind drunk. You were not to be found at first, Giles, and by the time you did turn up, the damage was done. And Kingscote – Kingscote can be impenetrable. Place sufficient men around its perimeter, and you've got yourself a fortress. I did go to Kingscote with some foolish idea of confronting Carleton, and was forcibly ejected before I so much as reached the door. I returned to Amyott to receive much the same treatment from my father – disinherit-ance, go and never darken my doors again, you know the sort of thing. I expect he would have been as physically abusive as Carleton's servants had been if he could have remained on his feet for long enough. After all, we had never been exactly close. And by that time rumours had been well spread around our neighbours. Bleating incoherently about it being someone else's fault did not seem too promising. I had more doors shut in my face during the weeks following Jeremy's funeral than I have had since I was fourteen and attempted to court a woman twice my age.'

Giles did not look at him. Jeremy's funeral – he remembered every detail of it – an intolerable, rain-swept November day. Lady Amyott haggard, wraithlike; Lord Amyott tear-sodden, drunk, ridiculous.

He said stiffly: 'I know that there were rumours. That you were responsible for Jeremy's death. That you corrupted him. That you were a coward. But hell, Richard, could you not have trusted *me*?'

The snow had begun to fall thickly, settling on the shoulders of Richard's cloak. Slowly, as if forcing the unwilling words from his mouth, he said:

'But I *was* responsible for Jeremy's death.' Giles's bent head jerked up. 'No – not as Carleton put it about – but it was *I* who took him away from Carleton, *I* who brought him back to Amyott. I underestimated Carleton – I miscalculated then just as much as I have now miscalculated with Mall Conway.'

The watch rounded the corner. The brothers began to walk again, Giles unsteady in the mud and snow that smeared the street. They stopped outside Molyneux's lodgings in Holborn Street, where the soft glow of candlelight from the badly fitting shutters illuminated the snow gathering in the gutters. It was bitterly cold, but Giles no longer noticed. There had been things, he was forced to admit, that he had avoided facing, avoided thinking about. Three years previously he had seen his family almost destroyed. He had watched one brother die, and seen another exiled, perhaps forever. Slowly, carefully, over the past year he had begun to pick up the pieces, to gather together the fragments of a better future.

He said thickly: 'So what now? We must bring Carleton to justice.'

Richard grabbed Giles's hand, staying him from using the door knocker.

'Not "we", Giles, "I". If anyone is to send Sir Nicholas to the headsman or to put a bullet through his brain, it will be I, and I alone. I have earned that right, I have bought it with three years exile. You have Anna and Mother and Amyott – keep them, and leave this to me. I have no ties or loyalties to hold me back.'

Angrily, Giles banged the door knocker. 'So what do you propose to do? You called Kingscote a fortress. What can you do now that you could not do three years ago?'

The first genuine smile of the evening lit his brother's beaten face. 'Carleton has been party to other crimes besides that of Jeremy's death. Reynardine's first victim, the Countess's messenger, presented me with the key: a nice, enigmatic, *useful* piece of information. I, my dear Giles, am arranging a beautiful and poetic justice for Sir Nicholas Carleton. That was why I was at Belford and at Saffron Walden. I had to be sure before I moved against him.'

The door opened.

Richard said softly, as they crossed the threshold: 'I am going to persuade one of Carleton's erstwhile friends to betray him. The red queen will checkmate the white king. But first – first I must call on Lady Carleton.'

CHAPTER NINE

An evil spirit, your beauty haunts me still,
Wherewith, alas, I have been long possessed,
Which ceaseth not to tempt me to each ill,
Nor gives me once but one poor minute's rest.

(DRAYTON)

S*EATED* by the fire in the draughty hall at Kingscote, embroidering gold thread around the cuff of a sleeve intended for a new gown, Mall, for the first time in three months of marriage, allowed her thoughts to wander. Sir Nicholas was still at the table; his friend, Mr Holland, had arrived from London that morning, so she could reasonably hope that the encroachments into the bottles of Kingscote's best wine would continue for some time yet.

She pushed the needle through the delicate cream coloured material where tiny exquisite flowers blossomed around the hem of the cuff. There were two rings on her hands. One, on the third finger of her left hand, was an enamelled hoop, set inside with three small diamonds. I take thee, Nicholas, for husband . . . and she was back in Belford's cold chapel, wearing Alice's hastily adjusted russet silk wedding gown, her hair loose to her waist, a garland of ivy and evergreens from Alice's garden crowning her head. Lover's knots of Conway green and Carleton blue and gold had been stitched to the gown, and the pearls Mall had worn at Alice's banquet had been strung round her neck. The ceremony had been quick; the guests few. A hurried, quiet wedding was what Carleton had stipulated, and, fearing to let the fine fish her stepdaughter had netted slip through her net, Alice had reluctantly agreed.

Mall had felt nothing there, standing in the chapel, repeating the vows that would bind her to this stranger for life. Neither had she felt anything when, after a strained and difficult parting with her father and stepmother, she had ridden over the crest of the hill and had her first sight of Kingscote, golden and perfect, her future home. The house was beautiful, she had been able to recognize that; its proportions and stone as natural a part of the shallow Essex valley as the ancient wood that covered the twenty acres to its side. Kingscote was immaculate; if Sir Nicholas was capable of feeling love, then Mall knew that it was love he felt for Kingscote, nothing else. There were no cobwebs to be seen inside the house, no weeds to jar the symmetry of the extensive gardens outside. And although some of the paintings and hangings were contemporary, they had been chosen with a collector's eye, to complement and enrich their surroundings.

Sometimes, during the endless, unfamiliar weeks that followed, Mall had suspected that that was how her husband thought of her: as a collector's item. They had dined together on their arrival at Kingscote, and at the end of the meal Sir Nicholas had dismissed the servant, leaving them alone in the withdrawing room with its frieze of painted musicians and dancers. The painted revellers, with their stiff Henry Tudor clothes and their winding stylized leaves and flowers, had watched with blank, pitiless eyes as Sir Nicholas had beckoned Mall out of her chair, and stood her by the fireplace. He had looked at her then as he had looked at her by the pool; and had unclasped the pearls from around her neck. There had been hunger in his dark eyes, almost desperation, and his hands had shaken slightly as he unlaced the bodice of her gown, and it had fallen from her shoulders, leaving them white and half-naked, only covered by her shift. 'Let down your hair,' he had said, and Mall, her arms stiff and cold with apprehension, had done as he had asked. Then he had stood and looked at her, small and dark, silhouetted by the orange glow of the fire, and his eyes had been as empty of love or affection as those of the painted figures frozen forever on the walls of the room.

But still she had felt nothing. Her hand went to the other ring, the one she wore on her right hand. Richard Galliers had worn the chrysoberyl on his smallest finger, but it fitted Mall's middle finger perfectly. It seemed to her that she had felt very little at all since that day at the beginning of December when Hosea Dockerill had lifted her down from his horse and left her to walk alone through Belford's main gates. Then she had experienced everything – relief, despair, a wild uncontrollable joy. Relief and joy, on Alice's and Sir Thomas's part, had rapidly changed to bewilderment, followed equally rapidly by anger. For the inventions that usually came quite easily to Mall's tongue had failed her then. If Reynardine is caught, what would happen to him? she had asked her father. Why, he'll swing for it, Sir Thomas had answered, his hand gripping his daughter's shoulder. The penalty for highway robbery is death, my dear; the fellow would be hung, drawn and quartered, and that would be the least he deserved. And she had tried to lie, to invent a highwayman and a deserted cottage, but her story had not convinced her father for a moment: they knew each other too well. When Sir Thomas realized that no satisfactory description of the highwayman or his whereabouts was to be forthcoming, the fury that he vented on Mall made him seem like a stranger to her. For a fraction of a second, then, Mall had considered explaining the whole thing to him, hoping that he would understand. But, looking at his clenched fists and red angry face, she had realized that she could not take the risk, that she must stay silent, that she must never, never tell anyone that Reynardine the Fox and Richard Galliers were one and the same.

So she said nothing more, being too tired to think of any better lies, longing only to be left alone. And left alone she was, confined to her room. The only face she saw was Lucy's anxious white one as she hastily deposited trays of food in her bed-chamber. After almost a week, Alice had come to see her. She brought Ralph, and for the first time in ten days Mall had been able to take the frail little boy on her knee, and shower on him all the hugs and kisses she was unable to offer elsewhere. She had cried at last, and it was when the slow, silent tears were flowing that Alice had told her she was to be married. For one brief ridiculous glorious moment she had imagined that it was Richard Galliers who had asked for her hand, Richard Galliers magically recovered and reformed. But the short-lived happiness had died when Alice had spoken the name of Sir Nicholas Carleton, and the frenzied beating of her heart had calmed, and she had pressed her wet cheek into Ralph's soft golden hair. She had said nothing; there was nothing she could say. Alice had repeated that it was an excellent offer, and that only marriage would silence the rumours her abduction had begun.

It was after Alice had left that Mall had burned the handkerchief, had watched that single betraying 'R' abruptly flicker in the flames, and the scrap of silk and lace twist, scorch and turn to ashes in the fire. But the ring she had kept, half despising herself, the enigmatic cat's eye a reminder that those few strange days in the Fens, that one half night in the narrow trestle bed, had really happened.

The bed to which Sir Nicholas Carleton had taken her on her wedding night had been a four-poster, carved and gilt, hung with blue and gold damask. The chamber adjoined the small withdrawing room with the painted dancers; like the rest of Kingscote it was elegant, harmonious, immaculate.

She had expected no pleasure and had found none. In the bedchamber, Sir Nicholas had watched as, one by one, she had removed her garments. Skirts, sleeves, bodice, petticoats, falling to the polished floor in a ripple of russet and green. Outside, the sounds of the servants in the courtyard and the stables, the rustle of the wind in the trees, the silence of the moat. As she had reached out to take her nightgown, he had stopped her, and instead sat her naked upon the bed.

He had not spoken then, but had looked at her for what seemed to Mall like an hour, a day, an eternity. And when he had touched her it had been to let the fine silk of her hair run through his fingers, to cradle her face in his palms and tilt it to the candlelight as though she had been a statue he inspected, assessing its worth. Only then had he let his hands run over her shoulders, her breasts, her belly and thighs. Only then had he loosened his own clothes and lain her on the bed, his breathing rushed and unsteady, his eyes void of all except his hunger. Then his hands had no longer been hesitant, careful; he had parted her thighs and forced his way into her as though it had been loathing he felt, not love; as though he sought to exorcise a demon, not welcome a wife.

If she had found no pleasure, then neither had he. She saw, glimpsing him as he finally turned from her, the dreadful emptiness in his eyes, the look almost of torment. Reaching out a hand, she had thought instinctively to comfort him, but he had recoiled at her touch, and instead trapped her hand between his two palms, pressing her fingers to his dry mouth until they hurt. She had feared him then, and she had feared him more when he had looked down at her, a small triumph in his eyes, and said:

'So whatever your highwayman did to you, it was not *that*.'

It was only when Carleton had gone, leaving her alone in the vast emptiness of the bed, that Mall had begun to feel something, to remember what she had almost had, and lost. Along with the expected physical pain had been a distress far more raw, more degrading. She had thought she had known little of love; but she found that she knew enough to be sure that what had taken place between those silken sheets had been a travesty of love. Then she had cried, her hands with the two rings, Nicholas Carleton's and Richard Galliers', pressed hard against her red and swollen face to muffle the sobs.

But by the following day, Sir Nicholas's blandness and composure had returned. He had shown her the house in the morning, every lovingly preserved room of it, and in the afternoon, the bitter weather having temporarily relented, they had ridden the bounds of the estate. Sir Nicholas and Lady Carleton had ridden ahead of their half-dozen servants, their clothes, rich deep reds and purples, trimmed with sable, flecked with the gold of chains and clasps, bright against the stark white landscape. They had travelled in silence, the only sounds the clinking of bridle and bit, the crunching of the snow beneath the horse's hooves. The sky had been a clear pale blue; the sunlight catching and sparkling on the snow like a carpet of diamonds.

But when they had begun the long ride back to Kingscote, the horses' breath white in the gathering cold, Sir Nicholas had said:

'The highwayman – Reynardine – you must tell me all you know of him, my dear. Such a rogue should not escape justice.'

Mall had given him the same lies she had given her father, and she knew that they had worked no better. Carleton had reined his horse in beside her, stroking the animal's neck with one expensively gauntletted hand, and said smoothly:

'When we find the man, you should be able to identify him. It should not prove too difficult; we know he was young, dark-haired, green-eyed –'

Mall had looked up, suddenly cold.

Sir Nicholas's eyes still bore the same unconcerned expression. 'I think we can disregard such things as red hair and trumped-up accents. He was certainly green-eyed – I spoke to Grosse, the first man he robbed, and he was most particular about that. Unusual eyes, he said, like a cat's. I am surprised you did not mention it also, my pet.'

Then he had spurred his horse, and ridden it hard back to Kingscote, and she had not seen him again until he came to her room that night.

The memory of that conversation still unnerved Mall, sitting in the Hall with her embroidery. But Sir Nicholas had not referred to Reynardine again; and he had been courteous to her, even considerate, during the three months of her marriage. The weather had been appalling, another harsh winter in a long succession of harsh winters. For most of January and February Kingscote had been blanketed under a thick fall of snow, isolated from the rest of the world. Mall had been confined within the walls of the house, and as the Hall and Gallery, with their high ceilings and vast empty spaces were always cold and draughty, she had adopted the solar as her particular retreat. It was a friendly room; its oriel window looked out over the courtyard. A window seat had been built within the semicircular oriel, and Mall could watch the comings and goings of the house through the small paned windows. If the fire was lit, and if she wore sufficient layers of petticoats, gown, doublet, and shawls, then it was really quite warm. Mall had occupied herself in the long cold weeks by sewing – the more complicated the design, the better – and by reading. Sir Nicholas's library was as extensive as her father's, and Mall had the freedom of it. In the afternoon, Sir Nicholas would sometimes play cards or chess with her. He was a good chess player, able to calculate and assess risks far in advance, and Mall was able to beat him only when one of her wilder schemes played off.

But still, despite the rides, the chess, the conversation, Mall did not feel she knew her husband at all. She had not expected love – heiresses did not marry for love – but she had hoped for friendship. He was kind enough to her, she had none of the household duties she had found so irksome at Belford (Kingscote had run quite smoothly for many years without a mistress, and would run just as smoothly with one); but she was unable to feel at ease in his presence. He did not completely trust her, she was sure of that, he was watching her, waiting for – what? Mall found that she longed for Sir Nicholas to leave for London, so that she could throw herself on the rug in front of the fire in the solar, in a less than perfect gown, and eat dates and almonds to her heart's delight whilst reading an unedifying book.

There had been few visitors since her arrival at Kingscote. Mall had seen neither her father nor her stepmother since her wedding day, and only a handful of neighbours had managed to brave the weather to gaze curiously and offer their congratulations to the newly married pair. But today, at midday, in spite of the grey, dirty snow that still lay upon the ground, a visitor had arrived. Mall had watched from the window of the solar as he had ridden into the courtyard, a solitary, bright figure, his long scarlet cloak draped over the rump of his chestnut horse, a fur-edged cap protecting his golden head from the weather. It was, she realized with a shock of recognition, the boy who had ridden with Sir Nicholas and had seen her at the pool last summer. She saw Sir Nicholas cross the courtyard and go to him, pleasure on his face, his jewelled hand touching the boy's gold silk hair.

His name was Lucas Holland, and he had, thought Mall as she offered him her hand in the Great Hall, quite the most lovely face she had ever set eyes on. He was perfect: cornflower blue eyes, a profile of Grecian purity, shoulder length hair clinging in small curls around his face. No rapier scars marred the smooth faultlessness of his countenance as they spoiled that of Richard Galliers, no shadows betrayed self-indulgence or suffering. He was tall, exquisite, and Mall disliked him on sight. There was a smile on the sculptured lips as Carleton introduced him, but no smile in the lovely blue eyes, only a look of reckoning, of assessment. They drank a cup of wine together and spoke of conventional matters, and then Sir Nicholas excused himself to Mall, explaining that he had business with Mr Holland. As they had left the room, Mall had seen the small unmistakable expression of jubilation on that Adonis face.

She had not seen her husband again that day until they had dined, the three of them together, in the parlour, in the early evening. Mall had risen from the table as soon as she could, leaving the men to their wine, and conversation which seemed to trickle mysteriously away in her presence. Later there would be music. Kingscote boasted its own musician, a small sour-looking man, whose magic at the lute and spinet were ill at odds with his expression of permanent resentment.

Tired of sewing, Mall put down her work and went to the window. Drawing the heavy curtains aside, she looked out to the still, dark moat, and allowed her thoughts to drift. Richard Galliers – Reynardine – she remembered him as she had last seen him, his hair blown about by the biting wind, wrapping her cold fingers about his ring. And, earlier in that same day, that sudden jarring realization that she had acquired some sort of affection for him, that she had allowed herself carelessly to slip into loving Richard Galliers, a man who would never be any good for her. That she no longer wanted to go home; that she wanted to be with one man, always.

But it was foolish to recall those days. She knew that, and had not allowed herself to think of Galliers since her marriage: only in her dreams had she been unable to forget him. For this was to be her life for the rest of her days – Kingscote her home; Sir Nicholas her husband; future children her joy. And if she was to be honest with herself, she must accept that Richard had felt nothing for her. He had been sorry for her – once. He had slept with her one night, but to keep her warm, not to satisfy desire or show affection. He had given her his ring . . . Mall looked at her hand again, touching the iridescent, lucent cat's eye as she had so often over the past months. He had liked her a little, perhaps, at the end: that was the most she could hope for. *I shall leave England and Reynardine will never be seen again.* That thought was bearable – just. The unbearable was that he had not reached safety, and might yet be un-masked. But in all probability, thought Mall, turning aside from the window, Richard Galliers was in some foreign country, and had forgotten her as completely as she should have forgotten him.

In the oak panelled parlour, the manservant opened another bottle of wine, and refilled the glasses of his master and his guest. Candles glittered in every corner of the room, their shadows dancing on the intricate plasterwork ceiling, enriching the colours of the draperies and hangings.

Sir Nicholas Carleton raised his glass to the golden-haired boy opposite him. 'To the future, then, Luke. To George Villiers' blossoming career, and all who may rise with him.'

Firelight reflected from the facets of the glasses, and Lucas Holland, colour in his cheeks, excitement in his azure eyes, said:

'And to your wife, Nick. She is your future.'

Carleton signalled to the manservant to leave the room. After the door had closed behind him, he said softly:

'Jealous, Lucas?' The small dark eyes rested on the boy's petulant face. 'You have no need to be, my dear. She is lovely, is she not? I could not resist it, she was there for the taking, and on such easy terms! Our highwayman did me a favour, perhaps. The addition of her dowry has been most welcome, most fortuitous. And the sight of you together! The fair and the dark, day and night, the moon goddess and the sun – the metaphors are endless. I do not require that you should *like* each other, although –' his hand caressed the bevelled stem of the glass '– if you *loved* each other, that would be perfect. I wonder I had not thought of it before. Celene and Apollo, making love in the moonlight –'

Sulkily, Holland interrupted, 'I thought you didn't trust her?'

'I don't.' There were, after all, those three days in Mall's life of which she refused to say anything. That, and an unexpected wilfulness in the girl. 'But neither do I trust you, sweet Luke. That does not prevent me appreciating your pretty charms.' There was silence for a moment, Carleton's face bland, Lucas's angry. Sir Nicholas rose, and stood behind Lucas, his hands resting on the boy's silk shoulders. 'Of the other tasks I asked you to perform for me –'

Holland looked down into his newly emptied glass, and said unwillingly, 'The rumours concerning Overbury's death are increasing. Galliers is now in England – in London. He appeared at New Year, and has since been drinking himself to death or early senility.'

Carleton fetched the bottle of wine from the buffet, and placed it beside Holland's glass. 'When you return to London, Luke, I shall come with you. I have visits to make, business to do. And Galliers –' he smiled thinly '– tell me more of him when we rejoin my wife. Do not modify your words for her sake – after all, she lived for three days with a highwayman, so we must consider her to be a woman of experience. You understand, Luke?'

The petulance had gone from the boy's lovely face. He smiled, then laughed, and poured the wine into the glass, a little of the claret spilling on to the dark oak table.

It was Lucas Holland's laughter that Mall heard, seated by the fire again, with her needlework on her lap. The musician had arrived, lute in hand, and he began to play as the two men came down the stairs and into the Hall. Carleton greeted Mall.

'You don't object if we continue to talk of London, my dear? I realize it may be a little dull for you, but Lucas has brought news of some of my acquaintances.'

They began to talk. Some of the names Mall had heard of, most she did not recognize. Soon she ceased to listen, concentrating instead on the tiny exactness of the golden flowers she formed with her needle, and the bravura runs and chords of the lute behind her.

'And the Galliers – our neighbours at Amyott. Have you news of them, Luke?'

The needle jabbed suddenly into Mall's finger, a small red ball of blood forming where the skin had been pierced. The boy's reply floated over to where she sat a little further back from the fire than the two men.

'Amyott is still attempting to patch up his tawdry estate. Apparently he hopes to become a pillar of the community when he marries. His younger brother I saw recently.'

'We speak of people my wife knows. You remember Giles and Richard Galliers, don't you, my dear?'

Mall replaced the needle, with its shining twist of gold thread, in the cloth. The calmness of her voice surprised even her. 'Galliers? Yes, I remember them. They were at Belford for my stepmother's banquet. I liked Lord Amyott, but I didn't greatly care for his younger brother. He was very rude, and drank a lot.'

And I haven't even lied, she thought grimly. Holland sniggered and continued. 'Then little has changed. I saw Richard Galliers in Whitechapel, drinking himself to the floor in a tavern. They say he has found himself a new mistress – doubtless she supplies him with money for his drinking and whoring.'

Carleton shifted in his chair to face Mall. 'I'm afraid that the entire family is dissolute. The youngest brother was knifed in a street brawl when he was fifteen. Did you know that, my dear?'

Mall could not speak. Her fingers, cold and nerveless, could no longer hold the cloth. She shook her head, knowing that watching her were two pairs of eyes: Sir Nicholas's dark, Holland's that beautiful, deep blue.

'Oh, yes, he was stabbed in the street like some common vagabond. It was his brother – Richard – who was the cause of it. He had corrupted the boy, and started some quarrel about a woman while the lad was with him. Then he was too drunk to do anything for Jeremy when he was set upon. That is why he had to leave the country, my dear. That time, the scandal was too great for him to remain in England. I am surprised he had the affrontery to come back – I doubt if his family can have wished to accept him again.'

Holland laughed again, as the manservant poured more wine in his glass. 'It seems probable that he will not be about much longer. They say he will drink himself to death – either that or catch some vile pox from one of the whores he lies with.'

'Or die knifed in a gutter squabble like his brother – an appropriate end for one with the morals of an alley cat.' At last, Sir Nicholas's gaze turned from Mall. He spoke to the musician. 'Use your voice, man, that is what I pay you for. Sing us something – a love song, perhaps. After all, we are newlyweds.'

The musician checked the tuning of his lute, and plucked a few soft chords. There was a thin line of red marring the white linen of the cuff in Mall's lap, mingling with the gold of the flowers. All that work for nothing . . . she would never wear it now. She put down the sewing, and walked to the window again, disregarding the eyes that she could feel still watching her. It had begun to snow again, large wet flakes that disappeared silently as soon as they touched the black unfriendly waters of the moat. She knew the song that the lutenist played, she had strummed it many times herself in the reassuring untidiness of Belford. Her lips moved, shaping the words as the man's unexpectedly gentle tenor voice sang:

'Since first I saw your face I resolved to honour and renown ye,
If now I be disdained I wish my heart had never known ye.
What? I that loved, and you that liked, shall we begin to wrangle?
No, no, no, my heart is fast, and cannot disentangle.'

Standing alone at the window, Mall struggled to halt the threatening tears at their source. Concentrate on the cold of the stone her clenched hands rested on, not the music. Think of the routine of the present, not the hopeless passions of the past. He was alive, and in England, that was what mattered most. But one thing she had, unavoidably, to face: whatever Richard Galliers had done, whatever Nicholas Carleton had said, Mall's heart was hopelessly, inextricably, entangled.

It should have been perfect: the dark succubus of his nights, the golden Adonis of his past, together under Kingscote's roof, at his beck and call. Except that she was not at his beck and call; she remained elusive, unobtainable. He had thought that once he possessed her the hunger would have gone; satisfied and satiated he would have been able to place Mall Conway where she belonged, a beautiful creature in a beautiful setting. But, apart from the crudest physical sense, he had not possessed her; it was she who had possessed him.

And that he did not like. Awake in the early hours of the morning in the oppressive stillness of his bedchamber, Nicholas Carleton looked down at the golden head on the pillow beside him. He should have sent the boy from his bed, have slept alone as he usually did. But when he had left his wife's room at midnight seeing, yet again, the indifference in those lovely dark eyes, he had needed company. He could have stayed with Mall, of course; for the first time slept the length of the night in his wife's bed. Except to see that indifference when he awoke . . . He recalled the previous evening when the three of them had sat together in the Great Hall. There had been both resistance and duplicity in her then, and it was these that kept her from him. Unable to bend her will to his own, he was forced into the humiliating posture of the supplicant.

He had never encountered resistance with Luke. Lucas Holland was his completely, happy enough to run errands for him in London, content to do his wishes providing his jealousy was appeased. And so had Jeremy Galliers been his. In the grey half light, Carleton rose softly from the bed, and went to the window, remembering.

Jeremy had been a beauty, too; dark-haired, like Mall, but hazel-eyed.

With increasing certainty he knew it was the episode of the highwayman that kept her from him. Something had happened then – something, someone. She had been obstinate, she had refused to tell him what he was sure she knew: the identity of Reynardine. She had not even lied particularly well, and yet he knew from the chess, the conversation, the books, she had a mind as quick as his. So she did not fear him: she did not even, perhaps, respect him.

He looked out of the window to the moat, then to the courtyard, and the stables and servants beyond. He could not remember when the conjecture that it had been Richard Galliers who had masqueraded as Reynardine had first crossed his mind. It had seemed too unlikely, too much a particularly ironic twist of fate. He still had not the slightest shred of proof, only a lingering, obsessive suspicion. But Richard Galliers had been out of the country from the end of November. The Conways' steward had thought one of his bullets had caught the highwayman. How long does it take a man to recover from a bullet wound?

In the heavy grey dawn a vision of Galliers and Mall came relentlessly into Carleton's mind. She might have tended him; those wild black curls would have brushed against that hated face, those small white hands have touched his enemy's body. If Mall was keeping her silence to protect Richard, he must not hesitate to use her to stop Galliers destroying *him*. He had been forced, in the end, to destroy Jeremy, and although it had angered and injured him to do so, it had served its purpose.

But perhaps such extreme measures would not be necessary. He turned from the window, knowing that he would sleep no more that night, knowing that he needed Mall now, but that his pride would not let him go to her. There was another way. He would wear her down slowly, her obstinacy would wither and die, and of her own free will she would tell him of the highwayman.

To Mall, riding beside Sir Nicholas Carleton in the early misty morning light, it felt as though the first faint beginnings of spring were in the air. She had slept badly for several nights, kept awake by fear of the future, by the gathering echoes of the past.

Carleton turned to her. 'You are very quiet, my dear. Perhaps this early start to the day has been too tiring for you?'

There was concern on his handsome, aristocratic face. Mall shook her head and smiled. 'Not at all – it's lovely to be out in the open air again.'

A servant rode behind them, a hooded falcon on his gauntletted hand. Sir Nicholas gestured to the falcon. 'I wanted you to see Dunyazad flown. This is the best time of day – before the sun is fully up.'

And it was the best time of day. The last of the snow had gone, and although it was still cold, the tightly furled buds and tiny snowdrops pushing through the earth held promise of warmer times to come. A soft grey mist swirled round the thin trunks of the silver birches, masking from view the frost-covered grass. Dew beaded the riders' hair and eyelashes, dampening the nodding scarlet plumes of Mall's velvet cap, patterning her red leather gloves, hanging like jewels on the bits and bridles of the horses. And in the sky the sun gleamed dully, its pale light picking out the spider webs festooning every bush and thicket.

They came out into the open, to a wide meadow dotted with a few old oaks. The mist was beginning to clear, the slight warmth from the sun starting to melt the frost. The man-servant rode forward with the falcon. The varvels of silver attached to the ends of her jesses caught and threw back the sunlight as the falconer prepared to fly her to the lure. She was a beautiful bird, proud and perfectly feathered, her yellow-brown eyes disdainful and cruel. Sir Nicholas reined in his horse beside Mall.

'She is exquisite, don't you think? Dunyazad was a ramage hawk. Do you know what that means, my dear?'

Mall shook her head. Falconry had never been one of her father's enthusiasms.

Sir Nicholas patted his restive horse, and said lightly:

'It means that she was a wild bird, a contrary creature that did not wish to be tamed. Ramage hawks are more difficult to train, but excellent birds if they can be managed.' His dark eyes looked straight at Mall. 'I shall tell you how their will is broken. First, they are handled gently so that they become familiar with their owner. They will then begin to feed on the scraps of meat offered to them. Then they are watched, day and night, kept awake and in the company of their master until their weariness breaks them. By then, my dear, their desire for independence and freedom has vanished, and they become docile. Still beautiful, still clever, but all that beauty and intelligence is put to the service of their master.'

At last Carleton's gaze turned to the falcon. Dunyazad was flying now, soaring high, a black speck in a white sky. The falconer swung the lure below. Dry-mouthed, Mall watched as the bird soared again, and perched in the topmost branch of one of the tallest oak trees. Mall did not move, but the words echoed in her head to the hurried pounding of her heart-beats: *Stay there, go free, go free*.

'She will take the lure.' At her side, Sir Nicholas spoke calmly.

And she did. As Mall watched, Dunyazad swooped and in a single breathtaking movement caught the lure.

'You see? They always do.'

The triumph in his eyes disturbed her.

'Perhaps you would like to see her at closer quarters.'

They rode forward. Dunyazad was perched on the falconer's arm again, her bright eyes hooded from view.

'Do you see these, Mall?' Sir Nicholas pointed to the silver varvels swinging from the end of the jesses. 'Now my name shall be engraved inside these. She is completely mine now, you see – she does not even desire her freedom any more.'

Three days later the weather brightened, soft intermittent rain alternating with spring sunshine, and Sir Nicholas Carleton left Kingscote for London. He took Lucas Holland with him. Mall watched from the solar as they rode over the small bridge spanning the moat, a retinue of servants behind them.

She would take advantage of the improved weather, and go for a walk. The woods beside Kingscote looked inviting, and it would be pleasant to explore them, alone. Throwing a cloak around her shoulders, Mall ran down the stairs to the Great Hall. The steward, a balding, pinched man called Matthews, joined her as she crossed the hall.

'You are going out, your ladyship?'

No, I normally dress this way when I wish to play the spinet, thought Mall crossly. But she smiled good humouredly, and replied:

'I am going for a walk. The weather is so much more pleasant –'

'Then I will come with you, your ladyship.'

'There really is no need,' Mall said, sharply. It was, after all, the freedom to be on her own again that she desired. 'I'm sure you have better things to do, and I do not intend to go out of sight of Kingscote.'

'Sir Nicholas's orders, your ladyship.' Matthews began to fasten his coat. 'He instructed me to accompany you when you went out.'

Matthews's impassive grey eyes met hers. She remembered the ramage hawk. Suddenly, the sun did not seem so bright. Proudly, Mall turned back to the stairs. 'I think it may rain again.' She fumbled with the clasp of her cloak. 'I do not think I wish to go out after all.'

And in the solar, Leah, the plump monosyllabic lady's maid, was waiting for her, needlework in hand, offering Mall her unwanted company. Mall did not attempt to refuse the offer again, for she suspected she knew what the answer would be. 'Sir Nicholas told me to make sure you were not lonely, your ladyship.' She would not court that insult twice; but a kind of revenge, sweet and apposite, occurred quickly to her. She would teach Leah chess, and Leah, she was sure, would find the game as tedious and incomprehensible as had Alice on Sir Thomas's short-lived attempt to instruct her. So Leah was ordered to abandon her needlework, and discover the fine arts of the knight's move, castling and smothered mate. I will make you play this damn game, or have you running from Kingscote's gates to plead for mercy from your precious master, thought Mall grimly, as she reiterated patiently, No, Leah, one along and one diagonal.

But what disturbed Mall, alone at night in the cold vastness of the four-poster bed, was – *why*? The lesson of the ramage hawk had been pointed in the extreme. She tried to recall what it was that Richard Galliers had said concerning Carleton, before he had collapsed in the doorway of Hosea's hut. He had implied that Carleton enjoyed the company of young men.

Mall thought of Lucas Holland, of her husband's hand touching the boy's golden hair, and she shivered again.

There were five of them, four men and a boy, riding through the soft late March rain. The track wound through the flat Essex countryside, skirting the copses, edging the fields with their patchwork of differently planted strips, rounding the occasional duckpond. The dress of the riders was uniformly chaotic; a mishmash of yellows, scarlets, greens and golds, haphazardly and over-indulgently decorated. Glorious primrose yellow doublets clashed with rough frieze cloaks, extravagantly slashed and striped breeches sat ill at ease with worn, patched leather boots.

They were not a quiet cavalcade. The boy, twelve years old and freckle-faced, sang in a pure high soprano; the older man who rode beside him occasionally joined in the chorus. Two other young men, both in their twenties, rode a little behind, deep in conversation. Only the fifth man, his long copper-coloured hair covered by a flat-brimmed, scarlet-feathered hat, was silent, riding somewhat ahead as he led the small party further into Essex.

The two young men were Nathaniel Brand and Benedict Daniel, more usually of the Red Bull playhouse in Clerkenwell. Only money – and a fairly respectable sum of it – could have drawn them from the comfort of the Red Bull to the miseries of the March countryside: both possessed sufficient luck and talent to keep them from the more precarious life of the strolling player. The Red Bull's company might still travel the roads in summer, especially if plague was rife in the city, or if the playhouse was particularly short of money, but fortune and fame were to be made in London, nowhere else.

Nathaniel Brand, a few years Benedict's senior, gestured to their silent companion ahead. 'He's quiet today, Bennet. Tried to pass the time of day with him, and I was sent away with a flea in my ear.'

Benedict Daniel, blue-eyed and auburn-haired, grinned.

'You should be thankful it was only a flea, Nat. The last time I spoke to him when he wasn't feeling conversational I ended up with his fist in my face. The dice must be rolling right for him to have financed this little expedition, and,' he added with feeling, 'I can only thank the Lord for that.'

'Which reminds me, Bennet – you still owe me for the last time I bought you out of the Marshalsea.' Nathaniel lowered his voice so that the boy – the latest of the Red Bull's long line of flat-chested, treble-voice heroines – and the older man, should not hear. 'And this small diversion, Ben – are we to be set the same task as last time?'

'Separating old women from their jewels?' Benedict's blue eyes, adored by the female half of the Red Bull's audience, sparkled. 'If only we were – but I can't think Richard would have brought Jack Adams and the boy along if it'd been highway robbery he'd had in mind.'

Nathaniel eased his horse over the potholes in the road. 'A pity.' His long, thin face was wistful. 'That was rare sport.'

'Aye, but we'd end our days with the hangman's noose about our lily-white necks if we played that game too long.' Benedict brought out a flask from the braided folds of his cloak, swallowed a mouthful, and passed it to Nathaniel. 'Doubtless he'll tell us what he wants of us in his own good time. At least he'd a civil tongue in his head today, unlike these past few months – and anything'd be an improvement on Ned's latest effort.'

Nathaniel swore, and spat on the ground. 'Twenty lines and I'm dead by the end of the second act! Then I'm back on as any potboy, goatsherd, third messenger, any damn odd or end.'

'*You* should complain! *I*, my dear man, have to journey to Africa.' Benedict's hat, an extravagant affair of purple felt and yellow feathers, slipped over his nose: crossly, he pushed it back. 'A prologue and an epilogue, and damn all between!'

'Perhaps you're losing your touch, Ben.' The freckle-faced boy ahead had slowed his horse in the happy expectation of a quarrel. 'Perhaps the ladies have wearied of carrot-topped striplings, and prefer something a little more mature – a little more sophisticated.'

The hat slipped again: Benedict caught it and tossed it into the air. 'If the truth be told, Nat Brand, neither you nor I have had a decent role the entire season. Now, last year . . .'

They fell to bemoaning, as players do everywhere, the playwright's inability properly to display their massive gifts. Their complaints kept them noisily amused, their voices rising over the boy's singing and the soft clip-clop of the horses' hooves in the mud, as the countryside gently swelled into a hill. At the top of the hill, their leader reined in his horse, and waited for them.

'Charlie Farrant, you had better hide that voice of yours, or you will be taken from the wicked Red Bull, and traded to one of the children's companies. Worthy Nathaniel and Benedict –' a cold green hawk's eye met Benedict's laughing blue gaze, 'Benedict – Bennet – sweet Ben – tonight you will perform a play that will do justice to your talents.'

A mixture of embarrassment and grievance crossed Benedict's face. 'You mean to say we have ridden all this way just to perform some play?'

The copper-haired man smiled. 'Just so. But hide your disappointment, my Bennet. It is not *some* play, it is *my* play. Had you hoped for more piquant entertainment, dear Ben?'

Benedict blushed, and said, mortified, 'But Richard, no-one travels the country in March! It's too damned cold, for one thing, and besides –'

'Besides, you will be sorely missed at the Red Bull?' The expression on the copper-haired man's face was almost sympathetic. 'Don't fret, beautiful Bennet. I only require one performance of you tonight, and then you may return to Clerkenwell and entrance the ladies again.'

Slightly appeased, Benedict said, 'So where is this performance to take place?'

The copper-haired man motioned Benedict to come beside him. 'Down there, my beauty.'

Benedict looked down through the broad sweep of the valley to where a moated manor house, mellow-stoned and ancient, stood cradled in the slight hazy greenness of the early spring

220

woods and fields. He glanced across at his companion, and noticed that any trace of a smile or sympathy had gone from the hard arrogant face, and that the thin rapier scar on his cheekbone stood out against the whiteness of his skin.

Benedict said quietly: 'Taking that old hag in the forest was easy. I hope you have no such venture in mind for that place. It will be guarded like a fortress.'

The other man shook his head slowly. 'I intend nothing criminal. All you will do is perform the play, talk nicely to the lady's servants, and return to London tomorrow. Oh, and you might perhaps assist me in seeing the lady of the house privately at night – but if you have no stomach for the task, I don't doubt Nathaniel would provide his services for a fee.'

'Seeing the lady of the house? At night?' Benedict's voice rose in a squeaky whisper. 'And where is her husband?'

The thin smile was back again. 'Sir Nicholas Carleton is in London. That is why we are here today. And I only wish to *talk* to Lady Carleton. Well, Bennet?'

The laughter had returned to Benedict's blue eyes. 'And who is to have the leading role in your play? Myself or Nathaniel?'

The copper-haired man clapped his heels against the horse's flanks, and started down the hill. 'Oh, you, of course, Benedict. The part calls for beauty, brains, and a serpent's cunning . . .'

And they were gone, riding down the hill towards the golden, moated house.

The players had arrived at Kingscote in the afternoon, a splash of colour in a series of grey days. Matthews had announced their arrival to Mall, pronouncing the word 'players' as though it tasted sour. She did not allow him to order them to move on, but told him to house them in the servants' quarters in the courtyard over the bridge.

So, in the evening, Lady Carleton and the entire army of Kingscote's servants took their place in the Great Hall, perched on chairs, stools, benches, huddled giggling on the cold stone floor, in eager anticipation of the performance. The Hall looked untypically disordered; the pile of gaudy hats and cloaks to one side of the room clashed with the muted elegance of the Carleton tapestries, and the laughter and noise from the group of brightly coloured strangers in the far corner announced the presence of the dramatic Lord of Misrule.

One of the players, bright blue eyes under curling auburn hair, stepped forward, swept off his preposterous hat, and bowed extravagantly to Mall. 'Our play, your ladyship, is called *The Poisoner's Tragedy*, or –' he paused impressively, '*The Victor Vanquished*. 'Tis an instructive tale, my lady – stabbings, mortifyings, lustings, bludgeonings – and we hope you will look kindly on the efforts of a band of poor players.'

The kitchenmaids giggled louder as auburn-hair moved back, replaced his hat, and assumed the character of the wronged hero, blighted by hopeless love. Poor players, thought Mall, and recalled herself standing at the doorway of Hosea Dockerill's hut, saying: *You are not a poet, Mr Galliers . . . No, Miss Conway, a poor player that struts and frets his hour upon the stage . . .*

She had missed the first scene, had failed to follow the details of auburn-hair's doomed romance with the piping-voiced, bosomless, heroine; had lost track of the precise ramifications of just why the wicked Duke looked quite so unfavourably upon their alliance. Something to do with incest, thought Mall, vaguely. She really must concentrate.

A song, the hero's pleasant baritone fusing with the heroine's eerily perfect treble, a quick change of cloak and hat for auburn-hair, and, joined by another player, he rapidly transformed into a Genoese courtier, sycophant of the wicked Duke. A swirl of unmistakably villainous black crowned with an appalling copper coloured wig, and the Duke himself hissed his way into the centre of the improvised stage. One short, suitably fiendish speech –

And the silk and ivory fan fell from Mall's suddenly nerveless fingers on to the heavily embroidered brocade of her gown. It seemed to her that everyone in the Hall must hear the manic thump, thump, thump of her beating heart encased in its unyielding buckram bodice; that Leah could not fail to see the hot scarlet that had risen to her cheeks, the shaking of the hands that wore Richard Galliers' parting gift.

Richard Galliers' voice, under the counterfeit Italian accent; Richard Galliers' face, under the white paint, the ridiculous wig, the tattered faded black trimmed with equally tawdry cloth of gold. There, in front of her, within Kingscote's four thick stone walls, watched by Matthews with morose distaste, by Leah with bovine incomprehension, was the object of Sir Nicholas Carleton's obsessive curiosity, that sly fox in another guise, Reynardine.

But – *why*? *That* question again, echoing in Mall's brain, until she would have liked to scream it across the few feet of stone that lay between herself and that dark, Satanic figure. He must have known Sir Nicholas was not here, he must have intentionally chosen this time to come here – to see her. Again – why? She had never expected to see him again – on a social occasion, perhaps, when the wife of Sir Nicholas Carleton might quite conceivably encounter Lady Amyott's reprehensible younger son, where memories would drown in etiquette, affections decay into ultimately painless familiarity. But not here, not at Kingscote, not so soon; for she might be forced to choose between the man she ought to love, but only, increasingly, feared; and the man she ought to fear, but, unable to take her eyes from him for a second knew, reluctantly, that she still loved. She would have to choose, she knew that – why else would he be here? But she did not feel ready to: he should not have come, she should have been allowed to forget him, and then, surely, eventually, she would have ceased to feel anything for him. Richard Galliers had taken her from her home and family; he had been indirectly instrumental in throwing her into Carleton's arms. He was, according to Sir Nicholas and others, a drunkard and a rake, and a murderer, and, if her husband had told her the truth, he had deserved every hour of his exile, every lost gold crown of his inheritance. She ought to despise him.

And yet, listening to the silence his words had created, her eyes, like everyone else's, fixed on that blanched devil's face, she knew that she did not.

223

CHAPTER TEN

In me it speaks, whether I sleep or wake,
And when by means to drive it out I try,
With greater torments then it does me take,
And tortures me in most extremity.

(DRAYTON)

*I*T was not until the early hours of the morning that Richard Galliers thought it safe to move. The servants whose quarters they shared had been merry; their revels, inspired by the play and the ale, had continued long past midnight. But now they slept. Groans of desire and indigestion had silenced, replaced by the gentle snoring of the deeply asleep.

Galliers moved silently to Benedict's side, shook him roughly awake, clamping a hand over his mouth at the first squawk of protest. Then they were out of the courtyard, running soundlessly through the woods to the side of Kingscote where they had hidden the small boat earlier in the day.

It did not take long for him to identify Mall's chamber: she had followed to the letter Benedict's instructions, whispered to her over the cold roast capon and veal and ham pie that followed the play. The curtains were slightly ajar, and a candle flickered dully on the sill. Galliers stood on the bank, looping the rope around his arm, light in his eyes, expectation on his face, as he estimated the height of the window from the moat. The weeks of waiting were past, the weeks of kicking his heels uselessly in London, trying to avoid venting his increasingly brittle temper on Esmé Molyneux, Kate Gilbert, or any other innocent bystander. No, perhaps his enforced stay in London had not been entirely useless. He had done what he could; he had watched, he had waited, and he had seeded rumours where rumours grow, in the taverns, the playhouses, the gambling dens. But the waiting had played upon his nerves; he had always found it hard to tolerate waiting. How poor are they that have not patience, he thought to himself, and smiled wryly in the darkness.

The rowing boat bobbed on the water, and Benedict, yawning, held an oar in each hand. With the rope coiled about his arm, Galliers stepped into the boat and pushed it away from the bank.

Benedict Daniel watched, steadying the boat as Galliers threw the rope upwards, and it snaked through the air to hit one-endedly against the candlelit window. A pause, a rattle, the window opened, and Benedict saw the dark-haired girl of the evening leaning out of the window to peer into the still waters below. She made no sound, and Benedict smiled to himself as he saw her reach out a hand and catch the rope as it soared towards her a second time.

'I hope the lady can tie knots, or you, my friend, will be taking a cold bath.'

Richard Galliers removed his frieze cloak and tossed it to Benedict. 'Hide the boat in the undergrowth, and wait for me.' He pulled the rope, it went taut. The boat jolted as Galliers began to climb, fast, silently, cat-like, up to the open window.

The rope was reeled in, the window shut. It occurred to Bennet that he had the poor end of the bargain; that whereas he would spend the next few hours huddled in the undergrowth at the edge of the woods, Richard Galliers would enjoy a pleasant time in that pretty girl's warm bed.

Now she was alone with him. The bright golds and scarlet plumes had gone, and he was Reynardine again, dark-haired, green-eyed, wary . . . dangerous.

She was silent as she watched him coil the rope about his

arm, place it neatly on the floor, and check Benedict's disappearance before he drew the curtains. He did not want her, she should not want him.

He did not sit, but stood in front of the fireplace, restless again, watching her. At last he said, 'How are you?', and she was tempted to laugh.

But she kept her answer equally conventional. 'Well – I am well.'

There was some slight change on his face; an almost imperceptible hardening, a barely acknowledged death of hope.

'So marriage suits you?'

Some of the unreasonable optimism that had stayed with her through the last few hours trickled away. 'Oh yes.' She spoke lightly, disguising her growing anger.

He should not have come here, to ask ridiculous questions, to talk of the weather, to unsettle her so that tomorrow, and the next night, and the next, she would cry into her pillow. She said, proudly, 'It suits me very well. I live in a beautiful house, I eat good food, I have a rich and noble husband. What more could I want?' But she could not keep up the pretence, the anger came through, and her voice cracked and changed. 'Oh, for God's sake, Mr Galliers. I *survive*.'

And there, she had not admitted that even to herself, that these past four months had been nothing more than an exercise in survival. She looked up at him, but his eyes were hooded, and he nudged at the embers of the fire with his boot.

'But you are not – happy?' He pronounced the word as though he had forgotten what it meant.

'Happy?' Through the blurring tears Mall stared at his shadowed profile. The question of happiness had long seemed irrelevant. 'No, I am not happy. I was given no choice in this marriage – perhaps you thought I was eager to be Sir Nicholas Carleton's bride? Perhaps you think I was only too willing to leap into the bed of the man so many other women had chased?'

Her voice was bitter; he had never heard that before. He forced himself to look at her, and to acknowledge that something had changed; that she was no longer the innocent child of Hosea's hut, or the thoughtless muddied beauty of the Gog Magog hills. She was still beautiful – more so, perhaps, for he could recognize that the months with Carleton had taught her to dress, to arrange her hair properly, to emphasise those fathomless eyes with kohl. And what else had Carleton taught her? No, *that* thought for some reason was intolerable – he would not allow it.

'*Mall*.'

Suddenly she noticed the whiteness of his knuckles, and the set line of his mouth.

He shook his head slowly. 'What can I say – that I'm sorry?' His voice was gentle, but Mall sensed the pain behind it. 'After the Fens – I went to France. When I returned, at New Year, I learned that you were married. And I know that it was my responsibility. I cannot undo those days we spent together – I wish to God I could – but –'

'Well, I don't!' She had forgotten that she should speak quietly, she had forgotten also to hide her feelings from him. Anger on her face, she said, 'I do not regret one minute of our time together, not one second of it! Oh, I know that I was cold and wet and frightened, and I realize that it helped bring me here, but I do not regret it, not one little bit!' She huddled back on the bed, shivering slightly, and added, almost to herself, 'And at least I was alive then . . . and I was not really afraid – perhaps a little bit at the beginning, but not later, not after you were ill, not when I knew you better.'

And not after I shared the bed with you, sleeping with your arm about me. That, thought Mall, was when you began to make me love you, and that was what made Carleton's greedy, loveless lovemaking so increasingly insupportable.

Richard Galliers had turned away from her now, his hands on the chimney piece, his back to her as he stared into the ashes of the fire. And Mall knew that, however little he might want to hear, she must finish what she had begun to say.

'I realize – that I mean nothing to you. I know that you did not want me with you. I am not asking anything of you. But please, *please* do not try and make me regret what happened. I could not bear that.'

It was what he had needed to hear, the obvious distress in her marriage, but it gave him no pleasure. There was, unexpectedly, a desire to comfort her. But that, ultimately, would be cruel.

He turned to face her. 'So if it were possible, you would wish to be free of Carleton?'

The question did not make sense. A thousand possibilities flashed through Mall's mind, all as quickly discarded. 'But it isn't possible. We are legally married. Nothing can undo that.'

'If I were to tell you that there might be a way by which you could free yourself of him, would you wish to take the opportunity to do so?'

He watched her impatiently, waiting for an answer. *No* – and he would do what he had intended to do in December, go away again, make himself some sort of existence abroad. *Yes* – and there would be nothing left to stop him using whatever came to hand to achieve the revenge he had sought for years.

But still she did not answer. He made himself speak evenly, made himself hide the rising sense of urgency. 'Do you remember that afternoon in the Fens – the last one, before Hosea arrived?'

She said nothing, just nodded. So at least she was listening.

Galliers continued: 'I told you that I had read a letter sent by the Countess of Somerset to a disaffected ally – someone living between Hinxton and London, someone frequently at Court, someone, perhaps a little short of money –'

The bent head jerked up suddenly, and her eyes met his, confused.

'Come on, Mall. Carleton cannot have taken your wits from you.'

She looked at him standing there, expectancy coiled in him like a spring, and like threads of different colours in a tapestry, the separate parts began to form a whole.

'You mean – not my father, not Mr Murray – but –'

'Sir Nicholas Carleton. Yes.'

That information could not sink in straight away. She sat completely still, her eyes on Galliers, but not seeing him, trying to understand. Sir Nicholas Carleton – her husband – had helped Lady Somerset rid herself of Sir Thomas Overbury: had helped Lady Somerset *murder* Sir Thomas Overbury . . . and since, realizing that the Somersets' days were numbered, was desperately trying to extricate all evidence of his involvement. And had married an heiress, of course, for her money . . . to free himself of the Countess's patronage, and to pay his debts. And to buy back the incriminating letters that the Countess held, poised like a spur to demand his compliance?

And of course he would fear Reynardine. Reynardine had read the evidence. And of course he would need to know Reynardine's identity.

Mall had not spoken yet, but Galliers had seen the shock on her face. There was no point in being kind to her now; she must fully understand the implications of what he had to say.

'If the Overbury affair were to be made public, and if Carleton's part in it were to come out into the open, then he would end with his head on the block. This crime comes much too uncomfortably close to the king himself, so those involved would have to be seen to be punished. If you will allow me to, I propose to try and ensure that the matter comes to trial. Someone, somewhere must have evidence that Overbury did not die a natural death. The rumours are rife already, it would only take one solid bit of evidence for the whole card house to begin to crumble. And if the Countess of Somerset is implicated, then I think she will betray as many of her past associates as she can. It would be her best hope of survival – to attempt to shift the burden of guilt on to others. And she would certainly have no compunction in exposing Carleton – he has angered her already, and she deals harshly with those who displease her. But it is up to you, Mall. If Carleton were to be found guilty, then you would likely lose Kingscote and its lands as well as the dowry you brought. And there would inevitably be a certain amount of disgrace which would probably also attach itself to you.'

She had not moved while he had spoken. She had watched him as flatly, dispassionately, he had explained to her what he had come here for. But although he gave little outward sign of it, Mall knew from the tension of his body that her answer was of immeasurable importance to him.

So she must choose now: choose between two damning, contradictory assessments. She thought of her instinctive fear of Carleton, first experienced when she had risen through the waters of his pool to see him on horseback, staring at her with that dreadful possessive hunger. And marriage had never dispersed that fear.

She said evenly, 'I would happily never see Kingscote again.' It had become cold in the room, the fire was completely out. 'But I don't understand – I don't understand why it matters to *you*.'

It was not, after all, thought Mall, wrapping the coverlet around her, as though Richard Galliers had wanted to marry her. It was not as though he and Carleton had been rivals, jostling for her hand, and ill chance, or fate, had given her to Carleton.

She looked up at him, and said, slightly unsteadily: 'You and Sir Nicholas hate each other – I have seen that. Perhaps you ought to tell me why.'

Galliers saw her, small, white-faced and shivering on the blue-and-gold-covered bed, and again had to resist the urge to go to her, to put an arm round those thin cold shoulders. He walked to the window, pulling the curtains aside to check the darkness, the silence. She had as much as told him she was in love with him, and he would not use that to make her decide against Carleton. He would not – she must choose rationally, not out of a young girl's short-lived passion. He would not manipulate her, use irrational affections to convince her of the course she must take. He had done that three and a half years ago with Jeremy, and he had lived to regret it.

Jeremy. He turned back to her, his face shadowed in the darkness.

He said, clearly, 'Then let me explain. Giles, my elder brother, you have met . . . but I once had a younger brother also.'

With a sick feeling in her stomach, Mall recalled that conversation in Kingscote's Great Hall. 'I know. Jeremy. My husband told me he died in a street fight.'

She could not look at him, but she heard him say lightly:

'Not quite. Perhaps I had better give you my version. Jeremy did not *die* in the street – I wish to God he had. He was wounded there, but he died three weeks later, at Amyott, of gangrene.'

She moved, suddenly. He saw the blue and gold covered shoulders jerk, and her mouth open and shut as if she had been about to say something and had thought better of it.

His face composed, his hands still, Galliers continued:

'I expect Carleton told you that I started the fight and was then too drunk to defend my brother.'

Mall nodded silently.

'Well, for once, I was perfectly sober. I admit that I have tried to avoid sobriety since, but I was sober then. I was taking Jeremy away from Carleton, you see, Mall. We were leaving the country.'

The coverlet had slipped on to the bed, and her face was bone white. 'What do you mean?'

He did not touch her, but said steadily, meeting the dawning horror in her eyes:

'Carleton wanted to possess something of mine, to possess it heart and soul. Our families had never been close – I'm not sure why, originally, no particular reason, perhaps, just differences in opinion and taste.' He paused, shook his head. 'But there was more. Carleton . . . pursued me. We came across one another at a banquet in London. He was . . . friendly – too friendly.'

His tone was bland, emotionless. But even now he could still recall the heat in Carleton's eyes, the heat that had cooled so rapidly to ice. He had not chosen his words carefully then, and for that insolence he had since paid, over and over again.

'Carleton was not used to rejection. He waited for a particularly apposite revenge. If I was not to be seduced, then perhaps my younger brother would prove more accommodating. Jeremy had just turned fifteen. He was at Cambridge. He was good-looking, intelligent, my mother's favourite. Carleton flattered him, and Jeremy was ill-equipped to resist his attentions. By the time I discovered what was happening,

231

Jeremy was as much Carleton's creature as that golden-haired boy is now.'

Two men standing in the courtyard, the older, darker one touching the boy's yellow locks . . . 'Lucas Holland,' she said, painfully.

'So I took Jeremy away. I intended to take him to the Continent, to get him as far away from Carleton as possible.' He sounded suddenly weary. 'I think. I have had so long to consider my motives that I have forgotten what they originally were. Perhaps my intentions were noble, selfless, perhaps not. Perhaps I wanted to make Carleton suffer, to prove to him that he could not have one of my family.' His voice was harsh, raw-edged. 'Perhaps I should not have interfered, but have left Jeremy where he was. If I had done that, he would still be alive.' His voice trailed off into silence.

Mall said slowly: 'So you took him away. What then?'

There was an unnerving cold violence in Richard's eyes. 'Unfortunately, Jeremy had made the mistake of leaving a letter for Carleton, announcing that he was leaving the country with me. We stopped overnight in the London house – he told me there. When we reached Gravesend the next evening, we were set upon by half a dozen men – Carleton's men. I was not hurt, but they beat my brother to a pulp. He had a knife wound to his thigh. I found a physician to attend to that, and took him back to Amyott. I wish to God I had not.'

He stopped for a moment, his mind far away from the silk-hung bedchamber. Then his eyes focused on Mall again, and he continued:

'He never began to recover. The physician had not done a good job, or the wound was too deep. They did everything they could for him, but he was dying. My God, it was a foul way to die, Mall, and a foul thing for my mother to have to witness.'

In the peat cutter's hut, at the height of his delirium, he had said the same words over and over: *My God, why did I bring him home* . . . she had not understood him then, but at least she had been allowed to comfort him. Here, she only had words.

'You could not know. You did what you thought best – there is nothing to be ashamed of in that.'

He laughed humourlessly. 'I have everything to be ashamed of – I did nothing right. Carleton was clever, I was not. Anyway, ultimately, there was my story against Carleton's. My lack of bruises didn't help, neither did my reputation, and, of course, my mother has never known of Jeremy's involvement with Sir Nicholas.'

'But why not? Surely she should have?'

'I don't think so.' He looked down at her and, gently, his hand touched her black hair. 'He was dying, remember, my dear – a foul, stinking disease that almost drove my mother mad. To tell her that he had been Carleton's plaything – that would have been cruelty beyond reason. As it was, by the time of the funeral, I discovered that Carleton himself had been busy. A girl had been found to swear that I had started a fight over her, and naturally, there was no trace of our assailants, no witnesses to the attack. I could not get near Carleton. It soon became obvious that my presence was intolerable to everyone around me. Giles knew something of the truth, but not all. So I left the country.'

He looked at her, saw pity in her eyes, and pulled his hand away from her instantly. Pity was not what he had intended.

He smiled, and said brutally: 'So there you are, sweetheart, a pretty tale, isn't it? I really could not understand why your stepmother summoned me to your dinner table in November – perhaps she doesn't keep up with the local gossip. I am not really much of a catch for any nubile maiden. I have been disinherited, by the way – not, being a second son, that there was much to inherit in the first place. My mother can hardly bear to set eyes on me and, I should tell you, Lady Carleton, that much of what you have heard concerning my sojourns abroad is completely, damnably, true.'

In other words, thought Mall, twisting the thread of the coverlet through her fingers, even if you are freed of your husband, *I* will not be there to carry you off into the horizon on my white charger. Perfectly plain, thank you, Mr Galliers.

'So what do you wish me to do?' He had taken the candlestick, ready to place it on the window as his signal to Benedict. He continued casually, as though it did not matter, 'I am entirely at your disposal. As you see, I have a considerable debt of my own to pay, but it is you who must decide. *You* would not be safe, especially if Carleton were to discover that I had played Reynardine.'

She remembered Dunyazad, plunging through the sky to take the lure, and she said slowly, 'Sir Nicholas does not trust me. He is watching me.' Another thought crossed her mind. 'And you, Mr Galliers, I think he is having you watched also.'

'By Lucas Holland? I thought so – I played the drunken rake for him.'

And I must play the virtuous wife, Mall realized. Continue to accept those fevered visits to my bed each night, to tolerate the watching eyes of the servants . . .

And if he succeeded, if Richard Galliers was able to bring Carleton to trial, there would be nothing at the end of it for her.

'Do what you have to, Mr Galliers,' said Mall, calmly. 'I want to be free of him. I do not care about the consequences.'

Galliers drew the curtains open, and placed the candlestick on the windowsill. Scarcely concealed excitement lit his face. He took her hand and kissed it.

'Untie the rope and throw it down as soon as I have reached the boat.'

He opened the catch of the window, and looked out into the darkness. The rowing boat was there, circling into position on the moat, Benedict's hair copper-coloured in the moonlight. The rope curled out of the window, reverberating on Kingscote's ancient walls. There was one last, very important thing he had to say.

He held her shoulders, fixing her eyes with his. 'You are to leave this to me, Mall. Just wait – that is *all* you must do. No creeping about in darkened passageways with a candle in your hand, this time. *Understand?*'

*

To win consistently at hazard requires either a combination of skill and good fortune, or loaded dice. Esmé Molyneux, watching the game from an adjacent table of the silent, smoky Clerkenwell gaming house, knew that Richard Galliers possessed the skill, and understood that his luck, poor since New Year had finally changed. Unfortunately, it seemed probable that the man opposite Galliers, whose originally large pile of crowns had shrunk almost to nothingness, would not agree. The man was a wintering mercenary with the build of a wrestler and the hands of a butcher. He was also apparently popular, for an interesting selection of his allies had gathered round the table to watch the play. The hour was late, the gaming house three-quarters empty, and the few remaining gamesters had abandoned their tables to witness the annhilation of one who had taken much money from them in the past.

Molyneux, his hand already hovering round the hilt of his rapier, wished he had not worn his green satin suit. A fight would spoil it so, and it had been expensive. If only Richard would lose just one throw, thought Esmé, mentally estimating the distance between the table and the door to the street. One throw, and honour might be vaguely satisfied, and they could leave this hellhole, and the green satin suit might remain intact. Having lost consistently for the past few months, and apparently not cared too greatly about it, it was unreasonable of Richard to return, bright-eyed and wearingly energetic, from some mysterious visit to the countryside, and proceed to win quite so convincingly. A increasingly loud rumble of discontent had accompanied Richard's every throw, and the mercenary had planted his uncompromisingly thick elbows on the table so that his face was only inches away from Galliers'.

Esmé leaned across and poured more ale into Richard's tankard. 'Lose, man. The knives are out, and they'll make mincemeat of us before we reach the door.'

Richard gave no indication that he had heard him. He leaned back in his chair – *smiling*, for pity's sake, thought Esmé – and called. Galliers watched lazily as the dice tumbled to the table, and Esmé winced.

''Tis a mighty obliging pair of dice you have there, sir.'

Indolently, Galliers' gaze travelled upwards to the scrawny, pockmarked man who had spoken.

He shrugged, and said gently: 'Fortis fortuna adiuvat – or, gentlemen, fortune's a right whore, and chooses tonight to bestow herself on the beautiful and the brave.' As he spoke, he slid the pile of coins into his hand.

The rumble of discontent intensified into a roar. The mercenary's powerful hands were fisted, his eyes small and hard, his face beaded with sweat.

A voice said: 'Give him another one to match the pretty scar on his cheek, Will!'

Someone laughed, the crowd surged forward, and Esmé's hand gripped hard round the hilt of his rapier.

'Aye –' the pockmarked man's voice again '– the ladies will think he wasted his bonny face fighting for one of them.' His voice rose in a squeaking falsetto. 'Oh, sir, let me kiss it and make 'ee better.'

More ribald laughter, and under cover of the whistles and jeers Galliers spoke quietly over his shoulder to Esmé.

'There's a back way – through the passage to your right. It leads through a baker's shop, and out into the Clerkenwell Road.'

He rose, flicking the lace of his collar and cuffs into place, tossing the dice in one careless hand. Sweeping his hat from his head, Galliers bowed, and said courteously:

'You do not like to lose, sir. My apologies – perhaps I may recompense you in some small part by offering you a drink.'

The jug that Richard Galliers emptied over the soldier's leathery-skinned face was filled with hot ale, sweetened with sugar, and spiced with cinnamon. The table rapidly followed the ale, tipped with one elegantly-booted foot, unseating the soaked and scalded soldier, throwing him and several of his comrades to the floor.

Then they were through the small back door, and down the narrow interconnecting passageway and into the bakery, where the ovens were warming for the day's bread-making, and sacks of flour and jugs of milk and water stood on the vast whitened table.

'The table, Esmé.'

Richard unloosened the ties of the nearest bag of flour.

To the men that sought them, ale-soaked, bruised and angry, down the dark passage, it must have seemed like one of Nature's fouler tricks: a sudden ill-announced snowstorm. The air in the passage was one minute dark, the next unexpectedly white, as clouds of dusty, billowing powder filled their nostrils and eyes, and obliterated the end of the corridor from view.

Back in the kitchen, Esmé had succeeded in hauling the enormous table towards the end of the passage. Butted against the door, it would take more than the strength of eight coughing, choking men to move it.

Out in the dark street, away from the chaos that the unfortunate baker would discover in only a few hours time, they ran through the maze of alleys and courtyards, emerging shortly to walk, gentlemanly and respectably, towards Esmé's Holborn Street rooms.

Or almost. Esmé, having recovered his composure, lost it again as he looked at Richard. Flour dusted his dark hair, the crimson velvet of his cloak was scattered with white powder as though from a volcanic eruption.

'God, Richard – tidy yourself up, man. You look prematurely aged.'

Richard grinned and leaned forwards, beating the flour from his hair and clothes. 'Damn it, I left my hat in that place –'

'But you have other hats,' Molyneux said firmly, taking his companion's arm, and steering him along the road. 'Let them keep it as a souvenir. Perhaps your soldier friend deserves some compensation for his losses. Your profit was two hundred crowns, two hundred and fifty? You can afford a new hat.' Esmé paused to fit the key in the door to the rooms. Cautiously, he looked at Richard. 'And were the dice loaded?'

'*Esmé.*' A wounded expression crossed his face, as Richard clapped a hand on Molyneux's elegant back. 'A word with you, my friend, if you please.'

Esmé led the way into the room. An unenthusiastic fire flickered in the grate. The ancient manservant lit the candles. A bottle of claret and two glasses were found, and Esmé collapsed, fanning himself, into a chair. He closed his eyes, thankful that the day's exertions were over.

Richard's voice said from somewhere behind him:

'What I require, my dear, is the name of an apothecary.'

Esmé's eyes opened slowly, and he raised one well shaped eyebrow. 'I'm not surprised, Richard – whorehouses are notoriously bad for the health.'

He heard the clink of glasses behind him as Richard poured out the wine.

'Why assume it is salts of mercury I require? I might have a rheum in my knee – or an excess of bile.'

'So you might.' Esmé took the glass that Richard held out to him. 'I know of a good apothecary in St Paul's.'

'I require a very particular apothecary. De Mayerne's, to be precise.'

'An expensive pox, Galliers,' said Esmé, dryly. 'I now understand why you had to win quite so excessively tonight. Why de Mayerne's?'

Galliers leaned back against the edge of the heavy oak table, the tips of his dark, flour-powdered hair lit by the glow from the fire.

'De Mayerne is First Physician to the king. He attends the rich and famous in their hour of need. He attended, for instance, Sir Thomas Overbury during his imprisonment in the Tower. So, the name of his apothecary, please, Esmé. Oh – and permission to use your address for a remedy I will send for.'

Molyneux looked at him suspiciously. 'And my name as well, no doubt?'

He took in the small graceful gesture of assent, the lack of any decent humility in the request, the light in those clear green eyes, and felt suddenly tired. The day had been long, the evening exhausting. There was a small triangular tear in the doublet of the green satin suit – probably the result of heaving that damned table about, he thought irritably. He said,

238

resignedly, 'As you wish, Richard,' and drank a little of the wine. He glanced across at the dark-haired man, noting with some chagrin that the unpredictable temper and edginess of the last months had completely disappeared and that, even now, in the early hours of the morning, Richard managed to look positively lively. Of the two extremes, Esmé was uncertain which was worse.

He said, tentatively: 'And I don't suppose you'll tell me, either, where you went last week?'

'Certainly not.' Richard replaced his glass on the table, and picked up his cloak. 'But it served its purpose.'

Esmé said thoughtfully, 'Had you enquired for an apothecary a week ago, I would have thought it was to cure an attack of melancholy. But now – you are quite unbearably vivacious, my dear. One might almost think you had fallen in love.'

'In love?' Richard grinned, and threw his cloak about his shoulders. 'Your poetry is addling your brain, my friend. I will admit that I saw a lady, but I am certainly not in love with her – though she's a brave enough little thing. But not my type – she's dark. And the adorable Mrs Gilbert satisfies all those needs quite adequately.' He flicked one expensively gloved hand against Esmé's embroidered sleeve and turned to leave the room. 'Besides, I have not been in love since I was seventeen, and have forgotten what it feels like.'

Days of endless grey cold rain; long hours of sewing in the unwanted company of Leah; longer hours spent searching uselessly for a way out of the cage that her marriage had become. Sir Nicholas was still in London. It was only from the servants that Mall must hide her thoughts, only the servants who must not know how much she now feared her husband. Kingscote had become oppressive: she had been too long shut in. Mall felt as though she knew every stone, every pane of glass in the rooms she used, every portrait, every hanging.

But when, eventually, deliverance from Kingscote's imprisoning walls presented itself, it was not in a form that Mall would have chosen. Watching from the solar's oriel window one wet April day, Mall saw Joshua's Joe and Martin Bartlett ride through Kingscote's gates, two friends from another life. It was only Matthews's small watching eyes that prevented her hugging them, after she had dashed down the stairs and out and along the bridge to greet them.

But the letter that Joshua's Joe extracted from the inside of his soaking jerkin dampened some of her happiness. The letter said, in Alice's ill-spelt childish scrawl, that Ralph was very ill, and had asked repeatedly for his half-sister. He had contracted an ague, which had gone to his lungs, and Alice feared for his life. The rain, or Alice's tears, had already blurred the rest of the letter.

Belford. Coupled with the new fear that Alice's letter had brought was an almost unbearable desire to see her old home again. She had not realized how much she had missed it – and Ralph – even Alice. And Sir Thomas might be there: their past disagreements nagged like an unhealed wound.

Mall folded the letter, and turned to Matthews to tell him to ready the horses for the journey. She was unprepared for the expression in his narrow eyes. His hand pulled her too roughly away from Belford's servants, as he said sharply:

'Sir Nicholas did not wish you to leave Kingscote.'

There was not even the conventional 'your ladyship'. Mall shook herself free of his hand, her temper, suppressed for so many long weeks, rising.

'I don't give a damn what he wishes. I am riding to Belford today – *now*. My baby brother is ill, possibly dying. So ready the horses, Matthews – oh, and tell Leah she will be riding with me. *That* should satisfy Sir Nicholas, should it not, *Matthews*?'

He did not attempt to restrain her. But it shook her, his insolently formal bow, and the look, almost of pleasure on his face, and she had to make herself brush her fears aside, and run back into the house to prepare for the journey.

It was not a particularly pleasant walk from Lime Street, near the Tower, to Holborn Street. The April rain was steady, filling the gutters and churning every passage and alleyway into a greyish-brown mud. To Gabriel Thorne, however, twelve years old, red-haired, freckled, and as smart as the one brass button that rakishly adorned the tattered blue coat he wore, it was good to be out, away from the dark mysteries of the apothecary's shop. Gabriel had been apprenticed to Mr de Lobell for just over a year now, but he still had doubts about his future profession. It was the smells that bothered him most – that, and a sneaking suspicion that the whole business, with its retorts and alembics and caudles and clysters, was something akin to witchcraft. He was happier out in the open street, despite the mire and the rain. Besides, these errands represented by far the most profitable part of his employment. It was sometimes possible to add a penny or two to the price of the remedy he delivered – once, he had even extracted an additional sixpence from a man far gone with the pox. Often, the sick were in no state of body or mind to calculate too precisely the cost of their cure. If Gabriel secured himself a profit, he compensated himself for his troubles with a hot pie, or a jug of ale, on the way back to Lime Street.

He had reached Holborn Street, and his sharp eyes searched for the address Mr de Lobell had given him. In his hand he held the twist of paper containing the remedy. Over the road was a fat matron selling hot oatcakes, the scent of which drove Gabriel almost dizzy with greed. He found the door he was looking for, and knocked. A very old manservant opened it, and the boy explained his errand.

'I've been sent from the apothecary's for Mr Molyneux, sir.'

He was shown into a room similar in size to his master's parlour, but more sparsely furnished. The chamber did not, however, compare with Dr de Mayerne's house, a very grand residence, the frequent destination of many of Gabriel's journeys. Sitting beside the fireplace was a man, dressed in dark breeches and hose and a white silk shirt. Silk meant that he had money, and, thought Gabriel optimistically, the fact that he was seated and not yet fully dressed indicated that he had, perhaps, only just risen from his sickbed. Gabriel thought of the oat cakes across the road, and mentally added several pence to the cost of the remedy he carried.

'I've come from the apothecary's, sir.' He took a deep breath and, nonchalance in his blue eyes, named his price.

The man in the chair looked up at him, and, unexpectedly, the boy began to feel uneasy. The eyes that studied him were only gently enquiring, but the face, with its thin scar along one cheekbone, did not look ill.

'Put the paper on the table.'

Gabriel did as he was told, and waited, fingers crossed behind his back, for the money.

But the money was not forthcoming. The gentleman beckoned to him to come nearer.

'What's your name, lad?'

No, Mr Molyneux did not look unwell. Gabriel swallowed, and said firmly, 'Gabriel, sir. Gabriel Thorne.'

Cold green eyes inspected him. 'And how old are you, Gabriel?'

'Fifteen, sir.'

There was a short silence in which Gabriel became conscious of his lack of height, lack of muscle, lack of beard. The muscles at the corner of the dark gentleman's mouth twitched almost imperceptibly.

'I don't think so. Ten, perhaps?'

Angered into truth, Gabriel said quickly, 'Twelve, sir!', and the gentleman's eyes finally left his face, and stared somewhere into the distance.

'Twelve. So you cannot have been apprenticed to Mr de Lobell for long?'

The boy shook his ginger head, wondering if he dared step back a few paces. 'I've been with him for just over a year, sir.'

'Which means –' the merciless gaze returned to Gabriel's face '– that you have been apprenticed since the autumn of 1613?'

'October of that year, sir.' The gentleman was smiling now, but it was not, thought Gabriel, a friendly smile.

'And your predecessor – Mr de Lobell's former apprentice – he is a journeyman now?'

Sweat was gathering in Gabriel's clenched palms, and he said rapidly, 'Oh, no, sir – he's gone away . . .' and then his voice trailed off uncertainly into silence.

The hard cold eyes flickered once, and the gentleman said slowly, 'Gone away? Well, that's very interesting. And where might he have gone, Gabriel?'

The boy took a step back, and an arm reached out, grabbing him, and holding him still. 'Where to, Gabriel?'

With a voice that did not seem to be his own, Gabriel replied, 'I'm not sure, sir. I think – I think he went to a foreign country –'

'Good.' The grip on his arm relaxed, and the gentleman smiled again.

Gabriel continued, gabbling: 'I've had to take a package to the docks a few times, sir – to Gravesend – for William, you see, sir.'

'William? Do you know his other name?'

Months of invidious comparisons with his irritatingly perfect predecessor rang in his ears. 'Reeve, sir. William Reeve.'

'Oh, well done, my Gabriel.' The gentleman released his arm, and stood up. There was no sign of sickness or unsteadiness about him as he placed one long finger under Gabriel's chin, and lifted his face. The boy stood his ground, ignoring the sudden wateriness of his knees.

'Now, Gabriel, you shall have your rose ryall and your few pence extra, and nothing more will be said of it.' The man took the coins out of his pocket, and placed them in the boy's shaking hand. 'And in return for my silence – apprenticeships can be hard to come by, and you like your post, don't you, Gabriel? – you will carry out a little task for me. I wish to know where William, who went abroad so conveniently, has gone. When you have discovered that, you will return to me here, and I will reward you most handsomely –' he held up an angel between finger and thumb '– with one of these. A very proper reward for a Gabriel, an avenging angel, don't you think?' He smiled again, a small humourless smile that gave Gabriel Thorne no reassurance whatsoever. 'And not a word to a soul, of course, my bonny lad. After all, you would have to run a great many errands to acquire such a handsome profit as this, wouldn't you, Gabriel?'

Out in the street, the coins in his hand, the sweat on his brow cold in the fresh April air, Gabriel Thorne looked across the road to the oatcake seller. He was surprised to find that he did not feel hungry at all. Instead he felt sick, and along with the sickness went a new-found sympathy for his formerly loathed predecessor, the absent William. To have *him* looking for you – with one last glance at the Holborn Street address, Gabriel picked up his heels and ran all the way back to the apothecary's.

In Essex, three days later, it still rained. The young Lady Carleton, crimson-cloaked and hooded, with an unusually severe expression on her smooth-skinned delicate face, guided her chestnut mare easily round the puddles, the pot-holes and ruts that littered the route from Belford to Kingscote. The servants – Kingscote servants – rode behind; the dark, dumpy maid squashing one of the men as she rode uncomfortably pillion. Her ladyship rode ahead, by herself and in silence, as she had done since they had travelled through Belford's gates.

Ralph, miraculously, was recovering, that was one thing to thank God for. She had sat beside his cradle for hours, giving some rest to the exhausted, over-strained Alice. And gradually, the little boy's cough had ceased to wrack him quite so violently, and his breathing had become gentler, more measured. And yesterday morning he had opened his eyes, and known who it was that sang lullabyes to him: his own Mall, and his tired pale little face had broken into an ecstatic smile. Whether it had been the efforts of the physicians (the child's ailment was due to an adverse influence in the constellations, and must be prescribed a remedy involving a lamb's caul and ants' eggs); or whether the gentler medicines of Alice's herb

244

garden had effected the cure, no-one knew, and it did not matter. Mall, taking the little boy on her knee, suspected that Ralph possessed his own reserves of strength that helped pull him through these frequent illnesses: a strength that few people, other than his mother, recognized.

But that morning Mall had left Belford, kissing Ralph's soft cheek as he slept, saying her farewells to Alice. The beginnings of a reconciliation with Alice hovered in the air, unspoken, painfully insubstantial, but there. Mall would have liked to have stayed longer: to greet her father, whose return from London was expected hourly, to play with Ralph, to cement the fragile relationship that had grown between her and Alice. But she did not dare stay any longer, and that was the truth of it. Sitting beside Ralph's cradle at night, she recalled her rash words to Matthews, and regretted them: they would have consequences she dared not contemplate. So Mall did not look back over the hill for a last sight of Belford, grey and ugly in the driving rain. Instead she kicked her heels to the horse's sides, and relieved her feelings by cantering hard the rest of the way back to Kingscote.

Sir Nicholas had returned.

In her bedchamber, trying with cold numb hands to unlace her wet and muddy gown, Mall's apprehension tightened like a knot in her empty stomach. He had returned from London the previous day – to find her gone, absent from Kingscote against his wishes. Perhaps if she went to find him, explained to him . . .

Her hair, soaked and curled by the rain, would not tie up: her fingers were too unsteady. So she left it, looped and curled and shining, falling over her shoulders to her waist. A gown – purple silk trimmed with silver ribbons – surely that should meet with his approval? And the sapphires, her mother's sapphires, around her neck.

And then along to the other side of the house, where Sir Nicholas's small withdrawing room, complete with painted dancers, stood next to his study. It had crossed her mind, while Carleton was in London, that the contents of his desk might make interesting reading; so, surreptitiously, she had tried the door. It had been locked.

She knocked on the door of the withdrawing room, and Sir Nicholas's voice beckoned her in. He was alone: he wore a loose embroidered crimson robe, and there was no smile on his face as Mall closed the door behind her. The transfixed lutenists, viol players, pipers, in all shades of red, orange, ochre, brown and gold, posed endlessly around the walls.

Sir Nicholas said gently: 'Your little half-brother – your father's heir – is he recovered?'

He was polite, courteous – why, then, did she feel so threatened? Because of what Richard Galliers had told her about him – or because she sensed that he waited, crouching, to pounce like a stalking cat?

'Ralph is much better, thank you. Alice believes he will make a complete recovery.'

'How delightful.' He moved behind her, and she felt him stroke her hair with the back of his hand, taking it in his fingers to feel its silky weight. His voice still quiet, Carleton said lightly:

'But I did not wish you to leave Kingscote. I was very distressed when I returned to find you gone –'

'I'm sorry – I had no warning – I didn't know –' She was gabbling, she knew, like a fool, but could not stop herself.

His hands had left her hair, and settled on the purple silk shoulders of her gown. 'You did not know that I wanted you to remain at Kingscote? Now, Mall. Don't lie to me, my dear. I know when you are lying. Matthews told me that you had said you did not give a damn for my wishes – that my particular request that you were to remain at Kingscote was of no importance to you. Was he not telling the truth?'

She could not speak: then Carleton's hands slid down her arms, and gripped her, hard. 'He was telling the truth,' she said, in little more than a whisper.

'Oh dear.' He let Mall go, and moved to face her. He was changed: the veneer of courtesy was almost transparent, his anger, his desire to hurt, showed through. He said slowly:

'You look lovely, my dear. The ride has brought colour to your cheeks, and that gown is just the right shade for you. And with your hair down you look pagan – amoral . . . Are you amoral, Mall, my dear? Do you have no loyalty to those who keep you, who feed you – who *bought* you? Have you already forgotten my ramage hawk? You have forgotten Dunyazad?' There was no expression in his eyes; they were dark, blank, empty. 'I had better find you another lesson, my dear. I have the very thing. You may assist – us.'

Us. For the first time Mall noticed that the adjoining door to Sir Nicholas's bedchamber was slightly ajar, and that on the table was a decanter, and two glasses, coloured red near their stems with the dregs of the wine.

'Assist you?'

He pointed to the table, the glasses. 'Yes. We are in need of a drink. I thought you might serve us.'

Mall did not allow herself to glance through that half-opened door again. She went to the table and picked up the decanter. She would pour it without spilling it, she would not dance to his tune.

One glass she handed, her eyes unable to meet his, to Sir Nicholas.

'Thank you. My dear – loyal – obedient – wife.' He moved aside. 'The other you will take in there.'

The bedchamber. And inside the bedchamber, with its blue and gold hangings, its French porcelain, its Italian marble, there was no need to draw back the heavy brocade curtains that surrounded the four-poster bed. They were already open a little at the side, and Mall had a perfect view of the person who reached out to take the glass from her, triumph in his azure blue eyes.

In the bed, his linen shirt unlaced to the waist, his golden hair dishevelled in loose locks and curls, sat Lucas Holland.

She did not speak when she saw him, but handed him the wine, scarcely controlling the impulse to throw the entire glassful into that gloating, beautiful face. She watched, hypnotized, as Lucas drank the wine, and placed the glass on the small table to the side of the bed.

And then, close behind her, she heard Sir Nicholas say: 'I have brought my wife to you, Luke. Get out of the bed, my dear.'

Holland stood up, tall and slender, wearing only shirt and hose. His eyes were bright, his parted lips slightly stained with red.

And a hand on the small of Mall's back propelled her forward.

'My wife does not obey me. But you obey me, don't you, Luke? Kiss her.'

Before she had time to cry out or run, Holland's mouth had found hers, his tongue forcing her lips apart, his hands at her neck, hurting her. She struggled, gagging, trying to twist away from him, unable to breath.

'*Enough.*'

Carleton's voice again, sharp, this time. Lucas fell back, and Mall spun round to look at Carleton, gasping for breath, barely resisting the urge to scream and cry out.

Sir Nicholas said, harshly:

'Just a foretaste, my dear – a sample. So that you understand that although you are not altogether to Lucas's taste, he can be persuaded to stretch a point if necessary. Now – go.'

She retained just sufficient self-control to leave the room and wait until she had reached the privacy of her own chamber, flinging wide the window before being exhaustingly and humiliatingly sick into the black mirrored moat below. And when at last the dreadful retching had ceased, Mall found that she had no strength at all left in her legs, and she slid down the wall to rest her hot dizzy head on her bent knees. The sapphires round her neck were choking her, she pulled at them roughly, unable to manage the clasp, and the necklace broke, its thin wires taut and bent, its blue stones scattered to the corners of the room.

Leave Kingscote – return to Belford – throw herself on her father's mercy – anything but see that laughing Greek god's face every time she closed her eyes, anything but feel his lips on hers . . . She scrubbed at her mouth with the back of her hand, staring at the room with wide, tearless eyes, at the jewels glinting on the Turkey mat, at the broken chain and setting flung against the locked carved linen chest. And she knew she must stay. *The penalty for highway robbery is death, my dear, the fellow would be hung, drawn and quartered* . . . that most vile, most sickening of punishments. To go to her father and explain the dereliction of her four month marriage would necessitate the betrayal of Richard Galliers. And that she could not do.

At last the dizziness passed, and Mall crawled over to the chest to pick up the broken necklace. It was her mother's necklace, of a lovely old Irish design. She had pulled one of the delicate gold settings in half: it would require a goldsmith to repair it. She touched the wires, long and sharp, trying to bend them back into position. And then her eyes strayed to the lock of the chest.

Martin Bartlett had taught Mall many useful things. He had taught her to swim, to row, to shoot.

He had also taught her to pick locks.

The door to her husband's study was locked, the desk would be also. Inside the desk would be documents, bills, receipts . . . letters. And perhaps among those papers, Richard Galliers' one solid bit of evidence against Carleton and the Countess: Mall's key to freedom.

Carefully, Mall gathered together the scattered sapphires. Then, using the protruding pieces of wire, she set about re-teaching herself to pick the lock of the linen chest.

Almost a week passed before Mall was able to put her rediscovered skill into practice. She had caught a cold, presumably on the chilly wet ride back from Belford, and after sneezing frequently and wetly over Lucas Holland, had been excused the nightly pleasure of dining with her husband and his friend.

The gold wire had proved unsatisfactory; it was too soft, and bent uselessly in the keyhole. So Mall had appropriated a small, narrow-bladed knife from the kitchens, a scaled-down version of Richard Galliers' main gauche dagger. She had been highly successful with that, especially with the heavy iron door lock of her chamber. A smaller lock on a desk might prove more problematic. Mall had struggled with a bodkin to pick the delicate fastening of her jewellery box, and eventually managed to open it. But there had been scratches left around the lock: not particularly noticeable, but visible, all the same.

Sir Nicholas and Lucas Holland would dine together that night in the small parlour. They had been drinking since mid-afternoon, and although Carleton never showed signs of intoxication, Luke's voice had been louder, his empty high-pitched laughter echoing in courtyard and hall. After they had dined, Carleton would come to Mall's bedchamber, as he always did. Since her visit to Belford, he had been less considerate; his clutching fingers had left bruises, the desperation of his kisses has left marks on her white skin. But never her face: he would hold her face between his two hands as she had seen him hold a fine piece of glass, imprisoning its frozen fragility, his eyes betraying his unquenchable need for ownership.

Mall did not know how long she could bear it. If only she could have some word from Richard Galliers, some indication that, if nothing else, he had not completely forgotten her. But that was impossible – she was alone, and she must do what she could, for herself: soon, tonight.

For she did not know how long she could continue to disguise her loathing of her husband. Mall thought of Lucas Holland, white and gold between Carleton's silk sheets, and she was afraid.

Tiptoeing quietly through Kingscote at midnight, candle in one hand, knife in the other, Mall fleetingly remembered Richard Galliers' parting words. She concentrated on stilling the rustle of her skirts, and ensuring that she did not sneeze or snuffle too loudly. The constant drumming rain masked what little noise she made, and the route to Carleton's study did not take her past any servants' quarters.

The lock on the study door was easy. It was the wetness of her palms, slipping on the thin mother of pearl haft of the knife that made the task more difficult than it should have been. The candle Mall placed on the floor, where it flickered in time to her almost audible heartbeats. But the knife, and Martin's conscientious tuition, achieved their aim: the lock clicked and slowly, achingly, Mall turned the handle.

Once inside, with the door closed behind her, she felt a little safer. There was another room, and two thick stone walls, between her and the bed where Nicholas Carleton slept. She sneezed, muffling the sound in a none too clean handkerchief. She was beginning to feel cautiously elated – it had been surprisingly simple to get inside the room, and the possibility of engineering her escape from the hell that her marriage had become excitingly presented itself to her. Richard Galliers must have felt like this when, as Reynardine, he had robbed the Countess's messenger, then the old lady in the oak copse, and later, the Murrays' house. The mad leap from the oak tree that Martin Bartlett had unsuccessfully tried to emulate, the glorious farce of bundling the Murrays' valuables into a foxes' earth. And, of course, a kiss, uncharacteristically and spontaneously stolen, on a dark, stormy night . . .

Mall blinked, and placed the candlestick on the desk. It was immaculate, no worm or rot weakened its carved and bevelled edges, no clutter of carelessly scattered papers marred its polished surface. Gently, so as to make no noise, she pulled at the handles of the drawers.

They were not locked. Unbelievably, wonderfully, it seemed that her husband put his trust in the stout locks of Kingscote's doors. Sitting on the chair behind the desk, Mall began to search through the papers.

Bills, a great many of them, neatly and alphabetically filed. Estimates, from picture dealers, jewellers, carpenters, goldsmiths. Receipts – from most of the above, plus wine merchants, hat makers, glove makers, tailors, boot makers. IOUs – a small collection of these, their signatures either unfamiliar or indecipherable. But no letters at all. Wiping her red and peeling nose, Mall sat back and considered. Either Sir Nicholas Carleton was unusually unsentimental, or he kept his letters elsewhere.

Her clear brow creased in a frown, Mall stared at the desk. When she had discovered Reynardine searching her father's study, he had been examining the cabinet's secret drawers. This desk might have a secret drawer; some niche in which to conceal the most private correspondence. Meticulously, crouching down beside the desk, Mall began to feel with the sensitive tips of her fingers for catches, springs, concealed fastenings.

Nothing at first, only smooth wood, jointed corners, polished edges. Until suddenly – there it was. Her probing fingers felt metal, there was a whirr and a click, and behind the shortened bottom drawer was a space, bound papers within it.

She could feel her excitement rising, almost unbearably. She had forgotten her streaming nose and sore eyes, had forgotten, even, Carleton. There were goosebumps on the back of Mall's neck, and her hand trembled as she took the papers from the drawer. She slid off the thin ribbon and opened the letters one by one, holding them under the fitful candlelight to read them. Some were signed, a few unsigned. Some love-letters, a few veiled threats, nothing of immediate interest to her. And then she opened the last, short letter.

The writing was uneducated, the hand foreign, the signature only initials: GLR.

After Mall had finished the letter she replaced it with the others, tied the ribbon back around them, and returned the bundle to the concealed space. Then she closed the drawer, checked that the desk was as she had found it, picked up the candle and left the room, slipping the lock with the knife.

But, almost running back through Kingscote's dark, uncaring chambers, she had to push her sleeve against her mouth to silence harsh, painful sobs. And the words of that letter repeated themselves mercilessly, over and over again: *I have done as you bade me. The hunt is almost done. You should have the letters and the Fox within the month.*

I have done as you bade me –

CHAPTER ELEVEN

Your beauty so enticed me
I could not pass it by
So its with my gun I'll guard you
All on the mountains high.

(REYNARDINE)

A *NNA* Murray's first visit to Kingscote, long postponed by the weather and the demands of her family, was made one warm spring day at the beginning of May. Her brother George, soon to leave again for London, rode with her through the tightly leaved woods and blossoming spinneys that decorated the path from Saffron Walden to Kingscote.

Anna felt vaguely remiss in taking so long to visit the new Lady Carleton. She did not envy Mall Conway her new role; the girl was so young, it had plainly been no love match, and that unfortunate business of the highwayman must have given her little choice in the matter. And Anna had never taken to Carleton – there was nothing she could put her finger on (except that Giles, recently, had spoken of the man with something close to hatred), but there was a lack of warmth, a suspicion that the attractive facade covered an unknown interior. An older woman might have understood the man, have found the underlying affections, if there were any – but an inexperienced girl?

And yet, Anna realized, cordially greeting her in Kingscote's impressive Great Hall, Mall was a child no longer. She had always been a pretty girl; Anna had recognized that when, years ago, she had seen beneath the sulky scruffiness. She had become a beauty – pale-skinned, shiney-haired, exquisitely dressed. But she did not, to Anna, look well. Discreet enquiries, when George was occupied in finding for himself the first drink of the day, established that Mall was not yet carrying a child, which would have accounted for the shadows under the eyes and the pallor. Other enquiries, all under the watchful gaze of Mall's black-browed lady's maid produced nothing but anodyne answers: she was well, she was happy, she wanted for nothing.

It was after Anna had been there an hour, and had hinted that she must leave soon, that Mall, desperation in her eyes, had said loudly, 'I think Miss Murray needs a little air. Open a window, would you, Leah?'

And then Mall had passed the quick-thinking, suddenly prostrate Miss Murray her fan, and something else as well, pulled rapidly from one of the fingers of her right hand, and had whispered, 'Give it to Lord Amyott. Ask him to give it to Richard. *Please.*'

Anna Murray had pushed the ring into the palm of her thin leather glove, and had weakly thanked Mall for the open window, commenting that spring was always so ennervating. And she had watched Mall sit back in her chair, a little colour in her white cheeks, her maid again by her side.

It was only when George and Anna had ridden through Kingscote's gates, away from an atmosphere that Anna had begun to find increasingly oppressive, that she had said, frowning, to her brother:

'George, I know that you intend to go to London. But do you think you could escort me to Amyott first?'

George, never one to notice atmosphere, looked at his sister and grinned. 'Too long without seeing him – eh, Anna?'

Anna shook her head, and her grey eyes, the mirror image of George's, looked troubled. She opened her hand, and held out the ring.

'Lady Carleton gave me this. She asked me to take it to Amyott.' She glanced back at the lovely old manor house they had just left. 'I'm afraid she is in some sort of trouble.'

254

George Murray took the ring that Anna held out to him. A funny little ring, green-stoned, of an un-English setting. And a recollection of a glittering Great Chamber, where the dice tumbled on a beautiful inlaid table, always right for his adversary, always wrong for him. And because that evening had been the beginning of a run of bad luck for him, the run that he must repair on this visit to London, every detail of that night had incised itself on his memory: the room, the table, the hand that had thrown the dice with such deadly accuracy. Wearing, on the smallest finger, this ring.

George handed the ring back to Anna, his mouth dry, his heart beating slightly faster. Pulling at the reins, he started northwards.

'Of course I'll take you to Amyott, my dear. We'll go directly.'

Even in London, the sky was a deep uninterrupted blue, the watermeadows dotted with white and yellow spring flowers. A new warmth could be felt in the air, and sunlight glittered on the roofs and windows and the waters of the busy Thames.

The information that Richard Galliers required of Gabriel Thorne was delivered, in quaking person, one early May morning. Much to Gabriel's relief, the unnerving dark-haired gentleman was not in the Holborn Street rooms when he called, the hard-sought scrap of information etched in his sharp young brain. Instead, the same decrepit manservant took him to a different gentleman, less intimidating than his predecessor, but much more gloriously attired. The gold suit that this gentleman wore outclassed, in Gabriel's eyes, Dr de Mayerne at his finest, and caused him momentarily to forget his errand and his manners. But, after a little gentle prompting, he gabbled his message so quickly that the gentleman had to ask him to repeat it all over again, slowly. What that was done, the gentleman smiled wearily, and reached into the capacious pocket of his coat to draw out – an angel. 'I believe this is to be your reward,'

255

was all he said, and thanking him rapidly, Gabriel made a hasty exit and ran fleet-footedly all the way back to Lime Street.

In Holborn Street, Esmé Molyneux fetched his hat, his gloves, and his cane, and walked out into the sunlight.

It took Esmé an unreasonably tedious hour to reach Kate Gilbert's house on the South Bank. Mrs Gilbert, a handsome woman in her mid thirties, had inherited from her late elderly husband a rather large fortune, and an equally large house on the South Bank of the Thames. She thus possessed sufficient money, as well as the independence that only widowhood might bring, to indulge her tastes with relative freedom. One of Mrs Gilbert's tastes ran to the Galliers brothers, and the intermittent, undemanding love affairs that she had enjoyed, at various times, with both Giles and Richard, had succeeded in convincing her that, despite a string of well-born suitors, widowhood was a state infinitely preferable to marriage. Richard Galliers had shared the pleasures of Mrs Gilbert's table and bed since his return from France in the New Year, a mutually agreeable arrangement in which neither enquired too deeply about the other's out-of-bedroom activities.

Mrs Gilbert had not yet risen when Esmé, exhausted by the rigours of battling with wherrymen for a reasonably priced journey across the Thames, was shown into the parlour.

'I shall never again, my dear Richard,' Esmé sank into a well padded chair, 'involve myself in your schemes in any way whatsoever. It is too fatiguing, far too fatiguing.' He pulled out his fan.

Richard Galliers, immaculately dressed in elegant russet silk, his dark hair falling neatly to brush the top of his restrained lace collar, was standing by the parlour window. The expression of amusement on his face was mildly irritating to Esmé, but the faint gleam of interest in his eyes was rather more gratifying.

'I take it my messenger has called?'

Esmé nodded. 'Your fiery-headed angel appeared on my doorstep at a horribly early hour this morning. He was in a mortal hurry to divulge the results of his investigations and be off and never darken my door again. What *did* you threaten the unfortunate child with, Galliers?'

'Oh, total ruin, that's all. If nothing else,' he said, indifferently, 'the experience will teach him to select his victims more judiciously in future. And did he earn his angel?'

Esmé fanned himself. 'A few days past the lad took a package to a ship sailing for Flushing. The package was intended for a certain William Reeve. There was no more specific address, so I would guess it is to be collected in person.'

Galliers left the window, and went towards the door.

'Flushing –'

'The ship sailed for Flushing. But that is not necessarily the package's ultimate destination.'

'No.' Richard picked up his hat from a nearby chair. 'Reeve could be in Middelburg, perhaps. I doubt if he would be much further afield, or they would use a vessel bound for a different port.'

'Zeeland has a sizeable population, and a good many foreigners,' said Esmé, reasonably. 'It might not be so easy to find one particular Englishman there.'

'Then I must hope,' Galliers opened the door, 'that my quarry pursues his former profession. There may be an excess of Englishmen in Zeeland, but I doubt if many of them are apprenticed to apothecaries.'

'And if you find him – what then?'

Their eyes met. The lightness of Galliers' voice belied the expression on his face. 'As you said before, Esmé, I will have a noose to knot around someone's neck. Mr Reeve will simply provide me with the length of rope.'

'At the risk of incurring your displeasure, Richard, I would hazard a guess as to the identity of your quarry.' Slowly, Esmé's long, thin fingers flicked the fan back and forth, back and forth. 'If it is Nicholas Carleton you mean to trap, tread cautiously.'

'I know. I have lost to him before. But I will not lose again.'

Hatred, anger, bitterness or even, remembering history, fear, Esmé Molyneux had expected to see on the finely structured face before him. But the expression of sheer, calculating pleasure was something that momentarily shook him.

This time, the game would be played to the death.

Giles Galliers, riding into London from the north in the afternoon of the same day, might have enjoyed his journey had he not been at least partly suspicious that he had been sent on a wild goose chase. The last few months at Amyott had not been easy; had it not been for Anna Murray, they would have been unendurable. Lady Amyott had been unwell and, despite his sympathy for her past and present troubles, Giles was beginning to find her constant complaints grating. There had been much sickness on the estate. Spring was always a bad time of year, and the servants and labourers seemed to have been falling like flies from one pestilence or another at distressingly frequent intervals. Then, as soon as the repair of the stables had been completed, the main staircase had shown signs of impending collapse. The crumbling stonework had been hastily shored up with an unpretty barrage of beams and wedges, and would cost a great deal of time and money to repair. Had it not been for Anna, Giles sometimes thought he would have let the whole antiquated heap sink back into the mire from which it had originally risen, and taken whatever money was left to him to live a life of glorious irresponsibility.

Like Richard. Momentarily, Giles bitterly envied his younger brother his freedom. Then, guiding his horse through the crowded, litter filled streets, he remembered his errand, and was not so sure. He had not seen Richard since the New Year (ruefully, he recalled the expression on Anna's face when she had seen his bruises). Since then, he had heard nothing concerning his younger brother except the occasional rumour about drinking or womanizing, which he had disregarded. With Richard, it was never easy to dissect truth from fiction. And he would have been happy to leave it that way for the time

258

being – Richard to his own, complicated troubles, he to his more mundane ones – had Anna not unexpectedly turned up on his doorstep the previous day.

She had arrived with her brother George, who had looked a little bit seedier, a little more puffy round the eyes than when Giles had last seen him. Giles had taken Anna to the gardens, away from the depressing sound of chisels and stonemasons' hammers that filled the Great Hall. And there she had shown him the ring, and given him Lady Carleton's message. It was undoubtedly Richard's ring – a small green-stoned one he had brought back from his travels. And it must, Giles realized, have some connection with the conversation that he and Richard had had, so memorably, at New Year. Uneasily, Giles had put the ring in his pocket, and had promised an equally uneasy Anna that he would set off for London at first light the next day.

His first problem would be to find Richard. He must try friends' houses and lodgings, the Dagger, Richard's mistress's house, the playhouses, the taverns, the gambling-dens . . . Sensibly, Giles decided to call on Esmé Molyneux.

There was a ship sailing for Flushing the following morning: a wool merchant's ship, happy enough to take an extra passenger when the right price was offered. It was a good four-masted ship, well built for the heady winds and deceiving sands of the Netherlands passage. It had taken Richard Galliers some time to find a vessel bound for the right destination amongst the tall masts and creaking timbers that crowded the docks at Gravesend. He was impatient to make this journey. For the first time in many years, he had even allowed himself to feel a little cautious optimism.

It was, therefore, with considerable reluctance that he looked back over the gunwale at the sound of his name being called. It was Giles, red-faced and dishevelled, guiding a plainly exhausted horse through the ropes and barrels that littered the quay. Richard paused; the brief flicker of impatience on his face was quickly suppressed, and he leaned over the railings.

'There was really no need to come and see me off, Giles.'

Giles slid off his horse, hitched it to a post, and, ignoring the sailor seated gnome-like at the bottom of the gangway, walked stiffly up to join Richard.

'Not the return fight?' Lolling against the gangway, aggravatingly neat in sober, well-cut, dark clothes, Richard sympathetically inspected his brother's mud-spattered clothing and dusty face. 'I wouldn't give much for your chances this time, Giles.'

Having ridden for almost two days, having barely stopped to eat or drink, and all for an errand that could well be a complete waste of time, Giles failed to find the appropriate words to wipe the annoyingly tender smile from Richard's face. Instead, he reached inside his pocket, found the ring, and held it out to Richard.

It was some consolation that that seemed to have a better effect than any words could have had. The smile vanished as Richard took the ring.

'How did you get this?'

Giles mopped his perspiring forehead with a handkerchief. 'Anna brought it to me yesterday. It was given to her by –'

'Lady Carleton. Anna called at Kingscote?'

Giles nodded, and sat down on a barrel to regain his breath. 'Lady Carleton asked Anna to give me the ring so that I might give it to you.'

'And did she say anything else – any message?'

Giles's eyes met his brother's. 'She said nothing else,' he said bluntly. 'According to Anna, she was not *able* to say anything else.'

Richard frowned, waiting for Giles to continue.

'Apparently some horse-faced maidservant hovered all the time, and they only had a few seconds alone.' He stood up, joining Richard at the gunwale, and said softly, 'Whatever she is trying to tell you, it appears she does not want Carleton to know. If you wish to find out, perhaps you should abandon this

260

voyage to – Flushing, is it? – though why on earth anyone should want to go to Flushing . . .'

Richard shrugged, picked up his bag, and started down the gangway. 'Flushing will have to wait.' He turned to Giles at his side. 'And you, dear brother, do you need to return to Amyott immediately? Or could you be in need of adventure – weary, perhaps, of the life of a respectable squire and husband-to-be?'

It was the voice of temptation whispering in the ear of the temporarily weak-willed. Giles, looked up, mistrust in his brown eyes.

'What sort of adventure?'

'Oh, I might need a little assistance in seeing Lady Carleton – someone to open the door, as it were.'

He had asked, of course, at a time when Giles's resolve was faltering. Months of restraining himself to kissing and holding hands, little more; months of tedious wrangling with servants, relatives, and the very fabric of the house he strove to keep standing. And that damned staircase . . .

Giles Galliers, fifth Lord Amyott, looked Richard levelly in the eye, and for the first time that day, he smiled.

'God rot you to Hell, Richard – why not?'

In the silence of the still, newly leaved woods covering the land to the side of Kingscote, only the occasional night-hunting owl or fox would have seen the two figures, darkly clothed and light footed, gazing through the trees to the manor house beyond. Rising Excalibur-like from the unrippled waters of its moat, Kingscote was impregnable on two sides, bridged on the other two. The bridges were gated, locked and barred, offering no easy access.

Giles looked away from the house, and whispered, 'Do you know where her ladyship's bedchamber is?'

Richard pointed to a dark window, twenty feet above the water, indenting the sheer wall of the house.

'And how in hell,' Giles scanned the wall for footholds, loose stones, anything, 'do you propose to reach that? Fly, perhaps, in one of da Vinci's contraptions?'

Richard, inappropriately, was pulling off his boots. 'Last time I had the lady's cooperation with a rope. This time, as I told you, Giles, *you* are going to open the door. We need a diversion to allow me to enter the house – something that will cause a lot of confusion, opening and shutting of doors, that sort of thing.'

'A fire.' Guaranteed to flush the prey from the coverts, thought Giles, pleased with himself.

'Exactly. It will be easy enough to get into the exterior courtyard, and the stables should burn well.'

'*I* shall set the fire,' said Giles, firmly. 'You would burn the whole bloody place down, given half the chance.'

Giles chose an empty stable, walled off from the rest of the block, conveniently strewn with dry straw, facing Kingscote's main gates. He had no difficulty in entering the courtyard, or, once the fire had gathered sufficient strength not to be too easily extinguished, in waking one of the servants with a few well aimed pebbles at a suitable window. He waited in the cover of the woods until he had seen the dark figure slip silent and unnoticed into Kingscote's courtyard, unseen in the gathering shouts and lantern lights; and then, with one last backward glance at the chaos he had created, Giles, too, melted into the night.

Inside Kingscote, Mall was woken from sleep by the sound of voices and footsteps. It was still dark, but there was something not right, the light in her chamber was not as it should have been. She went to the window and looked out. There was nothing to see, only the trees in the distance, and the moat, black and still, beneath . . . and fragments of smouldering straw, bright against the ebony sky, lifted high into the air by the breeze, floating wraithlike past her window.

Kingscote was on fire.

She was not frightened; instead, Mall smiled, as for one pleasurable moment she saw the answer to all her problems – burn the damn place to the ground, Sir Nicholas and all his works with it. But, as her brief exhilaration died away, she saw that it would not answer, that Sir Nicholas would always save his skin, and a new Kingscote would rise like a phoenix from the ashes.

Leaving her chamber, Mall ran to the adjacent withdrawing room at the corner of the house. She could hear from below the sounds of hurrying feet, the terrified neighs of the horses, and above the clamour, her husband's voice. Looking down from the window, Mall saw the unnatural orange glow of the fire, and the men's faces, weird in the eldritch light.

And then, with no warning whatsoever, a hand clamped over her mouth, and a familiar voice whispered in her ear:

'A pretty sight, is it not? Don't scream, darling, just listen.'

The hold over her mouth relaxed, and there at her side, as dark as the shadows from which he had materialized, stood Richard Galliers.

Pulling Mall into the far corner of the room, he said calmly:

'The hunting lodge at the edge of the wood – I will wait for you there tomorrow.'

Somewhere, not far away, someone called, and her name echoed on high ceilings, stone walls. She tried to speak, but Galliers silenced her, taking her hand in his. 'Don't worry about Sir Nicholas – Giles will take care of him. Do you think you can distract your maid?'

'Yes –' and the voice, Carleton's voice, called again.

The curtains were too short; the furniture offered nothing for a man to hide behind. Fear rose dry in Mall's throat.

'You must go. If he were to find you here –'

Richard Galliers grinned, the strange red light from the fire emphasising the slanting eyes, the long curling mouth.

He was on the sill of the open window by the time the footsteps had reached the withdrawing room door, and then, as Sir Nicholas Carleton turned the handle, he dropped impossibly backwards, heels over head, tumbling into the abyss below.

The hunting lodge perched on the far border of the wood, about a mile from Kingscote house. Had he been in the frame of mind to appreciate architecture, Richard Galliers would have admired the lodge's small, clever symmetry, its miniature geometric escutcheons and turrets, its high narrow lozenge-shaped windows, its flight of stone steps, delicately railed, leading to a front door five foot above the ground.

But, drenched in an ice cold moat, sentenced to an uncomfortable few hours on an unyielding stone floor (the lodge, though pretty, was not furnished), he was not in the mood to appreciate the loveliness of Carleton's hunting lodge. As ever, inaction wearied him, breeching the limited store of his patience. He should be halfway to Flushing by now, on what he instinctively felt to be a still warm trail, instead of waiting, in enforced idleness, for what could only be bad news.

So he had, since parting with Giles during the night, walked the bounds of the stone built lodge; had watched, unmoving, the dawn show through the high windows; and as soon as the day was decently light, had escaped the four confining walls to prowl, his face betraying only the faintest signs of a night unrewarded by sleep, the neatly manicured lawn surrounding the lodge. His horse was tethered to a nearby tree, his pistol and rapier beside his folded cloak. His hair, curled by its immersion in the moat, had dried, his shirt and breeches, dark-coloured and undistinguished, were still faintly damp. Richard Galliers sat at the top of the stone steps in the warmth of the sun, sleeveless doublet open to the waist, the main gauche dagger, as ever, to one hand, a pair of dice, idly thrown, in the other. And his eyes, predatory and wary, watched, alert for any movement not caused by bird or animal.

But a blue velvet skirt did not signify danger: retribution did not come in fine dark velvet edged with pearls. Richard Galliers saw Mall long before she espied him through the leaves and branches, sitting restlessly on the steps of the hunting lodge. He watched her as she moved rapidly beneath the tall, acid-green leaved trees, her gown cutting a swathe through the foot high grass, the sap filled bluebells, the star bright celandines. And then she was out in the sunlit glade that circumscribed the lodge and, seeing Galliers, Mall began to run towards him.

And for some reason that he could not quite understand, it caught him, almost hurting him, that carefree run, heavy skirts looped up in her hands, loose black hair flying behind her. Running, in all the cumbersome paraphernalia of the great lady, a glorious incongruity that forcefully, unexpectedly, reminded him of why he had once kissed her, so long ago, on the hills between Cambridge and Belford.

He had thought himself no longer prey to sentimentality.

He rose as she approached, and said lazily, mockingly:

'You will trip over your farthingale if you run like that.' He tossed the dice one last time, and then returned them to his pocket. 'You should have been born a boy, my dear, then you would not have suffered the encumbrance of skirts.'

Galliers stood, leaning on the rail, amusement in his eyes as Mall recovered her breath.

'Leah?' he prompted, gently.

She smiled, and brushed back her hair from her face. 'Rendered, in turn, hysterical by the fire, and unconscious by valerian tea.'

He gave her his arm, saying, 'I think we are safe enough here not to have to skulk inside that damned lodge.' They began to walk around the grounds.

Galliers continued: 'I assume Giles's messenger came.'

'About Giles selling his paintings?' Mall's eyes narrowed, watching Richard Galliers' unrevealing face. 'Yes, he arrived early this morning.'

She added, 'I understand that Lord Amyott sent the messenger to remove my husband from Kingscote for the day. But surely Giles is not so short of funds that he really intends to sell him his dearest painting?'

Galliers looked pleased with himself. 'I *knew* a collector like Carleton would not be able to resist seeing the Hans Memling.'

Mall pulled at his sleeve, slowing the relentless walking. 'But would Lord Amyott really sell it to Sir Nicholas?'

'Oh yes.' He paused at last, the sunlight catching the tips of his dark hair and glinting on the thin gold chain around his neck. 'If Carleton will buy, Giles will most certainly sell. The picture is a forgery – I picked it up in the Netherlands some time ago. But it's a good copy – I think it will take Sir Nicholas some time to be sure.' He added, looking down at Mall through sleepy-lidded eyes, 'Giles set fire to your stables, by the way.'

Mall had been casually occupied in picking daisies from the grass and piercing them with her thumb to make a chain. '*Giles* –'

'That's right – the responsible, the worthy, the soon-to-be married Lord Amyott, tempted briefly back into wickedness by one murmur from the serpent.'

'Meaning you, Mr Galliers?'

He inclined his head, watching her form the daisies into a circle. He was, he found, enjoying this assignation more than he had expected. The blue sky, the warm sun, the faint music of bumblebee and thrush must still work some magic on even the most restless soul. And she had always been a pleasant companion, quick to laugh (if also quick to anger), and blessedly slow to judge.

Sentiment again. God, old age must be creeping up on him unawares – he would be wishing her for a daughter soon! He was not here, after all, for the conversation. He pointed to the chrysoberyl ring, back in its original place on his smallest finger.

'I assume you have something you wish to tell me.'

The slender fingers holding the daisy chain clenched suddenly, and the chain fell in two halves to the ground. 'I had to talk to you. Miss Murray appeared unexpectedly, and the ring was the only thing I could think of at the time.'

'It served its purpose.' Galliers saw the unhappiness in her eyes, and then, for the first time, noticed the new shadows on her face, the pallor of her skin. And there it was again, that ridiculous avuncular urge to take her in his arms and comfort her. 'Tell me, Mall – have things been difficult?'

Mall could not meet his eyes, but she nodded, recognizing an unexpected gentleness in his voice. 'Sir Nicholas . . . does not trust me –' and then she broke off suddenly, shaking her head. 'I saw a letter. It was hidden in my husband's desk, in a secret drawer. The writing was foreign – it was unsigned, initialed GLR.' She took a deep breath. 'The letter said that a spy had been placed in the Countess of Somerset's household. A spy who will find my husband's letters for him. And that this GLR is on the Fox's trail. Reynardine's trail.'

She fell silent, her gaze fixed on the scattered daisies, the sun-strewn grass, anything but Galliers's eyes.

But this time, he found, it was not despair he felt, but an unreasonable pot-pourri of unexpectedly violent emotions: impatience, fast returning (this made the journey to Flushing even more urgently necessary); fear – how on earth had Mall managed to get her hands on this letter (and in a secret drawer)?; and finally, returning in double quantity, that old well-nurtured hatred of Carleton. For, looking at Mall's white face, and thin, bird-boned shoulders, he knew without doubt that matters between Carleton and his wife must have worsened considerably. What on earth had that bastard been doing to the girl? Richard moved away from her, attempting, inadequately, to hide the intensity of his feelings.

Misinterpreting his expression, Mall said edgily, 'I know you told me not to – not to creep about in darkened passageways, I mean. But I was desperate. I had to do something.'

Richard had a sudden vision of her, small and fragile, trying to hide her fear as she had once before, on that memorable winter flight to the Fens. He said, carefully, 'How did you do it, Mall? Carleton must surely keep his doors locked.'

'I picked the lock.' Her eyes, the same dark velvety blue as her gown, looked warily up at him. 'It was quite easy.'

Looking at the mulish expression that had accompanied her last words, Richard was ludicrously torn between crying with disbelieving laughter and losing his temper with her completely. When he had, after a brief inward battle, succeeded in controlling himself, he said, keeping his voice steady:

'It may have been easy, Mall, but it was not wise. Where was Carleton? Asleep next door, I suppose, and the rest of the household lurking round the corner?' His amusement left him abruptly, replaced by an unpleasant picture of just what her well meaning attempts at self help might have led to. 'For Christ's sake, Mall – you are no longer playing games of kiss-and-chase with the stable lads at Belford for a little harmless fun! Carleton is dangerous – he is clever and patient, and if he found you reading his private correspondence . . . I hate to imagine what he might do.'

He had spoken more harshly than he intended, fear lending an edge to his voice, a sleepless night subtracting from his judgement. He saw Mall bite her lip, saw her eyes sparkle suspiciously, and heard her say in a curiously blurred tumble of words:

'He would give me to Lucas Holland, that's what he would do.'

Like a stunning blow to the head, the full painful impact of her words did not register in the first numb second. The sky was still blue, the larks still soared high over the fields to the north, the early butterflies still floated on the warm air currents. But Richard Galliers saw none of it, he only heard himself swear, once, unrepeatedly, under his breath, and felt himself pull Mall close to him, her wet face against his shirt front.

Rather than an act of comfort, or affection, the gesture began as a solace for his empty arms. Had a sword been at his side, and Carleton at Kingscote, the solution would have been simple, satisfying, and be hanged to the consequences. But his sword was at the lodge, and Carleton at Amyott, so he must be content with one aching hand holding her shaking blue velvet back, the other stroking her wild black hair, as he stared sightlessly, into the darkness of the wood beyond.

And when he could trust himself to speak, his words were thoughtlessly kind, and his mouth brushed the crown of her head, and he felt the softness of her hair against his face. Hair like black silk, with none of the harshness that years of artistry had given to Madame Berthe's blonde locks; loose and long, escaping in untamable tendrils, not combed and restrained like Kate Gilbert's neat fair coiffure.

Not a little girl's hair, and his feelings were suddenly, compellingly, not avuncular. He lifted her face to see if she was crying, and seeing that she was not, and that her lips were slightly parted, he kissed her.

It was not a kiss like Reynardine's, mocking and careless, a kiss that had angered and teased and tormented Mall for weeks. But a real kiss this time, deep and passionate, showing her that at that moment Richard Galliers desired her just as much as she desired him. *Therewithal sweetly did me kiss, and softly said, Dear heart, how like you this* . . . Dear heart, thought Mall, dear heart, and her arms went about him, feeling the warmth of his body through the thin material of his shirt, burying her fingers in his dark hair, winding through the long locks that touched his shirt collar. And Mall's mouth returned kiss for kiss: on forehead, neck and breast, their skin, hair and fingers entangled, searching, hungry.

He did not speak as he untied the ribbons of her bodice and sleeves, but his darkened eyes said enough for her to know that here was joy, not torment, here was pleasure, not pain. And when he lifted her in his arms and laid her on the soft grass and knelt beside her, she saw that now his hands were not quite so steady, now his breathing more carefully controlled. His face banded by the bright sky and the shadow of the lacy branches, he said softly, 'Wake, now my love, awake,' and it was Mall who untied the laces of his shirt and drew him down to her, so that his mouth found hers and took the hurt and degradation of Carleton's usage from her soul.

If Nicholas Carleton had taken away her virginity, then it was Richard Galliers who took her desire and, igniting it, bound it about them so that all need for words, for thought, was gone. In lovemaking he was not impatient: his hands drew the music from her body as skilfully as they drew music from a lute, giving all time, all care, to their mutual pleasure. The mocking, careless rake of Belford's banquet had gone, but so had the highwayman, Reynardine. Reynardine's dangerous allure

269

might have led her to this grassy bank, this burning embrace, but now Reynardine was nothing more than a dark, flickering shadow of the past. In his place was a lover who could follow her own thoughts and desires before she even knew they existed, who could conjure, from a body innocent of love, a skill and joy to equal his own.

So, although it seemed to Richard Galliers that he had waited a lifetime for this, he did not satisfy himself until he was sure that their hunger was mutual, that they might die the little death together.

It would have been wise, perhaps, to return to the lodge, but they had forgotten wisdom, had forsaken caution. The grass was kinder than any silken sheets, the fretwork of branches and new spring leaves that sheltered them from the midday sun a better canopy than velvet and damask. The birds' song was music enough, the salt taste of the girl's skin under his questing mouth sweeter than any wine.

As they made love in the silence of the ancient wood, Richard Galliers discovered emotions he had long thought dead, buried under the destroying passions of hatred and loss. He was able, on that bright spring day, to leave a little of the bitterness of three years' exile behind him, and for a few short moments to forget the hatred that no pleasure – neither women, nor wine, nor battle – had even been able to vanquish. And Mall learned what she had suspected for many months: that the man she loved now she would love until the day she died.

Galliers looked down at the dishevelled head cradled in his arm, and thought, Oh Mall, what have we done.

Her eyes were closed, but she was not sleeping. Gently, he touched the back of her head and said her name.

When she looked up at him, she saw none of her own happiness reflected on his face, but saw instead that his eyes, as so often, were fixed on some unknown, disturbing, future. But she did not move or speak: she would not be the first to break whatever spell had briefly bound them together.

After a while Richard spoke quietly, his arm still around her, his hand absently stroking her hair.

'A spy inside the Somersets' house is not necessarily a disaster. It would still not be easy for anyone to find the letters.' He paused, collecting his thoughts, adjusting the truth to what she must want to hear. 'When Giles arrived with the ring, I was on my way to Flushing in search of someone whom I believe to have evidence of the Overbury murder – an apothecary's apprentice called William Reeve. So do not despair, Mall – it is simply a question of who is to find their quarry first.'

His hand stilled, he must be practical now, no more folly, no more impulse, he must not give in to the temptation just to lie here forever, holding her. He sat up, pulling his shirt over his head. 'If things should become unbearable for you, then you must leave – go to your stepmother, or to Giles – even Hosea Dockerill, if you are afraid Carleton should follow. I would ask Giles to call at Kingscote, but I doubt if he would be given admittance.' But Anna might, Galliers thought as he passed Mall her crumpled, grass-stained gown: Anna may be trusted to keep an eye on Mall.

He watched her as she sat on the grass, struggling with the complicated arrangements of her clothing. Helping her to her feet, Galliers stood in front of her, and took her hand.

'Listen to me, Mall. Lucas Holland was never anything more than a pretty face in search of a patron. If Carleton had not found him first, someone else, man or woman, would have paid to have that face on their pillow at night. Even Jeremy – he was very young, and easily led. You could never be like either of them. What I am trying to say is that Carleton cannot change you, but he could hurt you. So for God's sake, leave the rest of this to me.'

She thought, looking unsteadily up at him, how many weeks, how many months, until I see you again –

'When will you return to England?'

'As soon as I can.' He could offer no more; there were still too many unknowns. 'I can be in London tonight, and at Gravesend to find a ship tomorrow. A couple of weeks, with

271

luck – and I could be back with evidence that will send Carleton to the Tower. But you must be careful – if Carleton should know that there has been anything between us, that I was Reynardine, then that would be disastrous. Because, my darling, he would only have to threaten you to control me.'

Mall tried to smile. 'So no more creeping about in darkened passageways?'

'No.' He pulled a stray daisy from her hair. 'You promise?'

'I promise.' And what do you promise, Richard Galliers, she thought, what do you promise? No promises, of course, and she must ask for none.

So she left. No more kisses, no sweet words, no poetry. Her feet seemed to know the path back to Kingscote, which was fortunate, as her eyes, blurred with tears, refused to focus on the gaiety of the spring flowers around her. And a different verse of Wyatt's song chorused:

> *'It was no dream: I lay broad waking,*
> *But all is turned through my gentleness*
> *Into a strange fashion of forsaking . . .'*

CHAPTER TWELVE

The judge's men do follow me,
And my life they would destroy
So I'm seeking for concealment
All on the mountains high.

(REYNARDINE)

*G*ILES, watching Richard from across Amyott's small parlour table, thought his brother unusually cooperative. He had arrived at Amyott early that evening, having plainly ridden hell-for-leather, with the intention of imparting some message to Giles, and then leaving for London. When Giles had pointed out, reasonably, that Richard's lathered and white-eyed horse looked fit to drop, and that, although he could doubtless be provided with a substitute from Amyott's stables, it really would be much more sensible to have some food and some sleep, and set off early the next morning, Richard had glared at him furiously for a moment, and then relaxed, shrugged, and accompanied his brother into the house.

Borrowing some more respectable clothing from Giles, Richard endured the inevitable interview with his mother. The encounter was, as before, short and meaningless, but lacking in quite that glittering sharp edge of insult that Richard could add so adeptly to even the briefest verbal exchange. If there was no meeting of souls, at least there was no further severance of already overstrained ties. Indeed, it seemed to Giles as though Richard's mind was somewhere completely other than Lady Amyott's over furnished, under ventilated room at Amyott.

The two brothers dined alone in a small parlour at the back of the house, away from the demoralizing chaos that still littered the Great Hall. When the servants had gone, and the glasses had been filled, Giles leaned back in his chair, and unable to contain his curiosity any longer said, invitingly:

'Carleton wouldn't buy the Memling.'

Richard glanced across at him, glass in hand. 'Would he not? A pity . . . but it occupied him long enough.'

'Yes?'

It was darkening outside, the thin silver crescent of the moon lay on her back in the velvet sky overhead. Giles noticed the familiar hooding of Richard's eyes, the hard line of his mouth. He saw his brother stand and move to look out of the window, the shoulders of his borrowed doublet over large on his slight frame.

Bravely, Giles prompted, 'And you, Richard? You saw Lady Carleton?'

Richard looked out to the gardens beyond. *Oh, I saw Lady Carleton. I bedded Carleton's wife, on Carleton's green lawns, on Carleton's land . . .* He said, with difficulty:

'I saw her. She had some news for me.'

Turning back to Giles, Richard described the letter Mall had seen, the secret drawer in Carleton's desk. His plate of food lay untouched before him. It had become an effort of will to frame his words sensibly: his mind kept returning to the unreal events of the afternoon. He gathered his wits, and said:

'I would like you to do something for me, Giles. I would like you to ask Anna if she would call on Mall while I am away. She was received there before, so there should be no difficulty.'

Giles frowned and paused, his beef-speared knife midway to his mouth. 'Just to call on her?'

'Yes. Nothing more.' A brief silence, an impatient wave of the hand. 'Simply to see that she is – well.'

The beef found its way to Giles's mouth, and he ate for a while, expecting Richard to join him. He did not, however, but stood at the window, lost in thought, his hand cradling the wine glass. He was silent, but the face that was so nearly like Giles's

274

own, and yet by some extra stroke of the artist's brush so utterly, obliquely, different, was completely devoid of its customary expression of indifferent superiority. Eventually Giles, irritated by the silence, and by the monotony of eating by himself, recalled the last strands of their conversation, and said impatiently:

'Are you concerned for her – Lady Carleton, I mean? Do you think Carleton means her harm?'

He would give me to Lucas Holland, that's what he would do . . .

And it surprised Richard as much as it surprised Giles, that the stem of the glass he held twisting in his hand shattered suddenly, shards and fragments of glass shining like diamonds in the red pool of wine that lay dark on the old oak floor.

Richard's spurs touched the horse's flanks again, and he ducked to avoid overhanging branches as he galloped along Essex's leafy lanes. But speed could not block out the implacable workings of his mind. There had been no excuse: if he wanted sexual satisfaction there were plenty of women like Kate Gilbert, like Berthe, women who knew the rules of the game. Yet he had made love to her – to Mall, who should have married some pleasant, sensible squire her own age, who would have taken care of her and been able to give her the love she deserved and the security she needed.

Of course, there were answers, excuses if he cared to make them. There had been no doubt that in the oblivion of the moment she had wanted him just as much as he had wanted her. She was pretty, he would have had to be blind not to notice that. But, he thought savagely, pulling at the reins to swing the horse across a flat plain, he had been no young stripling, tempted by his first glimpse of available female flesh. He had known exactly what he was doing.

There was, unbearably, another motive, one he had to force himself to confront. If he had not been smitten with a sudden irresistible passion, then he had to consider the possibility that it was solely as the treasured possession of Sir Nicholas

275

Carleton that he had wanted her, an instrument of revenge for his brother's death and his own exile.

And that, Galliers thought, a grim expression in his cold, bleak eyes, *was* unforgiveable.

When, finally, in the middle of the following day, Richard Galliers arrived at Gravesend, it was to discover that there were no ships sailing for Zeeland until the end of the week. Exhaustive enquiries, tramping from one end of the crowded, bustling docks to the other, produced nothing more promising than a wool merchant's vessel that would not sail before Friday. Had he, Galliers reflected bitterly as he rode back towards London, wished to sail for any other far flung corner of the world – Cathay, the Americas – there would have been ships aplenty. But Zeeland? He must be patient, and William Reeve must wait a little longer for his unwanted visitor.

He did not return to Mrs Gilbert, who would have little forbearance either with restlessness or the qualms of a newly discovered conscience. Neither did he go to Esmé Molyneux, in Holborn Street: Esmé's indolent, bored gaze knew him too well. Galliers went instead to the Red Bull, scene of past conflicts and dramas, provider of bit parts in some comedies of his own staging. The Red Bull would be nearing the end of the season, preparing to close for the summer, playing out the leftovers of its exhausted repertoire, its players beginning to look forward to exchanging the growing heat of the city for the variety of the open road.

But there would be loyal company if he wanted it: undemanding, uncritical, and blessedly unadmiring. There would also be hazard and cards to occupy his mind and perhaps to line his pocket (necessary in view of the journey ahead), and, most important, an anonymous and solitary bed for the night.

But even that solace was denied to him. When Galliers arrived at the Red Bull late that evening, having entered the playhouse by dubious means, it was to find the tiring house already occupied. Overflowing with chests, baskets, piles of gaudy clothing, counterfeit armour and weapons, tables, chairs, stools, false beards and wigs, the chaos was further compounded by the presence of Nathaniel Brand and Benedict Daniel, noisily and aggressively occupying one corner of the room.

'My dear Galliers.' It was Nathaniel who spoke, accepting his arrival as though he had been the expected second lord in one of the Bull's less memorable plays. 'Richard, perhaps you would explain to our mutual friend here –' Nat's hand touched vigorously on Benedict's resentful back, '– that even if you have been denied the company of women for a year – a *decade* – you still do not bed the wife of one of the Bull's rapidly declining band of patrons and –'

Benedict swung from Nathaniel's grasp, out of the shadows and into the candlelight. And on his generally comely face blossomed a new and rapidly swelling black eye, of much the same shade of crimson as his doublet.

'– and be found out?' finished Galliers dryly. Under the dust and sweat of travel, the corners of his mouth twitched suspiciously. 'Oh, Bennet.' One hand lightly touched Benedict's bruised countenance. 'Her husband's mark, I assume?'

Benedict shook himself away and perched, shoulders hunched, on a nearby chest. 'The damned fellow would have been none the wiser if Nat had done as I had asked.' He scowled heavily, then regretted it, wincing.

Nathaniel, his face taut with exaggerated patience, retrieved his hat and gloves from a nearby chair. 'The lady's husband could only talk of the price of broadcloth and the incredible variety of diseases that sheep are subject to. He simply had no other conversation – and there is a limit to how long even I can talk to myself.'

'Really?' A fighting light had returned to Benedict's swollen sapphire eye.

'*Really*. There is also a limit to how much boredom I will endure to ensure the continuance of your love life.'

Benedict was on his feet, his hands, like Nathaniel's, fisted. 'Then that's the last damn time I –'

Galliers stepped between them, a hand on each man's shoulder.

'Gentlemen. Fascinating though this little divertissement is, I came here in hopes of a quiet bed for the night, not to witness unscripted melodramatics.'

His voice was mild, but there was an edge to it that they were both wise enough to recognize. The scene failed to reach its conclusion: fists relaxed, and Nathaniel plonked his battered hat on to his mousy hair, and said with justifiable glee:

'Then you'll have the pleasure of sharing the room with Bennet here. He daren't return to his lodgings, and I'm damned if he's going to sleep on my floor!'

In the silence that followed Nathaniel's final exit, Benedict Daniel and Richard Galliers eyed each other, green eyes speculative, blue eyes sour. Eventually Benedict spoke.

'And whose outraged husband are *you* hiding from, Richard? Or –' his irritation evaporated slightly as he took in the dusty riding clothes and slightly less than gentlemanly appearance, 'perhaps it's the *law* you're hiding from – the Red Bull today, France tomorrow?'

Galliers was unbuckling his rapier. 'I hate to disappoint you, dear Bennet, but I am escaping neither jealous husbands nor the hangman's noose. Besides, it is not France I wish to visit –' rapier, pistol and cloak found their way into an empty basket '– but Zeeland, so I must somehow pass the time until a ship sails on Friday.'

'Zeeland?' Benedict's voice rose in practised disbelief. Then, more thoughtfully, he said again, 'Zeeland . . . that's a long way from Clerkenwell.'

'Well done, Ben. Very perceptive.' Galliers heaved out a blanket from under a pile of multi-coloured costumes. 'I suppose the ladies love you for your quick mind.'

'Richard.' Benedict's voice had changed again, sweetly cajoling. 'Your business in Zeeland. Perhaps you would like some assistance – someone who has worked with you before.

278

After all,' he went on hurriedly, 'it may not be exactly convenient for me to appear on stage next week.'

'With the mark of Cain on your face, as it were?' It was on the tip of Galliers' tongue to give the refusal Benedict doubtless expected. Bennet would talk too much, and his company would be gratingly cheerful. On the other hand, he was cunning enough, and two would likely find William Reeve twice as quickly as one. And time was beginning to be in horribly short supply.

He was, he discovered, extremely tired. Amyott's linen sheets had not permitted him sleep, but a blanket on the floor of the untidy, undisciplined Red Bull might.

He slid down to the floor, hands cushioning his head, his eyes already closed. 'Very well, Ben. You may come with me. If –' his eyes opened a fraction, glittering darkly in the thin candlelight, 'if you do not snore.'

Late on Sunday evening, the *Flower of Norwich*, a seaworthy four masted galleon, put into Flushing's deep water harbour. The ship had sailed from Gravesend with the tide on Friday morning, and, the weather keeping fair, had made a speedy and happily uneventful passage. The *Flower of Norwich* was a wool merchant's ship, and she carried a mixed cargo of wools, dyes and leather, plus a little gold destined for the Continental headquarters of the Company of Merchant Venturers at Middelburg. The *Flower of Norwich* also carried a little extra, human, cargo, an easy profit for her master. Of the two men that had taken passage with the ship, the master had hardly seen the younger one. He had been an auburn-haired fellow, good looking if one were to ignore the disfigurement of the latter stages of an impressive black eye, but a poor sailor. He had spent much of the journey in his cabin, green and groaning. The other, a dark-haired man a little older than his nauseated companion, had prowled the decks, his eyes on the sails as though constant vigilance could ensure a favourable wind. The master could not quite place him: he was not dressed as a gentleman, although the thin jewelled dagger at his side, and the engraving on the ricasso of his rapier spoke of money. And although the dark-haired man knew the workings of a ship as well as any common sailor, the master doubted that he had earned his gold plying the trade routes. Attempts to satisfy his curiosity had proved unrewarding – any topic of conversation more intimate than the science of navigation or the positioning of a galleon's cannon was met with a polite but impenetrable reserve.

It occurred to Richard Galliers, leading an ashen-faced and wobbly-kneed Benedict along Flushing's tidy quay, that the master might not be the only one to be curious, so it would be advisable to find some occupation suitable to the town's more loquacious haunts. It would also be advisable not to be too obviously English.

Benedict, at his side, had recovered his voice. 'Never – ever – again. I shall remain on the Continent for the rest of my days rather than endure that misery once more.'

With rather unkind force, Galliers clapped him on the back.

'Cheer up, my friend. No more galleys charged with forgetfulness for you. Tonight you'll sing for your supper.'

Dark in the winter, in the early summer Kingscote's Gallery was bright yet cool. The Gallery was one of the loveliest rooms in the house, its proportions elegantly magnificent, its vistas of moat and gardens complemented by a fine collection of tapestries and paintings.

It was to the Gallery that Sir Nicholas Carleton went on his return from a week in London. His wife's presence was announced by the scales, trills and chords that swirled and soared from the spinet into the dust-moted air.

She did not see him: he made no sound as he stood at the door, still clothed in the black and scarlet he had worn for the ride. The spinet she played lay in a pool of sunlight, the quilting and ribbons of her yellow sarsenet gown caught and reflected the sunlight, giving her the appearance of some glorious and exotic summer flower. But a flower with a worm at its heart, rotten to the core. The ride had done nothing to lessen the anger he had felt since that memorable conversation of the previous day. A conversation in which he had paid to learn that his wife was betraying him. He watched Mall's neat dark head as she bent over the keys, saw her soft white hands touch the spinet with a gentleness she had never shown to him, and felt an almost intolerable sense of outrage infuse him.

He went over to her. He could bear the music no longer; its formalized happiness injured him.

His shadow fell over the keyboard, darkening the golden ivory of the keys so that Mall paused, her fingers suddenly disobedient. She turned and said his name, and he heard his own voice answer, 'Beautifully played, my dear. You have so many talents,' but it was her talent for deception that obsessed him, gnawing at his soul.

She began to rise from the stool, but he stopped her, one hand touching the smooth marbled skin of her shoulder, the other covering her right hand, still loosely fisted on the spinet keys. His fingers felt hers. There was no ring.

His impulse was to shake her, to break her until she could be moulded pliantly to what she should have been: he quelled it.

'I realize my return has been a little – unannounced. But I was given some rather unexpected information. Where is your ring, Mall?'

She looked up at him. She disguised fear well, he knew. Her lovely eyes would not cringe, she would brazen it out, defying him as she had in the pool, as she had after their wedding, lying to him. 'The ring, Mall,' he prompted. 'The green-stoned ring you usually wear on this hand.'

There was, then the faintest frisson of fear on her face, darkening her eyes, firming her mouth. But still she lied. 'I lost it – a little while ago, I must have taken it off somewhere, and put it down.'

'No.' He managed by an effort of will to keep his voice gentle. He let go of her shoulder, and lifted her hand, looking at the pale ovals of her nails, the small tapering fingers, the slightly

lighter skin where the ring had once been, and now, irredeem-
ably, was not. 'You did not *lose* it, my dear. You gave it to
someone.'

A cloud crossed the face of the sun, and the room momentarily grew colder. Carleton continued, 'I know that you gave the
ring to someone. To whom did you give it, Mall?'

She opened her mouth as if to speak, but said nothing. He
studied her, and knew that her mind was racing, burrowing in
culverts and blind alleyways, looking for an escape. She would
be calculating who had betrayed her; Anna Murray, Giles
Galliers . . . Richard Galliers? It angered him. His hold on her
hand tightened; he could feel the small bones move within his
grasp. His face remained a mask, however, drained of expression.

He said carefully, 'You can be so obstinate – and that is very
foolish, you know, my dear. I know who you sent the ring to.
You sent it to Richard Galliers. To Reynardine.'

And now, pleasingly, he could see fear on her face. But still
she tried, saying desperately, 'Reynardine? I told you – he was
just a brigand –'

Some of his control snapped, for a fraction of a second his
anger showed. He said, harshly, 'I'm sorry, Mall, but it won't
do. Not any longer.' He lifted her chin, looking at her face as
though for the first time. 'You are very beautiful, my dear, and I
intend that you should remain so. I wanted you the first time I
set eyes on you. I do appreciate beauty, you see. But
occasionally, even the greatest connoisseur can purchase
something that is flawed. Exquisite on the surface, perhaps, but
of inferior quality beneath.'

Light flooded suddenly through the lovely old windows of the
Gallery, staining a square of the floor with sunshine, catching
on the golden edges of the miniatures, softening the dark
colours of the tapestries. He knew that she wished to shrink
back from him, but she had nowhere to go, he had imprisoned
her in the golden cage that Kingscote had become.

'I will not mark your lovely face – bruise those soft lips,
blacken your eyes.'

He broke off, turning from her so that Mall would not see that, though there was terror on her face, on his own there was pain.

He regained his control, and, shaking his head, said, 'Nothing so crude. But there are other ways. You could, like my late Lord of Essex's unfortunate wife, simply have a bad fall.' In his mind's eye he saw Mall, tumbling endlessly down Kingscote's curving stone staircase, red blood breaking the perfection of her face and body. He forced that vision away: there was a faint film of perspiration on his brow, he dabbed at his forehead with his handkerchief.

'Or there is Luke, of course.'

And that threat, he could see, really frightened her. What little remaining colour there was drained from her face. He sensed the beginnings of victory, and strove to push it home.

'Yes, there is Luke. He will ravish whomever I instruct him to.'

But that idea, once so compelling, had lost its magic. The prospect of sharing Mall even with Lucas had become distasteful to him. The scene in his bedchamber had shown him that.

He saw that Mall's pallor had become extreme: he went to the table, poured a glass of wine, and held it to her lips, saying insidiously, 'If the thought of lovemaking with Lucas Holland gives you no pleasure, then perhaps we had better start again. I have suspected Reynardine's identity for many months. All I require is your evidence. Which you will be sensible and give me, won't you, Mall? Richard Galliers *is* Reynardine, is he not?'

She was silent for a moment, and then, slowly, her head inclined in assent.

And the sickening spectre of Richard Galliers and Mall together struck him anew, colliding with the other dread that had haunted him since Frances Kerr had sent her indiscreet letter: that he would lose Kingscote.

But, at least Mall was no longer resisting him. 'Richard Galliers is Reynardine,' he heard her say almost imaudibly, as if she could not yet quite accept her defeat.

He should have been triumphant at her admission, but he was not. Carleton closed his eyes, blocking out the blinding reflection of the sun on the polished wooden floor. His fingers longed to enclose that small white neck, to make her beg for mercy. The man who had rebuffed him once, as though he were no more than a common harlot hawking for trade. Richard Galliers – always Richard Galliers. A man with the manners and address of a guttersnipe, the code of honour of a bawd. The man who had taken Jeremy away, and who now sought to steal his wife. The man who, perhaps, had it in his grasp to take Kingscote from him. Who should have learnt his lesson more than three years ago.

Carleton said, thickly, 'So you spent those three days with Galliers last winter?'

Mall had recovered a little of her composure. 'Three days and three nights,' she said, levelly. 'He took me against my will, but I stayed – voluntarily.'

His mouth was dry, but he forced the single word out. '*Why?*'

A faint wash of pink rose to her cheeks, and the long-lashed violet-tinged eyelids flickered once.

'He was hurt. He had a bullet wound in his shoulder. I helped him because, if I had not done so, he would have died.'

Carleton said nothing, but stood, weighing her words. Then he said: 'You have seen him since. You saw him a week ago, when I was conveniently out of the way viewing Amyott's spurious Memling.' He did not wait for her answer, he could see the truth in her eyes. 'Perhaps you should tell me, my lady, how many other times you have enjoyed Mr Galliers's delightful company.'

In the endless, all-encompassing wait that followed, he could hear the distant sound of the servants in the courtyard, see the pigeons swooping through the blue air towards the dovecote. At last she said, 'Once. I saw Mr Galliers one other time. In March, when you were in London.'

He tried to frame his next, most necessary question lightly, but his face betrayed him. 'So what is he to you, then – your lover?'

She stared at him, and then, improbably, laughed, a jarring sound with no nuance of humour. 'My lover? No – Mr Galliers certainly does not *love* me. Mr Galliers has no time for love. He has only one passion; to revenge himself for what you did to his brother, nearly four years ago.' She smiled bitterly. 'I do not believe Richard Galliers is capable of loving anyone.'

He believed her. He could see the truth in her eyes, her bearing. If Galliers had been courting Mall, she would have told him so, triumphantly, a challenge blazing in her dark eyes. Galliers did not want his wife, and he would not have her. But she, he realized, had wanted him. It was Richard Galliers who had occupied her thoughts these last six months, Richard Galliers who had taken her from him, taking the joy even from his marriage bed.

She read his thoughts, and said flatly, 'I had – some affection – for him. Calf love, he thought. I expect he was right.'

And at last Carleton retreated, sitting down on a chair to the side of the Gallery. His dark foreign eyes still studied Mall, noting that the yellow silk seemed faintly crushed, that there was a bruised, defeated look to her pale face. He forced a smile to his lips. 'So Galliers used you, my poor little country innocent. He used you to spy on me, playing on your pathetic infatuation to persuade you to help him.' She was silent, but he saw her hand shake as she brushed aside the stray curls from her forehead. 'Poor Mall! You really must grow wiser, my dear. You are not the first he has used in this way.'

But if Galliers did not intend to take his wife, then he would be seeking to hurt him in some other way. Ah, Kingscote, of course. His home, the home of his ancestors for hundreds of years – the threat to Kingscote had not diminished. His hands gripped the chair arms as he saw where Galliers would strike him. If the Countess's intrigues were to be discovered, her accomplices would lose their heads, and their estates would be attainted. And suddenly, as the white-hot anger returned, he saw through the other deceptions: Richard Galliers' drunkenness, the tales of debauchery and prodigality that had convinced his stupid, beautiful Lucas . . .

He looked back at Mall, and saw that she must tell him more.

'So where, my dear, is the busy Mr Galliers now?'

He rose from the chair, the palms of his hands damp with sweat. He said, trying to keep his voice steady:

'Tell me, Mall. Galliers does not appear to be in London. Neither is he at Amyott, I hear. Therefore it seems possible that he has left the country –' He paused, his fevered eyes studying Mall's face. 'For good? I think not. I think he still seeks to trap me. Where is he, Mall?'

She was mute: her lips slightly parted, her breathing short and uncontrolled. He went to her, pulling her roughly to her feet.

'I said, I need to know. Did you not hear me, my loving, faithless wife? Perhaps Lucas Holland can present my case more forcefully. I shall have him sent for today. Is Richard Galliers in France?'

He felt her shaking, quivering as a hawk does before she is tamed. Perhaps not France. How far might Galliers have already unravelled the tangled skein of the Countess's plots?'

'The Low Countries – is he in the Low Countries?'

He heard the sound escape involuntarily from her lips, and suddenly the pieces fell into place, and he knew where Galliers was, and what he was looking for. He said, softly:

'Richard Galliers is in the Netherlands. He has gone there to find that damned apprentice.'

And he felt her go limp in his arms like a child's rag doll, saw the blue eyes close with something like relief; and he held her to him, tenderly cradling her unsupported head against the scarlet passementerie of his doublet.

The glories of the Zeeland sunsets – pinks, oranges, reds and golds staining the plains of sand, sea, and grass – could only be equalled in England by the sunsets of the Fenlands. The low-lying land, the marshes, the creeks and inlets, the complicated tracery of the fiercely defended coastline, all these, too, were echoed in the east of England. But with geography the

286

similarity ended. The tidy, busy town of Flushing, with its valuable deep harbour, and its organized, well maintained system of dykes, dunes, barrages and windmills, was unmistakably Dutch, and had no English equivalent. Whereas in East Anglia there were still endless marshes, waving trees and thinly populated islands, in Zeeland there was harbour, town and house, perfectly kept up, meticulously clean, a monument to the housewifely spirit of the Netherlander.

It rained, though. Unlike the drier Fenlands, in Zeeland it rained, drizzled or misted almost interminably. It was not, therefore, a country hospitable to foreigners – the temperate climate, the winds and the humidity left them prey to many malaises, agues, and distempers. A good living, consequently, for the apothecary, of which there were many in Zeeland.

A good living also for the innkeeper. When the apothecary's remedy failed to give relief, there was always a glass of ale or wine to distract the miseries caused by living in a continually dripping country, almost as damp as the sea it had been stolen from. And there was music in the taverns, music to help you forget your aching legs and the bubbling cough that plagued the lungs after a winter in Zeeland.

The music in Pieter Van Uden's tavern was particularly good that night. There were two musicians. French, perhaps: they had performed a French folk song (*O fils du Roi tu es méchant, D'avoir tué mon canard blanc!*) with some finesse. But there had also been sad English love songs, clever Italian ballads, and, to the great delight of the tavern's patrons, a many-versed, loudly chorused song in their own language, robustly suggestive.

The older man played the lute, his dark head bent over the battered old instrument as a lover might court his mistress, coaxing for a kiss. And many a girl might envy his mistress, if his long fingers touched her body as expertly as they played the lute. It was the other man who sang – the good-looking lad, a tuneful singer with a roving blue eye, whose voice could bring tears of laughter or sorrow. And when occasionally the dark-haired man joined him in harmony, then even the card players listened, pausing in their hands until the end of the verse.

If he had wished to earn a living as a travelling minstrel, thought Richard Galliers as, dry-throated and sore-fingered, he laid aside the lute, then the week could have been regarded as an unqualified success. They had no shortage of money to pay for the sparsely furnished but extremely neat rooms that he and Benedict had taken in one of Flushing's back streets. They had been plied with enough drink to turn them into drunkards and enough food to make them gluttons. But of William Reeve there had been no sign.

There were plenty of apothecaries in Flushing, and plenty of apothecary's apprentices. Some of the apprentices were acned and gangling, some still retained the soft unblemished complexion of childhood. Some hovered in the back of the apothecary's shop, pestle and mortar in hand, others skulked unenthusiastically round doorways, watching the girls, waiting for errands to run. But all were Dutch; there had been neither sight nor sound of an English boy, formerly of Lime Street, London, England.

Benedict Daniel had found some enjoyment in searching the streets of Flushing for Richard Galliers' enigmatic quarry. Peering into the apothecaries' uniformly gloomy rooms, searching through the bottles and retorts and unidentifiable objects hanging from the rafters, he had been, in rapid succession, an Italian sailor with an unmentionable disease contracted in a Mediterranean port; an English merchant suffering from chronic melancholy; a French soldier of fortune with a recurring and embarrassing stomach complaint – described by Benedict to the black-coated apothecary in great and colourful detail. He had considered, briefly, an attack of the plague, complete with suppurating sores, but had regretfully abandoned the scheme as too likely to draw attention to himself.

But still, as he told Richard that evening in the tavern, no William Reeve.

'Perhaps we should ask for him by name. After all,' said Bennet, gazing unenthusiastically at the inevitable plate of herring before him, 'we may simply have missed him. And I'm sick to death of staring at those damned miserable apothecaries and their damned stuffed crocodiles. I am even,' he said plaintively, lifting a piece of smoked fish, 'running out of interesting diseases.'

'There's always food poisoning,' said Galliers unhelpfully, his voice low in the crowded tavern. He was silent for a moment, and then said thoughtfully, 'No, if we ask for him by name he will be out of the country by nightfall. I'm sure of it.'

'Then how much longer?'

How much longer indeed. It might already be too late – Carleton might have his letters by now, obtained for him in return for an undoubtedly generous sum of money by the faithful GLR . . . (GLR – who *was* he?) And if that was so, then the game was already won, and he would have lost the opportunity that Fate, in the shape of Martin Grosse and a drunken wager, had dropped so neatly into his hands.

'Tonight, then,' Galliers said, absently picking up the lute, and re-tuning its constantly slipping strings. 'Tonight we leave for Middelburg.'

The daughter of the house was waiting for them on their return from the tavern that night. She was a large, square-jawed, fair-haired girl called Amalia, and the most her parents had permitted her lodgers to see of her during their week's stay had been a stout ankle glimpsed from under a heavy wool skirt as she polished the already immaculate furniture, or a lowered face under a black headscarf as she silently served fish and vegetables to them at dinnertime. But tonight, Amalia explained in helpfully slow Dutch, her father was away on business and her mother was asleep following a sick headache. So she was, she explained, looking pointedly at Richard Galliers, free for the evening. And if the gentleman would care to sit with her in the parlour – and take a glass of wine . . .

Benedict, whose Dutch had improved rapidly during the course of the week, gave a sort of muffled snort, which he tried, unsuccessfully, to turn into a sneeze. The smile was already hovering on his lips as he slapped Galliers matily on the back, and retired tactfully to his own bedchamber. It was left to Galliers courteously to accept the lady's invitation and go with her into the small, black-and-white tiled parlour.

She was, he guessed, around twenty-eight years old, and of more use to her parents unmarried than married. She had, she told him as she poured out the wine, three elder sisters, all of whom had families of their own. Unspoken was the comment that whereas married daughters do not scrub and serve in their parents' lodging houses, unmarried daughters do.

Unspoken also, but plain in the pale-blue, light-lashed eyes as she handed him the glass, was Amalia's intention to take her pleasure where she could find it. She sat down beside him on the small hard bench, and, putting her glass aside, took Galliers' hand in hers.

'You and your friend are musicians, Mr Galliers.' She touched the tips of his fingers where the lute strings had left their indented mark. 'I could never sing. Mamma says I have no ear, but I enjoy other people's music.'

She continued enviously: 'Have you travelled all over the world, Mr Galliers? I'd love to travel – but I've never been further than Middelburg.'

He reclaimed his hand and drank some wine. 'Oh, all over the world, Amalia.'

'Earning your living by playing the lute?'

And a few other things besides . . . He nodded, smiling down at her pale freckled face.

She moved closer to him, nudging his arm around her shoulder, pressing her thigh against his. She had her best dress on, her Sunday dress, and she had abandoned the familiar black headsquare. Her hair, he thought, feeling it brush against his wrist, was really quite nice – a heavy, flaxen, blonde.

'But I can't imagine why you come to Flushing, Mr Galliers. Flushing must be the dullest place on earth!' And the discontent of too many years of spinsterhood showed in her voice.

He looked down at her: at the honest light blue eyes, at the coarse skin, at the voluminous sprawl of her bosom. He ought to make some pretty compliment, fudge a tactful excuse, and leave this house tonight, its daughter unblemished. But he had not come to Flushing to sing, he was here with entirely other motives, and it was time, he thought, to take a calculated risk.

'Amalia.' He took her plump, work-worn hand in his. 'Can I trust you? Would you keep a secret?'

She nodded enthusiastically, eyes shining, and squirmed a little closer.

'Then, I did not come to Flushing to play the lute. I came here for a different reason: to find someone.'

Her eyes were like pale blue saucers, her mouth parted to reveal uneven white teeth. 'Tell me. I can keep a secret – I promise! And I know *everyone* in this town!'

She would, of course, he realized. Her discontented, frustrated gaze would have taken in everything and everyone as she shopped in Flushing's streets, ran errands for her parents. To relieve the boredom of her own life she would have sought out scraps of other people's adventures and mysteries as a pig hunts for truffles.

'Then,' he said carefully, 'I am looking for an Englishman – not quite a man, perhaps – a lad of not yet twenty. In England he was known as William Reeve, although he may have another name here. And he was an apothecary's apprentice. He may still follow that trade.'

Her freckled brow creased in a frown, and she bit her lip. Then, miraculously, her brow cleared, and Amalia began to smile. At her side Galliers' heart began beating with ridiculous speed, and not because of the plump soft body squeezed close to his.

'Oh, I know him – William is his name, is it? I have seen him. He hides away all the time, though. I thought –' and then she broke off, the smile vanished from her face, and, frowning, she looked suspiciously up at Galliers.

'And if you find him – you'll be gone then, I suppose?'

What did she want of him – an offer of marriage? Galliers thought not. Twenty-eight years must have made her a realist. He took her hand in his and pressed it to his lips, and his other hand stroked her long fair hair. And unaccountably, a picture of Carleton's hunting lodge came to his mind: Mall, her gown awry, daisies tangled in her hair. Irritably, he ignored the faint sense of betrayal, and said, leaving no doubt as to his meaning:

'I had intended to leave here tonight. But if you, Amalia, can tell me where I may find William Reeve, then I need not go until tomorrow at the earliest.' He bent to kiss the white skin at the back of her neck. 'In other words, my dear, I can stay here all night.'

And that, as he had hoped, was just what she had wanted. The smile returned. She moved and, planting her large, well-padded rear in his lap, she put her arms around him.

'Then, Mr Galliers, I can tell you where to find your English lad.' Her hand reached down, loosening the ribbons of her bodice. 'I can tell you just where to find him.'

> *'I have a bower at Bucklesfordbury*
> *Full daintily it is deight*
> *If thou'lt wend hither, little Matty Groves*
> *Thou'lt lie in my arms tonight.'*

There was a soft knock at the door, and Benedict's curly auburn head peered round the doorway, the next verse already on his lips:

> *'Quoth he, I thank ye, fair lady*
> *This kindness thou showest me*
> *But whether it be to my weal or woe –'*

The singing was abruptly halted by a well-aimed cushion.

Richard, fully dressed, was lying on the bed. Outside, the sky was grey, thickened with the inevitable soft drizzle. Leaning on the bedpost, Benedict looked down sympathetically. 'Poor Richard. You look exhausted. Was she –'

'Bennet. Shut up.'

Shutting the door behind him, Ben confined himself to a scathing remark about the weather.

'The weather, my dear Ben, is beautiful, and Amalia Van Groot the most admirable lady that ever lived.' Galliers tucked his hands behind his head, and a beatific smile settled on his features. 'In other words, Bennet, the lady told me where to find William Reeve.'

'She *knows* him?'

'Mr Reeve resides in an apothecary's shop on the corner of Glassblowers' Street, a stone's throw from the main canal. You have called there already, I believe, Bennet. And he *is* frightened. Reeve skulks in the back of the shop – hardly ever goes out by day. He gives the apothecary some assistance, but another boy runs the errands.'

'If he's as retiring as all that,' said Benedict bluntly, perching on the end of the bed, 'how can she be sure that he's our William Reeve?'

The smile became positively smug. 'Because, my poor player, Amalia visited the apothecary to fetch some potion for her mother. Reeve, supposedly a Dutchman, was in the back room making up a prescription. She heard him drop something, which broke. And he swore – in English.'

The apothecary, who wore the customary black coat and robe and long pointed hat, and dispensed medicaments and advice under a somewhat dilapidated version of the traditional sign of the stuffed crocodile, had just sent his boy with a paper of pills for one of his wealthier patrons. It was then that the two gentlemen arrived, foreign gentlemen, one dark-haired and quiet, the other the talkative auburn-haired Frenchman who had visited him a few days previously. The medicine he had made up for the gentleman's stomach complaint had not, apparently, been effective; the gentleman demanded, in extremely fast and idiomatic French, further advice.

It was dark in the apothecary's shop; the windows were small

293

and dusty, and the clutter of phials, crucibles, alembics, pestles and mortars obliterated what little light there was. The French gentleman, it seemed, also suffered from a skin eruption, one that the apothecary could not clearly distinguish in the dim light of the shop. With a quick backward glance at William, safely hidden out of sight in the small closet behind the shop, the apothecary agreed to accompany the voluble Frenchman out into the drizzle to identify the nature of his affliction.

There was little to see: even when the French monsieur had dragged him halfway down the street in an attempt to let the feeble rays of the sun illuminate his freckled, hairless chest, the apothecary could see nothing. He concluded privately that the man's stomach complaints and skin diseases all stemmed from the same source – the workings of an over-imaginative mind. But, naturally, he did not say this; instead he murmured soothingly about an imbalance of humours, and pointed out that the unhealthy miasmas from the marshes could have a deleterious effect on the constitution of a native of less low-lying regions. He promised an expensive specific, and returned to the shop, leaving the Frenchman while he went to the tiny back room to speak to William.

It took the apothecary only a very short time, peering into the house, the yard and, finally, the street, to conclude that William, unaccountably, had vanished.

William Reeve was, at that moment, walking very fast through the rain-soaked backstreets of Flushing on the arm of the dark-haired gentleman, a stiletto dagger at an uncomfortably close distance from his quaking ribs. He was a mousy-haired lad in his late teens, pale from too little sunshine, bronchitic from two Zeeland winters, with the transparent-skinned, drawn face of a frightened baby rabbit. His legs had ceased to function normally when he had realized that what he had dreaded for so many months was finally, unbearably, happening, and it was only the iron grip of the green-eyed man's hand on his elbow, and the nagging itch of the knife's point through his jerkin, that kept him on his feet at all.

Fear rendered the familiar streets of Flushing unrecognizable to him: clammy-browed, he had lost all sense of direction long before he was pushed through the doors of a tall wooden house, across its tiled floor, and up the well-scrubbed staircase. The knife was hidden from view, but it was still there, sharp as a bee's sting, reminding his resisting legs to bear him up the stairs. A dour middle-aged woman said something to his dark-haired captor, who replied in Dutch, charming the ghost of a smile on to her severe face. But he was not Dutch: the man was English, of that William Reeve was horribly certain.

The door of the chamber slammed behind him; he was pushed on to the bed; he heard the key turn in the lock. The dark-haired man leaned, almost indolently, against the bedpost, looking down at him.

'So, William Reeve – no –' as some muffled incoherent protest broke from William's frozen lips, 'forget the denials. You are William Reeve, and you have no need to be afraid *if* –' and there was a long, unnerving pause, '– if you do as I ask.'

Somehow, fighting nausea, he found his voice. 'What do you want of me?'

The man indicated the small table, on which lay a pen and paper. 'Simply to cast your mind back to England, eighteen months ago. I want you to write down, on that piece of paper, everything you can remember concerning the murder of Sir Thomas Overbury.'

William's stone-coloured eyes jerked up to meet those infinitely menacing green ones. Speech gargled in his throat, bubbling up into an uncontrollable coughing attack. There was a quiet knock on the door.

It was the other man, of course, the ginger haired one.

The dark man motioned him in, and, locking the door behind him, said lightly: 'I have been trying to persuade Mr Reeve here to do a little writing for me.'

He could hear noise and bustle in the street outside, and the sour-faced woman's sweeping-brush beating against the steps. Some semblance of rationality reasserted itself.

Gathering the tattered rags of his courage, Reeve said: 'I don't know what you're talking about. I don't know anything about any Sir Thomas Overbury.'

Irritation flickered in the dark gentleman's eyes, but his voice was still mild. 'Now, William, I think you do. You were apprenticed to Mr de Lobell, weren't you? And he made up the remedies that Dr de Mayerne prescribed for Overbury in the Tower. And then, when Overbury died, by coincidence you disappeared. Eighteen months later you turn up in Flushing, regularly supplied with letters and money from London, and still afraid to put your nose out of the door. What are you afraid of, William? Me? You should be, you know.'

His stomach had turned to water. Sitting on the edge of the bed, William Reeve's glance darted, fluttering, from one man to the other. The auburn-haired man still stood by the door, his eyes fixed on some vague middle distance. The green-eyed man moved closer, lolling against the window, arms folded.

'Oh, we could spend a tedious half hour with you denying all knowledge of Overbury's death, and me prompting your faulty memory. But I, William, am in a hurry. And I am not a patient man.

He pulled over the chair, and sat down on it next to the bed, leaning over William in the solicitous confidential manner of a doctor with his patient. The thin dagger was in his hand; it glittered evilly in the weak sunshine. He said softly, in a voice that must have been only just audible to his companion standing by the door:

'Come, William. I have killed a good many men in my time, and it would not trouble me to kill one more. This must be all very confusing – after all, you don't even know who I am. My name is not important, but you should understand how important that confession is to me, and know that I will have that confession from you, William, one way or the other. A little confidence for you, my boy. I have sailed with the Dutch corsairs on the Mediterranean – there, you are one of the few people in the world I have told that – and they are artists in death. I have seen how they hang their victims from the yardarm, then decapitate them, and then mount the dismembered head on the jack staff until it is all rotted away. Shall I tell you some of their other inventions, William? That cough is bad, my dear, you should see an apothecary.'

Galliers took the boy's cold, shaking hand in his. 'You see, if you sail with the corsair, then you do as the corsair does, don't you, William? When you have killed a hundred men in a hundred different ways, another one ceases to make much difference. Of course –' He looked down, studying that pale, quivering hand with a lover's attention, '– of course, I would not kill you straight away. I would do it slowly, very slowly, and soon you would beg me to allow you to write your confession. You would, my dear.'

Benedict, standing by the door, unwillingly listening to that soft, hypnotic voice, did not doubt that, at that moment, Richard Galliers meant every word he said. This was no play-acting, no entertaining diversion with a trick dagger for a weapon. This was real – and Benedict Daniel, who had not, after all, much experience of tragedy out of the protective wooden circle of the Red Bull, found that it sickened him. If this was what the other escapades had been for – the robbery of the old woman in the wood, the midnight rowing on the moat of that black-haired girl's house – if this, the systematic terrorizing of a weak-faced unbearded lad in a Flushing lodging-house was what it had all been for, then he, Benedict Daniel, wished he had taken no part in it.

But it was too late for squeamishness. William Reeve, coughing with an intensity that wracked his thin body, was walking shakily to the table, and Richard Galliers, his face blank of any expression, was looking across at him, saying:

'Benedict. Find me a witness – a doctor, a notary, a scholar – anyone who can sign this.'

Benedict unlocked the door and left the room, slightly galled by the unsteadiness of his own legs.

In the end, it was Benedict who wrote the confession: William Reeve's hand trembled too much to hold the pen. So it was Benedict's looped schoolboy script that described, in the greatest possible detail, the poisoning of Sir Thomas Overbury. When Benedict had finished writing, Reeve signed the paper, his face blue-white with fear, and the ageing, protesting scholar whom Benedict had bribed from his books witnessed it, his name, the date, and his occupation and rank neatly recorded in decorous Latin at the bottom of the paper.

Throughout, Richard Galliers stood by the table, prompting, questioning, ensuring that the events were set forth with the greatest possible clarity. And several times he moved to the window, looking down to the street below, shadowed, so that none should see him. When all was complete, he thanked the witness politely and requested Benedict to escort him downstairs to the street below.

When Benedict returned, the scholar's confusion and complaints still ringing in his ears, Galliers was at the window again.

Benedict did not join him. He said, softly, 'Trouble?', and put a firm but kindly hand on William Reeve's shoulder as the youth tried to rise from the chair.

Galliers nodded, his eyes still on the street below. 'Two of them – they have been outside in the rain for the past half hour, one in a doorway across the street, the other at the corner.'

'Enjoying the sunshine?' Outside the rain had begun to gather in the gutters, and to run in small rivulets along the cobbles.

'Perhaps. Or maybe they are friends of Mr Reeve's. Let him go to the window, Bennet.'

Benedict took his hand from the angular shoulder, and Reeve darted across the room to peer out of the window. 'I don't know them – they are no friends of mine –' and then he looked into Richard Galliers' face, and understood.

Shaking his head, his lips pale and parted, Reeve backed away from the window. A film of sweat bathed his contorted face, and he pressed his hands against his mouth to stifle the convulsive cough. His words tripped over themselves.

'Oh God – they'll kill me – get me away from here! Please, sir, I beg of you – don't send me out there.'

Richard Galliers' face was callous.

'He's right, Richard,' said Benedict angrily. 'Perhaps we can get him out a back way – smuggle him out of the Netherlands –'

Galliers pointed to the sheets of paper lying on the table. 'Not that I give a damn, but you have just bought your safety, William. If you had not so obligingly written those for me, then doubtless your body would have been at the bottom of the canal by tonight. As it is, it is not *you* they will follow.'

Galliers went to the table, folded the pieces of paper, and put them inside his doublet. The boy watched, his eyes distended, hardly daring to believe in the possibility of safety. 'I will take these,' said Galliers, 'And you, Bennet, will take Mr Reeve downstairs.'

Amalia was in the kitchen. Her mother was still cleaning the bedchambers, her father had not yet returned from Middelburg. She was gutting fish. She sent the maid out as soon as Galliers entered.

'For the room.' Galliers put a few coins on the table.

Praying that his guesses were somewhere near the truth, he went over to Amalia and put his arms around her, trying to judge the honesty behind those light-lashed, pale eyes, using the brief bond they had shared last night to make her do as he wanted. Then, from the inside of his doublet he pulled out the papers, and pressed them into her hands. 'Give these to my friend – Benedict – when he comes back. Tell him not to return to England, but to take them to – let me see – Brussels, perhaps. Yes, to the British Resident in Brussels.'

She nodded slowly. 'For your friend. Of course.' She picked up the roll of papers, and hid them in the depths of her cleavage.

He kissed her once, on the lips, for what she knew would be the last time, and she watched, a suspicion of pain in her heart as he dragged aside a kitchen stool and wormed his way through the high, narrow pantry window, out into the shadowed alley beyond. Then she turned from the window, and went back to gutting the fish, her plain, heavy-jawed face made plainer by distress.

CHAPTER THIRTEEN

Her hair was black, her eyes were blue,
Her lips as red as wine,
And he smiled so gaily upon her
Did that sly bold Reynardine.

(REYNARDINE)

*T*HEY saw him enter the alley and climb into the adjacent yard, and they pursued him, their boots (not Dutchman's clogs) slipping on the wet cobbles. He had known they would see him, and he had wanted them to, for they must be drawn away from the house and the papers within it. There were three of them, hard on his heels, close enough for him to hear their rasping breath as they chased him through the streets of Flushing. He would lose them somewhere in the centre of the town and then go to the docks, and let there only be a ship for England . . .

Over another wall: then, to the proprietor's considerable surprise, through a draper's shop and out into the busy street. A desperate glance to locate the bridge over the canal, and into the market square, the dogs always snapping at his feet. And through the market. Behind a crowded stall he flicked out the black coat he had stolen from the draper's, lifted a flat cap from the nearest unwary head, and he was Dutch, and invisible to his pursuers.

Standing on the deck of the unromantically-named *Corncrake* the following day, avoiding the garrulous company of her master, Richard Galliers watched Zeeland's flat outline retreat into the absolving distance. He had set the play in motion: let the players take what chances they could find. William Reeve would, he thought, lie very low for a while, and then when the air had cleared and the consequences had been taken, he would slither back to the surface. Reeve was an opportunist, a nervous one, no doubt, but Galliers had noticed that the clothing he wore had been of good quality, and that the gold ring he had sported on his hand had not been appropriate to a humble apothecary's apprentice. He had profited by his involvement and his exile. Amalia – Galliers remembered her as he had last seen her, standing in the kitchen, her hands and apron smelling of fish, her face confused, slightly forlorn. Amalia might well hand his papers to Benedict as he had asked; she might equally well consign them to the furnace, a fitting epitaph for a love affair of less than one day. But he rather thought, remembering that one long night, that she would give them to Benedict.

Benedict. And there lay the greatest unknown of all. Dear, beautiful, irresponsible, carefree Benedict. Benedict, whom he would trust with the glorious task of leaping from a tree to rob a sour old lady of her jewels; Benedict, who would help him keep a midnight assignation with another man's wife. But the long, wearying grind of a journey through foreign territory to Brussels? There was little of romance or novelty in that. And besides, he had seen the look of sickened distaste on Benedict's face when they had been closeted with William Reeve. Somewhere under the auburn curls and sanguine disposition there was integrity: and in the oppressive air of that lodging house bedchamber, Benedict had hated him for a while and pitied Reeve.

And then there were his followers, those grey nameless watchers in the street. Had they always been there, paid to protect the apothecary's apprentice? It seemed unlikely; too expensive, for one thing. And they had been English, he had been convinced of that. And if they had been visitors from England, arriving just too late to stop Reeve making his damning confession, who had sent them, and why? And if they had been Carleton's men, then how had Carleton known him to be in Flushing? Through Giles? Through Mall?

He turned, his eyes bleak as they left the infuriatingly endless waste of the sea, and focused instead on the masts and decks of the ship. Thoughts of Mall were unprofitable now. The *Corncrake* was bound for Portsmouth, but he would ride for Kingscote as soon as it docked, and check, somehow, that she was safe. He would be on English soil in two or three days, and he could do nothing for Mall or for himself until then. The *Corncrake*'s sail and pennants billowed encouragingly in the breeze; but speed was not a quality the vessel possessed. She had been built to carry cargo and withstand the North Sea's gales, not to make a fast passage.

The master was coming towards him, eager for conversation. Galliers rearranged his features into something like a welcoming expression, and went to meet him.

The threat came at night time; a clear, moonlit night when the dozing watch really should have noticed the pinnace that sailed, silent and unlit, towards the unconcerned, slowly tacking galleon. Years of easy passages, their only enemy the wind and the weather, had made the crew complacent of any possibility of danger from a human source. By the time the ship had been sighted, it was already too late. Had Richard Galliers been on deck he would have known what to do: to ready the cannon, to adjust sails and rigging so that the heavy, long-keeled vessel was less at the mercy of the fast manouverable pinnace that scudded lightly across the tranquil sea like a pebble bounced on a flat, still pond. But Richard Galliers was not on deck. He was sleeping, fitfully, in his cabin, after a dull and difficult evening of wine and conversation with the master. So it was left to the look-out tardily to raise the alarm and rouse the master, his head throbbing, from his bed.

And by that time, it was too late. The pinnace, small, dark and infinitely menacing, was positioned, broadside to broadside, alongside the disorganized *Corncrake*. And even across the black gulf that lay between the ships, it could be clearly seen that the pinnace's gun ports were open, its cannon armed and pointing at the galleon.

The master, not a fighting man, began to pray. He had given the orders for the crew to ready the creaking demi-culverin, and to arm themselves with weapons from the hold, but it would be too little and too late. Too late also, to turn and run, for the pinnace would have stove in the galleon's side long before the larger vessel could ready herself to take advantage of the breeze. Then, as the master watched, the pinnace let down her ship's boat into the gently lapping sea. So they were not about to fire – not yet, anyway. The master stood, silently gripping the gunwale, attempting to keep at least a semblance of dignity as the small craft rowed soundlessly ever nearer them. His mesmerized eyes strayed back to the pinnace, trying to discover her name or nationality, but he could see nothing.

Neither could Richard Galliers, newly on the quarter deck, attempting to find any possibility of salvation in an essentially hopeless situation, identify the nationality of the ship that threatened them. He was armed, and if necessary he would fight. As he had fought in many such situations, he thought with grim humour, but on a different side.

But the master would not fight. Galliers watched as, after a short, muffled exchange of words, the intruders were given easy access to the *Corncrake*. The master obviously intended to survive the encounter with his skin intact. No doubt a sufficiently well-embroidered tale could be concocted to satisfy his employers when the ship finally reached Portsmouth. He would hand over cargo and money, unprovocatively submissive, and in the circumstances that was probably the wisest thing to do.

There were six oarsmen still in the ship's boat; their companions stood on the main deck with the *Corncrake*'s master. The master's eyes slid along to where Galliers stood on the quarter deck, and the smaller, thinner, of the two intruders followed his gaze. It was then that the unease that had haunted

Richard since leaving Zeeland began rapidly to increase. His eyes scoured the small group on the main deck.

There was, he knew, nowhere to hide on a ship. You might run and skulk in the foulest, darkest, filth-ridden corner of the bilges, but they would hunt you out as a ferret hunts a rat, prising you from your stinking hole. And there was really no point in fighting. An anonymous, unwanted passenger was no loss, an easy bargain for a defeated master.

Leaning against the railings, Richard Galliers put away his pistol, and waited.

He had not long to wait. When the master came towards him, confusion in his voice, relief in his eyes, he went with him quietly, handing his weapons to the small, olive-skinned, liquid-eyed man without a sound.

He was silent until, rowed in the ship's boat, they reached the pinnace. He did not bother to look back at the *Corncrake*. He waited instead for the inevitable question that he knew he must not yet answer.

'Reeve's confession, Signor. Where is it?'

The accent was Italian. Galliers turned, noting the dark, cruel eyes – sadist's eyes – and the criss-cross pattern of scars on one side of the face. Then, softly and specifically, in his own beautiful poetic Florentine Italian, a smile on his long arrogant mouth, Richard Galliers cursed him, making particular reference to the Italian's dubious parentage and unnatural sexual practices.

The back of the Italian's hand hit him hard across the mouth and, as he tasted blood, his own fist lashed out, flinging the Italian sideways into the companion way, crushing his arm, so that the single scream of agony reverberated throughout the ship. His second blow, aimed for his opponent's damaged arm, never reached its target. He no longer had time to think: for the blow that struck him on the back of the head was annihilating, stupefying, and he crumpled to the pinnace's deck without a sound.

He thought he was on the corsair's ship: that the swelling seas the

305

vessel sailed were the blue waters of the Mediterranean. When that nightmare, and its customary feverish panic had receded, he made himself uncurl from his foetus-folded position, and separate the lapping of the sea against the pinnace's clinkered sides from the over-fast beating of his heart. Slowly, Richard Galliers opened his eyes, and remembered.

Somehow, he pulled himself into a sitting position. His head hurt badly. When his fingers gingerly touched the back of his head, he found his hair caked and knotted with dried blood. He had lost the Dutch coat he had stolen from the draper's – of course, they would have searched him and, failing to find what they were looking for, had let him live for a little while longer. How long had he been unconscious? He found he had not the least idea. They would come for him soon, and question him again, but he had learned, over the years, the art of silence. And they had already once made the mistake of beating him into unconsciousness: if necessary, and if his skull could withstand it, they could be persuaded to make the same mistake again. And, after all, the task he had set himself was accomplished. Providing no mischievous Deity intervened, the wheel that would roll Carleton to his ruin was already set in motion. It was no longer necessary for Richard Galliers to scheme, to plan, to act; it was no longer necessary, even, for him to remain alive.

Yet that thought gave him no comfort. He found that he wished very much to remain alive. Six months ago he had not cared. Why now? Because it was important for him to witness the destruction of the man he had hated for three – no, four – long years? Or because hope, in some frail, bruised form, had unexpectedly reappeared . . .

His eyes had become accustomed to the darkness: he inspected his prison. There was no port-hole: he was well below decks. The floor was bare except for a few barrels and a dirty blanket thrown down in a mockery of compassion. A store room, then, in the bowels of the ship. Rising unsteadily, fighting nausea, Galliers went to try the door. It was locked, naturally, and attempts to squint through the small spy hole showed him nothing. But had the door stood wide open, it would have made little difference. A ship was a floating prison, the worst kind of prison, for it offered no hope of escape.

So he sank back down again in a corner of the cabin. He felt in his pocket, and found that they had left him his dice. There was just enough light to make out the markings: he leaned his back to the wooden walls, and soon the small ivory cubes were tumbling to the scuffed floor as they had so many times before in countless glittering chambers and filthy hovels, in France, in England, in Italy . . .

The cruelty that Richard Galliers had recognized and played upon in the Italian was not tempered by a badly broken and ill-set arm. The cross-hatching of white scars on the olive-skinned face were emphasised by pain, the pupils of his eyes unnaturally large. Opium, Galliers realized, the pleasant effects of which were beginning to wear off.

But for the time being, the Italian was assuming civility. The two men (recognizable as his pursuers from Flushing), who had brought Galliers from his cabin stayed, the door closed behind them, silent as the prisoner was brought before his captor.

The cabin had a port-hole showing that outside it was daylight, that the sky was a clear blue flecked with small puffy clouds, and that the pinnace was making rapid progress – somewhere. Distantly, Galliers could hear the sounds of a ship in full sail – ropes and flapping sails, creaking timbers and men's voices. It took him a few seconds to acclimatize himself to the light, then his gaze wandered in the direction of the Italian, and he smiled sympathetically.

'You seem to have hurt your arm, Signor. My commiserations.'

The Italian's one good hand clenched suddenly, and his lips parted to show small pointed teeth. 'You know why you are here, Mr Galliers. If you are foolish enough to waste my time in making frivolous remarks, then I shall not hesitate to use methods that are a little less than – gentlemanly.'

There was a short pause in which Galliers seemed, irritatingly, to be absorbed in unknotting the tangled laces of his shirt.

Without looking up, he said, 'Then, if you are feeling in a gentlemanly frame of mind, perhaps you would be so good as to let me know whom I have the pleasure of addressing?'

The Italian smiled. 'Certainly – Mr Galliers, is it not? Or Reynardine – the Fox, perhaps – ?'

The question hung, unanswered, in the stale air of the cabin. 'My name is Rizzo,' added the Italian, softly. 'Gian-Luca Rizzo.'

Gian-Luca Rizzo. GLR? *The writing was foreign, the letter unsigned*, Mall had said. Yes: so this was the man who procured compromising documents for the noble Sir Nicholas Carleton, and this was the man who hunted the troublesome Fox. So you and I, my fine friend, have spent the best part of a year searching the country for those few incriminating pieces of paper –

Swiftly, in the middle of a particularly intransigent knot, Galliers looked up.

'Is Carleton your paymaster?'

'At present, yes.' Rizzo gestured to one of his men to pour the wine. 'I am a mercenary – as I believe you yourself have been, Mr Galliers? I had a short – conversation – with our mutual friend Mr Reeve, and he told me that you have sailed with the corsairs on the Mediterranean.'

The glass of red wine on the table was a torture to one whose head ached and throbbed with all the persistence of a three-day hangover. Galliers kept his voice perfectly polite.

'For survival, Signor. Unlike you, I have not yet sold myself for money.'

Anger flared in Rizzo's soft dark eyes. 'We are wasting time, sir! I want William Reeve's confession – the one you forced him to make.'

'A good Italian proverb for you, my friend. *Se non e vero, e molto ben trovato.*'

The Italian took a few mouthfuls of wine, and smiled thinly. 'Very apt, sir. But the apprentice's confession was not a happy invention, was it? Why should Reeve lie to me?'

'Why should Reeve lie?' He had succeeded in untangling the knots: Galliers began to thread the laces through their eyelets. 'Reeve lied, Signor Rizzo, because if he had not, your excellent stiletto knife would have slit his throat.'

Rizzo rose from the chair, wine in hand, and crossed the room to stand at his prisoner's side. The Italian was several inches shorter than his captive.

Rizzo said softly: 'My knife could just as easily slit your throat, my clever friend.'

A faint, mocking smile hovered about the bruised lips. 'I don't doubt it. But I'm sure your master reserves that particular pleasure for himself.'

Rizzo ignored him. 'William Reeve wrote a confession for you, Mr Galliers, and you have hidden it somewhere. A lad like Reeve would not have the wit to lie to me.'

Galliers paused, as if considering, his eyes lazily wandering the length of the Italian's body. 'You could be right. After all, you're not exactly the Chevalier sans peur et sans reproche, are you?'

He had his wine then: flung full in his face with the anger that the jittering, cold aftermath of opium had given to Gian Rizzo.

The Italian's voice hissed in his ear: 'I have been commissioned to stop that apprentice bleating, or, failing that, to destroy his confession! Your room in that lodging house was thoroughly searched, so was your cabin on the *Corncrake*. And you have been searched. Where is Reeve's confession, Mr Galliers?'

The wine stained the front of his already dirty shirt; he wiped the remaining drops from his face with the back of his sleeve. The effort of standing, a pressing need for food and drink – particularly drink – and the steady pounding in the back of his head were making it hard for him to retain his concentration.

He said, dreamily: 'Therefore let us sing and dance the galliard, to the remembrance of the mallard –', and then he blinked once and gathered his wits, and said, 'It is somewhere in Europe, Signor Rizzo. I can't be sure exactly where.'

The Italian relaxed slightly, and his smile returned. 'So you gave it to someone? You sent it somewhere –'

309

Galliers glanced out of the port-hole once, but the uncaring featureless expanse of sea told him nothing. Rizzo followed the direction of his gaze.

'Yes, you would like to know where we are, wouldn't you, Mr Galliers? We could be anywhere – in the North Sea, in the Channel, five miles from Gravesend, five miles off the coast of Zeeland . . . If I were to tell you we were sailing off the Netherlands, and that you might be released if you were to tell me who you gave those papers to – what would you say then, Mr Galliers?'

The offer hovered in the air. Cradling his arm, Rizzo waited for an answer.

Galliers said inconsequentially: 'And as the mallard dives in pool, then let us dabble and duck . . . I would say that you are a liar, Signor Rizzo. We are not off the coast of the Netherlands, and you will not set me free.'

The Italian's patience was diminishing as the pain in his arm increased. He drew his thin dagger from its sheath, and balanced it carefully in his good hand. 'No,' he said softly. 'I will not set you free. Shall I tell you what I will do with you? I will give you to Sir Nicholas Carleton. How will you like that, sir?'

Sweat was gathering prickling on his brow, running down his neck to mingle with the dirt and wine stains on his shirt. He said, lightly:

'As a sort of consolation prize for having neglected to kill the apprentice or to find his confession? Or –' another thought struck him, light in the considerable gathering darkness around him, 'or having failed to retrieve Carleton's letters from the Countess? You cannot have succeeded there, either, or you would not be here. Dear me, what a considerable trail of failure, Signor Rizzo. Remind me never to purchase your services.'

The knife was suddenly at his chest, glinting in the bright sunlight that streamed through the port-hole. Light sparkled also on the sea outside, dazzling him. All he had to do was to remain silent, and remain alive, nothing more . . . even consciousness was unnecessary.

The knife pricked his skin, releasing a thin trickle of blood. He could see the sweat on the Italian's face, and smell, increasing his own nausea, the Italian's breath. He looked downwards and said insolently:

'How fearful and dizzy 'tis to cast one's eyes so low. Perhaps if you were to *grow* an inch or two, sir, you might find greater success in your ventures. Might I recommend –'

But Rizzo never heard his tormentor's generous suggestion. Like many small men, he loathed allusions to his stature. Maddened by the twin hornets of pain and ridicule, he lost control. The sharp point of the knife scored Galliers' skin, and he scarcely heard one of the two men standing by the door cry, 'Careful, Gian! Carleton wants him in one piece!' But the words penetrated his consciousness enough to make him drop the knife, and to grip that hated throat. 'For the final time – where is Reeve's confession?'

But Richard had just remembered the last line of that ludicrous song, and it seemed quite marvellously apt. And besides, it was difficult to breathe, and darkness would be closing in, and it simply did not much matter.

He said, hoarsely and gleefully, 'It was a swapping, swapping mallard,' and the Italian saw the laughter in his eyes, and howled with rage, his fist and feet striking him where they might.

Lucas Holland, riding from London to Kingscote on a hot June day, was weary with the task of messenger. It had not rained for a fortnight. The always inadequate tracks were dusty and hard, and the insects had begun to gather in profusion. He wore only breeches, shirt, and a sleeveless doublet, and no cap covered his bright golden hair, but he was still uncomfortably hot. His clothes – of the palest blue silk piped with scarlet – had been immaculate when he had left London; now, after hours in the saddle, and an unpleasant night in a rather crude tavern, they had begun to look crumpled and dirty, a foolish choice for such a journey.

He had two messages to give to Sir Nicholas: one from that loathsome Italian Carleton paid to do his dirty work, the other a personal message, from himself, concocted and perfected over the length of this tiresome journey. His courage, never his greatest quality, had begun, now that Kingscote was so close, to fail him; the words he had so bravely mentally flaunted were not, perhaps, sounding quite so confident. But he made himself think of George Villiers, recently encountered in London, now a Gentleman of the Bedchamber, soon to rise, it was confidentially predicted, to heights of unimaginable greatness. And he thought again of Nick, of that hateful little black-haired wife of his, of Nick's unpredictability of late, of Nick's obsession with that cold-eyed man on whose antics he had been forced to spy, and he knew that, however much he might quail at the task, he must give both messages.

The first message was not verbal; Lucas handed the folded piece of paper the Italian had given him to Sir Nicholas Carleton, watching his features as he read. The bearded, handsome face, as ever, told Lucas nothing: but the soft curse after he broke the seal and glanced at the short note, told him that the words were not wholly to Carleton's liking.

'Still, it's not all bad news.' Methodically, Carleton tore the note into small pieces, and scattered them from the window into the moat below. 'It seems we are to have a visitor. You shall take a letter to Rizzo, Luke –'

'No.' Without realizing it, Lucas had placed himself behind the protective cover of one of the library's sturdier chairs. The single word, unnaturally loud, echoed around the book-lined room.

It took a moment for the refusal to register. Then Carleton turned towards the boy and, raising one thin eyebrow, looked at him as a bird might a worm that questions its fate. '*No?* I don't understand, Lucas.'

It was too late for retreat. He pressed his sweating palms together as he said:

'I will not run any more errands for you, Nick.'

'You will not run any more errands . . . And what cataclysmic event has inspired this unusual independence of thought, my dear?'

Holland flushed, a dark red that stained his pale unblemished skin. 'It's over with us. I have other friends.' He floundered hopelessly, trying to recall the phrases that had sounded so fine on his ride to Kingscote. 'You have paid me no attention recently – you only think of *her*.' And there, he had spoilt it, sounding for all the world like a sulking schoolboy.

There was, Sir Nicholas realized, a certain amount of truth in the boy's complaint. He said, softly, 'So you are jealous, Luke? And you wish to take your charms elsewhere? I suppose you think nothing of loyalty – of the clothes I have bought for you, the introductions I have arranged – one of which you doubtless intend to misuse now. I suppose all these mean nothing to you?'

'I have paid for all that! You had what you wanted of me!'

He almost expected the older man to hit him; he feared the violence that Carleton rarely allowed to surface. But the blow did not fall, Carleton only said silkily:

'So that is how you see our relationship? Some sort of a – trading agreement?'

'Well – isn't it?' There was a tense silence, then Lucas, unequal to the thought of Carleton as a future enemy, softened the defensiveness in his voice. 'Oh, things were well enough until the New Year. Then you took *her* to wife . . .' His words trailed away into silence. He took the silk handkerchief from his pocket and wiped the perspiration from his face, wishing that it was not so hot, that there was more air in the room. He had spoken the truth, though, it had been since New Year that things had begun to go wrong. Although, now he had begun to think about it, it was strange he had not yet seen the black-haired bitch today. She was usually hovering somewhere, with her sour looks and her sharp tongue.

'Dear Luke. And what if I do not see fit to let you go?'

His head jerked up, the yellow hair clinging damply to his forehead. 'You cannot stop me.'

Carleton looked at him speculatively. 'If my little – indiscretion – ever becomes public knowledge, I will make sure that your name is mentioned.'

Ah, but he had him there. Holland smiled triumphantly.

'But I know nothing of your intrigues, Nicholas – you have told me nothing. I have been your errand boy, that's all. I will not lose my head for running the odd message, eavesdropping on the occasional conversation. You never trusted me, Nick – and now I am glad of it!'

Carleton's dark face suffused with blood: Lucas blanched and edged to the door, panic constricting his chest.

But the moment passed. Carleton turned his back to the boy, and said smoothly, 'Then go. Sell yourself to another, my dear, and quickly, before your looks begin to fade.'

Carleton heard the door close behind Lucas, and then, his hand shaking slightly, he poured himself a glass of wine. Matthews could take the letter, that presented no difficulty. And if Luke wished to try his luck elsewhere, then let him. It would only be a matter of weeks before he came running squealing back. And besides, Lucas had become unimportant.

For he was aware that the world had narrowed inexorably into only two matters of importance: Kingscote and Mall. Nothing else was of any consequence. His house and his wife: they were the two possessions that mattered, he owned them and he would keep them, and no-one, least of all Richard Galliers, would take them from him.

Carleton looked out of the window, down to the cool, dark moat. The swans glided mirrored on the still surface of the water, and around them a few tiny fragments of paper floated like white rose petals. The apprentice had given his evidence, it could only be a matter of weeks, a month or two at the most, before the whole fragile edifice of the Overbury murder tumbled finally to the ground, taking the Somersets and the Howards with it.

But not the Carletons. His family would continue to live at

Kingscote, and his lovely faithless wife would give him what he needed: sons. For he could see his way out of the maze, and it delighted him: for Richard Galliers would free him, and Mall would be the bullet he would hold to his enemy's head.

Mall rose at dawn. Her fear had not allowed her to sleep. Her bed was a hot tangle of sheets and covers; she left it, opening the window to look, as she had done every morning, down the sheer wall to the crystal clear moat below. It was going to be another hot day; June, for once, was living up to the promise of the poets. The water looked so cool, so tempting. If things became any worse, Mall had more than once thought that she would jump out of the window as Richard Galliers had done on the night of the fire, swim that imprisoning moat, and run for her freedom. But where would she run? Since that dreadful scene in the Gallery with her husband, she had been confined to her room, shut out from the sun, no longer even allowed the freedom of the house. She had spoken to no-one other than Leah: even Carleton himself no longer visited her. She had a few books, but even they offered no solace, for she had become unable to concentrate on them, the words dancing before her, meaningless squiggles on the white paper.

Once or twice she had woken up in the night, hot and frightened, and thought that she was already lost, that Richard Galliers was gone or dead, and there was no longer any hope of escape from her marriage. And then it had been difficult not to cry out loud. To retain some vestige of dignity, some fragment of hope. And to blank out the panicking, disjointed thoughts she had lain there, reciting every line of poetry she could remember, until sleep returned.

But there would be no more sleep tonight. The sun had risen, pale and strong, brightening the leafy treetops in the wood beyond. The swans already circled gracefully in the moat, a barely perceptible wake rippling the water around them. Sounds in the servants' quarters opposite told her that the day had begun, that fields would be tended, bread would be baked, life would go on.

Mall turned away from the window, and began to comb out her hair. Leah would be here soon to help her dress. Leah must not be allowed to witness her distress but, oh, sometimes in these last two weeks of solitude, Mall had been glad to see even that unsmiling face.

But today Leah was not Mall's only visitor. When she was dressed (in the lightest gown she possessed, for it promised to be a blisteringly hot day), and her hair was tied up, and the breakfast dishes cleared away, Sir Nicholas Carleton knocked at her door.

He made no reference either to their memorable interview in the Gallery or to the two weeks of Mall's isolation. It was almost as though none of that had happened; she was complimented on her gown, and a polite remark was made about the weather.

'But we must not stand here talking.' Carleton offered her his arm. 'You have a visitor waiting for you, my dear.'

A visitor? From her bedchamber Mall could see neither of the bridges, and had lost track of callers to the house. Perhaps Anna Murray had called again, or Alice, or even Sir Thomas. Perhaps she had been punished sufficiently . . .

But Sir Nicholas did not lead her to the Great Hall or to one of the smaller parlours. Instead they walked, Mall silent, Carleton talking lightly of inconsequential matters, to a little-used corner of the house. And then down stone steps, where Mall could almost feel the waters of the moat crushing in on the damp windowless walls, where the only lights were rushlights, not the kind, friendly warmth of the sun. Her dread was rapidly returning; she pressed her lips together, and did not move her hand from her husband's arm, but her limbs seemed suddenly heavy, moved by will, not instinct.

They had reached a large cellar. A man that Mall did not recognize sat there, a deck of cards on the small table before him. He stood and bowed as Carleton and Mall passed, but said nothing, and returned to his game of patience. Mall did not know this part of the house. It was unlike the rest of Kingscote: here there was no beauty, however superficial; only darkness and an unaccustomed chilliness that made her thin gown hopelessly inadequate.

They were at a wooden door. Despite the cold, Mall felt sweat form on her brow, icing the surface of her skin. Carleton began to push open the door. She looked at him once, about to cry, even to him, for pity: but there was nothing on that darkly handsome face, no human response.

'Your visitor, my dear.' He opened the door wide. 'I trust you have an enjoyable conversation.'

It took a few paralysing minutes to make out anything at all in the grey-green gloom of the tiny cell. Two rushlights glowed on the walls, their malign orange light picking out the dark stones, the dirty straw on the floor, the bundle of rags in one corner of the room.

But that was not a bundle of rags. Mall felt a hand at the small of her back push her forward, and, as the shapeless mass resolved into a human form, her legs would no longer carry her, and she sank down beside the inert body, kneeling on the cold stone floor.

She knew who it was before she had even touched him, even looked at his face. She heard herself say brokenly, 'Oh, my dear –', and her shuddering hand touched his cold arm, as she struggled not to faint. Then she heard the door close behind her, and her husband's footsteps, walking away.

He was not dead, and Mall did not let herself faint. She knelt for a few moments, her head bent, waiting for some measure of self-control to return. And when her breathing had calmed slightly, and she felt able to move, she reached out and felt his wrist for a pulse.

It was there, not particularly strong, but definitely there.

Mall began to cry, tears streaming soundlessly down her cheeks. With infinite care she brushed back the dark matted hair from his forehead, and tried to say his name. Her voice would not work, however, only the phrase *dear heart* echoed over and over again to the pounding of her own heart. She stroked his face, and tried again, her halting voice saying the baptismal name she had so rarely allowed herself to use. She bent and kissed his bruised cheek, her tears dampening his face. She said again, 'Richard. It's me – Mall. Wake up, my dear – *please*.'

Something in her tone seemed to penetrate his unconsciousness. The long eyelashes moved slightly, and she saw his brow furrow. She spoke again, and kissed him again, taking one of his cold hands in hers. Then his eyes opened slowly, the same eyes, even though the skin around them was dirtied and bruised. He did not seem to see her at first, only the incomprehensible darkness of his prison, and Mall saw him begin to drift away from her again.

'No! Wake up, Richard. It's Mall – you remember, don't you?'

She was crying again; she could not stop herself, but at least his eyes opened properly, and his gaze fixed, this time, on her.

There was sense, if not understanding, behind those confused green eyes. She said, seeing that she must explain this strange reality to him:

'You are at Kingscote – in one of the cellars. Sir Nicholas brought you here.'

'I was on a ship . . .' He closed his eyes again, wearied by the effort of remembering. 'A ship –'

Keep him talking – keep him awake. 'You went to Flushing. To look for the apothecary's apprentice. I'm so sorry – I let him guess.'

Mall let go of Galliers' hand, and pressed her own palms against her wet face, recalling the bitterness of that betrayal. 'It was my fault – it was I who brought you here – I who gave you to him –'

And gradually, it came back. William Reeve – the confession – that damned crawling ship. Rizzo, his face contorted with rage, kicking him into unconsciousness . . . And now he was at Kingscote, with Mall.

She was crying; he realized that she must have momentarily

318

given him up for dead, so he tried to sit up, dragging himself into something like an upright position against the moist walls of the cellar. 'Christ – my *head* . . .'

She said, shakily, 'It does have a rather large lump on the back.'

He saw the wetness on her face and, recognizing the concern in her tone, made an unconvincing attempt at light-heartedness. 'Don't look so worried, little one. Giles has often accused me of having a skull an inch thick.' He grimaced, feeling pain as he breathed, and then smiled crookedly. 'It is my ribs that have been rearranged.' He paused, gathering his scattered thoughts, and with a visible effort said, 'Perhaps you should tell me what happened, Mall.'

'My husband found out that I had sent the ring to you.' Her voice shook as she saw Galliers' torn and filthy shirt, the untended wound on his chest, the dark bruises on his face and arms. 'But don't know how he knew – I cannot understand it. I have thought about little else this past fortnight, and it still makes no sense. Anna wouldn't have told him – neither would Giles.'

But Galliers had begun to think more lucidly now, to guess what might have happened. One person might have known who the chrysoberyl ring belonged to, one person might have had opportunity and reason enough to wish to betray both Mall and himself. He looked again at Mall, and saw that even with her reddened eyes and her gown dirty with kneeling on the wet straw, she was still beautiful to him. Throughout his interrupted, disastrous flight from the Netherlands, there had been one fear that had driven him: that Carleton might have hurt her to discover where he, Richard Galliers, had gone. But although Mall was pale, and the dark hollows under her eyes had deepened, she did not look injured. Her despair he recognized, and wanted to alleviate, but her physical wholeness made him feel almost cheerful.

He offered her the best comfort he could find. 'Whatever Carleton does, it no longer matters very much. I found Reeve, he wrote me a confession. Sir Thomas Overbury was murdered by the Countess of Somerset, with the help of various accomplices. It is all written, signed, and sealed, and on its way to the British Resident in Brussels. It can only be a matter of weeks before the evidence is brought before the king himself, and he will be forced to lay charges against the Countess – possibly Somerset also.' He pushed the damp, tangled hair out of his face, willing himself to remain coherent. 'Frances Howard has already told Carleton that she will betray him if the affair comes to light, and he can't have retrieved his letters from her, or his hired assassin wouldn't have been sent to follow me. There is nothing Sir Nicholas can do except wait for his fate – nothing at all.'

Mall said nothing for a while, but sat under the rushlight, the orange haze illuminating her profile and the soft wavy aureole of her hair. Then she said gently, 'But you don't believe that, do you?'

He frowned, and then smiled wryly, and beckoned Mall to sit beside him. 'I had forgotten you have brains as well as beauty, my dear.' He sighed. 'No, of course I don't believe it. Benedict – my player friend, you remember? – may not reach Brussels, he may throw away Reeve's confession, he may lose it, he may simply decide he has better things to do. And Carleton – Carleton has some special treat planned for me, I'm sure. Otherwise I should not be availing myself of your hospitality here – I should be somewhere at the bottom of the North Sea.' And Carleton had specifically wanted him kept in one piece. Which he was, more or less, if one discounted the odd cracked rib and bruised skull.

Mall's hand touched his; in the darkness of the cellar their fingers linked together. 'What do you think he intends to do with us?'

Galliers shook his head slowly, conscious of the dormant pain. 'I really haven't the faintest idea, sweetheart,' and his eyes, troubled, met hers.

'And why has he put us together like this? Just to taunt me? To prove that he has won?'

'But he hasn't. Not yet.' *Think*: Carleton wishes to show me something, that he can use Mall as a *pawn*. That angered him, and he said, gently and coldly:

'Whatever Carleton intends, you shall soon be free of him. It will all be over soon, Mall, one way or another, and you'll be safe, I promise you that.'

There was no time to say any more; they both heard the footsteps in the cellar outside. Galliers let go of Mall's hand, and she stood up, her heart beating fast.

The door opened, and Sir Nicholas Carleton stood there, the candlelight in the room outside darkly silhouetting him in the doorway. He gazed into the room, the amber underlighting from the rushlights emphasising the small pointed beard, the slightly arched eyebrows, and most of all his eyes, black and empty.

'I see you have returned to the land of the living, Mr Galliers. Charon must wait a little longer for his next passenger. I hope you have enjoyed a pleasant hour with my dear wife.' He took Mall's arm, and pulled her sharply to his side, repeating, 'My – dear – wife. Mine – till death us do part. Isn't that right, my dear?' He held Mall to him, not failing to notice the scarcely dried tears on her cheeks, and then kissed her roughly full on the lips.

'Now you will return to your chamber, my precious. Mr Galliers and I must talk.' He beckoned to the man outside to take Mall from the room. 'I have a proposition to make to him.'

The door closed behind her, and they were alone together, only a few feet of dirty stone floor separating them. Carleton was the first to speak.

'It's a long time since we have talked in private, Mr Galliers. Three – no, four years, I believe?'

The long-lashed lids flicked once, and Galliers looked up.

'Four. It was a few weeks before Jeremy died.'

So the verbal swords were unsheathed, the weapons – Jeremy, Mall – would be brought out into the open. Carleton said meditatively:

'I did not enjoy having to get rid of Jeremy. You must understand that, Mr Galliers. But the letter he left me – it was unforgiveable. You – both of you – left me no choice.'

Strangely, sitting because he could not yet stand, listening to Carleton talking so calmly about the murder of his brother, Galliers did not feel the hot familiar anger. Those events seemed so long ago – dead and buried, literally, in Amyott's green-mossed churchyard. Unexpectedly, he felt sorrow and pity, replacing that dreadful destroying thirst for revenge. Unexpectedly, he could remember that there was, perhaps, still a future, somewhere.

Again, it was Carleton who broke the silence. 'You are not very talkative today, Mr Galliers. You are not usually so short of things to say. Were my men too rough with you? I'm afraid that Rizzo has a very bad temper. You must have annoyed him considerably, I think – I doubt if even my beloved wife would find you beautiful now.' He paused, his face filmed with perspiration even in the cold air of the cellar, looking down at Galliers, his small eyes avidly inspecting the bruised face, the cuts and scratches, the torn and dirty clothes. 'Perhaps a glass of wine, Mr Galliers, would restore you to some semblance of your former self.'

He went to the door, and called to the servant, and then turned back to Galliers. 'And let us continue our conversation in the next room. This place is fit only for rats.'

With concentration and perseverance, Galliers found that he could stand. Walking was another matter, but it was only a short distance, and the thought of a drink was a considerable incentive. He could not remember when he had last eaten. He recalled briefly regaining consciousness somewhere between Gravesend and Kingscote, and having water poured down his throat, but that was all. Using the wall and doorposts as support, he found his way into the next cellar. The candles seemed intolerably glaring. He blinked and swayed in the doorway.

'Help him to the seat, Johnson. Our visitor still seems to be a little under the weather.'

The wine revived him, warming the pit of his stomach, but he must not drink too much, at all costs he must keep a reasonably clear head. He drained his glass, and then food was brought before him, bread and cheese and ham.

'Eat it. You must recover your strength, Mr Galliers.'

The goose to be fattened for the slaughter . . . He found he could trust himself to speak. He said, calmly, 'Why?'

Carleton laughed, his voice cracking slightly, echoing round the vast damp stone cellars. 'Why? The clever, the witty, the dashing Richard Galliers has not yet managed to work out why I have been at such pains to preserve his life for a little while longer? Did you think it was for love of you, sir?'

Galliers finished the bread he was eating. 'Not exactly. After Jeremy, that might seem a little – incestuous.'

Sir Nicholas's fist hit the table once, hard, making the plate bounce, and the remaining food scatter. '*Don't* do it! Don't make me kill you – not yet – I have a better use for you by far than that!'

Carleton stood up and walked to the far side of the room, dabbing at his face with his handkerchief. Galliers returned to his food. It was like a duel, he thought, fought with no weapons but words, each of them circling, waiting for the other to move.

Carleton regained a superficial calm. 'My wife admitted that you were the highwayman, Reynardine. How did you know what Martin Grosse was carrying?'

Galliers looked across at him, eyes wide. 'I didn't know what Grosse was carrying. It was pure luck. A gift from a benevolent god.'

Covertly, he watched Carleton swallow that bitter draught. For a man like Carleton, used to calculation and minute planning, the interference of damnable, unpredictable chance would be an almost unbearable irony. Galliers continued, his voice level, his body still:

'I was not at first sure that Grosse's letter referred to you. But you made a mistake in having me followed by those blundering footpads after the Countess's banquet last October. Murray I had already discounted, so it had to be someone else who was

323

also at that banquet. Either you or Conway. Mall's innocent knowledge of her father cleared Sir Thomas. So, having eventually confirmed that it was you whom the Countess was threatening, I had to find some real proof of the Overbury murder. Before you retrieved your letters, of course.'

'Reeve.' Carleton's back was to him, Galliers could not see his face.

'Yes, Reeve. One of the untidy loose ends that always spoils such ambitious schemes. I am surprised that you did not have him killed months ago.'

Carleton's long tapering fingers flexed, shaking out the lace at his wrists. 'I would have, Galliers, but unfortunately the apothecary and his wife had become fond of the boy, and had made arrangements for his exile and protection. But it was a mistake, I can see that now. Sentimentality should have no place in these affairs.'

The food was almost finished, some life had returned to his battered limbs. Galliers crumbled a crust of bread between his fingers. 'Reeve's confession is on its way to the appropriate authorities,' he said, gently. 'I did not go alone to Flushing, you see, and it seemed safest to give the confession to my companion.'

Carleton spun round, his face distorted with anger. 'And so I suppose you think you have won? That I will be ruined, and *you* – with your drunkenness and whoring and damnable insolence – will survive? I tell you, Richard Galliers, I tell you, you have not won, and you never shall!'

Sir Nicholas pulled out the chair and sat opposite him, and Richard Galliers could see on the handsome, noble face something he had never noticed before: the faintest touch of unreason.

'God knows why you ever returned to this country. Your family did not want you, the better part of society abhors you. You should have learnt your lesson – you are a penniless nobody, Galliers, and you will never be anything more. Oh, I know that you want revenge, sir, but you shall not have it! You are trying to take what belongs to me, but you will not.' And the image of Lucas, beautiful and frightened, saying *I will not run any more errands for you* entered his mind, and he knew that, for that too, Richard Galliers must take the blame.

Carleton had buried his head in his hands; he looked up and said in a quieter voice, 'You shall not have your revenge, Galliers. You shall not have Mall, and you shall not have Kingscote. I know what you intend. You think you can send me to the headsman, and then marry my widow so that you can have Kingscote. I know you have nothing of your own. You are disinherited, landless and penniless. It would seem a perfect revenge, would it not, Galliers, to have my wife and lands, but you shall not. You are not worthy of them.'

Galliers pushed the plate away, and leaned back in his chair. 'The wheels are set in motion, Carleton. Even if I wanted to, I could not alter that.'

Carleton's face was close to his, Galliers could feel his breath on his cheek.

'I shall tell you what you will do, Mr Galliers. You have a penchant for stealing, do you not?' He smiled, his eyes dark and excited. 'You shall steal my letters for me, and you shall bring them to me. You shall play Reynardine again, Galliers, for one very last time.'

CHAPTER FOURTEEN

Follow her, while yet her glory shineth,
There comes a luckless night,
That will dim all her light;
And this the black unhappy shade divineth.

(CAMPION)

*G*ALLIERS looked at Carleton, at the greed and pleasure on that aristocratic, saturnine face, and then he shrugged and the corners of his mouth curled.

'The biter bit, Carleton? How appealingly symmetrical.' He already knew the answer to his next question, but he still must ask it.

'And if I refuse?'

'You will not refuse, Galliers.' Carleton threaded his heavily ringed hands together in front of him. 'You can't have forgotten your brother, your mother's darling . . . You wouldn't want anything similar to happen to Mall.'

'Ah.' Galliers' gaze left Carleton, and he stared into the middle distance, eyes hooded. He had a choice, of sorts. He could refuse Carleton, do nothing, wait for events to take their course. That way he would have his revenge, he would see Carleton go to the block.

Carleton's voice reverberated in the empty cellar.

'The Countess has left London. My letters are in her house in Blackfriars, I know that, and there will only be a skeleton staff there. With a little ingenuity – and incentive – Galliers, you should not find the task beyond you.'

Galliers hardly heard him. Something of Carleton's desperation he noted and filed away for future use, but his train of thought was hardly interrupted. He cradled his head in his hands, his reflection dimly before him in the scratched surface of the table. He could not doubt that Carleton would carry out his threats to Mall. He had too much blood on his hands already to balk at another death. So, he could have his revenge or he could save Mall from injury. He could not have both.

'I will get your letters for you.'

That was all. No curses, no recriminations, no anger. It was almost – disappointing. Carleton looked intently, examining the shadowed, disfigured face before him for hatred, pain, despair. But there was none; and, what expression there was, was to Nicholas Carleton totally incomprehensible.

'I will get your letters for you, but you in turn must assure me of Mall's safety. I won't ask for the word of a gentleman, such niceties are long over between us. But I will promise you that if you so much as harm one hair of her head, I won't rest until I see you dead. No matter what cost to me.'

Ice cold words in an ice cold room. Carleton smiled thinly. 'When you bring me my letters, she may return to her father's house. Will that satisfy you, Mr Galliers?'

He nodded, and the bargain was complete. The tension relaxed, and exhaustion washed over Richard Galliers again, swamping him, renewing the dull pain in the back of his head, making the dark cellar swim before his tired eyes. But he must stay awake a little longer. There was something he did not understand, something nagging him, something new –

His glass, refilled with wine, was pushed into his hand, and Carleton's voice, distanced by his own dizziness, said:

'Drink, Galliers. I have a better room for you. A few days food and rest and you'll be well enough to ride to London.'

The wine revived him, and he was able to follow Carleton slowly up the stone steps, through confusing passageways and anterooms, to a small but comfortable chamber whose sloping wall showed him that he was in the roof of the house.

Sunlight streamed in the one oblong window, motes of dust floated carelessly suspended in the beam of light. He heard the sound of the key turning in the lock behind him, and Carleton was gone.

The bed, a narrow truckle to one side of the room, felt wonderful. Galliers sank down into it, his hands cushioning the back of his head, his limbs relaxing as they touched the feather mattress. But he must not sleep, not yet. He must refuse to allow his eyes to shut; keep them instead fixed on that small square of blue sky he could see through the window.

He was Carleton's prisoner, in Carleton's house, and in a few days' time he would risk his neck in an improbable scheme designed to save Carleton from the gallows. For almost four years his entire existence had been lit by one thought: that he would have his revenge. Lying on the small bed, he could remember the foul smell of gangrene, he could hear his brother's screams, and other screams: those of his mother, when Jeremy had died, those of the corsairs' captives, when they had longed for death. He could remember his father's drunken anger, his stumbling, pathetic attempts to punish his second son for the death of his third and, most clearly of all, he could remember Lady Amyott's face, unrecognizably ugly with grief. When he had fled the country, alcohol, women, and, at his lowest ebb, opium, had blotted out the passage of days, weeks, months. But he could recall some of that misery. Eventually he had washed up in Calais, and Madame Berthe had scolded and cajoled him back to some sort of sanity. And after that it had been anger that had fuelled him, had kept him alive, and functioning, and waiting. Waiting for a chance to destroy Carleton. And that chance had come, carefully nurtured by him, brought to fruition little more than a week ago when his own brutality had frightened William Reeve into confessing. And yet, in one simple sentence, he had thrown all that away.

And he did not care. That was what he did not understand; that was why he lay awake when his exhausted, mistreated body screamed for rest. He did not care a jot. He should be feeling despair; he should be feeling the utter hopelessness he had last experienced on the soaking deck of the *Eglantine*, when for a few seconds the prospect of death, of oblivion, had seemed so desirable. No, it did not make sense: a choice that should have been hard to make had been ridiculously easy.

He had chosen Mall. And down there, in Carleton's prison, with Carleton watching him, longing with hungry eyes for his protestations of hatred and defeat, he had begun to realize why he had chosen Mall. He had kissed her last September because she had been a pretty girl and he had been elated with the prospect of adventure, and he had found her irresistible. Later, in the Fens, he had come to know her better, and he had slept with her, feigning sleep while his arm cradled her slight body. And in May he had made love to her. Not because she was Carleton's wife, and not because he needed something of Carleton's.

But because he loved her.

He loved her for herself, for her black hair and blue eyes, and her loving words and her sharp tongue. He loved her because she was Mall, and for no other woman would he ever, had he ever, felt the same. He had not intended to love her. Neither did he know when he had begun to love her – perhaps in the Fens, when she had run away from him, and he had followed her, searching for that indomitable small figure through the wind and snow. Or later, in London, maybe, when he had first heard of her marriage to Carleton, and he and Giles had fought, rolling over and over in the mud and snow and dirt. Or perhaps when he had held her in his arms on the silken-green lawns of Kingscote's hunting lodge. It did not matter. Mall was all that mattered, nothing else; not Carleton, not even Jeremy. And he had just bought her safety, and that was why, even here, he could feel happy.

And Mall's safety must be sufficient for his own happiness. He could never have her, never, as he had once bitterly suggested to Giles, go down on bended knee and ask for her hand in marriage.

For Mall was Carleton's wife, and she would still be Carleton's wife even when Sir Nicholas had his letters, and when, providing he kept his half of the bargain, Carleton released her to her family at Belford. The marriage contract that had been signed in December in Belford's chapel would be as valid tomorrow, in six months' time, in ten years' time, as it had been on the day it had been written.

He had told Mall months ago that he had nothing to offer her, and for once he had done the right thing. Perhaps it would be enough to know that she was safe. No, it would not, of course not, he could not lie to himself. It would be intolerable to go away from her.

Galliers rose stiffly from the bed, and crossed the room to where the single small window looked down to the moat outside. Love – it was nothing but a ludicrous, deriding trick of nature, one last mocking reminder of his own humanity. He had not expected to find love again, nor to have to abandon it so immediately. He would not see Mall again, and perhaps it was better that way, better that they had parted already. He leaned his forehead against the small cloudy panes of the window, knowing that now, when he needed it, sleep would not come. All the poetry, all the songs that cluttered his memory, laughed at him, reminding him that, though his music could give solace to the broken hearts of others, it could offer no comfort to him. He would not sing so carelessly again.

His face was still, and his lips did not move, but the song was there, indelibly etched in his memory . . .

> *Therewith all sweetly did me kiss,*
> *And softly said, Dear heart, how like you this?*

The weather did not break: the sky remained a pure unsullied cobalt blue, the air pleasantly lightened by a gentle breeze. It was an English summer at its rare best, and only the farmers and landowners, seeing the crackled glaze form on the drying earth, voiced concern. Along the track by the edge of Kings-

cote's wood rode a woman and four manservants, their horses
and clothing dusty in the heat. The men wore the black and
white livery of the Murrays of Saffron Walden, the woman
was tall and graceful, her unbound chestnut hair flowing
rippling down her straight back.

To Anna Murray, turned politely but firmly away from
Kingscote's doors for the second time within a fortnight, the
warm midsummer day had lost its charm. Her first refusal,
over a week ago, had been given by Sir Nicholas Carleton's
steward, an unpleasant-looking man whom Anna had disliked
on sight. Her second had been imparted by Sir Nicholas
himself, standing on Kingscote's bridge, elegant as ever in
black and scarlet silk, his measured voice telling her that Lady
Carleton was feeling a little under the weather, his small dark
eyes telling her – Anna was not quite sure what. But he had
looked at her with hatred; there was no other word for it, and
Anna, accustomed to being universally liked, had felt shaken.

She looked back over her shoulder, searching through the
branches for a last sight of Kingscote, a golden jewel set in a
silver moat. But the windows, unrevealingly blank, stared
back at her, keeping their secrets. Suddenly Anna reined in,
and spoke to the manservant beside her.

'No, we are not going home. We will ride to Amyott.'

She insisted on leaving Amyott that evening, even though
Giles begged her to stay. Neither did she allow Giles to escort
her home, for what she must say to her brother George must
be said in private. Besides, she knew now that she had nothing
to fear from the highwayman, Reynardine.

George was seated in the parlour with her father when
Anna returned, dusty and weary from her day's travels. The
sun had not yet set, the air in the parlour was heavy with the
scent of dog roses and honeysuckle that filtered through the
open windows. George rose from his chair to greet her, a book
and an empty glass on the small table beside him. George,
who never read . . .

He had been home for a week now. He and Anna had always been close: they were the only two of seven brothers and sisters to remember their mother clearly, and perhaps that common bond of grief had welded them together. Anna was not unaware of George's faults. She had bailed him out of trouble with their father too often not to know that he drank too much and gambled excessively. But this week she had suspected something more than money troubles; George had been quiet, not his usual carefree self, unable to look her in the eye, avoiding conversation. And his debauches were beginning to spoil him, to register in the puffiness of his ruddy skin, the bloodshot eyes and blurred features of too many late nights and too much to drink. Anna had thought it would pass: a week or two and George would confide his latest foolishness, she would scold and advise, and they would return to their usual pleasant cameraderie.

But not this time. Anna kissed her father, dozing in his favourite chair, and John Murray, seeing that his eldest daughter had returned safely, was happy enough to retire to bed. Anna shut the door behind him, and began to light a few candles to relieve the dim light of the room. She heard George start to speak, but disregarded him, her own voice clear and cold in the twilight.

'I went to Kingscote today, George, to see Lady Carleton. I was not allowed to enter the house. It's the second time within a fortnight that I have been refused admission. Have you any idea why?'

Anna could see him more clearly now that the candles were lit; their yellow glow illuminated the creases and hollows of his face.

She continued, 'Sir Nicholas says that his wife is ill, George. Do you think that Mall is ill?'

'I don't know, Anna. It's some time since I called at Kingscote.'

'But you've seen Sir Nicholas recently, have you not, George? In London, perhaps?'

His eyes dropped. Pretending to gather his book, his hand-kerchief and his empty glass he turned his back on her, saying, 'I'm not sure, my dear. One sees so many people in London.'

332

They were so alike: tall, grey-eyed, chestnut-haired. And slow to anger. George could count on the fingers of one hand the number of times he had seen Anna lose her temper, and she could probably do likewise with him. But she had lost her temper now; anger sparkled in her clear eyes, and the candle she held guttered and threatened to go out.

Controlling herself, Anna fixed the candle into the brass candlestick. Her anger upset her, and it extinguished as quickly as it had appeared, leaving her feeling only frightened and miserable.

'After I had been to Kingscote, I went to see Giles,' she said, tightly. 'It was Giles who asked me to visit Mall, and it was Giles I gave the ring to. You remember that ring, don't you, George? The little one with the green stone, the cat's eye –' Anna knew that she was going to cry, but could no longer stop herself. 'I asked Giles about the ring today. I made him tell me everything. That ring belonged to Richard Galliers, and Mall Carleton sent it to him to ask for help. And you, George – *you* told her *husband*!'

Anna groped for her handkerchief, neatly folded in the wide sleeve of her crimson gown. She blew her nose and dabbed at her eyes, and taking a deep breath, said unsteadily:

'Giles has not seen his brother for nearly a month. No-one has seen Lady Carleton for a fortnight.'

There was a hunted look in George's eyes. He brushed at the air wildly with his hand. 'If her husband says she is ill, why should we doubt him?'

But the words fell on the scented air like stones dropped in a still pond. George had never liked to see his sister cry. He saw the tears roll down her soft cheeks, and swore violently, a luxury he rarely permitted himself in his father's house. Striding to the open window, his hands fisted at his sides, he looked out at the tangle of flowers, greyish-pink and ochre-gold in the twilight.

'Why did you do it, George?'

His lids shut tight, blocking off the light, the garden, his sister behind him.

333

At last he said, slowly: 'Because I owed Carleton money. Too much money. He was pressing me for repayment. I have lost – continuously – at dice since October last.'

Too long a run of bad luck: he had ceased, even, to enjoy the game. At night he dreamed of hazard, of the numbers coming right for him, only to turn, impossibly, wrong before his frozen gaze. And that game with Galliers had begun it: he had lost more than a hundred and fifty crowns to Galliers that evening, and it had seemed to him when Anna had showed him that strange dull chrysoberyl that at last he had the chance to turn his luck, to exorcise the demon that had cursed him.

He said, hoping for sympathy, absolution: 'Carleton was threatening to go to father. When I saw the ring I thought perhaps he would buy the information in return for my IOUs. And he did, Anna. I don't owe him a penny now.'

Absolution was not to be granted. 'So to save yourself you let Nicholas Carleton know that his wife was seeing Richard Galliers.' George flinched at the scorn in her voice. 'Have you any idea how much Sir Nicholas *hates* Richard?'

George said weakly, 'I know that they don't get on –'

'Don't get on! They loathe each other, George! And, from what Giles tells me, they have good reason.' A gentle woman, her palms itched to strike his evasive, uncomprehending face. 'Did you forget that our families are soon to be joined, that I am to marry Richard's brother?'

George's mouth was dry; he still retained a small child's dislike of censure. 'Galliers is a good man with a sword. He can take care of himself –'

'And Mall? I suppose she, too, is armed to the teeth, and ready to defend herself?' Anna's sarcasm rang in George's ears. She sat down heavily in her father's chair, bitterness on her finely cut features. 'I thought you liked Mall, George. You said you did, at Lady Conway's banquet. But for Heaven's sake, even if you detested her, there was no need to betray her, to *sell* her for your thirty pieces of silver!'

Her voice dropped, and she looked desperately at him. 'I

334

am afraid for what Carleton will do – perhaps already has done – to her.'

And he could no longer escape the real anxiety on her face. Forced to consider the consequences of his actions, for the first time he felt shame, and a dawning horror. 'You think that Carleton might hurt her?'

She did not answer immediately. He saw that she looked tired and strained, the fine lines and shadows on her smooth face reminding him that she was, after all, nearer thirty than twenty.

She pressed her hands together, and said unhappily: 'Giles wanted to ride straight to Kingscote. I stopped him. I couldn't see what good it would do, and besides, I was afraid . . .' Her voice faded into the warm evening air, lost on the soft breeze. It had been the nearest thing to a disagreement that she and Giles had ever had, and it had shaken her.

Anna straightened herself visibly in her chair, and looked, white-faced, at George.

'*You* must go to Kingscote tomorrow, George. You must.'

He had chosen three in the morning because it was the worst time of night, the worst watch on board ship, when even the most conscientious lookout might doze and wake, uncertain whether he had been asleep, uncertain of why exactly he was afraid. For him it did not matter: the nights and days had become blurred, all time leading to this one focus, this gate through which he must pass.

Galliers had ridden down from Kingscote to London that afternoon, keeping to the lesser known tracks and byeways, anonymous in old and borrowed clothes, only his knife and pistol his own. It had taken him longer than he had expected to recover from his injuries: almost a week before the dizziness from the head wound and the pain in his ribs no longer plagued him. He must be growing old, unable to bounce back as once he had. But the previous morning he had known he could ride; and with ice cold clarity he had also known that the journey to London must be put off no longer.

In an alleyway near the river at Blackfriars, his eyes searched the Countess's house for the side door, the Judas gate, that Carleton had told him would be open. There were many ways, Galliers thought, pulling the hood of the thin dark cloak over his head, in which this could simply be another betrayal, in which he could be looping the noose about his own neck. He saw the door: heavy, studded with iron nails. Swinging himself lightly over the wall, he landed silently on the grass beneath, listening to the sounds of the nearby Thames, the gentle lapping of water on wood and stone. And as the old elation returned, he knew that Carleton was right, that this was a certain pleasure: to be Reynardine, a thief in the night.

The door swung open easily. Knife in hand, he stood in the darkness for a moment, recovering his bearings, recalling the map Carleton had sketched for him, remembering what he himself had seen of this house in October. It was different now: no ranks of bright candles, no music or laughter, only silence, and the passages and chambers ill-lit by a few gleaming rushlights. But the light was enough for him; his eyes had accustomed themselves to the dark, and he began to move forward.

Silently past the servants' quarters – but no sounds from within. Dagger in hand for anyone rash enough to wake; he must kill if necessary. Two, three, four doors along, and into a square antechamber. Monstrous beasts – cameleopard, dugong, basilisk, firedrake – glared open-mouthed at him, their stitched tapestry faces leering yellowly down at him in the shadow of a single rushlight. Through the end door; and then he flattened himself against the wall, throat taut and heart beating fast as he heard a flutter of sound. But it was only an old brindled greyhound asleep, half covered by the curtains, tail beating against the floor as he dreamed of long-past chases. A small flight of stairs, Carleton had said, and there they were, wooden steps, and his heart surged faster with the consciousness that even the most silent thief could be betrayed by a creaking wooden staircase.

336

And there was the door. The Countess's withdrawing room, adjoining the Countess's bedchamber. He pushed back the hood of the cloak; the dark hair clung damply to his face. But his ungloved hands were perfectly steady as he slipped the tip of the main gauche knife into the lock.

A turn, a click, the lock had slipped, and he could push open the door. There was music in the sound of a lock yielding, and relief and ecstasy in shutting the door silently behind him, and leaning momentarily, lips dry and slightly parted, against the closed door. But it had only just begun: now, in comparative safety, he must search the room. He could dare light a candle now, first checking that the curtains were drawn and the shutters tight (he would not make the same mistakes he had made at Belford), then, wiping the dampness from his hands on the rough frieze cloak, taking the candle and tinder from inside his shirt. The candle flared and lit the room; he fixed it in the empty candlestick on the desk, unclasped his cloak, throwing it over a chair, and sat down, his shirt clinging wetly to his back for, even at this time of night, the air was warm and heavy.

He was methodical in his search, opening each drawer in turn, forcing the locks, but not, like Mall, caring whether the marks of his despoiling showed. Writing materials, bills, letters, receipts, inventories, invoices, all the paper detritus of a rich woman's life. Every piece of closely written paper to be examined, every sample of handwriting to be studied to see whether it resembled Carleton's small angular script.

Galliers was seated behind the desk, the chair swung back and balanced on two legs, papers in hand, when the door behind him opened. It was not the sound that told him he was no longer alone, for there was no sound: it was the light, sudden and shocking, pouring into the darkness from a branched candlestick.

A voice said coolly, 'Put down your knife, sir. I have five men nearby, and they will kill you if I so much as click my fingers.'

A pause, and then the knife was tossed to the other chair, landing uselessly and silently on the crumpled cloak.

'And your pistol.'

The pistol skittered across the floor, its powder impotent, its spark unlit.

Galliers could sense a figure behind him, and he felt hands, a woman's small flexible hands, run lightly over his body.

'No rapier, sir?'

'A rapier would get too much in the way for – this sort of thing.' His voice was light, natural, as unthreatening as hers.

'Ah.' Those same small hands, expensively jewelled, exquisitely manicured, flicked carelessly through the discarded papers littering the desk.

'And did you find what you were looking for Mr –? Let me see who you are –'

He looked up slowly, his slanting amber-green eyes rising to meet the Countess of Somerset's unnerving ice-blue ones.

Her beauty took his breath away. She was still fully dressed, but those great curtains of shining honey-coloured hair tumbled over her shoulders and back, reminding him forcibly of the Botticelli angels he had seen in Italy.

'Well, Mr Galliers, this is a surprise. I must confess I hadn't expected to find *you* here. From the way Nicholas Carleton spoke of you last October I wouldn't have thought you one of his pets. But then, loyalties change.' She swept some of the papers to the floor, making room for her candlestick, and studied him calmly for a moment. 'Or perhaps not. I have a good memory for faces, Mr Galliers, especially men's faces, and it seems to me that you have acquired a few more bruises and scars since we last met.' She perched on the edge of the desk and reached out her hand, tilting his face towards the light. 'No, I didn't think you and Carleton had any affection for each other. So why are you here, Mr Galliers, in this –' she touched the coarse linen of his shirt '– this rough clothing, sitting at my desk, looking through my papers – and for Nicholas Carleton?'

He folded his empty hands in front of him, looked up at her, and said, 'I apologise for my appearance, your ladyship, but thieves do not generally wear silk and satin. And I am sitting at your desk, searching your papers, because if I don't, something very unpleasant will happen to Lady Carleton.'

338

Her aquamarine eyes narrowed, and she said curiously, 'And what is Lady Carleton to you, Mr Galliers?'

It was strange to make his declaration to this woman, in this house.

'I love her, Lady Somerset.'

Her eyebrows raised, a faint smile played on her small mouth. 'Oh, Mr Galliers, what follies we commit for this thing called love. And does the lady return your affection?'

He had not really considered that. 'I'm not sure. It doesn't make much difference.'

She slid off the desk, and began to walk around the room, watching him. 'But I still don't understand. You love Nick's wife – and yet you are here to steal Nick's letters. Am I right, sir?'

He inclined his head, but said nothing.

'And who did you intend to give the letters to?'

'To Carleton. We have a bargain. I will procure his letters and so release him of any complicity in the Overbury affair, and he will in turn allow Lady Carleton to return to her family.'

She was behind him, her small white hands rested on his shoulders. 'And do you believe he will keep this bargain, Mr Galliers?'

'I have no option but to believe it,' he said heavily.

'Keeping faith is not one of Sir Nicholas's more notable qualities. Perhaps it is fortunate for both of us that I discovered he had placed a spy in my house.' A hard edge crept into her voice, and her grip on Galliers' shoulders tightened. 'That he should believe me unaware of what happens in my own house! The girl he bribed will not get another place, that she can be certain of – she will end up whoring in the streets. So perhaps you had better abandon your sweetheart, Mr Galliers, for it seems you have failed in your errand.'

Almost to himself, his eyes fixed on the bright candles on the table, he said softly, 'I cannot abandon her.'

He sensed some of the tension drain out of her, and her hand almost casually stroked his hair. 'I think we are a little alike, you and I, Mr Galliers. When I first saw you – in October, was it not? – I thought that you were beautiful, but without a heart. Half the ladies in the room were dying for you, Mr Galliers, but you did not care a jot. But for one lady, it seems, you would do anything. And for Robin Kerr I would do – have done – anything.'

He was conscious of her warm body behind him, her hand still playing with his hair. 'Including murder?' he asked, gently.

'Including murder.'

The room filled with silence. She moved to face him, her eyes hard. 'Do you know what sort of man Sir Thomas Overbury was, Mr Galliers? He was the worst sort of man, the sort who will use friendship to claw his way to the top, and then spit on those who befriended him. He hated me – I read some of the letters he wrote to my husband, and they were vile, poisonous. He would have turned Robin against me, he would have destroyed me if he could. Robin is not very clever, you see, Mr Galliers, and Overbury was clever – very clever. But I love Robin, and I had to have him, so Overbury had to die.'

And he, Richard Galliers, knew how Sir Thomas Overbury had died in agony in the Tower. He had heard it from the apothecary's apprentice, William Reeve, the details of the poisoned clysters and draughts, the intrigue, the plotting, the witchcraft. But Lady Somerset must not know of that confession, perhaps already given by Benedict Daniel to the authorities in Brussels. He looked up at her, saw that her mouth was pursed with distaste, and saw also that she had no regret for what she had done.

'I am beginning to think Sir Nicholas Carleton to be a little like Sir Thomas Overbury. He is nothing but another fortune seeker, Mr Galliers, and, my God, he is in need of a fortune now!' She smiled, and the smile lit her whole face, emphasising the small pointed chin, the fine long blue eyes, the perfect white teeth. She said meditatively, 'He should have stayed with me, you see, Mr Galliers. He should have kept faith. I have helped him considerably in the past; he made a mistake in trying to break free.'

He watched her as she circled the room, her brow faintly

creased in thought, her hands cradled one inside the other, always moving. 'Whatever happens, even if this wretched affair comes out, the king will not punish Robin, and he will not punish me because I am Robin's wife. It will be the others that go to the block – the little people. Because the king also loves Robin, you see, Mr Galliers.'

And George Villiers? thought Galliers, but said nothing.

'That is why Nicholas Carleton was foolish. That is why he has miscalculated.'

The room had become too warm. 'So – if Overbury's murder becomes public knowledge – you will use Carleton's letters against him?'

In the shadows he could not clearly see her face, but he could hear the rustle of her heavy brocade skirts as she halted near the shuttered windows.

'Ah – if only I could, Mr Galliers. If only I could. But I no longer have them. They are burnt. Robin burned them.'

Imprisoned in the isolated luxury of her bedchamber, Mall struggled not to lose track of time. A week had passed, she thought, seven days had gone since she had seen Richard Galliers, bruised and beaten in Carleton's cellars. She did not even know whether he was still held at Kingscote. Or whether her husband was here, or whether *anyone*, anyone in this unfriendly world had cared to discover whether she, Mall Carleton, was alive or dead. If only she could see either of the bridges – then at least the arrivals and departures might give some clue. But she had seen only Leah, and she could not quite yet bring herself to beg for Leah's assistance.

She heard the footsteps and knew that they were Carleton's.

It was late morning, the sun was high in a sky that was clouded for the first time in weeks. Mall waited, standing small and proud, for the door to open.

Sir Nicholas was smiling, his eyes dark and feverish, his usually perfectly brushed hair slightly untidy.

'A busy morning – I have had an unexpected visitor.' He

came into the room, and closed the door behind him. 'I had hoped to see you earlier, my dear, to tell you my good news.'

Mall's stomach cramped sickeningly, and her heart began to beat painfully fast. She sat down heavily in the chair by the window, and folded her hands, her palms already hot and moist, in her lap.

'Look at me, Mall.' Carleton had come to stand beside her, and, unwillingly, she raised her eyes to meet his. 'That's right, my dear, let me see your face.' He cradled her chin in his hand, his fingers stroking her cheek. 'Yes, I think I have made the right choice. Do not look so frightened, Mall, you have nothing more to fear. In a few hours it will all be over.'

She was sure that he would see her heart hammering in her breast. She opened her mouth to speak, but no words would come. He took his hand from her face, and sat on the edge of the bed, his eyes not leaving her.

'A good choice.' he repeated slowly. 'Our marriage has not been the success I had hoped for. Too many other things have come in the way of our happiness. I admit that some of the fault has been mine – I should have got rid of Lucas long ago. But I am free of him now; I have sent him away. And you, Mall, you are free of Richard Galliers.'

She dug her nails into the palm of her hand, and said hoarsely:

'Where is he? What have you done with him?'

Carleton smiled again. 'Oh, he is not dead – not yet, anyway. I have sent him for my letters, Mall. He has gone to London to steal my letters from the Countess of Somerset's house, and he will bring them back to me today. Within a few hours I will have them.'

It hurt to speak. 'And – Mr Galliers?'

He leaned forward and touched her black curly hair, escaping as always from its bonds. 'My men will take care of Richard Galliers. I told you, we will be free of him.'

He stood up, kissed her once on top of her head, and walked to the door. 'So you need only stay in here a little while longer, my dear. Just until this affair is finally ended. Then we can start again. It will be like another honeymoon. But we will do some things differently. We will share the same bedchamber, I think – I wish to be with you when you are awake, when you are sleeping. All the time. And I want sons, Mall – you shall give me sons. I have no other family, you see, so you must give Kingscote sons.'

The door closed behind him: Mall heard the key turn in the lock. She opened her hands and saw the thin crescent of red where her nails had dug into the white skin. She stared at the marks, not understanding, watching her hands shake like autumn leaves in a gale.

She was hardly aware of the door opening, and Leah coming in with a tray of food. Mechanically, she stood up, not hearing Leah's grumble about the weather and her swollen legs. She knew what she must do, and she knew she must do it right. One last chance, that was all, just one.

Mall was smaller and lighter than Leah, but the force that sheer, uncontainable fury gave to her fist as she swung it into the maid's face more than made up for any deficiencies in weight or size. Leah gasped almost soundlessly, blood spouted from her nose, her legs tottered and the tray holding plates, food, key and all crashed to the ground. The key was in Mall's hand before Leah had fully realized what had hit her; and the knife – in one swift movement Mall stooped and took the knife. The door she locked from the inside, and then she ran to the window, pulling off her ruff, struggling out of petticoats and farthingale as she did so.

The sight of Leah, on the floor with her legs splayed out before her, would have been comical had it not been for the blood that gouted thickly from her nose on to her white apron. Mall hurled the key out of the open window, and it dropped with hardly a splash, covered forever by the dark waters of the moat. Leah was struggling to her feet: Mall held the knife in her clenched hand.

'You stay still – don't try to stop me. I will use this if I have to – I will!'

She scrambled on to the windowsill and looked downwards. It seemed so far. She had dived before, but never from such a height. But she had to; she had no choice.

She sat on the sill like Richard Galliers had, her bare feet bunched beneath her, and then, feet first, dropped into the moat below.

Her husband, the Countess of Somerset explained to Richard, had not her steady nerve. She had tried to reassure him, had tried to make him see that they had nothing to fear, but he had not believed her. And a few days previously his nerve had finally snapped, and he had ridden back to Blackfriars and burned whatever evidence of Overbury's murder he could find. The maid whom Carleton had planted in her house knew nothing of the destruction of the letters; Frances Kerr had let that little masquerade continue, waiting for Carleton's attempt to retrieve what was already lost.

Galliers rose from the chair then, and she made no attempt to stop him. Through the cracks in the shutters he could see the first pale glimmerings of sunlight. Somehow, sometime, what he had just learned would become a part of him, an accepted fact, an item of history. But not yet – oh no, not yet.

'Well, Mr Galliers – and what are we to do with you?' It was almost a relief when her voice broke into his thoughts. 'I should turn you over to the authorities as a common thief, and you would swing from the rope within the week. But it seems to me that perhaps that would oblige the good Sir Nicholas.'

Thin slivers of light from the shutters illuminated the diamonds at the Countess's throat, the soft sheen of her skin.

'You have given me a sleepless night, Mr Galliers, and that should not go unpunished.' Her words had become harsh, jarring. 'And Sir Nicholas – what punishment for a turncoat, a Judas? Does he forget that my family is still one of the greatest in the land? Does he believe that, if I choose otherwise, he will escape with his name, his inheritance, his skin?'

And then, suddenly, she began to laugh, a shrill mocking peal echoing on the high ceilings of the chamber, as her soft musical voice turned abruptly to dissonance. And her face was no longer beautiful, but distorted, ugly, and he had to force himself not to register his disgust.

'If I fall, so shall he.'

Her voice had dropped to a whisper, her eyes were wide, glazed.

'You, sir, will return to Sir Nicholas. You may go free, but you will remind Sir Nicholas that I have only to say his name, and he will crawl in the dirt. Yes, Mr Galliers. Only to say his name.'

The water, ice-cold and breathtaking, surged up, filling Mall's nostrils and ears, forcing its way into the thin line of her screwed-shut eyelids. It dragged at her remaining skirts: Kingscote's last attempt to imprison her, trying to pull her to the oblivion that lay in the silty secret depths of the moat. But she fought back, kicking to free herself, refusing to allow her muscles to freeze uselessly in the icy grasp, opening her eyes to see the surface of the water above her, a barrier between herself and the summer blue sky. Her lungs would burst – the water was too deep and too cold – no; she was through, and she gulped in the warm air, freedom in every glorious breath.

But she had no time to spare. Leah would start caterwauling. Mall struck out for the bank, her bare arms cleaving the water, making for the comparative safety of the woods.

It required a monumental effort to haul herself on to the bank, but she managed it. Then, stumbling into the trees, shuddering with cold and reaction, she stopped and wrung some of the water from her soaking skirts. Where to? She had had no chance to think of that, she had only known that she must escape from Kingscote, and run – somewhere. Where to?

And then she knew. To Amyott, of course. To Giles.

It was a matter of immense relief to George Murray to see the single horseman riding along the bridle-path ahead of him.

It had been the worst gamble of his life, the gamble that would cure him forever of his addiction, to have to guess that Richard Galliers would return to Kingscote, to have to guess what route he would follow. He had almost given up, convinced that he was wrong, and that Galliers was already dead, fled abroad, or whoring in London. And then Mall would suffer, and Anna would always look at him as she had the previous evening: a look of utter contempt that he hoped never to see again. So he had wheeled his horse desperately round, taking a chance that Galliers might after all have ridden the quickest, most public route. And then he saw him, a pale cloud of yellow dust, riding like a bat out of hell across the flat dry Essex plain.

George put his spurs to his horse, and galloped along in the rider's wake. Galliers' horse would be tired, it should not be impossible to catch him. As he drew nearer the dust thinned, and Murray could see the dark hair, the set shoulders. He called out, but his voice was lost in the heat, drowned in the thunder of galloping hooves. He called again, and Galliers' name echoed against the trees and parched fields.

And this time Galliers heard. George saw him glance once over his shoulder, and his hands pull at the reins. Rider and horse slewed to a halt, and Murray drew level with them.

'George. What an unexpected pleasure. Sorry – no time for conversation.'

George grabbed at the reins, stilling Galliers' flight. He saw the wildness in his eyes, the grim set of his mouth, the dust and sweat that covered horse and rider.

He said, desperately:

'You must not go to Kingscote, Richard.'

The slanting eyes, impossibly green in the sunburnt face, widened slightly. 'I have to go to Kingscote. Let go of my reins, George.'

There was a scarcely concealed threat in Galliers' voice: Careful, George, or you'll end up sprawling in the dust with a broken jaw. There must be *something* to stop the man, something to make him listen –

'It was I who betrayed you, Galliers. I told Carleton about Mall's ring.'

For a fraction of a second, Murray thought it was inevitable, that the iron fist would strike him. But the moment passed, and Galliers said, 'I know.'

Richard wiped the sweat from his face with the back of his shirt sleeve and pulled at the reins again. The hard leather slipped painfully through George's palm. But George, steadfast for once, did not let go.

'Listen to me, Galliers. I regret what I did – I regret it deeply. I have just spoken to Carleton – I tried to make him see reason. But it was no use. I think he is no longer quite sane.'

Galliers' hands, dusted ochre with the powdery Essex earth, gripped the reins harder. 'I know that also. Which is why I must get Mall away from there.'

George shook his head, despair in his voice. 'But you don't understand, Galliers! I've been there. He's ready and waiting for you. You would never cross the bridge alive. His men are on the gatehouse, in the courtyard, at the windows – and they are all armed. You would have a bullet through your head before you so much as dismounted from your horse. Carleton has no intention of releasing Mall – Anna says he's going to found a damned dynasty with her – he talks of *sons*!'

The clouds were gathering heavily in the sky; dark, dappled shadows on the young green-gold corn.

'Why are you telling me this?'

Because – because I had not realized that the game was being played for such high stakes. Because, watching you and Carleton, I know that I am outclassed. There was shame in his voice when he answered:

'Anna guessed. She made me go to Kingscote. She was concerned for Mall.'

Galliers looked up sharply.

'Mall – is she safe?'

'I don't know.'

The first drops of rain began to fall, dark circles on the dry surface of the bridlepath. For a moment George thought that

Galliers had given up, that whatever had happened to him in that past month had finally taken its toll. But then he saw that his eyes were coldly fixed on the horizon, that he was assessing chances, weighing odds.

He turned. 'Perhaps you would let me have your horse, George – mine is tired, and I still have some distance to ride.'

'But Kingscote is just –'

'I'm not going to Kingscote. Your horse – and your rapier, please, George.'

Dumbly, George dismounted, and began to fumble with straps and buckles, slippery in the gathering rain.

'Now.' Murray's rapier was at his side, and Galliers swung himself into the saddle. 'I want you to take a message to Carleton from me. Tell him that I have his letters. Tell him that he must collect them from me – alone. Tell him that if he brings anyone with him – anyone at all – I will know, and I will not so much as wait to speak to him. I will simply go to Sir Ralph Winwood, the Secretary of State, and hand all the letters to him. Will you tell him that, George?'

Silently, his hand calming the lathered, shivering horse at his side, George nodded.

'Now listen carefully, George. You are then going to tell Carleton where to find me . . .'

CHAPTER FIFTEEN

> Her rosy cheek, her ruby lip
> They lost their bloom so fine,
> She fell into his arms again,
> All on the mountains high.
>
> (REYNARDINE)

*S*HE had walked, run, scrambled, it seemed, for hours, attempting to keep to the cover of tree and bush, hiding at the slightest sound. She knew now, she thought grimly, how the fox must feel, hunted to earth by hounds. Amyott was not so great a distance from Kingscote on horseback: on foot, it seemed like the substance of dreams, slipping steadily further and further away no matter how hard she tried to hurry.

The sun had gone, engulfed by thick black clouds, and the rain sheeted down, scattering her with runnels of water every time she pushed through the leafy branches, turning the ground under her bare feet to a greasy mire. Like last autumn, she thought, pausing at the edge of a copse to recover her breath, like that day when the thunderstorm had broken, and she had met Richard Galliers for the first time.

And that memory spurred her on her way, refusing to allow her to give into exhaustion. *My men will take care of Richard Galliers* . . . Giles – only Giles could help Richard now, if anyone could. She could do nothing.

She reached the top of the hill, and looked down. Somewhere in the grassy plain threaded with rivers was Amyott, and sanctuary, if not salvation. Her hair clung to her face in flat black tendrils, the hem of her gown trailed damply in the mud. No more the point-device Lady Carleton now, she thought wryly, pushing her hair out of her eyes. There were still jewels at her breast and arms. She unclasped them, Carleton turquoises, and threw them carelessly into a ditch. Now she could be anyone, any country maiden walking in the rain, looking for a ride on the saddlebow of a farmer or yeoman.

The track wound downhill, edged by a thick hedgerow. She was halfway along when she heard the sound of a horse's hooves, thunder to accompany the rain. For a moment her limbs would not move, and her heart thudded painfully in her chest. Cold and wet, she froze to the ground, her eyes desperately searching for a place to hide. Sir Nicholas – it would be him, or one of his men. Matthews perhaps, with his awful rat's eyes and cold hands. But there was a ditch. Movement returned, and Mall flung herself into the ditch, heedless of the inches of yellow water at the bottom, and the scratches and thorns of guelder rose, blackthorn and spindle.

She crouched in the hollow, shivering with dread, hardly daring to breathe. The rider was nearer now, the horse rounding the corner. One quick, hardly bearable peep upwards to see the rider's livery –

And it was not Kingscote's blue and gold. Nor was the rider Sir Nicholas Carleton. Mall jumped up and shouted as the horseman galloped past, waving her hands above her head.

'Mr Murray! *George!*'

She saw him rein in, the horse rearing as he turned to look over his shoulder. Grasping the soaking grass, Mall pulled herself out of the ditch and ran down the track to join him.

The expression on George Murray's face was almost worth the nightmare of the past few hours.

'God's blood! Mall!' He slid out of the saddle, and looked at her, open mouthed. 'How in hell did you get here?'

She grinned, gasping with relief and exhaustion, 'I jumped, I swam the moat, and I ran. Very fast.'

'*Christ.*' He managed to shut his mouth, and then opened it again to say, 'But where are you running to?'

'Amyott.' Her smile faded as she remembered Carleton's threats. Tears of tiredness and relief pricked at her eyes, mingling with the rain, and she grasped George's arm, hardly able to stand. 'Please take me to Amyott, Mr Murray. I must get help – Richard Galliers is in great danger.'

George looked at her, his mind working as fast as it was able. Yes, Amyott was the place to go to. He had given his message, and by now Carleton would be riding to his rendezvous with Galliers in the Fens. And Galliers had a pistol, knife, and rapier.

'Hop on to the saddle, my dear.'

It was somewhat reminiscent of Zeeland; the Fens in the pouring rain. They had known the Fens since boyhood: he and Giles and Jeremy. They had ridden here, swum here, hunted here, hawked here. He knew this wilderness as well as he knew Amyott's crumbling passageways or London's dark alleys and courtyards. The Fens had been a place of refuge to him in the past. Today they would be a battleground: a flat, patched, patterned board for a deadly endgame.

He had chosen an isthmus, raised a little above the rapidly swelling water level, crested with willows. Soaked by the teeming rain, the ground was slippery underfoot – a disadvantage, but a disadvantage for both of them. And Carleton, he suspected, would have practised most of his swordplay on Kingscote's smoothly jointed floors. He had tried George's rapier, balancing it, flexing the long thin blade, and he knew that the weapon was good, that George had not wasted all his money on dice or drink. Because it would be a swordfight, he knew. The chances of a pistol firing in this cloudburst were remote.

Galliers leaned against the trunk of the willow, his eyes always fixed on the flat, grey horizon, waiting for Carleton. His horse was tethered on the lower side of the isthmus, out of sight. If Carleton did not come alone, then he would have to try the pistol, shielding the powder from the falling rain, trusting that his one shot would be good. Unlikely, though; the light was bad and growing worse, the sky heavy and overcast. So he must hope that Carleton was desperate enough: that he would come by himself for the letters that no longer existed.

He saw him first as a small black moving dot on the skyline travelling, not particularly fast, along the path he had described to George. Carleton would not go fast, of course, the conditions were too bad, the route too unfamiliar, the rider too wary. Galliers waited, hidden by the long pale leaves of the willow. Carleton was unaccompanied; no-one could be hiding to protect him in that flat wet desolation. The final scene would have no audience.

When Carleton was within shouting distance, Galliers moved from the shelter of the trees to the bare grassy rise of the isthmus. His shirt clung soaking to his back, and small rivulets of water ran from his wet, rain-curled hair on to his collar. But he noticed none of this: his eyes, hard hawk's eyes, were fixed on one man, and his hand was already at the hilt of his rapier.

'Galliers!' Carleton's horse shied and skittered, uneasy in the oppressive weather and unfamiliar countryside. 'Galliers – give me my letters!'

Richard came out into the open, black against the vast grey sky behind him. He called over the water that separated them:

'Leave your horse there, Carleton.'

A moment's pause, eyes estimating the dark figure ahead of him, and Carleton swung himself out of the saddle. And the horse turned and bolted, back to dryer land behind.

Galliers watched Carleton circle the edge of the water and climb the shallow rise to reach him. A rapier, knife, and a pistol. The same as him. And Carleton's hand, like his, hovered within an inch of the rapier's hilt.

They were level, facing each other, standing on the sparse muddy grass.

'My letters,' said Carleton, softly. 'Give me my letters, Galliers.'

'We had a bargain. Your letters for Mall's freedom. According to George Murray, you have not kept your half of the bargain.'

352

Carleton laughed, a strange, unreal sound in the soft patter of falling rain.

'George Murray is a liar and a fool, but in this instance he told the truth. Did you really think I would set her free? You must be an even greater fool than Murray. You have lost, my friend. I will admit that it was a little too close for comfort in the end, but you have lost. Perhaps you should consider putting a bullet through your head here and now, for I don't believe you have too much to live for. You have lost your reputation, your family disowns you. Soon, all England will know that Richard Galliers was Reynardine. Remain in the country of your birth, and you will find your neck in the hangman's noose. And you have failed to take my wife from me. Go on, *Reynardine*, load the pistol – why wait?'

Galliers moved a little closer, his long mouth curling in a smile. 'Failed to take your wife? Why, I've had your wife already, Carleton. In May, when you were inspecting Giles's paintings – remember?'

Carleton's rapier was unsheathed, his eyes dark with hatred, his jaw clenched. Galliers moved back, out of the reach of the silver blade.

'I will kill you for this, Galliers. I will kill you and *take* my letters from you –'

'There *are* no letters.' Galliers circled round behind him, his voice taunting him, mocking him. 'The letters are destroyed, Carleton. You have been chasing a chimaera. All that money, all that effort, wasted on something that has ceased to exist. You could have had me killed in the North Sea, Carleton. Garrotted by Rizzo – he'd have enjoyed that – and dumped quietly overboard. No-one would have known. You missed your chance.'

The rapier lunged forward, slicing through the curtain of rain.

'What, Carleton? I thought you were a gentleman. If we are to duel, let us at least do it properly.' And suddenly Galliers' rapier and dagger were in his hands, and he lifted the rapier hilt, blade pointing skywards, to his face. 'A gentlemanly salute. My family, if not yours, observes the proprieties. *En garde.*'

And Carleton's sword cut through the air, narrowly missing Galliers' rolled up sleeve. A parry, a thrust, and they parted, and Carleton drew out his knife and pulled off his cloak to fling it to the ground.

They circled, looking for weaknesses in each other's guard. They were well matched. Carleton was an excellent swordsman, Galliers knew, and in other circumstances – in someone's empty Great Hall, with buttons on the rapier tips, and money on the outcome – this would have been rare sport. But now it was not sport: within seconds, minutes, at the most, an hour, one of them would die, painfully. One of them would fall, finally, to the cold wet ground. Kingscote, Mall, four years of hatred and feud, all were forgotten, and the only thoughts were of balance, of opportunity, of remaining upright and not slipping to certain death in the mud.

The blades clashed, crossing like silver wires high against the lonely sky. Push to the side – God, Carleton's arm was strong! – ignore the fast returning, flickering pain hovering in the cracked ribs – concentrate on not allowing the hand's grip on the rapier hilt to slip fatally as rain and sweat mingled together, trickling down the flexed wrist. Move to the side, parry with the dagger – and there was Carleton's weakness, in the left hand – *there* he would have him.

Carleton evaded the main gauche dagger, its long deadly blade hissing against the quilting of his doublet. His breath was coming hard, his eyes narrowed and hot. *There are no letters . . . I have had your wife already . . . You could have had me killed . . .* But he would kill him now, this blade would draw red blood from that loathsome exquisite face – *too* like Jeremy's. And Mall, too, what would he do to Mall . . . ?

Galliers had seen the small slip of concentration. Expertly, efficiently, he took advantage of it – cut, thrust with the dagger (Carleton's weak point, *remember*), and the rapier again, and hear the satisfying sickened gasp: first blood, only a scratch, but first blood nevertheless, staining Carleton's sleeve. Not so pretty now, Carleton, not so damned immaculate, not the elegant courtier. Mud and rain and blood and sweat take us to the same level.

Galliers backed, pushing wet hair out of his eyes, wiping the damp palm of his hand on a shirt that was scarcely any drier. Lips parted in a smile, eyes narrowed glittering green, he said softly:

'First blood to me, then, Carleton. An omen, do you think? Do you believe in omens, Carleton? This is *my* land – you'd rather fight in Kingscote's courtyard, wouldn't you, Carleton? I had your wife on your land. It was very agreeable.'

He did not hear what Carleton shouted. His entire being must concentrate on the sword; on the repeated, fast and furious, clash and cut of the whirling rapiers. On keeping that swooping deadly blade from his throat and heart – too close that time – on disregarding the frenzy on Carleton's distorted face.

And then he saw them. Two horsemen, grey in the twilight rain, riding fast through the Fens.

Giles had known exactly where to find Richard. When George had appeared with Mall, soaking wet and exhausted, on the brim of his saddle, he had had no difficulty in following George's garbled directions. He knew the place: they had sailed there as children, a small flat boat, frequently capsized, pretending to be Christopher Columbus, Marco Polo, Sir Francis Drake. Richard had led, and he had followed. And, damn it, he was still following.

Giles had thrown down the pen and paper with which he had been writing, bundled Mall, protesting, into the arms of the startled housekeeper, and had found his weapons and a fresh horse for himself and George within minutes. And then, to the Fens: through tracks and reeds and waterways that he had not seen for years, but that still, even allowing for the natural movement of time and tide, remained much the same.

Giles saw them before George did. They were silhouetted on

the small rise, black against the brightening sky – it must be clearing from the east – fighting for their lives. Giles reined in, and George drew up behind him. Giles dismounted from his horse – the path had become too narrow, wet and dangerous – and he ran towards the isthmus.

He did not call out, did not run too close. The wrong movement, a glimmer of distraction, and Carleton's knife or rapier could go through Richard's breast. He strained to see more clearly through the rain. Carleton was wounded: only slightly, but one sleeve of his shirt was pink, not white. Richard did not appear to be hurt, but –

'Oh Christ, he's tiring.'

His words were barely audible, but George heard and looked again at the duellists on the hill, concern on his face.

'I doubt if he has slept for thirty-six hours –'

It was true: he was tiring, he could feel it in the less than perfect arc of his rapier strokes, in the deadly ache of his muscles. He knew Giles and Murray were there, but it made little difference now. And Carleton was not tiring, not yet. God, he had strength, that man! Strength and hatred, and they fuelled each other.

Carleton closed in; the pain in Galliers' side was like a sword thrust, distracting. The danger was that his reserves were gone, that he might cease to care, that Carleton's words, insidiously echoing to his thudding heartbeats (*you have lost your reputation your family disowns you you will find your neck in the hangman's noose*), might destroy his will with the ring of truth, as fatal as any death knell. His sword arm, more and more leaden, parried Carleton's heavy thrust. Mall –

He had forgotten the ground, for a fraction of a second he had forgotten that the grass was slippery, perfidious to the smooth soles of his boots. His legs buckled under him, he heard Giles's involuntary cry, he saw Carleton's face above him, dark and gleeful. With all his remaining speed and strength he rolled, and Carleton's dagger, plunging downwards, downwards, clipped his shoulder, missing its target, impaled in the soft earth. No more the gentleman . . . Galliers' head, wet, muddied, and hard, butted into Carleton's stomach, winding him. And through the rain and mud he heard Giles's voice again, but clearly this time, good music to his ears.

'Mall's safe, Richard! She's at Amyott!'

Their eyes met for the last time, Galliers' green and Carleton's brown.

Galliers kicked the hard heel of his boot, striking the rapier from Carleton's hand to land uselessly in the mud. He had lost his own rapier somewhere in that moment of carelessness, but he kept the dagger in his left hand. Carleton was on top of him, his weight pressing him to the ground, a grotesque parody of love. His right hand gripped Galliers' throat; he wanted, Galliers knew, to choke the life from him, to hear the death rattle. Blackness – cold – Carleton's thumbs, forcing down into his windpipe – Carleton's face, inches away from his own – blocking out the sky – *Now* –

The dagger, clutched in his left hand, stabbed downwards, through skin, muscle, and bone, severing Carleton's spinal chord at the neck.

Carleton made one last unearthly noise as the air rattled from his lungs; his hands relaxed, slipping from Galliers' throat, and his head toppled forward like a puppet's head when the strings have been cut, his dead face falling against Galliers' face, his lifeless body a nightmarish, sickening burden.

One moment of paralyzing suffocation, and then Galliers, screaming, pushed him away, gasping for air, every hair standing on end, a cold sweat icing his skin. And Carleton's body rolled, slowly at first, and then gathering speed, down the incline and into the dark peaty water of the Fen. The main gauche knife still protruded pruriently from the neck wound, and blood, slow and scarlet, stained the water around him. Black spots swam before Galliers' eyes, and nausea rose in his bruised throat, and he knelt in the mud at the crest of the isthmus, looking down.

It seemed a long time before Giles's voice penetrated his consciousness. George was there, wading through the black and red water to turn (and Richard shook again, uncontrollably) Carleton's body in an unnecessary attempt to check that he was really, finally, dead. Giles was saying something, but he could not hear it, and when Giles's hand reached for his uninjured shoulder, he shuddered, recoiling at the touch. It was over, Carleton was dead, he was revenged, Mall was safe. Why then was there no triumph, only that terrible voice of disillusion saying *I don't believe you have too much to live for*; only – he looked at his shaking hands, the fingers spread out, palms upraised – only Carleton's blood, mingling with the grass and mud stains.

It was Giles who drew him away from the chasm, throwing his own wet cloak about his brother's shoulders, dragging him to his feet and turning his pallid face to his own, forcing aqua vitae from his flask into Richard's mouth. And when Richard had sat for a while, quiet, eyes closed, his damp dark hair tumbled on to his folded arms, beneath the kindly shelter of the willow tree, Giles had taken Richard's hand in his, and said simply, 'Come home, Richard. Please.'

Richard did not answer immediately, but he opened his eyes at last. Then he said, his voice unsteady:

'They had their own punishment for criminals here. They would bind them hand and foot and bury them alive in the embankment. So the body would become part of the sea defences . . . evil put to good use . . .'

His voice faded away, and he buried his head again. Then he looked up, and said:

'But the Fens do not deserve – that.'

Giles nodded, understanding. 'We will take the body away – George can do it.'

So that you may ride home with me. But he would not, could not, go back to Amyott. Richard said, very carefully: 'Now go, Giles. Leave me alone.'

'But –'

'Go. *Please*.'

For a long moment Giles did not move, and then he stumbled to his feet, looking down at his brother, searching for words. But Richard was no longer looking at him, his eyes, empty of everything, stared into the grey misty horizon where the Fens mingled eternally with the North Sea.

So Giles left him there, under the willow, and went to help George.

When they were halfway along the long flat trek across the Fens, Carleton's body slung across the bow of George's saddle, Giles looked back. Richard was still sitting there: he had not moved since Giles had left him. He looked as though he would never move again.

She returned to Kingscote once only, for that last ordeal, the funeral.

Mall recalled little of it afterwards; only the day's derisory beauty, the deep sapphire blue of the sky, the pinks and lavenders that scented the warm air of the tiny churchyard. There were few mourners, surprisingly few for a man who had mingled with the great. But he had been loved by none, thought Mall, her hands clenched tight inside her black kid gloves. Loved by none, and mourned by none.

And Richard? Only when she was quite, quite alone did Mall allow herself to think of Richard. Giles had left him in the Fens, and no-one had seen or heard of him since. If his face still haunted her dreams, and if, sometimes, a phrase of poetry or the melody of a song made her want to cry out in pain, then she must teach herself to live with that.

Looking out of her window, at the black sky speckled with stars, and the trees lit with the moon's yellow light, Mall thought: I have nothing now. She had had a handkerchief once, and a ring, once, but now there was nothing. The episode was over. Reynardine had gone to earth.

But there was, she realized one bright August morning,

something she could do for Richard. And she must do it before Giles's and Anna's wedding in September, and whether the Galliers family wanted her interference or not. The thought of what she intended to do dismayed her at first, but then Mall remembered Lady Woodroffe, Richard's first – no, second victim. She had stood up to her: Alice – kind, well meaning Alice – had been intimidated, but not Mall. So if Lady Amyott turned out to be another miserable old battleaxe, Mall Carleton could also stand up to her.

To call on Lady Amyott, she must dress in her best. Black silk, appropriate to a widow, but made to show wealth and position by the perfect lozenge-shaped quilting on the full sleeves, the silver stitching and beading on the low-cut bodice, the small round pearls edging the sculptured points of ruff and wrist-bands. A ludicrously wide farthingale, designed to make riding difficult, if not impossible; chains – silver, gold and jet – around her neck; bracelets, rings, and a net of fine silver thread holding her wild black hair uncompromisingly in place. Only a little kohl and powder – enough to satisfy the demands of rank, insufficient to jar with the pose of mourning widowhood.

And the letters. Letters that Sir Thomas Conway had taken from the desks and cabinets of Kingscote's study. Letters mentioning Richard, letters from Lucas Holland. And one letter, pathetically brief, from Jeremy.

The magnificent and haughty Lady Carleton was attended by Joshua's Joe, Martin Bartlett and six other manservants, all unusually and uncomfortably resplendent in immaculate Conway livery.

Mall entered the dark, stifling room. It was a well proportioned room, and would have had a pleasant view of Amyott's untidy gardens and sweeping woodland beyond, had not the heavy brocade curtains been drawn, blocking out the light and the beauty. Despite the fine summer weather, a fire smouldered feebly in the grate, producing more smoke than flames. Portraits crowded the walls, jostling for space with tapestries and discoloured hangings. Furniture cluttered the oak floor – tables and stools in styles of fifty years ago, cupboards and chests crammed with relics and treasures.

Lady Amyott was not in the four-poster bed, was not huddled under its swathes of greyish-yellow silk. She was near the window, sitting iron-backed in a heavily carved, uncomfortable chair.

'Lady Carleton, I believe.' And the voice edged with distaste about the name, Carleton.

Mall moved out of the darkness towards the window, face to face with Lady Amyott, and instantly her courage, fortified by her gown, jewels and title, dispersed. This was no Lady Woodroffe: this faded, fragile beauty bore no resemblance to the forbidding old tyrant who had unexpectedly visited Belford a year ago. Neither was Lady Amyott, as Mall had conjectured on the ride from Belford, an invalid, enfeebled by ill-health and sorrow. But what shook Mall, silencing the conventional greetings before they reached her lips, making her breath catch in her lungs, were the eyes that stared at her, coldly, dispassionately, from the delicate face. Green eyes, older and weary, but still, unmistakeably, Richard's eyes, looked proudly at Mall from his mother's face. And Richard's expression, his worst one, arrogant and insolent, was echoed in the old countenance, emphasised by the lines of age and grief.

'Yes, Lady Carleton? To what do I owe the unexpected pleasure of this visit?'

Richard's tone. Mall collected herself, and found her voice.

'I have come to talk to you, your ladyship, about your son.'

The old lady looked at her, uninterested. 'Giles?'

Mall's throat was dry, she licked her lips. 'No, not Giles.'

Lady Amyott's eyes, Richard's eyes, hooded instantly. 'I have no other son, Lady Carleton.'

'Oh, but you do, Lady Amyott,' Mall said clearly. 'You have Richard, your second son.'

'Richard is no son of mine.' One old, silk-gloved hand reached for the bell. 'There is only Giles now.'

Stubborn old woman, thought Mall, struggling to keep her temper in check. 'Richard is most certainly your son,' she said firmly, 'Just as much as Giles is, just as much as Jeremy was. And it is pointless ringing that bell. No-one will answer. Your maid has gone temporarily deaf – upon Lord Amyott's orders.'

Abruptly, Mall's anger was mirrored in the older woman's face. Stiff-necked and furious, Lady Amyott glared at Mall.

'How dare you, madam! How dare you come into *my* home, talking of *my* family, issuing orders to *my* servants. With your ridiculous finery, and your unwelcome name! *Carleton* – the Galliers have never liked the Carletons, and never will. What right have you, madam, to come here at all?'

'No right whatsoever, Lady Amyott.' Mall pulled over a spindly stool and sat down. 'I am here because I love your son – I love Richard.'

The thin eyebrows raised, the disconcerting eyes narrowed, travelling slowly over Mall's black clothing. 'But you are in mourning for your husband, Lady Carleton,' said Lady Amyott, pointedly. 'What possible interest can you have in Richard?'

Mall did not let herself shrink from that piercing gaze. 'I hated my husband, your ladyship. I wear black as a concession to propriety, but I assure you, if I was allowed to behave as I feel, I would be dancing on Sir Nicholas Carleton's grave. My husband was a wicked man, and he deserved to die.'

'Then so is your lover wicked, Lady Carleton. Perhaps you should know that it was Richard's neglect and dissipation that led to my youngest son's death.' As she spoke, Lady Amyott's eyes strayed to the gold-framed miniature on the wall beside her. Mall rose, and went to the miniature. A young face, dark-haired like Richard, but with eyes of a hazel somewhere between Richard's green and Giles's brown. A good-looking, gentle face, but perhaps, even accounting for youth, lacking in strength. 'Jeremy?' Mall asked, gently.

There was a silence. Lady Amyott nodded, her white, slender hands twisting the folds of her gown. After a while she spoke:

'He was my youngest son . . . my baby. There were eight years between Richard and Jeremy, and I knew I would have no more children.' The anger had gone, leaving only grief and regret. 'My daughters died at birth, but Jeremy and I were as close as mother and daughter. Perhaps I spoiled him – I don't know. When he had to, he could not defend himself. Richard should have defended him!'

Mall knelt down in front of the old woman, taking the fragile, unsteady hands in hers. 'Richard was not responsible for Jeremy's death. My husband – Sir Nicholas Carleton – was.'

A slight rallying. Lady Amyott shook herself free of Mall. 'Nonsense, madam! I do not believe you!'

But you want to believe, thought Mall, who had noticed the sudden, hastily suppressed flicker of interest in Lady Amyott's eyes. You know you have lost one son, and you are beginning to regret that you have turned away another. Underneath all that unyielding bitterness, you still love him, perhaps.

It was unbearably hot in the stuffy bedchamber. Ignoring the spluttered protests from behind her, Mall pulled back the thick curtains. Clouds of dust rose in the brilliant sunlight that flooded the room.

She took the letters from her pocket. 'If you are going to be able to read these, Lady Amyott, then we must have some light. And –' Mall struggled with a stiff window latch, unopened for too many years '– and if I am not to collapse from the heat, then we must also have some air.' The window opened, and a distant scent of thyme and chamomile wafted in from the herb garden below.

'Now, your ladyship, you are going to listen to *my* story . . .'

Mall did not go into the house on her return to Belford; instead, she went to the orchard. It was hard to climb a tree in the appalling stiff black clothes, but she managed it, disregarding the occasional rending sound and the dusty lichen stains. Some of the apples were ripe enough to eat, so she sat on her favourite old wide bough and crunched, looking down to the courtyard and stables below.

As she had done a year ago, watching Martin at the stables, then riding with him, swimming in Sir Nicholas Carleton's pool, dreaming of the highwayman . . .

And Martin was there again, rubbing down one of the horses, whistling. And in that year Mall had been both married and widowed. Martha had also married; she had had to. Not Martin, though, but Sam Hollis, five years Martin's senior. Martha would have her baby in December.

And Mall had nothing. At last, some of the dulling misery had begun to transform into anger, a more familiar emotion. She must sit here and wait for a man who might never return, who had not even bothered to say goodbye. Neither wife, nor sweetheart, nor, if she listened to the gossip, an entirely respectable widow. Other rumours gathered like dust in dark corners: *They say that Amyott's younger brother was the highwayman* . . .

But it was unreasonable of Richard Galliers simply to disappear, expecting her just to accept it. Giles did not know where Richard was, she had asked him at Amyott, and there had been no letter, no word, nothing. It was unreasonable to leave her ignorant of whether he was living or dead. It was unreasonable to leave her wondering whether that brief, bittersweet hour at Kingscote's hunting-lodge had been just a freak consequence of spring and despair, or whether, perhaps, it had meant a little more. Richard Galliers had spent the last year appearing and disappearing from her life in the most inconvenient fashion possible – on the Gogs, in her father's study at Belford, rowed on Kingscote's moat by that auburn-haired player.

Benedict – my player friend. Where was Benedict? In the Netherlands, in Brussels, back in England? Mall frowned as she finished her apple, core and all. Benedict was one loose end in too many loose ends. It was September – and the London playhouses opened in September, she thought. So Benedict should be in London. And she had never, she realized bitterly, seen London, although she had always longed to. Neither her father nor Sir Nicholas had taken her there. She, who had read every travel book, had studied every map, had dreamed of galleons, mountains, seas and deserts, had never travelled further than Kingscote in her entire life.

She watched Martin saddle the horse, tightening the girth under its belly. Picking another apple from the branch, she cradled it in her palm, frowning. And then suddenly, Mall saw what she must do. Tossing the apple high into the air, a whirling rosy globe against the deep blue sky, she caught it in one hand, and then jumped to the ground, and ran all the way to the stables.

Benedict Daniel, removing scarlet doublet and hose in the rapidly emptying tiring room of the Red Bull playhouse, felt distinctly pleased with himself. The play had gone well, he thought: his own performance had been particularly affecting. It was good to be back – the summer had been interesting (rather too interesting, on occasions), but this was where he belonged, on the stage of the dear, disreputable Red Bull. Travel. He substituted the scarlet doublet for a scarcely more restrained blue one. He never wanted to travel again: those lengthy, exhausting wanderings through the Low Countries had cured him forever of any desire to see the world. He still felt some lingering satisfaction, however, in the knowledge that he had performed his task well, that he had passed William Reeve's confession into the right hands. He had said as much in the letter he had sent in reply to Richard's own short enquiring missive, received, by circuitous means, at his Clerkenwell rooms in early August.

The tiring room was almost deserted. Benedict bundled the discarded doublet and hose into a basket, and began to buckle on his rapier.

'Mr Daniel! Mr Daniel! There's a lady to see you!'

Charlie Farrant, still fetchingly garbed in wide skirt and ruff, ran into the tiring room, a white mouse clutched in one freckled, dirty hand.

'There's a lady outside, Mr Daniel.' Charlie grinned. 'A *rich* lady.' He opened his other palm to show a gold crown nestling on the paint and dirt stains.

A rich lady . . . After the early summer's debacle, Benedict had been unusually judicious in his amours. But a wealthy mistress – the Red Bull had never paid well . . .

He looked up and caught a glimpse of a neat ankle, a cloud of black hair ill-contained by a feathered and veiled hat half in, half out of the tiring room door. Adjusting his clothing, he ran a hand through his auburn curls, and went to meet his admirer.

'Mr Daniel?'

Charlie Farrant had been right: a dark blue silk gown trimmed with silver lace, a necklace of ridiculously large sapphires.

'Benedict Daniel, madam. Bennet to my friends.' He sketched a bow, and then as the veil was lifted back, paused, looking harder at the black hair, the blue eyes, the small neat figure.

'Yes, Mr Daniel. We have met before. At Kingscote, in Essex.'

Richard climbing to where this girl leaned, enchantress-like, out of a high stone window. 'Of course. You're Richard's –' He silenced himself just in time, and recalled his manners sufficiently to lead her into the tiring room, dusting a stool with his sleeve for her to sit beside a large pile of Greek armour.

'That's right. It was Richard I wished to talk to you about. Oh –' she smiled at the fair-haired youth who had followed her into the tiring room to stand protectively at her side. 'This is Martin Bartlett, a friend of mine. We have spent a very enjoyable three days in London looking for you, Mr Daniel. We have visited all the playhouses – it has been *wonderful*.' Her smile broadened.

Benedict looked slightly anxious. 'And which performance did you enjoy most, Mistress –'

'Oh – Lady Carleton.' She considered. 'This afternoon's, Mr Daniel – I cried at the end, you know.'

Benedict thought seriously of falling in love with her. He

tried not to look too smug, and edged a little closer, leaning against the wall in front of her, ignoring the scowls from the fair-haired lad.

'You have a discerning soul, Lady Carleton. Perhaps we should share a meal together somewhere, and have a nice long private talk about the theatre. I could tell you some very amusing stories.'

She looked up at him, wide blue eyes fringed with luxurious black lashes, and said:

'That would be delightful, Mr Daniel – but another time. The play has been most enjoyable, but my real reason for coming to London was to find Mr Galliers.'

'Richard?' Aware of a vague feeling of disappointment, Benedict shrugged. 'He's not in London.'

'Then where is he, Mr Daniel?'

He sighed inwardly. She was such a sweet little thing, with her pale oval face and her adorable smile – what a shame that she should have this unfortunate preoccupation with Richard. Still, perhaps he could do something about that.

'Richard's abroad, Lady Carleton. In France.'

'France.' Her jewelled hand played idly with the papier-mâché of a Greek shield. 'Perhaps you could be a little more specific, Mr Daniel.'

Benedict managed to drag his gaze away from those large enquiring eyes. 'I had a letter from Richard a month or so past. He's in Calais, my dear. In a – house – in Calais.'

'A house?' The perfectly arched eyebrows raised en-quiringly. 'Whose house, Mr Daniel?'

He did not answer immediately, searching wildly for a suitable way of explaining Madame Berthe's establishment to this elegant small creature before him. 'A friend's house,' he said at length, weakly. 'An old friend.'

'A lady friend?'

Benedict shifted uncomfortably, untypically lost for words. 'Yes.'

'Then please tell me the address of this house, Mr Daniel. I have to see Richard.'

'Oh, no – you can't do that –' He had a sudden appalling vision of this girl crossing the Channel in all her finery, and knocking at the door of Richard's favourite brothel.

'Why can't I do that?' She looked at him narrowly. 'Has he been drinking, Mr Daniel? Is he in a temper? Has he a mistress? I assure you, I know Mr Galliers very well. I would hardly expect to find him both sober and celibate.'

There was nothing for it, he would have to tell her the truth. 'Richard's friend runs a brothel, my dear,' said Benedict, baldly. 'He's staying in a French whorehouse.'

'*Oh.*' The faintest blush rose to her cheeks, and her eyes met those of the tow-headed youth beside her. She rallied, and said firmly, 'Well, then, Mr Daniel – the address of this brothel, please.'

Benedict was beginning to feel a little hot. It was all a little too reminiscent of a bad audience on a wet afternoon. 'No, Lady Carleton – it won't do, you know –'

'Why not, Mr Daniel?'

'Because, my dear girl,' said Benedict severely, 'well-dressed young ladies do not go jaunting about the Channel with only a –' he looked critically at Martin Bartlett '– a stable boy for company. Neither do they pay calls on French bawdy houses! Besides,' he added feelingly, 'Richard would probably kill me.'

Mall said nothing. She did not even, thought Benedict irritably, appear to be listening. Her eyes had fixed on the far corner of the tiring room, on Charlie Farrant. His white mouse safely imprisoned in a box on the floor, he had unlaced the skirt and bodice of his gown to reveal dark coloured breeches beneath. The sleeves and bodice of the gown fell to the floor, a shirt and jerkin were pulled on, and he was no longer the lisping heroine of the tragedy, he was a boy again, freckled and carefree.

Mall turned triumphantly back to Benedict. 'But my stable boy's younger brother would be free to sail, wouldn't she, Mr Daniel, and to visit where she pleased?'

Benedict, confused, followed the direction of her gaze to Charlie Farrant. Understanding dawned. 'Oh God, no – you mean –'

'Mr Daniel, if you do not tell me where Richard Galliers is, I shall simply tour the brothels of Calais until I find him. Every one of them.'

Benedict's eyes met Martin's. 'She would, you know,' the boy said.

Benedict sighed, out loud this time.

The sea voyage was wonderful, glorious, marvellous. The weather was fine, the wind breezy, and neither Mall nor Martin had felt remotely sick. It had taken Mall a little while to get used to breeches and hose, and longer to stop wanting to giggle when Martin addressed her as Tom, but really, it had all been surprisingly easy. A lack of bosom was, at last, a positive advantage, as was lack of height. It had caused Mall some misgivings to see a considerable length of her hair fall under Benedict's deftly wielded shears to the floor of the Red Bull's tiring room. But it had been worth it in the cause of authenticity, and even Bennet, belatedly entering into the spirit of things, had unwillingly admitted that she had looked quite convincing. Rather more misgivings had been evoked by the brief note she had sent to Alice, a masterpiece in equivocation.

It was, however, when *La Mignonne* docked in Calais that some of Mall's optimism began to falter. First, it was by no means certain that Richard Galliers would be here: as Mr Daniel had emphatically pointed out, the Calais address was merely a letter drop, a point of contact, hardly an assurance that the man was in permanent residence. Secondly, Mall had no very clear idea of what she intended to say to him: she could already hear the crushing sarcasm that might meet any honest attempt on her part to explain her mission. Thirdly, the French that Sir Thomas Conway had taught her at Belford, in order that she might read the poetry of Pierre de Ronsard, was not, she discovered, quite the same as the French spoken in the streets of Calais. With Martin at her side, she had stopped and asked the first likely looking seaman for directions to the address on the crumpled piece of paper she held clutched like a good luck charm in her hand: but the sailor had looked at her and laughed, waving his arms about in a suitably Continental fashion, saying something totally incomprehensible before moving on. This happened several times before Mall hit on the idea of sending Martin, complete with a single phrase of primitive French, to beg for directions while she hid behind some barrels. The scheme proved successful; directions to the Rue St Louis were provided by means of the universal language of gesture and mime, peppered with a few roguish masculine winks and nudges.

It was late evening, and the sun was beginning to set, sparkling amythysts and carmines reflected on the quiet sea. The town was still busy, the harbour and streets laced with sailors and their sweethearts, respectable burghers and their wives, with children, soon to be dragged protesting off to bed. It occurred to Mall, walking with Martin through the unfamiliar, strangely named streets, that she was very tired. She was also grubby – the brightly coloured breeches and shirt, purloined from the overflowing costume baskets of the Red Bull, had been none too clean to start with: after three days travel they looked positively filthy. Her hair felt oddly light, and her aching legs still rocked with the motion of *La Mignonne*'s heaving decks. They turned into the Rue St Louis, an alleyway of tall crooked houses, noisy taverns and rubbish-strewn cobbles. Mall looked down at herself – at the frayed edges of her gaudy sleeveless doublet, at her flat chest, lost in the voluminous folds of an over large linen shirt – and thought of Richard Galliers, in his most dislikeable mood, lecturing her in the peat cutter's hut. Suddenly, she began to feel nervous.

'This is the one,' said Martin.

Madame Berthe, when she emerged from the depths of the house to the doorstep where the blue-frocked maid had left them, was not quite as either Mall or Martin had imagined. Dressed in a simple black gown, the coils of yellow hair elaborately piled on her head, decorous ropes of pearls strung round her capacious bosom, she would not have looked out of place in Kingscote's withdrawing room.

She took one look at her callers, and said crisply: 'Come, come, mes petits, this is not a place for children. You, young man,' her sharp blue gaze alighted on Martin, 'take your brother home –' and then she stopped, frowning, looking at Mall.

Mall swallowed. 'No, madame, we're not here for –' and then her voice petered out, the precise words, the delicate nuances of what she had to say unobtainable in French.

'No?' The experienced eyes swept from Mall to Martin, and then back to Mall again. 'Then what are you here for, my dear?'

A deep breath. 'To see Mr Galliers.'

A beautifully Gallic shrug. 'To see Richard? Well, that's easy. What name is it?'

'Carleton. Lady Carleton.' And then her hand flew to her mouth. 'Oh hell.'

Madame Berthe, however, did not bat an artistically painted eyelid. 'Little brothers have dirty hands and bitten fingernails, chérie. And their pockets overflow with stones and shells, and catapults and apple cores.' She added smoothly, 'If you would care to come with me, Lady Carleton – and, oh – Toinette –' the maid came hurrying down the passageway – 'take madame's *brother* to the kitchens, and find him something to eat.'

Mall, shown into Madame Berthe's private sitting room, was glad she had been spared the offer of food. It would have choked in her gullet, turning to sawdust in her dry mouth. Her gaze flicked panicking round the room – simply furnished, tastefully decorated in blue and cream, it was an oasis of quiet in an extremely noisy house. Shrieks of laughter, singing, foot stamping, echoed from the other rooms. And somewhere, lost in the tall thin dark winding house, someone played a lute, extremely well.

Her hands, used to the folds of a heavy gown, nervously sought and failed to find something to do. No beads to run through her fingers, no quilting or slashed sleeves to clutch at, as a drowning person clutches at driftwood. So he was here – at least he was here – but who would he be this time? The acid-tongued, exquisitely dressed drunkard of Belford's banquet, the bruised and beaten body on the floor of Kingscote's cellars, the dark dangerous highwayman of the hills – or the lover, gentle, considerate, passionate, of the hunting lodge's green lawns? For they had never, Mall thought as she pressed her cold shaking hands together, met as a man and a woman, unhurried, in the open, with time and peace at their disposal. Stolen kisses, secret love; that had been their portion. No chance for understanding. No chance to see whether those dreams, those hastily taken pleasures, were anything more than a talisman against an evil future.

The lute playing had stopped. There were footsteps outside, the door opened. 'Lady Carleton,' said Madame Berthe's accented voice, and then the door was shut, leaving them alone.

And if this was another guise, it was a better one. He was well dressed. Dark, well fitting clothes. No jewellery. His face was sunburnt, the cuts and bruises long gone. Only the eyes were the same, green, long-lashed, heavy-lidded, hawk's eyes, cat's eyes.

'Christ –' and then a short, dazed glance at the breeches and shirt. 'I was about to say, Mall – but perhaps Ned – or Kit –'

'Tom, actually.'

He circled round her, eyes wide, the beginning of a smile playing on his mouth. 'I would salute your hand, Mall – Tom – except that I would feel like some ageing pederast –'

He reached out to touch her hair. The short, feathery ends slipped through his fingers. He said, his voice slightly unsteady, 'A considerable sacrifice in the cause of veracity? Let me guess – the handsome cabin boy? A mile out of port and half the crew's doubting their masculinity because they've fallen in love with you –'

'Mr Daniel,' said Mall, evasively, 'thought sailors might not like a woman on board.'

'Did he, by God.' He was standing in front of her, laughter in his eyes. 'Well, it suits you, my dear. You look positively elfin. Robin Goodfellow, putting a girdle round the earth in forty minutes –' He perched on the edge of Madame Berthe's walnut desk. 'So Benedict told you where I was?'

'He didn't want to,' said Mall, hastily. 'He was most unwilling.'

'Poor Ben. What did you use – thumbscrews?'

Reddening, Mall dropped her gaze, staring at the patterns on Madame Berthe's best Turkey rug. She heard Richard say, 'Sit down, my dear,' and saw him go to the table and pour a glass of wine.

Three large gulps of claret, and then courage began, fleetingly, to return.

'I came to ask you – to find out –' she began, and then said crossly, 'Well, Mr Galliers, what can you expect if you disappear with no clue whatsoever as to where you have gone? A short note to your family would have been civilized, at least!'

He said dryly, 'I would have thought that most of my family were only too glad to see the back of me.'

'Not at all, Mr Galliers. They are *all* concerned for you –' Draining the rest of her glass rather rapidly, Mall added, 'I went to see your mother –'

'You did *what*?'

Mall braced herself for the blistering sarcasm, the few well-chosen words on the evils of interference. They did not come. Instead, she heard herself gabbling nervously:

'Lady Amyott and I got on rather well, in fact. I've asked Alice to visit her – she could revive your mother's interest in gardening – I thought it might help –'

'You mean, weed Amyott's overgrown knot garden, whilst convincing her ladyship of her younger son's true nobility?'

Her eyes slightly blurred, her heart heavy, Mall nodded. Unexpectedly, she felt his hand ruffle her short curls, and heard him say gently:

'My dear, it was a kind thought.'

Kindness did not help. The wine had made her head ache. Mall blinked to clear her sight. 'So –' she had found her voice at last '– will you come home?'

A small silence. Then:

'No.'

She saw him shake his head, and walk to the window. Her own fists clenched, her nails dug into her palms.

'No, Mall – I can't. However industrious – however thoughtful – you have been on my account, it really makes little odds. You cannot undo the events of the past year – of the past four years. Oh, I know that Carleton is dead. I know also that Lady Somerset and her collaborators will be brought to trial. Some will die; the lady herself will not. Comfortable imprisonment in the Tower, perhaps, or put out to grass on some obscure country estate. Though that,' he said, turning back from the window, 'might for a Howard be a little worse than death. We are no longer of any significance – perhaps we never were. Just –' he shrugged, '– just minor characters in someone else's drama.'

Her head jerked up, her eyes dark and angry. 'So, Richard Galliers – is that all you think we were? Minor characters in someone else's drama? So nothing has changed? Well, I'll tell you what has changed. *You* have changed, Mr Galliers, and so have I. You have a family to return to, if you so choose. You have friends, you have people who love you. People who *need* you.'

'*No.*' He moved, taking her restless hands in his. 'No, Mall, I don't have a family to return to. There is nothing in England for me except the hangman's noose. Carleton told me that before he died, and he was right.'

At last she understood what he was trying to tell her. His voice was gentle, patient. Her fingers curled in her palms, her eyes closed tight.

'There are rumours already, I would guess?'

Mall's head inclined once in single, damning assent. *They say Amyott's younger brother was the highwayman* . . .

'Then Carleton won in the end, you see, Mall. I can never go back to my country or my family.'

Giles and Anna and Lady Amyott. Her own family: Thomas and Alice and Ralph. She pulled away from him, shaking her head.

374

'*Don't* say that! Don't ever say that he has won –' The tears were flowing freely now, she scrubbed at them with the back of her sleeve. 'We have come through it all, you and I. Can't you see?'

'Here.' A handkerchief, a beautifully embroidered R nestling in its corner, was passed to her. Mall blew her nose and forced the tears back to their source. '*You and I*, Mr Galliers,' she said, fiercely.

He stared at her, and then he said:

'No. No, my dear, I will not ask that of you. Go back to your home and your family. Start again.'

She knew then what he intended to do: open the door, find her some respectable room, see her on to a ship bound for England the following morning. Back to Belford. Back to her own family. Back to the aching, terrible emptiness.

But she would not let him.

Mall rose from her chair. The handkerchief, rolled in a wet ball, fell to the floor. 'My father is selling Kingscote for me,' she said, steadily. 'There were debts. And besides, I never, ever wanted to see the place again.'

He had distanced himself from her, standing by the door, one hand already to the doorknob. But his eyes, which once she had thought cold, he could not distance. There, his feelings were as naked and undefended as hers.

'I'm not going back,' said Mall.

She saw him throw his hands into the air in a familiar gesture of exasperation. '*Listen* to me, Mall –'

'No. *You* listen to me.' Her voice was firm, but the anger had gone. She saw him pause, silenced for once.

'After my husband's death, I went back to Belford. There was nothing for me there, nothing at all. You say that you cannot go back. Well, neither could I. I tried – but too much has happened. If I go now, it must be because you do not love me. No other reason will do.'

She saw him pause, searching for words. Soon she would go to him, hold him, and finally erase what the past had done to him. The noise of the house had receded, becoming as gentle as the distant whisper of the sea. She knew that the words he thought he should say would not come, that he had, at last, to abandon all disguise.

'I know I'm an inconvenience,' she said, softly. 'But I can no longer bear the prospect of seeing you only for the odd half-hour, in a peat-cutter's hut or in someone's dirty cellar. Richard, you really will have to make up your mind.'

The faintest trace of a smile touched his mouth. His eyes, which had never left hers, flickered. 'Indecisiveness has never been one of my faults,' he said, and she let herself go to him, let herself take his hand in hers, folding his fingers and kissing them one by one.

'A runaway,' he said. 'An outlaw. Is that what *you* want?'

His arms had encircled her, she had laid her head against his breast. She looked up. 'Oh yes,' she said. 'Oh yes.'

'Travel,' he said. 'France – Italy – the Sublime Porte itself, complete with harem and sultan. Deserts and seas, galleys and carracks. If that is what you want, I can give you that, with all my love and all my heart. But I cannot give you a home, Mall. I cannot give you your family.' Fleetingly, his lips touched her forehead. 'Perhaps in time I may hope for a pardon. But not yet. Maybe never.'

If he thought that he offered her a choice, then she knew that choice had already been made. Long ago, when she had accepted a stranger's kiss; in springtime, when they had both known love.

Her fingertips traced the path of the scar across his cheekbone as though their touch might wash it away.

'*You* are my home, Richard. You are my family. Without you, dear heart, it is all worthless, all dust.'

And there was joy in his eyes, a joy she knew her own face mirrored. And when he bent his head to kiss her mouth, all need for words perished, blown away on the soft air with the swirl of a man's black cloak, the sound of horses' hooves in the night.

But, far away in England, the wind blew in the Fens, swirling the reeds and grasses into whorls and curlicues, always moving,

376

always changing. And the final verse of the old song threaded, half-heard, between the rustling willows and dark, ancient waters.

> *Sun and moon, she followed him*
> *His eyes did brightly shine*
> *And he led her over the mountains*
> *Did that sly, bold Reynardine.*

THE END

HISTORICAL EPILOGUE

William Reeve's confession was sent via Trumbull, the British Resident in Brussels, to Sir Ralph Winwood, the Principal Secretary of State. It was Winwood who set the Overbury trials in motion.

Both Robert Kerr and Frances Howard were accused in September 1615 of the murder of Sir Thomas Overbury. They were tried, found guilty, and sentenced to death in May 1616. The sentences were not carried out, however, and the Somersets were eventually pardoned. Released from the Tower in 1622, they then lived in retirement in Chiswick. Frances Howard died in 1632.

Mrs Anne Turner, Frances Howard's accomplice, was tried for the death of Overbury in 1615. She and her associates, including the Lord Lieutenant of the Tower at the time of Overbury's death, were found guilty of murder, and hanged.

De Lobell, the apothecary, was examined, but not brought to trial.

The fall of the Howards was completed in 1618, when Frances Howard's father, Thomas, Earl of Suffolk, was disgraced by financial scandals concerning his role as Lord Treasurer.

George Villiers continued to rise in the king's favour, and became Duke of Buckingham in 1623. He was assassinated in 1628.

J. L-S.
1988.